MARRYING
A ROYAL

NINA MILNE

SUZANNE MERCHANT

MILLS & BOON

First published in Great Britain 2025
by Mills & Boon, an imprint of HarperCollins*Publishers* Ltd,
1 London Bridge Street, London, SE1 9GF

www.harpercollins.co.uk

HarperCollins*Publishers*, Macken House, 39/40 Mayor Street Upper, Dublin 1, D01 C9W8, Ireland

Marrying a Royal © 2025 Harlequin Enterprises ULC

Secret Royal's Napoli Reunion © 2025 Nina Milne

Conveniently Engaged to a Princess © 2025 Suzanne Merchant

ISBN: 978-0-263-41756-2

09/25

MIX
Paper | Supporting responsible forestry
FSC
www.fsc.org
FSC™ C007454

This book contains FSC™ certified paper and other controlled sources to ensure responsible forest management.

For more information visit www.harpercollins.co.uk/green.

Printed and Bound in the UK using 100% Renewable Electricity at CPI Group (UK) Ltd, Croydon, CR0 4YY

SECRET ROYAL'S NAPOLI REUNION

NINA MILNE

MILLS & BOON

To Suman: you are an inspiration.
You always find the positives.

PROLOGUE

Seven years ago

MARCO OPENED HIS EYES, aware of an unfamiliar sense of anticipation, a knowledge that the day ahead held something precious. He stared up at the ceiling, memories of the previous days ranging through his head, felt his smile widen as he thought of Sonia.

Not that he believed his unexpected visitor, the young woman he'd rescued from unwanted attentions on the streets of Naples, was truly called Sonia. As for a surname, she had refused to give one, said she had no wish to know his either. So, days after he had brought her back to his student digs he was none the wiser; all he suspected was that Sonia was running away from something or someone.

All he knew was that somehow the dark-haired nineteen-year-old, with her rare smile and expressive blue eyes, had got under his skin and he liked her, truly liked her. Wanted to protect her, make her smile, be with her. Hoped that as time went on Sonia could be persuaded to trust him with the truth of who she was. Maybe even today, after the kiss they had shared the previous night, a kiss that had been so glorious, so beautiful that his whole body, his heart, his soul was still buzzing with the after-effects.

What could they do today? Plans fizzed through his head; even as he reminded himself that he should be going to university, that lectures awaited. But for once he couldn't bring himself to care—he'd catch up. He enjoyed his course, had chosen international business management because he knew he would need a sensible job whilst he pursued his real dream. A dream to become a sculptor, to follow in the footsteps of Italy's famous artists. To this end he had undertaken courses in pottery, blacksmithing, jewellery making, sculpting. As many as he could afford, financed by a part-time job in a local artist's shop. But today not even his current project could lure him. Right now, nothing was more important than Sonia.

A sudden question entered his head. Was this how his father had once felt about his mother, this elation, this joy? He blinked the thought away; he wasn't going to get carried away by this, whatever this was. But neither was he going to compare it to whatever his parents had once had. Because his parents' love had withered and shrivelled, leaving behind nothing but the fruit of bitter regret.

But that was irrelevant, those were thoughts he didn't want to harbour. Not today, when the day stretched before him, before them. Perhaps he could take Sonia to see the botanical gardens; she had mentioned that her sister loved gardens, the one bit of information she had dropped.

Outside the early morning sunshine scattered the sky with motes of yellow and orange and he decided to get up. He'd go to the bakery and bring back the *sfogliatelle* pastries that she loved for breakfast.

An hour later Marco surveyed his efforts with approval. The shell-shaped pastries with their creamy filling were carefully arranged on the table, alongside a bunch of flowers. The smell of freshly brewing coffee beans pervaded the air. But there was no sign of Sonia. Qualms touched him; had their kiss spooked her? The anxiety tautened—after the time they had spent together, the hours wrapped in each other's company, surely she knew he would never do anything she didn't want? That he wanted to help her, for her to trust him. He hadn't meant to kiss her, but he hadn't been able to help himself. They'd been standing overlooking the panoramic vista of Naples, the stretch of history from the ancient fourteenth-century bell tower to the towering recent skyscrapers all bathed in the orange glow of a glorious sunset. She'd looked up at him to ask a question, her long dark hair ruffled in the breeze, her blue eyes sparkling, and temptation had been too much. He'd leant down and a tentative brush of his lips against hers had evolved, deepened into the type of kiss that fairy tales were made of.

That had been yesterday and they'd walked back, hand in hand, in a dazed silence neither had wanted to break. And he'd been so sure that the magic of the kiss would cast its spell onto this day, onto the future. But now that certainty faded with each tick of the clock; he glanced at his watch and then headed to the spare room, knocked gently on the door. No answer. He knocked again, louder. Still nothing. Worry and foreboding twisted inside him as he tried the door. Not locked; he had no idea if Sonia locked the door at night or not. A moment's hesitation and he pushed the door open and stepped over the threshold. The room was empty.

Marco strode over to the wardrobe, pulled the door open. Nothing. He spun round; the bed was made. Walking over to the desk, he searched for a note, a clue, any indication of what had happened. The window was open and he stared outside; had she snuck out through there? Anxiety clenched his gut. Where would she have gone? Turning, he raced to the bed, stripped it down, searched for something, anything. Perhaps the note had slipped to the floor. Surely, she wouldn't have just left. Oh God. Was it his fault? He shouldn't have kissed her.

But no matter how frantic his search, all Marco found was a single strand of jet-black hair.

CHAPTER ONE

Present day

PRINCESS SOFIA OF PALOSIA stared at her reflection in the mirror, decked out in all her bridal finery. The duchess satin dress was straight from a fairy tale, designed to combine elegance with luxury, with a hand-beaded, long-sleeved bodice, corseted waist and a full ivory skirt that fell in soft folds to just brush the floor. To complete the picture-perfect image, an extravagant train extended behind her, to be held by the array of bridesmaids assembled to showcase the aristocracy from both the bride's and groom's sides.

Was she really going to do this? Sofia gritted her teeth, clenched her hands into fists. Yes, she was. She'd thought this through and marriage to Prince Eduardo of Sarcos was the only choice.

The alternative was to remain on Palosia, trapped by her father into an existence, a lifestyle she didn't want. She loved her country, surrounded by the sparkling blue of the Mediterranean, the island a quixotic blend of so many terrains. Majestic-peaked mountains touched the skyline, sun-kissed beaches swathed with white sand stretched along the lapping waves. There were lush olive groves and valleys where fish-laden rivers flowed. The lazy drone of bees hummed in the flower-scented air. Palosia was a truly beautiful place. But there was no future for Sofia here.

Here she was hedged in by rules and restrictions, not allowed to pursue a career. Largely ignored but wheeled out on public occasions because, to her father's irritation, the people loved her. Despite the fact she had commoners' blood running through her veins. Despite the fact her mother had brought scandal and disrepute to the royal name. Perhaps the people felt pity for the princess who had been abandoned by her mother. The then Queen Flavia had run away, fled her distasteful marriage and gone back to the arms of her true love when Sofia was a baby.

And King Fiero had never forgiven his daughter for the humiliation of her mother's desertion. So, he in turn did his best to humiliate Sofia, had even written her out of the line of succession. Women could not rule in Palosia, but King Fiero had excluded Sofia completely, decreed that any sons born to her could not ascend the throne either.

Sofia could still taste the revelation of that bitter truth, when she'd learnt what he'd done. Had wondered if her mother could have envisaged the depth of King Fiero's anger when she'd fled, back—so it was rumored—to Naples.

Naples.

The word evoked the memories she had buried deep down, summoned images of Marco. The boy, the man, who had rescued her, taken her in and with whom she had shared her first kiss. His lips against hers, diffident at first and then…demanding, glorious. It was a kiss that had awoken desire, had dizzied her head, touched her heart, heated her body with unfamiliar sensations.

Not now. Now she was about to marry a prince. Create an alliance. Escape Palosia and hopefully she and Eduardo would be happy together. Have a family. There was no question of love. They both understood that, both happy with the idea of building a union based on convenience, liking and respect. A marriage that would work, unlike her parents'. That marriage had been based on one-sided love. King Fiero had been smitten by Flavia's beauty. Had wooed and pursued, showered her with gifts and promises of wealth and power for her and her family and she had eventually agreed.

But she had never forgotten her true love and in the end that love had won. Had trumped her maternal love for Sofia, assuming she in fact felt any. Perhaps she hadn't. Perhaps she couldn't love a daughter begotten by a man she had grown to loathe.

Sofia didn't know, but she did know that love turned your head, messed up your priorities, made you act in ways that were wrong. And she wanted none of it.

There was a gentle knock at the door and she turned as her half-sister, Rosabella, known as Rosa, entered. A familiar wave of protective love surged over Sofia, along with worry at leaving Rosa. An anxiety she doused— reminding herself that her little sister was twenty-three now, would be twenty-four in the not too distant future. Plus the possibility that Rosa's mother, Queen Chiara, would repeat history and flee an unhappy marriage was now over. Gone too was any real danger that their father would divorce or banish Chiara; he knew the people wouldn't stand for it. So, it was finally okay to leave the sister who meant so very much to her. Rosa was the reason that Sofia had buckled down and submitted for so long to her father's tyrannies.

But now she would still see Rosa on visits to Palosia and perhaps the king would allow Rosa to visit Sofia on Sarcos. Still, the anxiety persisted, deepened, when she saw her sister's worried face.

For a moment illogical hope sprung—maybe something had happened, a reason to postpone the wedding? She shook the feeling away, reminded herself that this marriage was her salvation. A chance to build a life, to *have* a life. A chance to pursue her interest in interior design, even if she was only allowed to decorate and furnish a single royal residence. On Sarcos she could hopefully make a difference, work for good. Achieve something. Not be sidelined any more. Most importantly she hoped to be a parent, a good mother, whose head could never be turned by love, who would stand by her children through thick and thin.

Rosa stepped forward. 'There's someone here to see you. A woman. She managed to get through to the gardens. I was getting some fresh flowers for your bouquet and there she was. She asked to see you. I know I should have called security, but there is something about her. I think you should see her.'

Sofia nodded, trusted Rosa's opinion. 'It will have to be quick, but bring her now and you stay in the antechamber, make sure no one interrupts us.'

Minutes later Rosa returned, accompanied by a heavily veiled young woman.

When they were alone the woman stepped forward. 'Thank you for seeing me.' Her voice soft, her accent a regional one. 'I…need, you need to know something.'

She lifted her veil to reveal a sweetly pretty heart-shaped face, with cornflower-blue eyes smudged with tiredness.

'Go ahead.' Foreboding trickled through her, but Sofia kept her voice even, wanted her visitor to feel able to speak freely.

'Prince Eduardo loves me. I love him. This marriage to you, he believes it is his duty to go through with it, but…what about his duty to me?' The woman turned wide anguished eyes to Sofia. 'He doesn't know, but I am pregnant.'

The words echoed as Sofia forced her brain to assimilate their meaning, to think logically.

'How do I know this is true?'

'I have pictures, messages. I swear to you, Your Highness, that what I say is true. I understand the importance of a political alliance but what about the baby? What will become of him or her? Perhaps it is right to sacrifice my happiness and Eduardo's but I will not sacrifice my child's. So, I have come to you. I cannot get to Eduardo and he will not take my calls.'

This could not be happening and for a craven instant Sofia wanted to cover her ears, close her eyes, in the hope this was some sort of hallucination. But she knew it wasn't. Intuition told her that this woman was speaking the truth, but logic told her she might not be. She had to keep her dignity, keep her cool, push down both panic and the impetuosity that was telling her to simply get up and run. Or better yet, put this woman into the wedding dress and send her in her place.

The bottom line was if this woman was telling truth Sofia could not go through with this marriage. Would not enter a rerun of her own parents' marriage. Her mother should never have agreed to marry King Fiero when she loved another and King Fiero should never have married a woman he knew to be in love with someone else. Sofia would not make the same mistake. Especially not when there was a baby involved. She'd been abandoned by her mother, understood the bitterness and the pain that ensued; she wouldn't allow this baby to suffer a similar fate.

'What is your name?' she asked

'Luciana.' The woman met her gaze. 'What are you going to do?' She placed her hand on her stomach as if to protect her child from whatever was to come next.

'I am going to call Eduardo.' She kept her gaze on Luciana's face, saw her flinch slightly and then straighten.

'Will you tell him about the baby?'

'No. But I think you should.'

Sofia pressed the button, held the phone to her ear. 'Eduardo. I have Luciana with me. She wishes to tell you something.'

There was a silence on the other end, a silence that spoke volumes.

'I'll pass you over.'

'Sofia...wait, I need to explain...'

'You need to talk to Luciana.'

She handed the phone over, aware that her nails were digging into her palms as she watched. Wondered why she wasn't more distraught, assumed it was because there was no love involved. The betrayal was still real and she knew the hurt would come later, along with an assessment of the consequences, but now that wasn't important as she watched Luciana's face, heard the tremble in her voice.

'Eduardo. It is me. I... I need you to know. I am pregnant.'

She couldn't hear his reply; it no longer mattered. She knew what she needed to know. and that meant she knew what she needed to do next.

One hour later...

'You've done what?' Rosa's brown eyes were wide open in shock.

'I've called off the wedding,' Sofia repeated.

'But Father will be furious, he is going to…' Rosa trailed off, clearly unable to even picture the extent of King Fiero's potential rage.

'I know.' Sofia tried to find some courage, told herself that she had no choice, even though she knew that no one else would see it that way. Especially not her father. Even Rosa looked shocked. But, 'I can't go through with it. Please help me out of this dress.' The feel of the material was restrictive, confining, a weight she wanted to be rid of. 'If I have to face the music, I would rather face it in clothes I can run in.' She tried to smile, knew the joke had fallen flat, because there was every chance she would have to run.

But before Rosa could even move towards her, the bedroom door crashed open and King Fiero strode in, his face apoplectic with rage. Various court officials hurried in after him, along with palace security and Queen Chiara, her face even paler than usual. The queen glanced first towards her daughter then at Sofia with worry writ large on her face.

'Is this true?' the king demanded. 'Eduardo has told me the wedding has been cancelled.'

'Yes, it's true. I have called the marriage off. Prince

Eduardo is aware of my reasons, but the official line is that I have been taken ill.' Sofia had no intention of betraying Luciana's story, would leave it to Eduardo to make the decision as to how much of the truth to reveal.

'Pshaw…not a soul is going to believe that. Every court official knows you were ready to head to the church.'

'An illness is better than the truth.'

'There is no illness. And I have no wish to know the truth. Because it is irrelevant. Eduardo will still marry you if his father and I tell him to, despite this fiasco. He knows what is due to his country.'

'But… *I* cannot marry *him*.'

'Why not?' The timid intervention came from the queen.

The king swung round and Chiara flinched. Years of marital bullying and rage had prepared her for what was now a ritual humiliation. 'Be silent, woman. I do not care why not.' He turned back to Sofia. 'I am telling you right here and now, you will go to that chapel and marry the prince.'

For a moment she almost agreed, just as she had agreed to whatever had been demanded of her all her life. Oh, she tried to stand up to her father, tried at the very least to stand between him and Rosa, but, in the end, King Fiero held power over all of them. Apart from that one rebellious week of escape in Naples, when she had temporarily broken free of her father's control. The memory gave her a sudden surge of courage. Eduardo might be willing to sacrifice love for duty but Sofia had seen what happened when a one-sided marriage went wrong. Did she want Luciana's unborn child to pay the price she herself had paid? The answer was no. So somehow, she had to stand up to her father.

'No, I will not. This marriage is wrong. It would bring unhappiness to too many.'

'Unhappiness?' the king raged. 'You are indeed your mother's daughter, mewling and whining about happiness. A commoner through and through, your blood even more tainted than I believed. I always knew you weren't a true princess and yet I gave you one chance to do something for your country. And you have failed me. If you refuse to behave as a princess, your title will be rescinded and you will be banished, like your mother before you. You will leave Palosia tonight and you will not return.'

'Leave?' Sofia faltered; the idea filled her head with fear. How could she leave Rosa with no prospect of seeing her again? On a practical note, how would she survive? She had no money, no real knowledge of how the world away from Palosia worked. The royal family had wealth but that was controlled by her father. He paid her bills, granted her a small monthly allowance and had consistently vetoed any idea she had come up with to earn her own money. The only qualification she had she had obtained from an online interior design course that she had done in secret.

Panic pounded her temples, yet buried in the strum of anxiety was a barely discernible note of exhilaration at the prospect of freedom.

Her father nodded. 'Yes. Leave.' He turned to his security chief. 'Remove Princess Sofia from this palace. I want her to be off the island within twelve hours.'

There was a murmur of consternation from the courtiers and Rosa stepped forward. Instantly Sofia shook her head at her sister; she did not want the king's wrath to fall on Rosa.

'But, sire, the press…' The words from a chief counsellor.

'The people…' This from another advisor.

'They will see that Sofia has disgraced and humiliated our country.'

Sofia dug her nails into her palm as she heard the murmurs of agreement, realised that to all these spectators it looked as though she had thrown away political gain, a marriage that would have helped her country. Her father and Eduardo's had made a lucrative trade deal that was to be cemented by the marriage. A deal that would now be in jeopardy.

'I do not want to see her face. Carry out my orders.' The king turned. 'Chiara, Rosabella, come with me.'

'Could I stay to help Sofia pack?' Rosa's voice was small. 'It may be better to keep things in the family.'

The king hesitated. 'You have half an hour.'

They waited until the room emptied, the security guard positioned outside, and Rosa headed to her, deftly starting to help her remove the bridal gown.

'Sofia, what are you going to do?' Sofia could see the worry, anxiety and doubts in her sister's eyes, wanted to allay all three.

'I am going to go and have an adventure,' Sofia said. 'I will not let Father ruin my life. I am sure at some point he will allow me back. The people will not like my banishment to be for ever.'

'But how?' Rosa stepped back. 'I will give you all the money I have but it is not enough. Where will you go?'

Incipient panic threatened again. She had to go somewhere. A choice had to be made. Her brain scrambled together a plan: she would complete the mission she had been forced to cease seven years before. She would find her mother. Return to Naples.

But it wasn't Flavia who came to mind—after all the only image she had of her mother was constructed from her own imagination and Internet research. When she thought of Naples she thought of a young man with over-long blond hair, grey eyes, a passion for sculpture, and she thought of a magical sunset kiss.

But that wasn't why she would return. She didn't even know Marco's surname. He had been a student in Naples, and could be anywhere in the world right now. But Naples was where she would go.

'I will be all right,' she told Rosa. 'I will get a job. I'll manage. On my own two feet.' She glanced at her watch. 'Now I must pack and you must go. Before Father turns his anger on you. It is better if you don't know where I am going.'

She stepped forward and hugged her sister, just as the guard knocked on the door.

Four days later...

Marco Stewart glanced at his watch and quickened his stride as he headed for the upmarket estate agency situated in the centre of Naples. He was en route to pick up the keys for the villa he'd purchased, not so much for himself but for his mother and her husband. The man he supposed was technically his stepfather, even though his mother had married Lorenzo only five years before when Marco was twenty-three.

His mother would protest at the purchase but Marco knew she would love it and he wanted her to be happy; after all, Giulia had sacrificed a lot for him. Both his parents had. And despite the knowledge it wasn't his fault, he couldn't eradicate the guilt he felt.

His parents were individually both wonderful, loving parents. But as a couple they'd brought out the worst in each other. Marco had never understood it. Once his parents had undoubtedly been in love—their wedding photos showed two people who thought the world of each other. Yet somehow that love had died, leaving behind a scorched earth, a place where even civility became an impossibility. Marco's childhood had been experienced against a backdrop of constant drama, screaming matches, tears, thrown ornaments and insults. Where he was always in the middle, an unwilling referee, in a constant attempt not to be caught in the crossfire or, worse, still have to pick a side.

He'd asked them once what had happened, to be met with a shrug. 'Who knows? Love couldn't survive real life, I suppose. Bills, nappy changing, responsibilities.' And, 'I mistook attraction for compatibility. I think your father missed Scotland.' The place Alec Stewart had been born and grown up in, until a work placement to Rome where he'd met Giulia and fallen in love. But long after love died, Marco's dad had remained in Italy for Marco's sake, spent decades away from the homeland he missed. Another layer to Marco's guilt.

But despite everything they were amazing parents; Marco had never felt unloved or unwanted or a burden. What he did feel was guilt at the knowledge that his parents had stayed together for him, embroiled in an ever downward spiral of misery, but determined to remain together for Marco's sake. So that all Marco had wanted to do was grow up, to enable his parents to be freed of the misery of their marriage.

Which they had duly done as soon as he'd finished university. His dad had returned to Scotland, bought a remote place in the Highlands.

And his mother was happily remarried, to a widower who had a brood of children, all grown up but they had welcomed his mother in with open arms and she seemed to have become one of them, absorbed into a close-knit happy family. Something she had always wanted; another reason for Marco's guilt. He'd known his mother would have loved to have more children, but she had given that up for him.

But at least now she was happy; he recalled her excited voice as she discussed her stepdaughter. 'Louisa and Juan are expecting a baby. It will feel like being a gran...' Then her voice had trailed off. 'I am sorry, Marco. I...'

'It's okay, Mum. I am happy for you and for them. Say congratulations from me.'

And he *was* happy for them, though the news had prodded the hurt, the pain that he had tried to bury over the past three years. Had brought back memories of Leo, the baby he'd believed to be his son. He closed his eyes, grounded himself. That was over. Leo was not his son, and never had been. All that was left were the memories of those precious six months when he'd thought he was a father. Now all he could do for Leo was to stay away, allow him to live his life with his real father.

As for Marco, he had spent the last three years focused on becoming a success. Rich beyond belief. A life where he could mingle with the rich and famous, could buy whatever he wanted…including this villa.

As he neared the estate agency, he saw a woman standing outside looking in the window, a woman with a cascade of dark hair, a way of standing, straight-backed, graceful, but as though she were always poised to run.

The sight triggered a memory of a woman he'd once known, and never forgotten.

His feet dragged to a stop; his heart hammered his chest even as his brain told him to cool it. How many times had this happened to him before? A glimpse of a dark-haired woman, a certain sway of the hips, a certain way of lifting a hand to tuck a tendril of hair behind an ear…and in seven years the woman had never been the woman he'd hoped it would be. The woman he'd worried about, had sleepless nights over. For months after Sonia's disappearance, he'd scoured the streets of Naples, revisited every place they had ever been, but all to no avail. He'd painted all sorts of scenarios, terrified that their kiss had driven her away to some awful fate. In the end, he could only hope that she had found sanctuary elsewhere.

Now…he remained still, watched the woman, waited for the inevitable disappointment as she turned away from the window, saw her profile and almost froze before urgency propelled him forward and he heard his voice. 'Excuse me. *Scusi.*'

The woman turned and now he did freeze, as her dark blue eyes widened.

'Sonia?'

CHAPTER TWO

SOFIA'S TUMMY WENT into freefall, instincts colliding, fight versus flight, but her feet seemed rooted to the pavement, the two of them caught in an immoveable tableau of shock. Could it really be Marco? But as she stood here, looking at him, every bone in her body told her it was. Even though this man was a far cry from the young man of yesteryear. The over-long hair was now cut ruthlessly short, his features seemed harder, the jaw more pugnacious, the grey eyes full of shock.

Now her gaze lingered on his lips, sct in a firm linc. Lips that had given her such joy in that one glorious kiss. 'Marco?' The more her gaze drank him in, the more familiar he looked, and for once all the years of royalty, of knowing the right thing to say at the right time, the correct smile, the things drilled into her in lieu of an actual education, deserted her and she knew she resembled nothing more than a puffer fish. 'I...'

He took a deep breath and relief dawned in his eyes at the unspoken confirmation that it was really her. 'You're okay?' he asked. 'Thank God. All these years I've wondered, hoped...that you were all right.'

'I'm fine.' As she looked at him, still hardly able to believe that this was Marco, she became aware of something she couldn't quite define: a beat of her pulse, a race of her heart and an almost irresistible urge to step closer to him. 'I didn't think you'd even remember me.' The inanity of the words struck her as she saw his expression change, relief now mitigated by incredulity.

'Not remember you? You vanished without trace. I was worried sick.'

Sofia tried to work out what to say. 'Sorry. I don't know why I said that. Maybe I hoped you'd forget about me.' The only way to mitigate the guilt she'd felt at the impossibility of explaining the circumstances of her rapid departure. An explanation that was still not possible. All she could think of to do was to close this down as quickly as possible. 'I am truly sorry that you were worried, but now, as you can see, I am fine so, if you'll excuse me, I'd better be on my way.'

'Huh? You're kidding, right? You're going to go, disappear again?' Now a hint of anger entered the mix and he took a deep breath and, with what was a clear effort, he stepped back, hands raised in the air, ran a hand over his face, and when he spoke his voice was softer and she glimpsed *her* Marco, the man she had remembered for all these years, tucked away in a small private space in her heart. Her secret—she'd never told anyone about Marco, not even Rosa. 'Look, I'm incredibly relieved that you are okay, but after all these years I guess I would like some explanation for what happened. Especially...'

He broke off and she became aware of a woman waving at him through the estate agency window. 'I have an appointment. It shouldn't take long or I can postpone.'

Sofia turned away from the window slightly; so far there had been no publicity about her race from the altar, but there had been some publicity about the engagement and she had no wish to be recognised.

'So, give me five minutes and then how about a quick catch-up over a coffee? A latte, extra milky with chocolate sprinkles.'

'You remember?' The idea surprised and warmed her.

'I do.' And in that instant, something changed, crackled in the air, fizzed and popped. Marco remembered how much she had loved the local lattes—what else did he remember? Right now, as their gazes met she'd put money he was walking the same steps down memory lane. To a kiss that was seared on her memory. But surely not on his. To him it must have long since faded to insignificance. He must have kissed hundreds of women since then.

Whereas she...well, never mind the actual statistic. Because the only other person she had ever kissed was Eli... The memory caused distaste, the bitter tang of betrayal, the knowledge of her own foolishness, and she pushed it away.

'And you have a double espresso with a drop of milk. And I said...'

'That you couldn't see the point.' His eyes rested on her face and he gave a sudden smile, and Sofia blinked. His smile had always made her want to smile as well, but now, seven years later, it did more than that. It made her tummy dip, her toes curl, and heated her whole body. 'So, what do you say? One coffee for old times' sake?'

She should turn and walk away. That made sense. Because she couldn't give him what he wanted—couldn't explain the truth without revealing her identity. And she had no intention of doing that. For some reason the press hadn't so much as mentioned the jilting of a prince at the altar; instead, there had been a brief statement from the Palosian palace that Princess Sofia had been taken suddenly ill, that the family would appreciate privacy at this difficult time. Accompanied by a picture of Prince Eduardo, his face etched with concern. Though knowing what she knew, Sofia wondered exactly who the concern was for. Not for her, she was sure.

She didn't know what was going on, assumed it was a publicity spin, in which case the best thing she could do was to stay under the radar. At least until she found her mother; she had no wish to bring the glare of publicity down on Flavia, and had no wish for the press to interrogate her as to her reasons for ending her engagement. Problem was, the real world was hard to navigate if you were unable to show a passport or proof of identity. If you didn't want to admit to who you were.

So coffee was a bad idea. Yet temptation beckoned. Put it down to loneliness, to wanting human contact, wanting a distraction, or perhaps sheer curiosity. She wanted to know what he had done with his life. He seemed harder but he'd also clearly done well for himself. Her practised eye discerned the discreetly expensive cut of his clothes, the equally discreet brand that displayed wealth but without the need to be ostentatious about it. Maybe this chance meeting was fate, an opportunity to put the past to rest.

'One coffee sounds good, but I can't offer any explanation. I'm sorry.' And she was; his concern was undoubtedly genuine and the idea that he had cared was…nice.

Understandable confusion creased his brow and then there was that smile again. 'I know now that you are safe and well and unharmed. That will have to be good enough. Seven years ago, if I'd been offered that I'd have taken it. One coffee, no explanations it is. Give me a minute. Or you can come in?'

Sofia shook her head. 'I'll wait.'

She watched as he went inside, the easy stride, the breadth of his shoulders, saw the woman smile at him, an exchange of words, and then Marco frowned, the woman looked apologetic and then he smiled again, she handed over an envelope and then he turned and headed back to the door, pushed it open and her gaze dwelled on the shape of his forearm, the strength of his hands.

And Sofia admitted the truth to herself. She also wanted to prolong this contact because something she'd only latently recognised in her youth was glaringly obvious now. This man was gorgeous. Now qualms surfaced; perhaps coffee was a bad idea. Marco might be gorgeous but that was irrelevant. She was in Naples to find her mother, and learn how to live her own life, stand on her own two feet. Not to be distracted by good looks and an amazing body. Seven years ago, attraction had distracted her, made her lose perspective. But she hadn't identified it as attraction back then. Back then all she had known was a consuming desire to be with Marco, with the young man who was so passionate and so kind, who'd looked at her as if she mattered, as if she was important. Now she could dimly perceive that the tug, the connection she felt, was physical.

And she still had no idea how to navigate the shoals of attraction and no desire to learn. Attraction was too complicated a landscape; her mother's beauty had been what caught King Fiero's eye, caused him to fall in love and pursue a woman who didn't want him.

'Ready?' Marco's deep voice cut through the thoughts.

Get a grip; she was going for one coffee. 'Ready. That was quick.'

'I just needed to pick up some keys; the agent had also said she could find me an interior designer, but it turns out he's not available after all.'

Sofia opened her mouth and closed it again. She could hardly offer her services, based on an online course and a sketchbook full of ideas. The idea was preposterous. She had no experience, no website, no references; hell, she couldn't even tell him her true name.

So, she remained silent as they negotiated a busy road with its preponderance of cars weaving and merging, cheerful horns blaring as scooters zoomed in and out in the organised chaos that characterised the city's traffic flow. Then made their way down a couple of narrow alleyways, strung with washing pegged out to dry, walls bedecked with posters and graffiti, and balconies dotted with vibrant potted flowers. The walk triggered an avalanche of memories, of seven years ago when they had walked together along similar streets. The contrast seemed stark; back then she'd felt as if she were floating on air in his company, they'd spoken about so many things or walked in a silence that had been so full of contentment there had been no need for words. But then, as now, she'd always been achingly aware of him, his proximity, only then she hadn't understood the significance of her feelings.

Not until he'd kissed her, his lips unlocking the answer, unleashing a burn of need, one they had never had a chance to explore. And never would.

It somehow seemed important to remember that as they reached a bustling café, joined the throng of customers, and she was even more aware of his proximity, the hard swell of muscle, the breadth of his shoulders. Tried to focus instead on the aroma of coffee and baking, the bricked arches behind the glass-fronted cabinets that housed an array of pastries, the foliage and flowers that wreathed the ceiling above.

'I'll get the coffees,' he said. 'Would you like something to eat?' His grey eyes way too discerning.

'Just coffee is fine,' she said, even as she tried to remember when she'd last eaten. Her appetite had vanished in the aftermath of her furtive departure from Palosia, the need to find a cheap place to stay, the dawning realisation that finding a job of any sort was difficult without a useable bank account, any form of identity. But she was managing. She was staying in a cheap hotel and working night shifts as a cleaner for cash. Thankfully on her own, so no one could see how much longer it took her than the allocated hours. Simply due to inexperience. But it was a job, her first job, and she felt a sense of pride in it, a thrill at receiving money she'd earnt. 'I'll grab a table.'

A few minutes later he made his way over.

'I brought food,' he said. 'I couldn't resist.'

She opened her mouth to protest and then she saw the tray he placed down on the table and as if on cue her tummy gave a rumble of hunger.

'Sfogliatelle,' she said.

More memories washed over her, of other cafés, of ending up with cream from the pastry on her upper lip, the feel of his finger gently rubbing it off. 'Thank you,' she managed. 'I'll give you some money.'

He shook his head. 'No. You didn't ask for them. Anyway, I skipped lunch. It's as much for me as you.'

'Then thank you,' she said, aware that she was suddenly ravenous. Had a suspicion it was because for the first time in days she felt safe, even though she knew that didn't really make sense. Or maybe it did, because that was how he had made her feel seven years ago. Safe. She reached for a pastry.

Marco watched as she ate, realised that Sonia, or whatever her name was, had been hungry, whatever she had said. He studied her face, saw how her beauty had matured, her face more slender, the slant of her cheekbones more accentuated, a few more lines around the arresting dark blue eyes. Her hair was longer, fell in sleek waves past her shoulders. His gaze went back to her face and now he couldn't help but focus on her lips, generous and, oh, so kissable. Did she remember their kiss? Or had she wiped it from her memory because that had triggered her to run away? *Forget the kiss.* Curiosity resurfaced. What had happened seven years before? Maybe a better question would be, why did it matter? She had said she was fine. All that had happened was that she'd moved on. And yet…he studied her face again, saw the smudges of tiredness under her eyes, and the questions kept coming. How could he have got it so wrong? Why couldn't she explain now? Tell him she'd regretted their kiss and so she'd done a midnight runner. And why did his instinct tell him something was wrong?

Stop it, Marco. Surely he knew by now that his knight-errant instincts were misplaced. When he'd met Leila, she'd purported to being down on her luck, the victim of a bad break-up. He'd taken her story at face value, agreed to let her stay in his spare room. That had been the start of a path that had led to a world of grief and pain.

He wouldn't do that again; Sonia had said she was fine, so he'd make polite conversation and be on his way. 'What brings you back to Naples? A holiday?'

'Business,' she said, but didn't elaborate. 'What about you? Tell me about yourself,' she said. 'Did you graduate? Are you a sculptor now?'

'No.' The question a bolt from the past; he'd long since abandoned those ambitions and dreams. Dreams he'd harboured since childhood, when he'd made things out of putty, out of clay, cardboard tubes, anything. Models, building blocks… It had been a way of blocking out his parents' arguments, the accusations, the hurled objects, the slammed doors and the tears. He'd always believed being an artist, a creator, was his raison d'être, his career, his calling. But life had turned out differently.

Soon after Leila had moved in, they had fallen into a brief relationship. Soon after that she'd told him she was pregnant. And his world had changed. He'd got a sensible job with a steady pay cheque but he had kept sculpting in his spare time. Happiness had fed his creativity. He and Leila had decided not to continue any form of romantic relationship, had wanted to focus instead on being parents, but they had remained living together so Marco could help, be part of the journey. Leo had been born and Marco had loved every minute; for six wonderful months he had been a hands-on dad, filled with love and pride in his beautiful, adorable little boy.

Then Leila had dropped her bombshell and his world had exploded and all his creativity had dried up. As if it had never been. He'd gone to his studio and it had all seemed so pointless. Things he'd made when he'd been deluded, when he'd believed himself to be a father, now looked tawdry, fake, rubbish. And he'd destroyed them all.

Leila had moved with Leo and Leo's real father to Australia and, left behind in the now, oh, so silent flat, Marco had felt his loss crystallise into a hardness, had realised that all his creativity had gone for good, buried in the avalanche of bleakness, loss and betrayal. So, to keep sane, to keep going, he had determined to succeed in a different way. A way he could control, a way that made sense, could be measured in cold, hard currency. Instead of iron, he'd forged a global business and become a tech billionaire.

'I set up a company instead. I am a businessman.' He looked at her closely; it seemed clear that she had no idea who he was. True, he wasn't an instantly recognisable figure, his only brush with celebrity a brief relationship with a supermodel three years before. Since their split he'd kept a low profile, had no need or desire to court celebrity status or public recognition.

'You really don't sculpt any more?' Her voice sounded shocked. 'You were so…focused, so passionate about it and so talented. Your ideas, your sketches, the pieces you showed me.'

'That was then,' he said shortly. 'I was young. It turns out I am better suited to business.'

'What sort of business is it?' she asked.

'Sales,' he said. There was a silence and her frown deepened.

'What sort of sales?' Her dark blue eyes focused on him. And then she blinked. 'It's okay. You don't need to tell me. I know. You set up a company, an online platform for people to sell things. You're Marco Stewart, aren't you? I should have recognised you. You are the founder and CEO of Krafty.'

'Yes.' He wondered why he hadn't wanted her to know. Perhaps it had simply been a tit-for-tat response or perhaps he had wanted her to remember him as he had been, an idealistic dreamer who'd been dedicated to art. Ridiculous. Idealism and dreams had taken him to heartache and misery. Being a businessman had brought him success, status and wealth. 'I am. You look surprised.' But she looked more than that, she looked a bit edgy, glanced round as if checking to see if anyone was watching them. Relaxed slightly when she saw no one was.

'Of course I am surprised. It's quite unusual to discover the first…someone you knew briefly years ago has become a billionaire businessman.'

'To be fair, it surprised me. I knew from experience how hard it is to sell your own products. So, I decided to set up an online community, an online marketplace for small businesses and entrepreneurs. It started out being for artists but I've expanded it now, to offer other goods and services. The whole thing took off.' Krafty was now a global phenomenon.

'So you don't sculpt any more? At all?' It was clear that she was having a hard time coming to terms with the idea and he felt his arms cross his chest in a gesture he recognised as defensive. Why, when he had nothing to defend? He'd made billions.

'There's no point. People would want to buy my work because of who I am, not the work itself.' There was truth in that even if it wasn't the whole truth. Again, her dark blue eyes looked into his and just like seven years ago he felt as though she could read his soul. The idea set him further on edge. 'I'm not the person you knew briefly all those years ago.'

'No,' she said, and he heard a near sadness in her voice. 'Of course you aren't. You've moved on. That's why I didn't recognise you; I mean, I've read the odd article about Marco Stewart, billionaire entrepreneur, at various red-carpet events, but it never occurred to me that Marco Stewart could be my Marco from all those years ago. I always imagined you as a sculptor, the same long-haired dreamer you were then.'

'So, you imagined me?' he asked.

She bit her lip in clear annoyance, then shrugged. 'Of course I did, you helped me, you looked out for me, of course I remembered you sometimes, wondered how you were, how your life had panned out. Now I know.'

'And what about you?' he asked. 'How have the past seven years treated you?'

Her gaze wavered, went down to the now empty plates, and she lifted a finger and began to move the remaining crumbs into a little pile. 'I'm afraid I can't present any comparable achievements.' She glanced up. 'But I intend to change that.' Now her voice was steely, the tilt of her chin defiant.

'Is that why you're here?' he asked.

'Yes.' But he could hear a waver of doubt now, as if reality was vying with the scale of her determination. But before he could question further, her phone beeped.

'Sorry. I'll need to have a look. It's my sister,' she explained.

'No problem. The same sister who loves gardens?'

Surprise flashed across her eyes as she looked at him, nodded and then looked down at her messages.

Her face paled as she inhaled sharply, and instinctively Marco leant forward in concern. She looked round the café, scanned the crowded streets and then pushed her chair back in an abrupt movement, rose to her feet and swivelled as if to flee. Recalling herself, she turned back. 'I have to go.' Her voice slightly breathless, though she managed to pull a smile to her face. 'I'm really glad you have done so well, but I have to run.'

She stretched out a hand and on automatic he rose, put his own hand out and as he clasped her fingers something shot through him. Desire sparked and buzzed but it was more than that. Her touch ignited memories. The first time he'd seen her, facing down a crowd of adolescents, her body poised for flight, her blue eyes wide with fear as she'd slowly backed away. Back then she'd been a stranger in the city with no more than the clothes on her back.

As her gaze met his now, as he looked down at their clasped hands, Marco suspected that not a whole lot had changed. Tried to tell himself he was imagining it, that this was a simple case of trying to recapture something from his past, a misplaced moment of nostalgia. That he should let her go. But almost against his will he retained her hand in his. Knew he couldn't do that. Seven years ago, he'd betrayed her trust by kissing her and she'd left. He couldn't let her walk away into the unknown, into potential danger, again. Perhaps he was overreacting, but he had to know.

'Are you in trouble?' he asked.

CHAPTER THREE

SOFIA STARED DOWN at their linked hands as sensations zigged and zagged through her, a mistimed, unwanted raw zing of attraction. She closed her eyes, told herself she was just mixed up. This was panic engendered by her sister's message, nothing to do with Marco.

The message on repeat in her brain

Dearest Sofia. You must take care. Father wants you to come back. The prince still wants to marry you. I think they have sent people to get you. I am so very glad I don't know where you are. Belle

At least she knew the message was authentic, the signature proved that. She and Rosa had agreed a code. Rosa would sign herself as Belle, not Rosa or Bella or Rosabella and that way Sofia would know the message was from her. As an additional precaution Rosa would use the phrase 'so very' in all her messages.

That meant the palace guards were looking for her. Most likely en route to Naples. Her father wasn't a fool. If he had decided to rescind the banishment, he would send people to the place he'd found her before.

So now was not the time to stand here staring down at

a pair of linked hands, or to worry about what that touch was doing to her. She had to answer Marco's question in the negative. And leave. No way could she let him get mixed up in this whole mess. Not again.

'Are you in trouble?' he asked again, her hand still in his, that tug of awareness still shimmering a connection, igniting a spark in her tummy.

'No.'

'Is that a no you are not in trouble or a no you don't trust me enough to tell me? I'm sorry I betrayed that trust seven years ago. You can trust me now.'

Sofia frowned, wondered what Marco meant, saw genuine contrition in his grey eyes as he released her hand and she tried to ignore the foolish sense of being bereft. 'What do you mean? How did you betray my trust?'

'Seven years ago, I kissed you, and made you feel you weren't safe with me. I drove you away.'

'No!' This time the denial was completely true, the syllable wrenched from her. 'How could you think that?' When the kiss had felt like the very best thing that had ever happened to her. A kiss that had awoken something in her, dizzied her, turned her knees to jelly, had filled her with glorious, wonderful sensations and a desire for more. That night she'd gone to sleep with a smile on her face, and dreams in her heart. The kiss was still one of her most treasured memories.

But Marco believed that the kiss had triggered her departure, that he'd done something wrong, scared her away. Sofia felt a pang of regret, of guilt that he had believed that for all these years.

'Our kiss…it had nothing to do with me going. I promise. That is the truth.' For a moment her own predicament was forgotten in the need to get him to believe that. 'That kiss…' Now, as if of their own volition, her feet moved her closer to him, she put a hand on his arm and froze, would swear a current was flowing between them as her fingers felt the sculpted muscle. 'That kiss was magical.' Now somehow her other hand was reaching up to touch his cheek and it felt as though time somersaulted, somehow fusing past and present, the Sofia and Marco of yesteryear and today. 'It didn't scare me or drive me away and it didn't betray trust. I trusted you implicitly.'

'Then trust me now.' His voice was deep, the sincerity palpable and the strength and warmth of his body, his sheer proximity, dizzied and reassured her at the same time. 'If you are in trouble let me help.'

Sofia saw the intense focus in his eyes. Knew she couldn't lie to him after what he had just said. 'I am in trouble, but you can't help. This time I need to deal with it on my own.' Stand on her own two feet, not simply be a damsel in distress. 'I won't involve you.'

'Why not?'

'Because it's not fair on you.'

'Maybe you should let me make that decision.' He hesitated. 'When you left last time, I truly was terrified something had happened to you. I can't watch you walk away now knowing you are in trouble or danger. At least let me try to help.'

Sofia's mind whirled as she tried to decide what to do. The problem being she *was* a damsel in distress and, like it or not, fate had brought her to a knight in shining armour. One her father could not possibly suspect as being her ally. Right now, there was no one else. Seven years ago, her father had tracked her down with ease; it would be even easier this time because she hadn't really tried to hide her trail. After all, she'd been banished, for cripes' sake.

Thoughts followed one after the other: realistically the security guards would be in Naples within hours and she had to make a choice. Leaving Naples was the best option but she couldn't afford to do that and, anyway, where would she go? She gritted her teeth; she would not go back yet, not go back to have pressure exerted on her to do her duty, to marry a man in love with someone else, a man who had a responsibility to his unborn child.

A sudden anger filled her. What right had her father to demand this of her? Her whole life he had made it clear he regretted her very existence, that her blood was tainted, so tainted he didn't want it to poison the royal bloodline. Had never once treated her with kindness or civility, yet always expected her unquestioning obedience. Dammit, she would not be dragged back ignominiously. Not this time.

But surely it still wasn't right to embroil Marco in her mess. Plus, how did she know she could trust him? He himself had said he was not the man she'd known seven years ago and had she really even known that man? How could she trust someone on the basis of one week? A week seen from a nineteen-year-old's perspective, through a rose-coloured filter.

After all, she had used the same filter in her relationship with Eli and look what had happened. That pink-tinged vision had led her to the precipice of disaster, had led to betrayal and humiliation. Because Eli had not been the man she'd believed nor hoped him to be.

So how could she trust this man? When she knew her

desire to stemmed from a shallow *physical* desire for him, or perhaps an even more foolish romantic desire for a chivalrous knight.

But what was the alternative?

As if sensing her indecision, he took her hands back in his. 'Why don't you tell me what is going on? Even if you don't want my practical help, perhaps I can at least give you some advice.'

The café door swung open and instinctively Sofia swung round as panic surged. A scenario flashed through her brain of the guards crashing in. But it was okay, simply a woman entering, pushing a stroller. But it underlined the fact that she had to get moving. She turned back to Marco, her decision made.

'Okay. If you are sure. But can we go and talk somewhere more private, somewhere where we won't be spotted?' The last thing she needed was for someone to recognise either of them.

He nodded. 'We could go back to my hotel. I've been using it as a base to work from as well as a place to stay. If anyone even notices us, which I doubt, they will assume you are a business colleague.'

Sofia hesitated, then nodded. Once inside they could be sure not to be observed and her father's guards would not come looking for her in Marco Stewart's suite. That was all that mattered. Once there she could at least have some time to think. 'That works. Thank you.'

'Let's go.'

They left the café, retraced their steps and then emerged onto a narrow iconic street that she recognised as one of the main roads that originated from the ancient city millennia before. Even as her mind raced with her own predicament, she couldn't help but wonder what the people from back then would think of the present-day Naples, her eyes absorbing the piazzas, a spectacularly decorated fourteenth-century church, the palaces all interspersed with lively vibrant shops and bakeries, the air scented with both traffic fumes and the waft of pizza dough and sugar.

But all the while the question remained of how much to tell Marco. She had to remember that this version of Marco was different. No longer a dreamer, no longer a sculptor; he was now a billionaire entrepreneur who rubbed shoulders with influencers and celebrities. If she shared her identity, it was possible he would share that secret.

They came to a halt in front of a hotel that stopped her in her tracks, the building steeped in history, a grand old house, with a sweep of balustrades and a majestic stone entrance, set in a tiled courtyard lush with potted palm trees and flower beds. 'It's beautiful.'

'It's a renovated aristocratic house,' Marco said. 'And a protected historic site. The inside is even better.'

Sofia understood what he meant as they entered the lobby. The furniture was sleek and modern, the floors wooden, the reception desk made of gleaming metal and glass. Yet the ceiling boasted an ancient fresco that was somehow complemented by the minimalist décor. Her interior-designer eye took in all the detail even as she realised the need not to linger, to gain the privacy of his suite.

To her relief the area was busy enough that it was easy to head to the lifts without much notice being taken of them, bar a cursory wave to the man behind the desk. Then, within minutes, they entered Marco's suite and once again her brain absorbed the décor. 'I love how they've renovated it,' she said, taking in the sleek curve of the kitchen bar and the state-of-the-art chrome refrigerator, one gleaming white wall contrasted with a wood-panelled wall and feature wall of unadorned brickwork. A half-open door showed a spa-themed bathroom. 'It's a fabulous mix of past and present, contemporary but with whispers of history interlaced through.'

It was also, she thought, a marker of how far Marco had come, from the cheap and cheerful student digs of seven years ago to this boutique exclusiveness. It emphasised the changes in him, and increased her anxiety about how much she should trust him. 'Would you like another coffee?' Marco asked and she shook her head.

'No, thank you.'

They walked over to the glass-topped mahogany table by the large window and she caught her breath at the panoramic vista of Naples, the contrast between the narrow alleys and the iconic beauty of buildings dating back so many centuries. One last look and then she turned to face Marco, still not completely sure what she planned to say.

A deep breath and a last moment to filter her words. 'There is something I would like to accomplish. A personal thing and Naples is where I can make a start.' Had already made a start; she'd tracked down the address of a potential relative of her mother's. 'However, for various complicated reasons my…family would prefer it if I go home. Much the same as seven years ago, they are going to send someone to take me back.'

There was a silence. 'By force?' His voice held an edge of anger. 'Is that what happened back then?'

'It's not that straightforward.' Her father's security

guards had tracked her down and given her no choice, but, equally, 'Seven years ago I didn't resist.'

'Why not? Why didn't you call out? I could have helped.'

'I couldn't. It was important that no one knew about you.' She'd been scared what her father, what the guards, might do if they discovered Princess Sofia was sharing a house with a male, completely unchaperoned. Knew it sounded ridiculous in this day and age, but Palosian royalty hadn't moved with the times, her father determined to keep his family in a time warp. Now she was transported to seven years before. The sound of the window-pane slowly edging up, opening her eyes and feeling a frisson of fear. Her mouth open to scream for Marco. Then the figure at her bedside, the low voice—'Your Highness'—the recognition of a member of her father's palace guard. From then all her fear had been for Marco. And perhaps it was the memory, the vestige of her fear, that made her reach out now, to touch his hand.

An instinct she regretted as the touch ignited a fizz of something unfamiliar, a need, an urge to leave her hand where it was or better yet to trace the swell of his forearm, to feel the muscle under her fingers, to… Oh Lord, she had to get a grip. She took a deep breath and removed her hand. 'I know this sounds melodramatic, but it was for your own safety.'

She ran the words in her head, could hear how improbable they sounded.

'So you didn't call out, you didn't resist, you went with them to protect me?' Marco's voice held way more outrage than gratitude.

'Yes. But there is more to it than that. There was no

point resisting. I always understood I had to go home at some point; I wasn't running away for ever.' Her place, as a Palosian princess, was in Palosia. She had duties and responsibilities. But, more than that, she would never leave Rosa. 'When they found me, I accepted the inevitability of having to return before I was ready to.'

'And when you got home?' he asked. 'What happened then?'

'Nothing. No one hurt me or harmed me.' Or not in the way he might be imagining. She had been assigned extra security, exposed to the invective of her father and then life had continued as normal, only with even more restrictions in place. A life where her father continued to grieve the fact he had no son to succeed him, so tried to consign his daughters to a non-life, as if by doing so he could forget their very existence. In truth, nothing very much *had* happened in seven years.

'I don't understand why you didn't get in touch. Let me know you were okay.'

'How?' she asked simply. 'I didn't even know your surname. I didn't have your phone number.'

'You could have written a letter to my address.'

It was a fair point. 'I couldn't.' If she'd written there was a chance he would have worked out who she was, however hard she tried to hide it. And how could she have explained anyway? 'I'm sorry. Truly I am. Somehow, once I got home, my time in Naples…it started to feel like a dream.' A treasured dream rather than a memory. The time they'd spent together, the kiss they'd shared that had meant so much to her, a sheltered princess. It had all been so incredibly magical she'd wanted to keep it as a dream, untouched by reality. Because she'd known it couldn't mean the same to Marco. To him a kiss was just a kiss, one of hundreds he'd have shared before and since. 'I'm sorry,' she repeated. Took a deep breath. 'But here and now I am worried the same thing will happen again and this time... This time I want to at least buy some time so that I can achieve something.'

The idea that so little had changed was dispiriting, sent a wave of frustration over her. Seven years later and she was still buffeted at the whim of her father's wishes, constrained and hedged by duty and royal protocol. Banishment had given her hope, the possibility of escape. That window was now slowly closing.

She wouldn't let it, not yet.

She became aware that Marco was studying her face. 'Maybe I can help,' he said.

Hope warred with pride. She truly wanted to stand on her own two feet. But, more than that, she wanted to find her mother, wanted to evade detection for at least a little longer, didn't want to be dragged back at her father's decree. 'How?' she asked.

CHAPTER FOUR

MARCO WONDERED IF he'd lost his mind; Sonia's story had so many holes he could drain pasta with it. It was a tale of melodrama and intrigue. People creeping in by night, a twenty-six-year-old woman unable to leave home, a chance reunion outside an estate agency.

The thought snagged. Was it chance? He had no idea who this woman was. Further doubts unravelled, warning him that he was perhaps being a fool. He more than anyone knew how easy it was to be led astray, conned, duped—for all he knew, Sonia had discovered that the man she'd once walked out on was now a billionaire, a man of wealth and means. It could be that it was no co-incidence that she had been standing outside that estate agency. This could be a trap.

Logically that was more likely than her story being truth.

And yet…and yet…*surely*, he had seen genuine panic and fear in Sonia's dark blue eyes when the message had pinged through on her phone, seen sadness, frustration and heard resignation in her tone as she'd told her story. Enough to trigger a protective urge, a desire to help. Or was he being played, governed by attraction? Yet another unwelcome thought.

Because seven years on and the attraction between them was still there, only now he was more able to recognise it for what it was. Back then he'd had half-baked notions of romance and chivalry. But even in his youth he'd known the folly of both, had known that romance didn't last and when it sloughed away it left behind bitterness and regrets. Had seen that in his parents' marriage. And since then, he'd learnt another lesson. That even without the flowery veneer of romance, your world could be tipped from happiness to bleak disbelief and despair by the stark betrayal of trust. Had learnt of the duplicity of which people were capable. So *logically* the best thing to do was not get involved, to trust no one except himself.

But now, for the first time since Leila's betrayal, that principle was being tested. All because of a blast from the past, a time when he'd been more idealistic, more naïve. He studied Sonia's face, the wide blue eyes, the sign of strain and the still indomitable tilt of her chin, and he made up his mind.

He'd accept the chance he was being played, trust his instinct against the force of logic one last time; he'd go into this eyes wide open and keep his distance. Because he couldn't risk that she was telling the truth, that she was in trouble, however far-fetched it sounded. So, he'd help, but he would not get sucked into her orbit, would ignore the pull of attraction. He would not get emotionally or physically involved.

Realising the silence had stretched, he leant forward. 'You said you need to buy time. How did they find you last time?'

'I don't know. They worked out that I was in Naples and I think they literally combed the area; they must have got lucky and spotted me. That or there is a possibility my phone was tracked. I wasn't very good at covering my trail. This time I got a new phone when I arrived here and got rid of my old one. Only my sister has my new number. And she has a new phone as well.'

'Then what you need now is a place to hide out for a week or so. I imagine after that they will assume you aren't in Naples and move on to somewhere else?'

'I hope so,' she agreed. 'But a hotel is too visible and renting somewhere is…expensive and also requires some sort of identity and a bank account.'

He nodded. 'That's where I can help. You can stay in one of my properties. The villa I picked up the keys for earlier. No one will look for you there, or be able to trace you. It isn't even a rental property.' It was the perfect solution; he would take her there, make sure she had provisions and leave her there. If she was in trouble, it was the perfect bolt-hole. If she was a con artist, the most she would get out of him was a week's free accommodation and a grocery shop. He could check in with her daily, but there would be no danger of involvement. 'What do you think?'

Her face lit up. 'Are you sure? Won't that be inconvenient? Don't you need it?'

'No. I bought it as a holiday home for the family.'

'Family?' Her body tensed and she glanced round the suite. 'I didn't realise you were married. That changes everything. I can't expect you to help me if you have a wife, children…'

The words touched a nerve and he forced his body to stay relaxed; he had no child and he'd come to terms with it as much as it was possible to do so. No longer dreamt of Leo, no longer thought of him every day. Though the dull ache of loss remained, prodded into a flaring sear of pain by triggers that were unavoidable. The glimpse of a dark-haired baby boy, an innocent comment like Sonia's.

'I'm not married,' he said tersely. 'I bought the villa as a holiday home, primarily for my mother.' And her new family. He'd get something different for his father, a lodge in Scotland, a second home in the country Alec Stewart had missed so much and where he was happy now. 'She doesn't even know about it as yet. I'll tell her once it's redecorated. It is habitable now but it needs work and it's yours if you want it.'

'Thank you.' She folded her arms and he sensed her discomfort. 'I promise I will repay you one day; I can't pay much now but…'

He'd swear there was sincerity in her voice even as he told himself it could be fake. 'No need. It would be empty anyway. I'm not losing out.'

'Still, this time I will repay you.'

This time. The tacit acknowledgement of how things had changed. Seven years before neither of them had considered money or payment; their feelings, the sheer joy of spending time together, had transcended practicalities.

'Would it be possible to take me there now?' she asked. 'Or if you are happy to give me the keys, I can make my own way there.'

He glanced out of the window where dusk was throwing a gentle blanket over the skyline. 'We can, but it may be better to go in the morning. The villa is on Capri. We'll need to cross by boat.'

'Capri?'

'Yes. Is that a problem?'

'No…or at least…' She shook her head. 'It's just I won't be able to get to work.'

'Where are you working?'

'It's a cleaning job. In an office. A few hours a night. I enjoy it; it's good to…have found something. I don't like letting the agency down at such short notice.' She shook her head, and gave a quick smile. 'Sorry. That is not your problem. I'll call now and then I'll get out of your hair. If we could go first thing in the morning that would be great.'

He watched as she pulled her phone out and dialled and curiosity surfaced. Her clothes would be impossible to afford on a cleaner's salary, the long-sleeved blouse and skirt plain but well cut. He wondered what her usual job was. Thought back to their time together; she'd never spoken much about her own hopes and dreams, just listened to him spout on about his visions of becoming a great sculptor.

His thoughts were distracted as her expression changed and he heard the volubility of the person on the other side.

'I understand,' she said. 'And thank you. I appreciate it. No. Yes. Of course.'

She dropped her phone into her pocket, her face once again leached of colour. 'They're here,' she said. 'That was Maria. The agency lady. She said someone contacted her, asking about any recent new employees.'

'That doesn't necessarily mean it is the people who are after you. It could have been a survey, or something to do with tax, or a clampdown on giving jobs to people without identity or…'

'Or it could have been the…the people who are looking for me. It's not a risk I can take.' He could hear the tremble in her voice, the vibe of panic, and a protective urge touched him. 'But how did they know to target cleaning agencies? Unless…' She grabbed her phone again and quickly typed a message.

A second later the phone buzzed and she looked down, before dropping the phone.

'What's wrong?'

'They have found my sister's phone. That's how they worked out to contact agencies. I told her I'd got a cleaning job.'

'But how can you know?'

'We have a code. I just messaged her; I got a message back but it's not from her.'

She took a deep breath and rose to her feet. 'I don't know if they are already in Naples or not. Is there any way you could give me the keys and I'll manage? I assume I can go by ferry if they're still running?'

Marco rose too. Perhaps he should let her go. But there it was again, a glimpse of the young woman she'd once been. Fear in her eyes that she was determined to conceal, defiance in the tilt of her chin as she pulled a smile to her face and, in that moment, he knew he couldn't let her walk out of here into unknown danger. *If* there were people out there looking for her it wasn't beyond the realms of possibility they would find her on the way to the ferry. What then? What if she walked out of here and he didn't see her again?

'I'll take you today,' he said. 'I can charter a private boat.'

Her forehead creased. 'Would you mind if we did get the ferry?' A hesitation and then she continued. 'You're a well-known person. If you charter a boat, it may garner attention and when you get on the boat with me someone may question who I am.'

'That's fine. But we'll only just make the last ferry. You won't have time to go back to the hotel.'

Sonia shook her head. 'I don't want to take the risk anyway. I've got my passport and a few bits and pieces with me. I'll call the hotel tomorrow and ask them to keep the rest of my things.'

'Then let's go,' Marco said, with a glance at his watch. 'Give me a minute to pack some things. I'll stay on Capri tonight. In case there are any problems.'

'In the villa?' She blinked. 'Of course you'll stay in the villa. It's yours. But...' She stepped backwards and now her eyes narrowed with sudden ware and he sensed an awkwardness as she cleared her throat. 'I'd better make something completely clear. I know what I said earlier about our... About our kiss. That was all true, but it doesn't mean I want to pick up from there; it was a long time ago and we are both different people now.'

Marco exhaled. Marvellous. Whilst he was busy suspecting her of ulterior motives, she was doing exactly the same and he supposed he couldn't blame her. 'Understood,' he said. 'And agreed. But one thing hasn't changed. You could trust me seven years ago not to cross the line and do anything you didn't want. The same holds good now. There are no strings attached here. At all.' Quite the contrary, in fact. 'But I was planning on staying in a hotel.'

'Oh.' For a second he wondered if there was a hint of disappointment in her face. If so, it vanished so fast he couldn't be sure. 'Thank you.'

'No problem. I'll be ready asap.'

* * *

Half an hour later they reached the ferry port and Sofia tried to quell the urge to look furtive, to dart sideways glances at every person. Perhaps this wasn't a good idea: if they had worked out that she knew Rosa's phone had been rumbled, they might be expecting her to leave Naples.

She found herself shifting closer to Marco's reassuring bulk. Reminded herself that she couldn't rely on his presence. She was still annoyed with herself for her assumption he would stay in the villa, even more annoyed at the fleeting sense of regret that he wasn't.

Relief touched her as she saw the ferry was ready to board and they stepped forward and merged with the others all making the same trip.

Once on board she relaxed slightly, looked out at the calm blue water and tried to breathe naturally. Focused on the man standing beside her; his warmth, the strength in his face, and she vowed that she'd pay him back. Somehow.

'Would you like something to eat? There's a snack bar through there,' he asked.

She turned to answer him and froze, saw a man walking through the ferry, looking around him. Surely that was one of the palace guards, scanning each section of the room, and in a minute, less than a minute, he'd see her.

'What's wrong?'

'There's…he…a guard…' He was going to see her, any second now. Running would draw attention. What could she do? Hell, she wasn't even sure it was a palace guard, he was obscured by the other passengers and she'd only caught a glimpse, couldn't risk looking more closely. But *if* it was…if he saw her… *Think*. He'd be looking for a woman on her own… Her brain leapt an intuitive leap.

'Sorry,' she muttered and before Marco could respond she moved so she was facing him, his body shielding her from view, stood on tiptoe and brushed her lips against his.

And that was all she'd meant to do, to stay frozen in pose until the guard moved on. But somehow as her lips touched his, as his lips touched hers, all the seething, simmering awareness of the past hours simmered over. His hands clasped her waist, her hands snaked up around his neck and then he was kissing her, she was kissing him.

Sofia's world seemed to tip on its axis. His lips felt… Both familiar and unfamiliar. Familiar because she'd revisited their kiss in her dreams, in treasured waking moments, and unfamiliar because this kiss was different. This kiss started out almost perfunctory and then something changed as she tasted the hint of pistachio, the tang of lemon, the sensation of his lips against hers and all thought seemed to float away and she was caught up in every heightened sense, lost to where she was, who she was, why she was, lost to everything but the spin of desire, his hand in her hair now as he deepened the kiss, and she pressed her body against his, wanting more, to be closer, nearer…wanting something she couldn't define. Her whole being consumed with want, need, greed, desire.

And then the ferry lurched slightly and the rocking motion brought some sort of reality back into focus, a reminder of where she was. Marco stepped back, one hand on her arm to steady her. His grey eyes were dark and she could see shell shock in them, succeeded by surprise and, she would swear, a flash of anger, though who it was directed at she couldn't be sure. She exhorted her brain to work, to think, to cut through the fugue of desire that still hazed it. 'I'm sorry,' she said. 'I thought I saw someone looking for me.' Carefully she shifted so that she could scan the room as discreetly as possible. 'I can't see him any more.'

Marco stepped back, his body still shielding her as he studied her expression searchingly, his grey eyes hard now, and she met his gaze head-on.

'I figured he wouldn't be looking for a couple so it seemed sensible to act like one. It was a spur-of-the-moment decision, and I apologise.' Though she wasn't sure if she was sorry. How could she regret a moment that had awoken such glorious sensations inside her? Caught in that bubble of desire, everything else had faded to insignificance.

But now…as she saw the grim set to the lips she'd just kissed so recklessly reality dawned—she'd kissed a virtual stranger with an abandon that sent a sudden wave of discomfort over her, a wave that doused the adrenalin, the sense of wonder, the heat of desire. Surely she hadn't imagined the fact that Marco had kissed her too; it hadn't all been one-sided. Had it? Doubts began to converge and she pushed them away, would deal with them later. Right now, she had to figure out how to avoid being taken back to Palosia.

'As I said, I apologise, but it seemed like a good idea at the time.' Now anxiety started to gnaw. 'If there is someone on the ferry looking for me, I have a problem. How much longer until we get to Capri?'

'About twenty minutes.'

'Okay. I need to make sure I'm not spotted if he makes his way back through here, or when we disembark.' She forced herself to meet his gaze. 'Would you mind continuing the couple pretence? Until we get to the villa? If we stay close, hopefully he won't spot me.'

'Sure.' His tone was even but something about the set of his jaw, the hard light in his grey eyes, set her on edge. Perhaps he was regretting this whole escapade and his offer of help, perhaps the kiss that had set her alight with yearning had had the opposite effect on him. 'What did this guy look like?' he asked.

'He's dark-haired, about five feet eleven and he was dressed in jeans, T-shirt and a lightweight tan-coloured jacket. I realise that is a bit generic. But he's also quite clearly scanning people.'

'I'll keep an eye out for him. But I suggest we assume he's watching when we disembark, so we try to get lost in the crowd, and walk out close together. Usually, I'd hire a car but that's not possible on the island. So maybe we'd better walk to the villa rather than get a taxi. Just in case he is enterprising enough to ask taxi drivers if they picked up a fare with a dark-haired woman, or shows your photograph at the taxi rank or bus stop.'

Surely there was something in his voice, almost as if… as if he was humouring her.

'That works,' she said evenly.

CHAPTER FIVE

MARCO GLANCED SIDEWAYS at Sonia as they disembarked and then scanned the area to see if he really could see any suspicious-looking character lurking. Tried to decide what the hell was going on, but it was difficult when his whole body was still reeling from the after-effects of a kiss that had blindsided him, made it difficult to decide which way was up, let alone anything else. What had happened to the 'not get involved' policy? To the decision to ignore the attraction, and not allow it any scope?

Clearly it had been jettisoned. Because when she'd brushed her lips against his, instinct had taken over, and not a vestige of policy considerations had so much as crossed his mind. The glorious sensations evoked by her lips, the feel of her body pressed against his and he'd deepened the kiss, and then the sheer intoxication of her response had meant that all that mattered was the moment, the taste of her, the raw, visceral force of desire.

But as they exited the ferry, he could kick himself, knew he could not let himself be influenced by that kiss. A kiss that could have been a gambit taken from the cheesiest of films, a device to engineer a kiss, to mess with his head and distract him from the sheer improbability of her story. Codes and phone trackers and suspicious stalkers. It could all be designed to gain access to a billionaire.

Yet he scanned the crowd looking for the man Sonia had described and they both saw him at the same time. He instinctively moved to shield her from the man's line of view, but his quick glance showed him that the dark-haired man was talking with a crew member, gesticulating urgently as he spoke.

Could Sonia be telling the truth?

'Was that him?' he asked and she nodded, her stride increasing.

'Slow down. You're more likely to catch his eye if you don't act normally.'

'Is it far to the villa?' Her voice urgent.

'About a thirty-minute walk,' he said.

For a while they walked in silence, past the white-washed buildings, shops and restaurants, up the narrow winding roads that characterised the small cliff-laden island and meant there was very little traffic other than the elongated vintage taxis or the almost miniature orange buses that glided by at irregular intervals. Each one scanned by Sonia's anxious eyes and he sensed the tension in her body, had to counter the urge to step closer to her, to offer reassurance. Tried to remind himself there was a chance she was simply acting. How could he tell? He'd had no clue that Leila had been playing him from the first. Had been suckered in, clueless from start to finish. The memory hardened his resolve, his stride increasing slightly even as he tried to focus on the warming sun, the tangy citrus smell of lemons, the bright stretches of flowers that scented the Mediterranean air.

Yet the idea that he could be being played persisted,

caused an edginess he couldn't shake. The sense heightened by the sheer rawness of the desire that still seethed inside him, making it impossible to view Sonia with any clarity. His judgement clouded, making him easy prey if she was indeed trying to pull his strings. The idea he was dancing to her tune, the idea that by kissing her he'd ceded control of his own objectivity, galled him, caused his lips to set in a grim line, and he was aware of her sideways glance.

'Can I ask you something?' she said.

'Sure.'

'Why are you helping me?' she blurted out.

Perhaps he should have thought before he spoke, worded his answer better, but he couldn't, wanted her to know, wanted to remind himself that he wasn't utterly clueless now.

'Because you've claimed you're in trouble and I can't take the risk that you're telling the truth.'

'Excuse me?' There was anger in her voice, but there was hurt as well. 'What risk? Are you saying you are doubting my word?'

Marco considered his options and decided that perhaps the truth was the best way to go. Call this out here and now. 'It is hard to know what to believe when you won't even tell me your real name.' He could hear the derision in his tone. 'The story you've told me; it sounds like something from a soap opera.'

'But why would I make it up?'

He shrugged. 'You wouldn't be the first to target a billionaire with a story designed to elicit sympathy.' That was the truth. Leila hadn't been targeting wealth, she had wanted a father for her baby. But since his material and business success Marco had been shocked by the number of accidental meetings and overtures that had been extended to him.

Sonia slammed to a stop beside him and ire flashed from her eyes. 'You think... Oh my God...you think I've orchestrated everything, including what happened on the ferry. You think I'm trying to seduce you?'

Outrage dripped from every word and anger vibrated from her.

'Well, think again,' she said. 'Every word I have told you is the truth; I have no interest in your money. I have no interest in you. So, thank you for your offer of help but you can stuff it. I'll take my chances on my own.'

With that she spun on her heel and started walking, leaving Marco looking after her, his head reeling.

What the hell was wrong with him? He'd made a decision to offer help, and now, because he had messed up and kissed her *again*, he had goaded her into walking away. Bottom line was there was a chance she was in trouble. The guy at the ferry had been suspicious, Sonia *had* vanished without trace all those years ago, and, dammit, there had been the ring of truth in every word she'd said. He wasn't letting her disappear again, not this time.

'Wait,' he called, hastening after her when she didn't so much as break stride.

He strode after her, caught up and placed a hand on her arm, ignored her efforts to shake it off.

'Listen to me. You can't take your chances. You know that. If you are telling the truth, if that man was after you, you are walking straight back into his arms. Seven years ago, you said you went with them to protect me. Well, now it's my turn to protect you. If I don't and you disappear again, I'll have years more of regret on my conscience and this time the regrets would be justified. So, my offer of the villa still stands. Don't pass that up because I have a few legitimate doubts about your story.'

Her pace slowed and she glared down at his hand. Stepping back, he removed it.

'Surely I am entitled to have doubts? In the past two years since I've made my money countless women have engineered "accidental" meetings with me, have tried to seduce me. Yes, it has made me wary. But that doesn't mean my offer of help isn't valid. Plus, you've made it clear you don't trust me either. You didn't seven years ago and you don't now.' He halted now. 'It's up to you.'

Up to her. Sofia tried to focus through the haze of righteous anger. Realised her anger stemmed from hurt. She'd felt safe with him, touched that he still wanted to protect her just as he had years before. Now it turned out that he thought she'd fabricated her plight as a ruse to target his wealth. That she'd kissed him as part of that ploy.

The idea was abhorrent, the whole scenario reminiscent of Eli. Eli, who had professed undying adoration, all because he had an eye to marrying royalty. Eli had kissed Sofia, cold-blooded kisses, part of a ploy. Now she wiped her mouth with the back of her hand and took a deep breath, actually thought about what Marco had said. Had to concede that maybe, just maybe, he had a point.

Quite a few points.

Her story did sound fantastical and he clearly had been targeted before for his wealth. But…she studied his expression now, and she sensed that there was more at play here, that something bigger had destroyed his ability to trust, that the shadows she had glimpsed in his grey eyes stemmed from baggage that was truly heavy.

And yet despite all that he'd still chosen to offer help, to give her the benefit of the doubt and a sudden sense of appreciation defused her anger.

She looked up and met his gaze.

'If the offer stands, I'll take it. Thank you.'

To her surprise and perhaps to his, her reply garnered a smile from him. A smile that still made her tummy give a funny little lurch of desire.

'I'm glad,' he said simply. 'Truce?' He held out a hand and for an instant she studied its shape and strength and goosebumps shivered her skin as she reached out and shook it.

'Truce,' she repeated and offered an answering smile, though she was quick to withdraw her hand. No way would she give him any reason, however tenuous, to suspect she was trying to seduce him, to give credence to the idea she was a gold-digger. So, as they walked, she was careful not to get too close.

Fifteen minutes later, Marco gestured. 'That's the one.'

Sofia stared at the sprawling elegant edifice, the tall arches and white plaster walls, set within a mosaicked courtyard surrounded by a stone wall, sectioned with Roman columns. She looked up at the roof of curved terracotta clay tiles and the jut of the balconied terrace, the whole thing another stark reminder of how wealthy Marco was if he could make a purchase like this as a holiday home for someone else. 'It's stunning,' she said, aware of an urge to sketch it to capture the Mediterranean architecture on the page.

A tiled pathway lined with colourful pots containing

shrubs led to a front door that made her come to a halt. The arched door made of heavy Venetian glass allowed a tantalising glimpse into the interior of the house. 'I've never seen anything like this.'

'It was one of the reasons I bought the house. Well, that and where it's located.' He opened the front door and stood back so she could enter. 'I can show you around straight away if you like?' he offered.

'I'd love that.' The interior designer in her was eager to look at the rooms, come up with ideas, even though she knew the exercise would be done solely for herself, aware of a wish Marco were bringing her here because she was a bona fide interior designer.

She followed him along an entrance tiled with what looked like original ceramic tiles, through to a living room and a reception room both sporting high vaulted ceilings, featuring gold leaf and wooden beams, and cool marble floors. Massive arched glass windows showcased a view of a garden where rose bushes and lemon trees abounded and the lounge boasted an immense glass door leading onto a large covered terrace.

'Your mum will love this. It's truly beautiful and has such potential.' She glanced at him and a pang assailed her as she tried to picture having a mother who had done so much for you that you wanted to give her a gift of such beauty.

'Thank you,' he said. 'I'll show you the rest of the house. There are four en suite bedrooms as well,' Marco explained. 'Two of them are furnished, though like in all the rooms the furniture is a bit basic, a hotchpotch of things the previous owner didn't want.' He took a deep breath. 'So, I thought I'd stay tonight. You can choose whichever room you prefer and I'll take the other.'

'Stay?' Sofia shook her head. 'No way.' Not whilst he doubted her story and her motivation, and would probably barricade his door. 'There is no need. I have everything I need here and if I do run into any problems I can contact you.'

'I disagree. If the man you saw is looking for you there is a chance he will knock on random villa doors; he could be lurking outside, could knock on the neighboring villas' doors and ask if anyone saw any strangers or new people. Hell, he may stay in the same hotel as me, recognise me from the ferry and ask where the woman I was with is. It is better if I stay here.'

'Even though you have doubts about my story?'

'Doubts that I accept may be misplaced. If I leave here tonight and I return tomorrow and you're gone I'll never know what happened, won't even know where you are. Whether you have simply decided to leave or whether you have been spirited away.'

The words made her pause. The possibility that Marco would never know for sure that she wasn't a con artist made her skin prickle with the sheer unacceptability of it. Or what if he stayed and the guards turned up and he got hurt trying to protect her when he didn't even know who he was protecting? The idea horrified her.

Yet she hesitated. If she revealed the truth, she was putting her future in his hands and all her previous doubts resurfaced. Her own dubious ability to judge men's trustworthiness, amply demonstrated by how she'd believed Eli, the fact she barely knew Marco and even *if* she had been able to trust him years before that didn't mean she could now. But more than that was the knowledge that if Marco did betray her that would devastate her, would shatter the memories she had held so close to her of their magical week together.

Instinct told her she could trust him, but she couldn't be certain that her doubts were unfounded. Maybe she should channel her sister. Rosa always believed the best of people; that was what Sofia would do now. Take the risk in the interest of doing what she knew to be right. She couldn't ask him to put himself in danger without knowing the facts.

'If you are going to stay then you need to know the truth. I *want* you to make that choice knowing the truth.'

'Are you sure?' His face held a serious expression, as if he understood that this wasn't a decision she'd made lightly.

'Yes.'

'Then let's go and sit on the terrace. It's still warm and the previous owner has left a bottle of wine and some food in the fridge. We can have a picnic on the terrace and talk.'

'That sounds good.'

'You go and sit. I'll bring everything.'

She nodded, stepped towards the glass doors that led onto the terrace and stood, mesmerised by the sweeping panoramic vista before her. The famous rock formations that had been shaped and weathered over millions of years, the peak and jut of cliff faces, the spread of whitewashed edifices and the glinting aquamarine ripple of the sea. The whole thing took her breath away and as she gazed out, she tried to decide the best way to explain who she was, knew that there was no way to build up to the revelation of her identity. Hoped she'd made the right decision to trust him.

CHAPTER SIX

MARCO HANDED SONIA a glass of cold sparkling wine, and sat opposite her on one of the cushioned chairs placed under the wicker-ceiled covering, made sure he kept his body relaxed, his expression neutral, not wanting to overwhelm her or force anything. This was clearly a big deal and he wouldn't rush her.

'I'm a princess,' she said simply. 'Her Royal Highness Princess Sofia of Palosia, to be exact.'

There was silence as he looked at her, his brain reeling, because whatever he might have suspected, this was not it. 'You're kidding, right?'

'Nope. It's the truth. I mean, Palosia isn't a massive country or anything but it's a monarchy with a royal family.' She reached down into her bag and pulled out her passport, and he took it. Even now, at this moment of shock, a frisson ruffled the air as his hand brushed hers. And he realised whatever else changed with her revelation, this hadn't, the attraction impervious to rank or status.

He opened the passport, looked down at the unfamiliar official stamp, the ornate lettering, the crystal-clear confirmation that the woman sitting opposite him was a royal princess. The idea difficult to wrap his brain round. The woman he'd rescued on the streets of Naples seven years before was a princess. For all these years he hadn't known something so massive. Thoughts and emotions collided: a wish she'd told him before, a sense of the surreal but most of all an overriding happiness that she wasn't playing him. This wasn't a scam or a con, Sonia, no, Sofia, was on the level.

Marco frowned, aware the happiness was out of proportion, told himself it was simple relief that he could now ask questions, make decisions without second-guessing. And now he did want to ask questions, know more, understand exactly what was happening.

He trawled his mind for what he knew about Palosia. Not very much, just a hazy memory of an article once perused.

'Palosia is an island, a small island, a monarchy, growing in economic importance, due to its recent export of specialist olive oil.' But that was all he knew; the article hadn't detailed members of the royal family.

She nodded. 'Yes. About twenty years ago we discovered a whole new olive variety that thrives in Palosian soil. It's kind of lemony and nutty and it's unique to us. It's put Palosia on the global map, or at least Europe's. It's a beautiful place,' she said, and he could hear the pride in her voice.

'But why are you here? Is there unrest on Palosia? Is that why you have left?' His brain whirled with the idea of royal intrigue, revolutionary uprisings.

Sofia shook her head. 'There is no unrest. My father is not a popular ruler personally but the people accept his rule, accept that it is fair and brings Palosia prosperity. I left because…my father banished me.' She gave a small smile, a smile that held a wealth of sadness, and instinctively he moved his chair closer to hers. 'Another twist in the soap-opera plot.'

'What happened?' he asked.

'On Palosia the rules for royalty are very traditional, the customs date back years. Even though the women on Palosia are moving towards more modern ideas, my father has chosen not to allow this at court. He insists royal princesses adhere to the old ways, has made no attempt to catch up with the twenty first century. Women can't inherit the throne.' He heard the catch of frustration in her voice, but also a note of bitterness, the shadows in her eyes deepening. 'And my father doesn't believe in princesses having careers; he believes our job is to be royal, to carry out royal duties at his decree. The main royal duty being to marry advantageously.'

'An arranged marriage?' Marco didn't even try to keep the surprise from his voice.

'Yes,' Sofia said. 'Such marriages have taken place in royal families since the dawn of time. Rosa and I have always known our fate is to marry for the good of Palosia.' She sipped her wine, picked up an olive and looked out at the sky that was deepening to a navy darkness, obscuring the jagged cliff lines, the waves of the sea silhouetted. 'I know how old-fashioned it sounds, but if you look back at my country's history so many marriages based on an alliance worked, endured. Maybe because the people were well matched, had the same backgrounds, goals and an understanding of what they expected from a marriage. I believe that can work, but for it to work there has to be trust and both parties have to agree there can be no regrets or yearning for love.'

Marco considered the words, could see the logic behind them. Look at his own parents: love had turned bitter and that had meant they couldn't work out a way to coparent, to navigate a path to stay together in any sort of harmony. Or perhaps it had never been love, perhaps it had simply been attraction that had masked incompatibilities and in the end perhaps liking, having similar outlooks, did trump love or attraction.

'I thought about it long and hard and, in the end, I realised that marriage gave me so much. Freedom, a purpose and a chance to have a family. To bring up my children in security, in a peaceful atmosphere without drama. Love brings drama, it changes how you think, affects your decisions.' She sipped her wine. 'So, when my father arranged a marriage with a prince of a neighbouring island I agreed. And I would have married Eduardo, I was literally ready to go to the altar when… I discovered that Eduardo was in love with another woman. A woman who was in love with him. Whilst I knew our marriage was one of convenience, I couldn't marry a man who was in love with someone else. I pulled out of the wedding. My father banished me. Said I had let down my country, let down my people.'

'Is that what you believe?' He heard pain in her voice, an underlay of regret to the resolution, and his heart twisted as he moved his chair a little closer to hers, wanting to show solidarity.

'I don't think I could have made a different decision,' she said slowly. 'But yes, I do regret that it didn't work out as I expected. The trade deal my father made with Eduardo's father was very advantageous for both countries and the marriage was arranged to seal the deal. I wanted to do that for my country. And I understand that Eduardo wanted to do the right thing for his. According to my sister, he still does. That's why my father wants me to go back. Eduardo still wants to marry me.'

There was anxiety in her voice now and Marco felt a surge of protectiveness as he tried to understand her up-bringing. 'But they can't force you,' he said. 'Can they?'

She shook her head. 'It isn't a question of forcing me; they can exert pressure. My father is ruthless where Palo-sia is concerned. He won't use physical coercion but he will use leverage. As Eduardo's father will. I had hoped, assumed, Eduardo would hold firm. But if he doesn't, I will. I can't marry a man who is in love with someone else. Not when he may regret it for the rest of his life, not when it may impact any children we would have.'

Marco picked up his phone and did a quick search. 'The only publicity around the wedding is a fairly brief piece saying that "It is understood from the palace that Princess Sofia was taken ill minutes before she was due to leave for the church. The family requests privacy at this difficult time. Prince Eduardo is understandably con-cerned and is believed to be by his fiancée's side."'

Sofia nodded. 'They are buying time until they can find me.'

'Why doesn't your father simply ask you to come back?'

Her laugh was singularly mirthless. 'Because he doesn't work like that. He wouldn't deign to negotiate or ask. He believes I owe him complete obedience. But I hope the longer I stay away, the more likely it is that Ed-uardo will decide not to marry me. I would at least like to go back on my own terms.'

'To another arranged marriage?'

'Yes,' she said simply and he couldn't help his frown. 'Try not to judge.'

'I am not judging,' he said. 'I can see the sense in an arranged marriage, but I struggle with the idea of marriage full stop. And even in an arranged marriage, surely there is a risk that one of you will fall in love with someone else at some point? Eduardo could have met the woman he is in love with after you'd got married.'

'If he had, I hope that he would never have let it progress to the point of love, would have walked away at the first sign of danger. Marriage is my only real option. The only way I can have a family. As a Palosian princess, if I want children marriage is a prerequisite. And I do want children. In this type of marriage my children will have two parents who are committed to being loving parents, who aren't distracted by the drama of loving each other. I will provide stability, security and love for them.' Her voice was fierce with determination and he nodded acknowledgement.

'I get that. But...' He hesitated, aware that Sofia's upbringing, her culture, her country's traditions were important.

She gestured with her hand. 'It's okay. You can say whatever you are thinking.' Her lips upturned in a sudden smile, both genuine and sweet. 'It's nice to have a real conversation, to get someone else's take on things. I am very aware of how sheltered my life has been, so please go ahead.'

'I understand all the reasons on paper for you to accept an arranged marriage. Duty, family... But...what about the actual realities of marriage?' He might as well lay it on the line. 'What about attraction? Are you attracted to Eduardo?'

'Attraction is overrated,' she said flatly.

He raised his eyebrows. 'Are you sure?' he asked softly as a memory of the kiss they had shared just hours ago flooded his mind: the desire, her response to his touch. How could a woman as vital, as passionate as Sofia be willing to forgo attraction for the rest of her life? She had kissed him as though her life depended on it, a kiss that even now had his lips tingling. He looked at her and he couldn't help it, his gaze dropped to her lips and for an insane instant he wanted to kiss her again, *show* her the importance of attraction.

Heat touched her cheeks but she met his gaze full-on. 'I'm sure. Attraction messes with your head. It makes you make questionable decisions. Sparks cause fire.'

'Fire is a good thing. It creates warmth, gives pleasure.'

'Fires can burn out of control, cause hurt and devastation. I'll stick to central heating. Pleasure doesn't outweigh what is *really* important. Respect, liking, compatibility, those things make the bedrock of a marriage. I believed Eduardo to be a good man, with an understanding of how royalty works. He was even happy for me to pursue some sort of job.'

Marco wondered how it must feel to not be allowed to pursue a career. 'If you could have any job, what would you do?' he asked.

Sofia didn't hesitate. 'I'd train as an interior designer. I did an online course a year ago and I loved it. Eduardo said I could renovate some of the royal residences. I hoped to use that experience to branch out, get a real job. That means more to me than any spark.'

She tipped her chin out as if daring him to challenge her further. A challenge he had no wish to take up because he could see her point of view, could understand that for a woman in her position the benefits of an arranged marriage far outweighed the disadvantages. As for attraction, she had a point. His own parents had mistaken physical compatibility for real compatibility.

'Anyway,' she said now, 'that's enough about me. I'm assuming from what you've said that you want it all. Sparks, love, the "real thing"?'

'God, no.'

Her eyebrows rose at the vehemence in his voice.

'Then what is your take on relationships?'

It was a fair question. After all, he'd given his opinion on her take. She was entitled to do the same. 'I'm not sure I have one; I do know that commitment doesn't work for me.' It wasn't as though he minded being on his own; that was the safest way to be. Involvement led to complication and to pain.

'Why not?'

'Because whether it is based on an arrangement or love it doesn't come with a guarantee. Most people believe love conquers all, but love is not necessarily a long-lasting phenomenon; too many relationships break down and too many people race to the altar, floating on a delusional cloud of romance, and then real life kicks in and they realise romance isn't enough.'

She nodded. 'Or they race to the altar on a lava-hot floor of attraction. And that doesn't last either. The volcano stops and you're left with destruction.'

He grinned at her and raised his glass. 'To cynicism.'

'To realism,' she countered, before putting her glass

down and looking at him thoughtfully. 'But where does that leave you? I mean, what about children?'

'Not for me.' His voice terse. No way would he risk that again. His own experience with his parents and his short time as Leo's father had shown him that parenthood held too many pitfalls, too many paths to pain and grief. Before Leo, he'd believed that if a relationship went wrong joint custody could work. He still believed that, but he could now see that even if joint custody was best for the child, it could be heartbreaking for a parent. Even if Leo had been his in the end there would have been loss and pain when Leila met someone else. Watching his son being brought up by another man. Helpless to do anything if Leila had taken Leo halfway across the world.

Aware that Sofia was looking at him, he blinked the thoughts away and shrugged. 'Because I don't believe in love lasting or any long-term relationship lasting. So, it's not fair to risk bringing a child into that. It's not really even fair to enter any relationship.'

'You did try though? I am sure I saw a few articles about you and a supermodel. Cynthia Martinez.'

'I did date Cynthia and that's why I know relationships don't work for me. Krafty had just taken off and I was being asked to a lot of celebrity events.' And he'd decided to embrace the jet-setting, super-rich lifestyle as a way of showing himself that he'd moved on from Leila's betrayal, from the loss of a son he'd never truly had. 'I met Cynthia at some sort of gala. She asked me to dinner and I accepted. I shouldn't have. Or at least I shouldn't have let it go any further.'

'Why not?'

'I knew it couldn't go anywhere. I was still so caught

up with work, with taking the company to the next step, I didn't have time for a relationship.' That had been his official line, the one he'd finally told Cynthia.

'But it was more than that,' Sofia said softly.

'Yes.' In truth he'd spent the whole relationship feeling guilty, because each date had seemed to emphasise the fact that he hadn't moved on. Exacerbated the knowledge that he'd trade this life of celebrity dating and wealth to have Leo back. For Leo to be his real son. And he'd realised it wasn't fair to use a relationship to prove anything. To use another human being. He wouldn't do that again.

'Relationships don't work for me, because I feel like a fraud. If I am going into it not wanting commitment or long-term, knowing it can go nowhere, then what's the point? What do I have to offer?'

Sofia looked at him for a long moment. 'Do you really want me to answer that?' she asked. And just like that the atmosphere shifted slightly.

'Yes. I do. Go ahead.'

CHAPTER SEVEN

FOR HEAVEN'S SAKE, what was she doing? Had the wine gone to her head? Nope, it wasn't that—she'd only had a glass and a half. It wasn't the wine. It was the company, the heady exhilaration of feeling safe, of having a real conversation. Like it or not, it was also the undercurrent, a current that was zinging as they spoke, as the night fell in around them. Now she looked up at the glittering pinpoints of starlight, felt the soft warm breeze, the night-lit illumination of Capri, and she knew that, this time, these moments were precious.

Not for Marco, but for her.

Because she'd painted her future for him, a destiny she'd always accepted as her fate, a future she *wanted*. It was her way to prove to her father, prove to herself, that she was truly a princess, understood her duty to her country. But she knew that future wouldn't include evenings like this, a place and time where her status was irrelevant, where desire shimmered in the air as bright as the starlight from above.

There was more than that: she'd seen the shadows in his eyes, and she wanted to lighten the mood, make him smile, make him… *Make him what, Sofia?* Kiss her again? This time for real, because he wanted to.

No. Attraction *was* overrated, sparks could cause devastation. But that didn't mean she couldn't indulge in a little flirtation; after all, she was a long way from home and Palosia's rules and etiquette.

And she was aware now that whilst she had been thinking she had also been studying him, and, somehow, she seemed to have shifted a little closer.

'Yes, I would like you to answer that,' he repeated. 'What *do* I have to offer?' His tone deep now, it shivered over her skin leaving a trail of goosebumps.

'Hm, well, let's see... You're...' deliberately now she let her eyes rove his face, let her gaze focus on his lips, and she felt her pulse rate ratchet '...pretty good-looking, you're young and...' Now her eyes dipped and lingered on the swell and breadth of his body. 'And you look like you're pretty fit, work out a lot.'

'You're saying I have stamina?' The low rumble of his voice held a note of banter and a deeper note of promise that triggered a stream of toe-curling images.

'I'm saying,' she managed, 'that you look good. You also have plenty of money to wine and dine a woman in style and pay your own way. As for your stamina, I'll have to take your word for it.'

'You have my word. I believe in stamina. And strength. And technique.'

Okay. She was getting way out of her depth here.

'Then you can put all that on the table too. The point I'm making...' What was the point she was making? It was difficult to know when he looked at her like this, his grey eyes dark with something that churned her up inside, her pulse rate now off the charts. 'The point I am making is...' She pulled herself together. Dammit, she would not let him see how he was affecting her. 'Why not be upfront with women and say you're looking for short term? I am sure there are women out there who don't want commitment either. Then you won't feel like a fraud. And you could enjoy a strings-free relationship. Just have fun.'

The idea sounded definitively appealing. And she gathered speed.

'There are so many things to do out there and you are free to do whatever you want whenever you want. I can't even imagine that.' As children she and Rosa had had some freedom, simply because their father hadn't cared what they were doing. But after Sofia's escape to Naples that had drastically changed. 'If I want to go for a walk, I have to tell someone where I'm going and most of the time if it isn't on palace grounds I have to take someone with me. Even on palace grounds there is always someone keeping an eye on me.'

She shrugged. 'You can get up and go for a walk anywhere. Hell, you can go for a run, a swim, catch a plane to anywhere in the world. Sightsee, visit historic sights, go out and eat pizza or whatever you like. And you can choose who you ask to do that with. You are free to ask any woman you like on a date, and I am sure there are plenty of women out there who would love to have some short-term fun. As long as you are honest with them it would work.'

For one sweeping instant she allowed her imagination full rein, imagined a different world where Marco and she were sitting here on this balcony because she was one of those women. That they were here to have fun, instead of here through necessity. But that was not possible. 'My choices are limited by who I am… Yours aren't.' She put her glass down on the table. 'So go out and have fun.' She stopped, aware that he hadn't said anything for a while. 'Sorry. I may have got a bit carried away there. It's just an idea.'

'No need to apologise. I appreciate the input.' His face serious now. 'When you said your life was full of restriction, I didn't realise the extent. Are princesses not allowed to date at all?'

'No.'

'So, you've never been out for dinner or to the movies with someone?'

'No.' She shrugged. 'But, much as I hate to admit it, there is a point to that rule. Another reason why I think an arranged marriage is best. I did have a relationship and it was a disaster. I met Eli at a court event, the annual summer dinner my father puts on for the aristocratic families.'

Sofia had always looked forward to these as a break in the monotony of their existence. It was also an occasion where, for appearances' sake, her father, the courtiers, had to show her at least some respect. Not that she would tell Marco this. She had no intention of moaning or complaining about the difficulties of her childhood. Those things were private. She would never risk confiding in anyone, couldn't bear to see the daily humiliations of her life made public.

'He was a couple of years older than me and the son of one of Palosia's leading families so it was okay for him to dance with me. We got talking and it was…nice.' In truth, she had been so starved of affection and attention that someone complimenting her had turned her head.

Made her believe that maybe Eli was like Marco. That she could recapture, re-experience something of the feeling Marco had evoked. 'He asked if I'd meet him. He was a younger son so we knew it wouldn't be allowed officially, so we used to sneak meetings. It was risky but it made me feel alive.' And good about herself.

'What happened?'

She sighed. 'I realised he didn't really like me. I'd already suspected something wasn't right.' When he'd kissed her, she'd anticipated the same magic she had felt with Marco, she'd tried to instil the kisses with even a vestige of the dizzying sensations Marco had evoked. But they had just felt awkward. 'Then I saw a message on his phone one day. It was a friend asking if he'd managed to get any pictures. I asked him what it meant and in the end he confessed. He was hoping to get compromising pictures of me, and get me to fall for him and then use both those things as leverage to marry me. I was furious. With myself even more than him. I should have seen through him.'

'It's not always that simple,' Marco said and she could see understanding and surely a light of empathy in his eyes. 'A betrayal of trust of that magnitude is difficult to accept, makes you feel like a fool. But you weren't. Eli is the one who was at fault.'

'Thank you. But at least it taught me a valuable lesson. That men will want to marry me for who I am. In which case the best thing I can do is accept that and make sure that there is also something in it for me. An arranged marriage allows me to do that.'

'Not all men are like Eli,' he said.

'No,' she conceded. 'But realistically all the men I am

destined to meet on Palosia, all the men my father would approve of, are going to want to marry me for my title. I have accepted that and I've realised that I can't expect attraction. With Eli… I thought kissing him would be like kissing you. I had a romantic belief that all kisses would be like the one I had shared with you. After Eli I knew that wasn't the case, that with the limited pool of eligible men magical kisses are unlikely to be part of the deal.' There was a silence and she jutted her chin out. 'I'm good with that. It works for me.'

He looked at her. 'For what it's worth, that kiss was magical for me as well.'

'You don't have to say that. I know you will have shared hundreds of other kisses.'

'Not like ours. I'll never share another kiss like that. It was my first kiss that meant anything. Even aged twenty-one I'd never believed in romance. You turned that on its head. That week with you I did believe that anything was possible; when I was with you nothing else mattered except you.'

The words were said with a depth of sincerity and the knowledge of their truth made her yearn to kiss him again, to relive the magic. But that wasn't possible. Seven years separated that moment from this and they were two different people now. Yet the temptation wouldn't cede; what harm could there be in one kiss?

Stop. What was she doing? Seven years ago, she'd let Marco and attraction and foolish ideas about romance mess with her head, distract her from her real purpose in being here. To find her mother. Not this time.

With a movement she recognised as abrupt she pushed her chair back, managed to pull a smile to her face. 'We seem to have wandered from the point. Now you know who I am, I understand if you would rather not stay.'

Marco blinked, ran a hand over his face and then pushed his own chair back a little as though he too wished to emphasise the space between them. 'I'm staying,' he said. 'I am not leaving you here to be found by the palace guards. And, Sofia...?' The sound of her real name on his lips seemed to resonate through her. 'Thank you for trusting me. I will do all I can to keep you safe.'

The idea that there was someone on her side gave her a sense of strength, an optimism that maybe she could hold out against her father.

'Thank you.'

He rose to his feet. 'Now I'd better check we have all we need. I suggest you have the first bedroom and I'll have the second one.'

She nodded, told herself that history would not repeat. This time the guards would not silently appear in her room. As if reading her mind, he stepped towards her, reached out and lightly touched her forearm, the touch retriggering awareness. 'They have no reason to suspect that their princess is hiding out with me. No way of knowing that we know each other.'

He was right and she smiled at him. 'Thank you. For everything, Marco.'

'You're welcome. Now what we both need is a good night's sleep. Then tomorrow we can come up with a plan of action.'

CHAPTER EIGHT

PLAN OF ACTION. Marco opened his eyes, took in the dingy white of the ceiling that needed a coat of paint, sat straight up on the double bed that had seen better days. He'd slept sketchily the previous night, on high alert for suspicious sounds or intruders. But before he'd dropped into an uneasy doze he had come up with a plan of action, one he wanted to run through in his mind before he shared it with Sofia.

But first he'd make sure Sofia was actually still here.

He rose, dressed quickly and gave only a cursory look out of the curved window at the early morning sunshine, the leaves and branches of the trees completely still under the haze of heat from the cloudless blue sky. He headed out of his room and stood outside Sofia's, anxiety heightened as he knocked, replaced by both relief and a flutter of anticipation when he heard her voice. 'Marco?'

'It's me.'

'Come in.'

He pushed the door open and saw her sitting at the desk by the window, a closed sketchbook in front of her. In the light of day he could see that her room was at least in a better state than his. The walls were also in need of paint but the king-sized four-poster bed with its gold-leafed bed coverings looked comfortable. The mahogany desk came with an office chair and in truth the view from her window made up for everything—the smooth azure sea, the scrub of Mediterranean shrubs—and the scent of bougainvillea and lemon that wafted in from the courtyard.

'Good morning.'

'Good morning. Did you sleep okay?'

She moved her hand in a so-so gesture and he could see tiredness on her face, hoped his plan would help dissipate it. 'I've had an idea I'd like to discuss over breakfast. Which I am about to go and get now. Is there anything in particular you'd like?'

'Whatever you choose will be fine. I'll set the table.'

'I won't be long.'

True to his word Marco made sure his shopping trip was as quick as possible, didn't linger at the bakery, with its display of pastries, or the market, and although the next items on his list were a little bit harder to find he was back at the villa within an hour. Once again, the relief palpable when he entered the kitchen to find Sofia standing at the marble-topped counter, carefully arranging flowers in a vase.

'I hope it's okay to have picked these?'

'Of course.'

'I thought we could sit in the courtyard. There is a table and some chairs out there.'

'Sounds good. I got freshly baked bread, butter, jam and *torta Caprese* as well,' he said, naming the speciality chocolate cake made with almond flour. 'And coffee.'

'That sounds lovely,' she said.

He moved to the counter to unpack the bags and he was, oh, so aware of her, of a light floral scent, the brush of her arm against his causing desire to ripple in his gut. A desire he knew he had to quell.

Sofia was in his care, she needed protection and he had no intention of making her feel he expected anything in return, the idea repugnant. Seven years ago, he'd been worried about spooking her with a kiss. That had not changed. Kissing her would be wrong; she was a sheltered princess destined for a political marriage. But the knowledge did nothing to lessen the tug, the allure, the way her vanilla scent dizzied his head.

Soon they were sitting outside at a small wooden table set on a mosaic-tiled area shaded by a canvas canopy and surrounded by thriving luscious bougainvillea and roses. 'You said you had an idea?' She buttered a piece of bread and spread it generously with jam.

He nodded. 'I've been thinking about what you told me and it does change things.'

She put her coffee cup down, her gaze direct. 'I understand. If you no longer feel you can help, I get it.'

'No.' He shook his head. 'That's not what I meant. At all. I want to help. But I think our original plan, the hide-out idea, won't work. Your father has too many resources. If he knows about the cleaning job and suspects you are in Naples, he will leave someone there. He may even leave someone on Capri.'

'But he won't find me here, in the villa.'

'Maybe not, but how long are you willing to hide out in this villa? And how will you achieve anything hiding out?'

Sofia bit her lip. 'But what else can I do?'

'I think you need to hide in plain sight.'

She frowned. 'I don't get it.'

'No one looking for you knows anything about me. They are looking for a woman on her own, a woman with no money, hiding out somewhere. A woman with long dark hair. So let's change it up. We cut your hair, maybe dye it and then you stay here with me, openly. If anyone shows any interest, we say you're an interior decorator and we're staying here for a few days for you to look at the house. Then instead of hiding out in the villa, unable to leave, you can be free. Free to look round Capri, walk where you want to walk, go where you want to go. Without asking anyone. Have some fun. If you're with me and you look different, even if there is a guard looking for you, they won't spot you. And I'll be with you the whole time as camouflage.'

'But someone may recognise you and wonder who the woman with you is and then work out it is me.'

'I have never been recognised in Italy. I am based in America and London mostly, and my only real claim to celebrity fame was my connection with Cynthia and that was years ago now.'

'So, you've no interest in being in the public eye?' she asked.

'None. When I was with Cynthia, I loathed the attention. People thinking they could ask anything they wanted.' His refusal to do a cutesy couple interview, his refusal in fact to do any interview, had been a bone of contention with Cynthia. But Marco had had no intention of discussing his childhood or his view on relationships and certainly didn't want any enterprising reporter finding out anything about Leo. 'I really don't think there is any risk. There is probably more risk of them finding you if we are hiding out. Someone will spot you through a window, wonder why you never go out, wonder why I am buying provisions for two people. I truly think my plan works. And it is definitely more fun.'

'But what about you? Surely you have better things to do than babysit me?'

'Actually, no, I don't.' The words were the truth. 'I'd taken some time off to sort the villa out anyway. Yesterday we talked about fun and I realised that I can't remember the last time I had any. This seems like an ideal opportunity for both of us. I would like to go around Capri with you, relax, have a real break. After a few days maybe everything will become clearer—you may hear from Rosa or something may happen on Palosia. We can reassess then, maybe you can go back to Naples. I want to do this.'

He held his breath, wanting her to agree. Her story last night, the wistfulness and urgency in her voice when she exhorted him not to take the everyday freedom to do as he wished for granted, had caught at him. Now he wanted Sofia to at least have a taste of those freedoms.

She smiled, a smile that lit up her whole face and seemed to light something inside him too. 'Then so do I.' She touched her hair. 'I did think about trying to look different, but I didn't want to risk a hairdresser so I bought some dye. I even did the allergy test. But then I was too chicken to do it. I mean, my hair is so dark, what if it goes orange or something and I look even more noticeable?'

'I'll do it,' he said. 'Cut it and dye it. Tell me what dye you tested.'

She looked at him doubtfully. 'Have you ever cut hair before?'

'No, but I'm pretty sure I can do it.' After all, once he

had sculpted clay, smelted copper. For an instant he recalled the feel of the clay beneath his fingers, the sheer joy of spinning it, moulding it, creating something with his own hands, the intensity, the feeling of fusion.

And whilst he didn't believe he could ever recapture that sense of creativity, he did believe he could do this. He looked at Sofia, his mind working out the angles, the best way to frame the beauty of her face, and he was struck anew by that very beauty.

The high slant of the cheekbones, the wide eyes, the blue so dark and so clear, the long lashes, the sweep of her nose and the cast to her jaw that combined strength with delicacy. His gaze lingered on her lips, lips that he'd kissed, tasted, revelled in. Lips that he wanted to kiss again, even though he knew he wouldn't, couldn't. Not now he knew where she was from, the mores and rules and etiquette of her life. Not now when he understood the extent of the trust she'd put in him by revealing who she was.

So he wrenched his gaze away, and tipped his hands up. 'If you're willing to let me try.'

'I'm sure you can do a better job than me. So yes, please.'

'There's no time like the present. I'll pop back out and get the dye. I bought everything else when I was out earlier.'

An hour later they were standing in her en suite bathroom, facing the gilt-framed mirror set into the marble-tiled walls.

'I'm thinking a bob down to just above your collarbone?' he suggested and when she nodded, he continued. 'I'll wash it first, if that's okay? I think it will make it easier for me, start the creative process.'

'I'm in favour of anything that does that.'

Once he'd rigged up the hand shower over the curve of the gleaming white double sinks, she sat with her head tipped back over the sink and he started to lather in the shampoo, aware of tension in her body. Not surprising given the amount of stress she was under.

Slowly he started to move his fingers in firm gentle circles and she exhaled and he felt the tension gradually seep away, only to be replaced by tension of a different kind.

The room was, oh, so quiet, just the sounds of the birds from outside, a gentle breeze wafting in carrying the scent of flowers, of verdant greenery.

And now the silken feel of her hair under his fingers, her sheer proximity were making the breath catch in his throat. She'd closed her eyes, and he could see the length of her dark lashes, the flawless creamy skin. As he continued the massage with circular rhythmic strokes she made a small noise; a catch between a moan and a sigh, and he knew she was picking up the sheer sensual pleasure, aware of the current that was now impossible to ignore. A faint flush crept over the high cheekbones and her eyes flew open, eyes that held shock and desire. Her lips parted and all he wanted was to kiss her.

But he couldn't, wouldn't.

Instead, he stepped back, even as desire twisted his gut, urged him to throw caution to the wind, told him there was no harm in one kiss. But there was. One kiss would never be enough, he knew that, the idea shocking—how could Sofia arouse such strength of feeling in him, something that felt like more than simple physical desire, something that drove him to almost want something he knew couldn't work? All the more reason to re-mind himself Sofia was off limits. 'Time to start the cut,' he said, aware his voice sounded over-hearty.

Somehow as he cut it was easy to work out exactly what to do, the best way to frame her beauty, to accentu-ate the impact of her eyes, to showcase the classic struc-ture of her face and the wide, beautiful smile.

'Right. You can open your eyes now.' Eyes she had kept resolutely shut. 'What do you think?'

He'd cut a lot, her hair now a sleek crop of glossy dark hair, cut close to her head, the ends reaching the curve of her jaw line, her graceful neck now exposed, and his fingers tingled with a desire to brush the nape.

'I've cut it so you can have a central parting and slick it down or you can get rid of the parting and push it back.'

As he spoke, he demonstrated both styles, tried to keep his breathing even as he felt her shiver when he did inad-vertently brush the nape of her neck. A shiver that seemed to reverberate back to him.

'What do you think?' he asked.

'I… I love it.' Her voice held a certain wonder as she stared at her reflection, one hand going up to smooth her hair. 'I look so different.'

'Wait until I've done the dye.'

And two hours later they both surveyed her reflec-tion and her eyes widened. The dye wasn't dramatic but her hair was a tone lighter, a deep brown highlighted with strands of copper that glinted in the late morning sun. Rising, she turned to face him. 'That's incredible. I don't just look different. I feel different. Like a different person. I think it will work. I really don't think a guard would recognise me.'

'Then your days of freedom start now. What would you like to do?'

'First? I need some new clothes, something to change my image. These…' She gestured to the long baggy navy skirt and long-sleeved dark blouse. 'These don't really make me blend in. I'd love to wander round the shops, maybe stop somewhere for coffee.'

'Free to do whatever you want, whenever you want.' He quoted her words from the night before.

'Exactly.'

'Then let's go.'

As they stepped out into the warmth of the late morning sunshine, Sofia tried to wrap her head round the concept of this sudden, unexpected freedom. As they walked along the pathway leading to the villa, past the grey stone walls and onto the pavement, she felt impervious to danger, able to revel in and appreciate the warmth of the rays, to inhale the hazy scents of sun and lemon, to look around and take in the brightness and vivacity of the flowers, the gloss and whitewash of the buildings.

But now more than anything she had an awareness of Marco, his proximity, his woodsy scent, the way the sunlight glinted on his blond hair… Everything about him causing ripples of desire to cascade over her skin. Her whole body still on high alert from when he'd massaged her scalp, the feel of his fingers, the strength, the tactility, the sensations he'd aroused still bubbling and seething inside her.

Made even more exhilarating by how different she looked, how different she felt, as though her skin were glowing, not from the Capri sun, but the sheer heat Marco generated, the memory of his fingers brushing the nape of her neck. Her whole body full of unfamiliar sensations, a yearning, a need, a heat.

Then they reached the winding narrow streets of Capri's centre and she truly was just one of the many, generating no interest, with no chaperone, no schedule, no timetable in a public place. And it was glorious to be able to walk with anonymity and security, taking in the beauty of her surroundings.

The stylish historic buildings, the abundance of cacti, aloe vera and exotic plants she couldn't name interspersed throughout, in alleyways and also atop the flat rooftops that characterised so many of the houses.

Then they arrived at the shops themselves, a street lined with designer shops, luxurious, exclusive brands displayed in glittering, artistically designed window fronts.

'This street has been around for a long time,' Marco said. 'Two thousand years ago it was where the cisterns were located. You can still see the bricks in the arches along the street. So once this was where rainwater was collected and stored, water that was vital for the island.'

'And now it's somewhere where the rich congregate to buy less than essential items. But I suppose you can argue it's what Capri is famous for so it is still essential. For its economy.' She glanced in one of the windows. 'But definitely out of my price range. Isn't there another famous shopping street with more local stores?'

Marco nodded. 'I know which one you mean. Once it used to be where all the local shops were, so the butcher, fishmonger and so on. Some of them are still there, but there are a lot of others now too, including some clothes boutiques.'

'Perfect.'

They made their way through narrow arch-covered alleys, vaulted houses, and soon enough Sofia gestured to a shop that at least looked relatively affordable.

'I'll try here.'

She stepped inside, felt a flicker of anxiety as the shop assistant greeted her. But the elegant woman gave no hint of recognition, simply offered help if needed. Relieved, Sofia picked two dresses that caught her eye and headed to the changing rooms.

Minutes later she surveyed her reflection, the clothes the finishing touch in her transformation. The dress was something she would never have been able to wear in Palosia, and she loved it. It was short by royal Palosian standards, the silk folds falling to just below the knee. The pattern reminded her of exotic plumage, orange, blues and reds, a pattern of flowers, trees and birds that was elegant rather than garish. The whole cinched with an orange sash-like belt.

She could just about afford this, another dress and a few other essentials. And she would still be left with enough if she eked it out so that she wouldn't have to ask Marco for anything over the next few days. But then what? She pushed the question away, didn't want to let the exhilarating sense of freedom dissipate, took one last glance in the mirror, and anticipation swirled inside her. What would Marco think of her new look?

After paying for her purchases, she exited the shop and a sudden shyness struck her, caused her steps to falter slightly. Then Marco turned, took in her appearance and shyness morphed into a sheer thrill of satisfaction at the look of appreciation in his eye. She heard the rasp in his voice. 'You look beautiful. Radiant.'

'Thank you.' She grinned at him and did a little twirl, revelled in the swirl of the silk around her legs, the sun on her bare shoulders. 'It feels so very different.'

'Shall we head to the square for lunch?'

'That sounds perfect.'

As they walked, he glanced at her. 'Different how?' he asked. 'What sort of clothing is traditional on Palosia?'

'Nowadays most people have relaxed the traditional approach and women wear a mix of the more traditional kaftans and more modern garments, jeans, T-shirts, sun dresses. But not Rosa and myself. My father insists on us "embracing tradition" to ensure we "keep the dignity of royalty and do not draw disrespectful attention".' The truth of it was that King Fiero didn't want his daughters to draw *any* attention, he would prefer them not to exist at all, their existence a reminder of the sons he didn't have. And Sofia a reminder of his own humiliation.

But now all such thoughts fled as they approached the *piazetta* and she blinked, felt as if she were entering a different world where time had stood still. The medieval church and picturesque bell tower, the scattered tables fronting a number of cafés served by waiters clad in cream jackets. She followed Marco to a free table and sat gazing round at the throng of people, inhaled the tantalising aromas of coffee, the pervading scent of lemons mixed with a baking scent redolent of sugar and spice.

She scanned the menu and smiled up at the waiter who appeared almost instantly.

'I'd like a Caprese salad, please.'

'Make that two,' Marco said and the waiter nodded and glided away.

'It's so...picturesque,' she said and she couldn't resist, delved into her bag and pulled out the sketchbook she carried everywhere.

'Do you mind if I make some sketches?'

'Go ahead.'

She opened the book to a fresh page and started to outline the scene, glanced up to explain.

'It's for ideas. If I draw the architecture, capture the lines, it sparks ideas for interior-design themes.' She sighed. 'I know there is a chance I'll never get to use any of them, but I enjoy sketching and it makes me feel like I am doing something positive about becoming an interior designer. Even if I know it's a dream that probably won't materialise.'

'Tell me about the dream,' he said. 'Do you have a specific goal?'

She nodded. It wasn't something she'd share with anyone but, here and now, sitting anonymously amongst the crowd of people, for a few hours she was going to allow herself to believe in a life where anything was possible. 'I'd love to work on fabulous places like palaces and villas, but also on different types of housing. On Palosia there is a housing shortage. People are still living in buildings that should have been condemned years ago. I'd like to knock them all down and start again, but I'd like the houses to be designed in an affordable, functional but also beautiful way. Beauty doesn't have to be expensive; it can be simple and comfortable without being stark or minimalist. I'd love to get involved with that. I'd like to design nurseries where women could have childcare so they could work. And I'd love to renovate historic build-ings as well.'

He gestured to the sketchbook. 'Can I see?'

Sofia hesitated, unsure about showing something so important to her to anyone, beset by fear that a negative judgement would destroy her enjoyment. But the hesita-tion was only momentary; if she was serious about in-terior design she could hardly refuse to show people her ideas. 'Sure, but bear in my mind these are just ideas,' she settled for as she handed the book over, tried to keep her tone breezy, to stay relaxed as he turned the pages, tried to look as though her nerves weren't on the rack.

Relief arrived in the form of the waiter bearing their salads and she looked down at the vivid red of the toma-toes, the bright white of the mozzarella drizzled with oil and sprinkled with basil that smelt utterly divine. Tasted a forkful and let out a sigh of appreciation. 'This is deli-cious. I have no idea how something so simple can taste so good. It must be the freshness and quality of the pro-duce. And this oil is definitely top-notch quality.'

Marco tasted his and nodded. 'This is pretty good,' he agreed, but his voice sounded absent-minded and he returned his attention to the sketchbook. 'And these are really good,' he said after a few moments. 'Really, really good.' Sofia released the breath she hadn't realised she was holding as she heard the sincerity in his voice. He pointed to the page he was looking at. 'That's the villa.'

She glanced at the page where she had sketched an idea for the large reception area of the villa. The wide arched window looking out at the garden showed the cur-rent patio adorned with a swinging basket chair, potted shrubs and plants and a sprawl of benches. The room itself with a striking rug, curved, elegant yet comfortable sofas and an arrangement of circular glass-topped tables. Arched art deco doors that complemented the architecture along with a dramatic hanging chandelier-type light.

'This is brilliant.'

'I couldn't sleep last night so I was just playing around with ideas.'

'I didn't know interior designers hand-sketched,' he said.

'Not all of them do. I can do computer drawings and plans as well. But, for me, there is something real, something authentic about hand-drawing. So here, if I sketch this square rather than take a photo or look it up on the Internet, I feel I am capturing its essence from my point of view and I can use that concept, which is unique.'

Marco pushed his empty plate aside and flicked through the sketchbook again. 'Would you consider drawing more sketches? I don't want to take away from having fun, but I'd love to have your ideas for the whole villa. If you stay long enough, I'd be willing to give you the project, providing the rest of your ideas are as good.'

Sofia stared at him. 'You don't have to do that. You can afford the best interior designer in the country.'

'I know I could. But I like these. I like your approach and I like your vision. If you don't feel able to commit to seeing through the whole project, I could still use your ideas as a blueprint.'

Sofia wondered if she should pinch himself, tried to think straight. 'You're sure this isn't charity?' Maybe he was humouring her, would accept the sketches but never ever use them.

'I'm sure. I wouldn't lie to you.' The words were deep

and she sensed how important his integrity was. 'So will you do it?'

'Yes. I would absolutely love to. To actually design something and know my ideas will be converted into something real… That's beyond anything.' Happiness bubbled up inside her.

'We'll work out a fee.'

'Absolutely not. After all you have done for me, I will not accept payment.'

'Then it's no deal,' he said. 'I offered you a sanctuary because I wanted to. I'm offering you a job because it benefits me and I will pay a fair price for it.'

'I…' She grinned at him. 'Then thank you.' And whether he liked it or not she would pay him rent for the use of the villa out of the money he paid her. Money she would have earnt doing something she loved. Her smile widened. 'I'd like to start as soon as possible.' She looked round the crowded square. 'Could we go somewhere quieter so I can ask you some questions?'

'Sure. I know the perfect place.'

CHAPTER NINE

MARCO WAS AWARE of a sense of anticipation as they approached the port, a buzz of hope that Sofia would like his plan for the next few hours.

She glanced around at the crowds, a small endearing frown on her face. 'Where are we going?' she asked.

'I thought we could take a boat trip round the island. I've chartered a private yacht so we can talk in peace and not be noticed.'

Her smile was all he could have hoped for, her face lit up as she emitted a small chuckle. 'I was thinking of a tucked-away corner in a garden somewhere, but this sounds way more...'

'Fun?' he asked and she nodded, before her expression clouded slightly.

'It's okay. The captain only knows me as Marco and he didn't bat an eyelid. I told him it was a business meeting so we'd appreciate privacy rather than a guided tour and he's good with that. He's probably used to it; Capri is full of people richer and more famous than I am.

'It's even easier to fly under the radar here. I guess that never really happens for you.'

She shrugged. 'Yes and no. Because my father insists on us having a very sheltered life there isn't anything very much for a reporter to ask about. But when we do carry out any public duty we are scrutinised in detail and if we generated even a whisper of scandal it would be frowned upon.'

Which must have made Eli's betrayal all the worse to bear and made her all the braver for refusing to marry Eduardo. Admiration touched him anew, along with a renewed determination to make sure she enjoyed the time she had to be free from scrutiny. Before she had to return. The idea of her leaving struck a sudden discordant note, a memory of seven years ago when she'd gone, leaving him...bereft.

He shook the thought away. That had been different. Back then he'd believed her to be in danger, hadn't known who she was or where she'd gone. He'd been worried, frantic. This time he knew the facts, understood the parameters.

And the most important thing now was fun.

'So let's get on board,' he said.

Fifteen minutes later they were sitting at the front of the fifty-foot yacht, cold glasses of champagne in hand as the boat glided over the water. Marco knew he should perhaps be looking at the scenery, after all it was incredibly beautiful, the sweeping heights of the limestone cliffs, the glimpses of hidden coves and caverns and the loom and jut of the overhead rock formations that protruded from the azure blue of the salt-tanged sea. But instead, he couldn't take his gaze from Sofia, saw the sparkle in her eyes and recalled her vivacity, the gesture of her hands as she'd spoken of her love of her work.

Work that intrigued him; he wondered if she fully appreciated the raw talent she had. The ability not just to capture proportion and detail but also to give her sketches life so they jumped off the page.

Her enthusiasm had reminded him of how he had once felt about his art, his creations, his dreams. Now, watching her, he wanted to etch her face onto his brain, because, one way or another, she would go back to Palosia and would be lost to him. And again, the reminder brought on a sense of loss. Not for himself, he told himself, it was the idea that her talent wouldn't be given its scope, that perhaps she too would lose the joy in her own creativity as he himself had.

She looked at him. 'What are you thinking?'

'How a princess can be so beautiful and so talented,' he answered truthfully, and was rewarded with a shy smile.

'With the help of a billionaire with a hidden talent for cutting hair.'

'That doesn't explain the talent.'

She tipped her head to one side. 'I'm not sure if it is a talent,' she said. 'Sketching buildings and interiors is something I've always done, something that I could do that was mine and no one could take away from me.' She sipped her champagne. 'You inspired me,' she said.

'What do you mean?'

'When I came to Naples all those years ago, I'd stopped sketching; there didn't seem any point. It wasn't bringing me happiness any more—I looked at the piles of sketchbooks and it all seemed like a monumental waste of my time. Sketches no one would ever see, that I would never be able to use. Then I met you and I saw your work ethic, your belief in yourself, how much you cared about art and sculpture and what you did. It made me believe that my dream was still worth dreaming. When I got back, it wasn't easy. My father was livid I'd run away; life became full of even more restrictions, but I started drawing again. Because I remembered your passion and belief.'

'I'm glad that I helped in some way.'

She hesitated. 'What happened? I know you said you changed, you stopped being that person, but it's so hard to believe.'

Marco looked back across the chasm of time, to a time before Leo, a time when the world had seemed a different place with different priorities. A time when he'd been naïve and idealistic. 'I grew up. My priorities changed. I changed. Needed to succeed faster, differently.' Because he'd known he couldn't succeed creatively, because his ability to be an artist had vanished, under the bitter weight of betrayal, the desolation of grief.

But he wouldn't share that with Sofia. It was over, done with, he'd moved on. Hadn't he? Yet today, seeing her excitement stirred memories of the soaring exhilaration, the sense of commitment that bordered on obsession whilst working on something. How time vanished, how deep frustration and light happiness could coexist.

Enough. That was gone. That had been a different Marco. 'Now I get fulfillment from my company, watching it grow, seeing it succeed.' And that was true; he did get a kick, a buzz from his business. His idea.

'I'm glad,' she said, but he could hear the soupçon of doubt in her voice. 'But could you still sculpt as a hobby?' she ventured. 'I know you no longer want or need to make it into a career, but don't you miss it?'

'No.' The word came out harder than he'd meant it to and he pulled up a smile. 'I've moved on,' he said. 'You just happened to meet me in my idealistic dreamer phase.'

To his relief the yacht approached the majestic iconic beauty of the Faraglioni rocks, which effectively brought the conversation to a close as they both gazed in awe at the three colossal formations that towered from the sea.

'They are incredible,' Sofia said softly.

He nodded, struck by the sheer beauty that seemed to enchant each stack, carved by nature millennia ago, sun hazed by the Mediterranean air.

'Legend has it that they were formed by Odysseus in ancient times. He was sailing through these waters and he was set upon by sea monsters. He escaped by throwing massive rocks into the sea and those rocks were the start of the Faraglioni we see today. Other myths say that mermaids lived around the rocks and used to lure unsuspecting sailors off course. The one I prefer though is the idea that the rock would glow luminescent in the dark and act as lighthouses to help sailors in distress.'

'Those stories make them seem even more magical,' she said. 'I can almost see the mermaids swimming through the arch, clinging to the side of the sailors' boats, trying to entice them. Maybe it wasn't their fault, maybe they didn't know what they were doing, thought they were leading them to a life of happiness. And I can see them glowing like beacons of nature offering a light towards a path of safety.' She looked at him. 'Because nothing is black or white in this world, is it? There is good and bad, temptation and safety in everything. Maybe that's why these formations feel so powerful, so significant.'

For a fanciful moment he could imagine her as a mermaid, a woman sent to tempt him. Shaking the notion away, he took one last look at the looming mystical shapes as the yacht resumed its course over the shimmering blue water.

Sofia smiled at him. 'Thank you for this. Seeing those, seeing all of this—' she swept a hand around to encompass the scenery '—it's beautiful and it is inspiring too. It's made me think of lots of themes and ideas for the villa.' She delved into her bag and pulled out her notebook. 'I can't believe I get to sit here doing this and you are proposing to pay me for it.' Her soft laugh pulled an answering smile from him. 'Do you mind if we get started?'

'Of course not. Go ahead.'

'You've bought the villa as a holiday home for your mum; ideally I'd meet with her but, seeing as that's not possible, can you tell me what she's like in terms of her taste? An overall idea to start with. There's no point me choosing an ornate chandelier or pursuing ideas of art deco if she is more of a minimalist. I am happy to do different ideas so she has a choice, but I'd like them to be ideas she would definitely consider.'

She looked at him expectantly and Marco opened his mouth and closed it again, realised he had no idea what to answer.

Seeing him struggle, Sofia said, 'Or I can try to be more specific. Does your mum prefer white walls or bright colours? Is her house cluttered or is she really organised? Does she like traditional or contemporary? What did you grow up with?'

'It's not that easy,' he said. When he'd been a child neither of his parents had given a damn about the interior of the house and their stance would always be to simply find fault with the other person's taste. 'My parents divorced when I was twenty-one and now this villa is for my mum and her new husband and family.'

She paused. 'I'm sorry about the divorce but you must be happy that your mum has found happiness.'

'Yes.' Marco could hear the flatness in his voice. 'I am, of course I am. Happy for her. She's married a nice man and she has three stepchildren who are lovely and have welcomed her in. But… I don't really know them very well.'

'So, she married recently.'

'Five years ago.' Marco realised he'd folded his arms somewhat defensively and quickly unfolded them. 'It was when Krafty was beginning to take off and work has taken a lot of my time ever since.'

'It's okay,' she said softly. 'You don't have to explain. It's natural sometimes to feel a bit strange if your parent remarries.'

He shook his head. 'I don't feel strange. I'm truly happy for her and I don't bear any resentment at all. I just wanted her to have time to settle in with her new family.' As soon as the divorce went through, he'd worked out the best thing to do was slip into the background of his parents' lives. 'It was perfect that Lorenzo came with a ready-made family. And I'm glad they feel like real family to her.'

'Have you got siblings?' she asked.

He shook his head. 'That why I am so pleased for her that she is so close to Lorenzo's children.' Again there was that defensive note in his voice and he frowned. The last thing he wanted was for Sofia to believe he was jealous. 'You see, my mum always wanted a big family. But she couldn't because fairly soon after I was born my parents realised that they should never have got married in the first place. They fell out of love and it wasn't pretty. But they both loved me and they decided the best thing for me was for them to stay together, to stick it out, however unhappy they were.' He could hear the incomprehension in his voice. 'They were individually wonderful parents who stayed together for me. They spent years living their lives for me, now they deserve their own space and time. Without me.' And he meant that, wanted his parents to live their lives.

'They stayed together because they both loved you,' she said softly. 'There's a difference.'

'No.' He shook his head. He knew Sofia was trying to make him feel better but he refused to hide behind that argument. 'There isn't. They endured twenty years of misery, wasted their youth. My mum lost her chance to have a whole brood of children. For me. It doesn't make any difference if it was done through love or if I wish they hadn't.'

'But it was their choice and it wasn't your fault.'

'It wasn't my fault, but if I hadn't existed, they could have split up, gone and lived their own lives. The least I can do now is try to make up for that.'

'By staying out of their lives?' she asked.

'If need be, yes. They deserve that, a chance to live those lives. My mum has remarried, she has a new life.'

'The life she may have had if she hadn't had you?' she asked and there was an underlay to her tone. 'And your dad?' she asked.

'He moved back to Scotland. That's where he was born and grew up and I think he always missed it. He's happy too; he's bought a ramshackle old place in the Highlands and he is doing it up.'

'I'm guessing you haven't visited?' she asked.

'Not yet.' He tried to explain. 'They are both finally happy. When I go round to see my mum it is all so different—everyone is relaxed and smiling, you can see Lorenzo's love for her. There is no shouting and there are so many family jokes. Then when I see pictures of where my dad is, see how happy he looks in the quiet and the beauty and the peace; I wonder how he managed all those noisy years. I don't want to…rock the boat.' Didn't want to intrude upon an idyll with reminders of their awful marriage, or with reminders of Leo. After all, his parents had lost a grandson too. 'I want them to enjoy what they have now.'

'You make it sound as though they can't enjoy their new life if you are part of it,' she said. She moved closer to him and, reaching out, she brushed his cheek with her hand, the gesture so sweet and yet somehow so sensual he blinked. 'That's not true. I know it.'

'I'm sure you're right,' he said but he could hear the lack of conviction in his voice and they were both silent, looking out to the cerulean sea and precipitous shore, at the white and grey hordes of gulls that thronged the coastal rock, at the glint of sunlight on stone villas built into the cliffs.

Then she turned to him, a hint of resolution in her voice. 'I *am* right.' She hesitated and then continued. 'Because I know how it feels if a parent truly doesn't want you in their life.' She made a gesture. 'If you read up on Palosia you'll see what happened. My mum…she left when I was a baby, not even two years old. She did choose to leave an unhappy marriage. The marriage was doomed from the start; my mother was in love with someone else when my father met her. But he didn't care, he believes his royalty entitles him to whatever and whoever he wants and being thwarted simply made her more of a challenge for him. He claimed to fall in love and it was inconceivable to him that my mother, a mere commoner, wouldn't be honoured by his love and love him back. In the end she did capitulate, under pressure from her family, and maybe her head was turned by wealth and promises, the fact that her family would benefit. That's why I know it is better to have an arranged marriage between equals, where both parties gain something, so they can both be content with the terms.

'Because my mother wasn't content. How could she be? They weren't seen as equals. The court looked down on her as a commoner, though the people loved her. I believe she regretted her decision from the start, and so did my father. It must have galled him that his bride was clearly unhappy and once he had the prize, he found he no longer wanted it, rued the marriages he could have made. Marriages between equals. And she must have deeply regretted giving up the man she loved. Then I was born, a daughter instead of the son he wanted, another disappointment and he took it out on her. In the end I think she couldn't take it any more; one night she ran away, went back to her true love.'

'Leaving you?' Marco closed his eyes, imagined the baby Sofia waking one morning and her mother was gone, could only imagine the void that must have left.

'Yes. I have told myself again and again that she must have had her reasons. I try to put the best spin on it but... at the end of the day she left. I can understand her leaving but I can't imagine leaving my child behind. To not at least have tried to take me. Perhaps seeing me reminded her of my father, reminded her of the wrong decisions she'd made. Maybe she couldn't love me. Or maybe she made the decision not to waste her life, her youth. And taking me was too complicated, would have jeopardised her love.'

Her voice broke slightly and his heart went out to her. 'I'm sorry,' he said softly. 'Sorry she left. But it's not on you.'

'You can't know that,' she said softly. 'The facts show that she left me behind. If she'd loved me enough she would have taken me. Instead, she made a decision that her life without me away from her marriage was preferable to life with me in her miserable marriage. Your parents chose to stay in their marriage. They did it because they loved you enough that for them the misery they brought each other was worth the joy they got from parenting you. So don't feel guilty and don't think that their life is now better without you in it. I know you are doing it with the best intentions but I think you're all missing out. You are lucky to have two parents in your life who love you, who tried to put you first.'

Her words resonated and he wondered if she was right, wondered if perhaps his decision to give his parents space from him was misplaced. 'Thank you,' he said softly. 'I promise I will consider your words.' His heart twisted anew at what she had told him, the idea that she had grown up in the knowledge that her mother had abandoned her, the belief that there was something lacking in her. *'If she'd loved me enough she would have taken me.'*

The words seemed to still linger in the air and he reached out and took her hand in his. 'I do know my parents made their decision with my best interests at heart. Maybe your mother believed she was too.'

'I'd like to think that. That she thought it was too risky. I may have cried, screamed, alerted the palace guards. Or she may have been depressed, not thinking straight.'

'Or maybe she genuinely thought leaving you behind was the best thing for you. The same way my parents believed it was the best thing for me for them to stay together.' Just as he'd thought he'd done the best thing to let Leo go. He squeezed her hand gently. 'I truly believe that is possible.' He hoped she could hear the fervency in his voice, wanted to dispel the clouds of sadness in her eyes, shifted slightly closer in the hope his proximity would offer a sense of solidarity. 'Have you ever tried to contact her?' he asked.

'That's why I came to Naples,' she said. 'To try and track her down. This time and seven years ago. I don't know if she is in Naples, but that's where her family came from. I thought if I could find someone in her family, perhaps they could at least get a message to her. I didn't manage it the last time, but this time I have tracked down an address of someone I believe is a relative. I was on my way there when I bumped into you, but now it is too risky to go back to Naples. This time I have to hope that I find her before my father finds me.'

He considered her words and he saw how he could truly help her, on a practical level.

'If you give me the details, I can ask my solicitor to act as a go-between, try to initiate contact with your mother. In a way that keeps your initial involvement minimal, keeps you distanced and doesn't make it obvious that you are actually on Capri.'

Satisfaction touched him as her eyes lit up. 'Really? You'd do that?'

'Of course I would. It makes sense for you to keep a low profile and it will allow you to keep working on the villa.' To enjoy her time, her limited time. And it allowed her to stay with him, whispered a small voice in the back of his head, one that he shut down instantly. Reminded himself that Sofia was leaving, had a destiny to fulfil. One that did not include him.

Yet for an instant he wondered what it would be like if Sofia didn't leave. Remained here, on Capri or in Naples. What would he do? Would they spend more time together having more fun? More…

His brain shut down the train of thought. There could be no more of anything. Sofia wanted different things from life than he did. She wanted a family. And if she didn't have the prospect of an arranged marriage ahead of her, perhaps she *would* want the real thing. Love, the happy ending… The works. Marco didn't want any of that. So, whatever he and Sofia had here and now he wouldn't act on it. Couldn't. The thought of getting involved was too scary. The idea of building something in the knowledge that it might well go wrong, change, morph into something bitter and desolate, was too risky. His parents' marriage had gone from joy to misery, his time with Leila, with Leo, had gone from a place of trust and partnership and joy to misery. Leaving him alone, and now that solitude was his strength. His protection against further hurt or abandonment.

But that didn't mean he couldn't enjoy the here and now with Sofia; more than that, he could try to make this stay on Capri special for her, ensure she enjoyed her taste of freedom. So enough of all this analysis of impossible might-have-beens he didn't even want. It was time to have fun and he recalled her wishes of earlier, to enjoy simple everyday pleasures.

'I'll call my solicitor as soon as we dock.' He could see the ferry port approaching. 'And then would you like to head back to town and find a pizza place? I am pretty sure we can find a crowded, local place where no one will give us a second glance.'

'That sounds perfect.'

CHAPTER TEN

AN HOUR LATER they *had* found the perfect place, were sitting on a restaurant terrace overlooking a panoramic view of the Capri shoreline. Sofia watched the rays of the setting sun shimmer and tiptoe across the water, the deep green fronds of leafy trees gently sway in the warm scented evening breeze and a sudden precarious happiness fluttered through her.

A happiness she suspected came not so much from the scenery, breathtaking though it was, but from the man sitting opposite her. A man she had confided in and who had confided in her. As she looked at him, he smiled. Her heart cartwheeled and, afraid her own answering smile was veering towards goofy, she hurried into speech.

'That is stunning and the vibe in here is perfect. Whoever designed it did a fabulous job.' She looked around at the tiled floor, the whitewashed walls, alleviated by arches painted a deep blue. 'The marble tables give a sense of both tradition and opulence and I love the lighting. It gives a touch of the industrial and then you have the traditional red and white checked cushions scattered round.'

'The menu is pretty good too,' he said as a member of the waiting staff arrived at the table.

'Is there anything you would recommend?' Sofia asked.

'*Signora*. To be truthful everything on the menu is beautiful. The chef uses only the best local produce to create a tomato sauce that is renowned through Italy. And here in the kitchens we have a pizza oven that is one of the oldest on the island.'

'Then I will keep it simple and have a margarita pizza, please,' she said.

'And I'll try the fried upside-down pizza with the speciality tomato sauce,' Marco said.

They ordered a glass of red wine each and the waiter left.

'There's something special about the idea you're eating a pizza that's so steeped in tradition. But in a place that is contemporary, with recipes that have a new twist to them. That's how I wish Palosia could be, a mix of the best of our traditions but with a contemporary twist.'

'How would you achieve it?'

She hesitated. 'Are you sure you want to know? You're not just being polite.'

'I am a hundred per cent sure. I know so little about your country and I'd love to know your ideas for it.'

The thought that he meant it, that he was actually interested in what she had to say, exhilarated her; the novelty almost fantastic. 'Well, for example, I'd love to promote the island for more than its olive oil. I know Capri has its own signature perfume; I wish Palosia would do the same. We have incredible flowers unique to the island and both Rosa and her mother are passionate, knowledgeable gardeners. I am sure they could work with a parfumier to create something wonderful.'

'Why don't they? That sounds like something that would be great for Palosia.' He leant forward and she could see his brain whirring. 'From an economic point of view as a business, but also it would increase the tourist trade, make Palosia better known and enhance the royal family's image.'

She sighed. 'My father wouldn't let them. Queens and princesses aren't allowed to work. He did allow Chiara, that's Rosa's mother, to set up a cooperative that helps Palosian women make traditional straw hats, but he only agreed to do that because it generated good publicity on the island at a time he needed it. But he definitely doesn't like what a success she has made of it.'

Marco looked puzzled. 'But your ideas would enrich the island. As its ruler he must want that. Have you ever talked to him about the ideas? Or could you talk to his advisors? Surely you of all people can persuade him— you're articulate, you're resourceful, you're bright, en- thusiastic…'

Sofia couldn't help but smile—the compliments warmed her in an unfamiliar glow and her smile morphed to a low chuckle. 'Don't stop. Keep going. It's all music to my ears.' Without thinking she reached out, placed her hand over his, and bit back a small gasp, the touch electric. The past hours, the freedom, their proximity had fed the simmer- ing attraction and now desire fizzed through her with a deep, unsettling heat. Her eyes roved his face, the strength and cragginess, the dark blond hair highlighted in the last dappled rays of the sun, and settled on his lips.

Then he smiled back, a long, decadent smile full of promise. 'I'm happy to comply. You're beautiful, you care about things, you're talented, you're kind, insightful…and right now all I want to do is kiss you.' He broke off and swore under his breath. 'Sorry. I shouldn't have said that.'

Maybe he shouldn't have but Sofia didn't care. The words had sent a thrill of sheer happiness, a satisfaction, straight through her along with an escalation of white-hot desire. All she could think about was how it would feel if he did kiss her. Because he actually wanted to, was consumed as much as she was. Now she was leaning forward and the only thing that saved her was the soft noise of their waiter clearing his throat.

Dammit. What was she doing? The whole point was to not draw attention to themselves, to look like colleagues. Colleagues would go out for pizza but they wouldn't end up in a lip lock.

The waiter discreetly deposited their wine in front of them and left and Sofia pulled a smile to her face, saw the rueful tilt tip his lips, saw too that desire still darkened his grey eyes. 'You don't need to be sorry,' she said. 'I...' Shyness tinged her cheeks. 'I'd like to kiss you too. But it's not a good idea.' Though suddenly she wondered why not.

'Not here and now. Or not ever?' he asked softly, echoing her thoughts.

She closed her eyes, opened them again. 'I don't know.' Honesty seemed to be the best policy. Part of her asked, could a kiss matter? The other part clanged a warning bell loud and clear. Attraction was a distraction and it wasn't something she could have, she knew that. Knew there were other things that were way more important. But those were things to think about whilst considering an arranged marriage. That wasn't on the table here. She shook her head; she'd said it herself—attraction was all about playing with fire. And fire was dangerous.

'It's okay.' Marco raised a hand. 'I'm sorry. I don't want to make things awkward. I really shouldn't have said any of that.' But now he smiled, a smile full of reassurance. 'Apart from when I said all the nice things,' he added. 'I meant every one. But now let's scrub all mention of kisses from the record and go back to our conversation. Deal?'

He lifted his glass and she smiled back at him. 'Deal.' She clinked her glass against his, unsure how easy it would be but determined to try.

He thought for a moment, clearly rethreading the conversational needle. 'So, to go back, have you tried talking to your father or his advisors about change?'

Sofia sighed. 'We don't really talk. If we have to have a conversation it is usually more of a shouting match but, in truth, he mostly pretends I don't exist. He certainly doesn't value my opinion enough to give my ideas any thought and his advisors take their cue from him.'

His forehead creased and she could tell he was going to try to come up with a strategy.

'Nothing will change that.'

'Are you sure? It's not like you to give up. Look at your interior-design aspirations.'

'This is different.' Hesitating, she sipped her wine then placed the glass back down. 'I'd like to explain, but I don't want to sound self-pitying. It is as it is and I know there are millions of people in the world who would think it's ridiculous for a princess to complain about anything.'

'You aren't complaining, or self-pitying,' he said. 'I'd like to understand.'

'Nothing will shift our father's stance on Rosa or me. He would never give us equality or freedoms. He resents us too deeply, both of us for being girls and he despises me because I am a reminder to him of his own folly in marrying my mother, a daily reminder of his own humiliation. That turned the disappointment he'd felt at my gender into something worse.' Her voice matter-of-fact. 'I brought him no joy at all to balance against the misery he associates with me.'

Shock and compassion showed in his eyes. 'But you are his daughter. His eldest child. That must count for something in terms of the succession.'

'Traditionally a woman cannot rule, but she can bear the male heir. But my father does not believe I am worthy, believes my blood is tainted. My whole life he has made it clear he doesn't consider me to be truly royal.' She kept her voice matter-of-fact, had absolutely no wish to invoke pity. 'When I was fourteen, I overheard a conversation saying that my father had cut me out of the succession. I didn't believe it.' Reliving it now, she heard her voice crack slightly. 'I went straight to confront him, challenge him. I can remember what he said, word for word.'

In that moment she was back in the royal stateroom, listening to King Fiero's harsh voice, heaping scorn and derision over her. '"You are the daughter of a commoner, a woman who had no principles or morals, your blood is tainted and I will not allow it to poison Palosia's royal bloodline. Your child will not so much as touch the throne. Rosa's son will be heir. You shall have no influence or say. Because to me you are nothing. I will support you because I have no choice and in return you will obey my bidding and in time you will marry who I tell you to marry. Remember your place or it will be far the worse for you. And your sister."'

There was a silence and she saw Marco's hands slowly clench into fists, his mouth set in a grim line. 'I don't know what to say. I cannot imagine what that did to you.'

'For a while it crushed me. Not because I begrudge Rosa her position. I don't.' That was the truth. She had felt saddened that she was deemed unworthy of the position she had believed was hers by right, that she would have no part in her country's future, but mostly, 'It was the idea that I was unworthy to have any connection to my country, that I was tainted. Sometimes it does feel that way to me. There was a reason she abandoned me. Either my own shortcomings or hers.'

'No.' The word was torn from him.

She shrugged. 'I know I look like my mother, but I don't know anything else about her. To my father, to the whole court, she is persona non grata, vilified as an adulteress, a person with no concept of duty. It was after that conversation with my father, when I realised the truth depth of his loathing of her and me, that I knew I had to find her. See her for myself. And now maybe I will. Thanks to your offer of help. I feel that if I can find her, meet her, talk to her, it will get me understanding and some form of closure. Then I can return to Palosia.'

Before she could say more the waiter arrived with their food and she sat back as he placed their plates in front of them and then in a deft movement tugged a handful of herbs from the plants growing in the terracotta pots that lined the terrace and sprinkled them over the food. The addition enhanced the already tantalising aroma wafting up from the plates.

She smiled up at him. 'Thank you. This looks incredible,' she said.

Marco nodded, added his thanks but he sounded almost absent-minded and she sensed his mind wasn't really on the food. An idea backed up when the waiter left and he didn't even glance downward, left his cutlery untouched. 'Or you could tell your father you aren't going back,' he said. There was a pause and her heart did a funny little hop, skip and a jump. Stay here. With Marco. Walks through Naples together, going out for dinner without fear of being identified, without the fear of being caught and dragged back. More pizza, perhaps cooking a meal together. A job, a real job, completing Marco's villa, meetings with Marco, with his mother.

But then he gave his head a small shake as if dispelling his own thought process.

'Don't go back,' he repeated. 'Relocate. You could go anywhere in the world, build yourself a life abroad. As an exiled princess.'

Sofia blinked, realised the absurdity of her own thoughts. Of course he wasn't suggesting she stay with him. The idea *was* absurd. Marco had his own life, had made it plain he wasn't on the market for *any* sort of relationship. More to the point, she didn't want to stay with him; what would be the point? There could be no future in it. She wanted a family, he didn't.

So his suggestion had nothing to do with them, because there was no them and never could be. He was simply suggesting she leave Palosia, relocate 'anywhere in the world'.

'I can't do that.'

'Why not? Your father has taken so much from you. You owe him nothing.'

'It's not about him. My father believes my blood is tainted, perhaps it is. But Palosia is my country and the thought of losing it, being exiled, isn't something I can allow to happen.' Images of the island came to her and she leant across the table. 'I wish you could see it. The olive groves, the lush beauty, the scent on the air from the trees and all the flowers. But it's more than that. If I leave then I am proving my father right. That I am like my mother, that I too have run away from my duty and responsibilities as a princess of Palosia.' And that was not a possibility, not a scenario she could ever accept or initiate.

'But what about your life?' he asked.

'That is my life. To be a princess. And it's more than that. I can't and I won't leave my sister.' Her own words triggered a sense of guilt that she had, however briefly, contemplated the idea. A further confirmation if she had needed it that attraction, the pull and tug of whatever it was she felt for Marco, was dangerous. Messed with her head and made her forget the things that were really important. Like Rosa. She must never risk any emotion that could cause her to make bad decisions, to prioritise love over family. As her mother had.

'If my father banishes me I may never see her again. And that is not happening. Rosa is—' She broke off, marshalled her thoughts, wanted him to understand. 'When Rosa was born, I was only three years old but the minute I saw her I felt this incredible urge to protect her. She looked so small, so vulnerable and I vowed I would always be there for her. And I still feel like that.'

'Of course you did.' Now his voice was deep with understanding. 'You must have believed that perhaps her mother would leave as well.'

She nodded, touched at how he instantly got it. 'I must have, and even when it became clear Chiara wouldn't do that I...could never be sure of what would happen. My stepmother is a truly good woman, but it is my father who calls the shots. He could have banished Chiara because he needed a son and after Rosa there were no more pregnancies. That made him dislike Rosa almost as much as he loathes me. So, I have always tried to be there for her. Tried to stand between her and my father. Because Rosa isn't like me. She is one of the gentlest people I know. She always finds the good in people and she also has so much inner strength; she is beautiful inside and out. I can see why Chiara did stay.'

'So can I but don't ever believe that Chiara stayed because Rosa is better than you in any way.'

'I don't believe that. Or not exactly. But...'

'It must have been hard for you,' he said. 'That Rosa's mother stayed when yours didn't.'

'Sometimes it was. I did question what it was about me that made it okay to abandon me, but in the end I was glad that Chiara stayed. Was there for Rosa.'

'Then that makes you a good person, because sometimes you must have had bitter thoughts but they didn't make you bitter. You didn't resent your sister, instead you were happy for her, cared for her, shielded her. That takes compassion and kindness and inner beauty.'

Sofia blinked back a tear at his words. 'But I was lucky as well. Chiara was not a wicked stepmother. She has always been kind to me and encouraged Rosa and me to be close. And I admire her for sticking out a marriage that diminishes her, where she is bullied and belittled.' She sighed. 'And over the years, as I've watched

Chiara get frailer and weaker as a result, I do wonder if perhaps my mother was right to leave. But then I see the bond between Chiara and Rosa and I know Chiara never would.' A bond that sometimes made Sofia feel excluded, sad that she would never have that bond with a parent. Made her all the more determined to make sure she had that sort of bond with her own child, a bond she would never let anything break.

'I understand why you couldn't leave Palosia whilst Rosa was growing up. But Rosa is an adult now. You said yourself that she will soon be married, that it is her duty to have the royal heir. Surely then she won't need your protection any more, surely you are entitled to your own life now?'

'She still may need me. What if her marriage is miserable? I don't trust my father—we don't even know the identity of the man she is to marry. In any case, if I defy him he has it in his power to make sure I never see Rosa again. I can't and won't let that happen. I won't leave her to my father's whims.' As her mother had left her.

'I understand,' he said quietly. 'But I hope one day the situation changes. That you can to some degree follow your own dreams.'

'I will.' She could see a sadness in his grey eyes, a frustration that he couldn't come up with a solution. 'Truly, Marco, I have come to terms, made my peace, with my life. I will negotiate a good marriage, have a family and some freedom. I will be there for Rosa.' And she would prove to her father, to herself, that she was a true princess. 'I'm happy with it.' She smiled now, wanted to lighten the mood. Reached forward and touched his cheek gently. 'And right now I am happy to be here, to have this chance, be it a few days or a few weeks, to not be a princess, to experience this time. Here.' She held her breath and decided to speak truth. 'With you.'

The feel of his cheek under her hand, the rough six o' clock shadow, made her catch her breath as attraction shimmered and weaved in the air. And suddenly Sofia didn't care, wanted to give this attraction a bit more free rein. She was happy with the future fate and birth had destined her for but, in the meantime, her body, her heart, craved to experience this. At least a little bit.

And perhaps he felt the same, because now the sadness went from his face and he smiled; a smile that seemed to hold an infinite promise. 'Then let's make the most of it,' he said. 'I have an idea where we can go next.'

'Where?'

'It's a surprise,' he said.

CHAPTER ELEVEN

TWENTY MINUTES LATER they were standing outside an un-assuming building, indistinguishable from any other trattoria, with its curved wooden door and low-key signage.

'Here we are,' Marco said as he pushed the door open. 'I know it would be easy to pass by but this is one of Capri's most visited nightclubs. I thought you may like the chance to experience some nightlife in a place where you can let your hair down if you want to or just watch and soak up the ambiance.'

'I'm not sure I know how to let my hair down,' she said quietly. 'As a princess one of the major rules is to always be dignified and calm. Though admittedly that isn't always my forte.'

'Apparently this is the sort of place where dancing on the tables isn't unknown. But its aim is to bring people from all walks of life together to simply enjoy themselves, listening to music in a place that combines history and the present day. That's why I thought it may appeal to you. It combines tradition and contemporary.'

She smiled, felt a happiness at the knowledge that Marco truly listened to her, heard her, saw her. Once inside, she looked around. The club was already crowded and there was a relaxed, inclusive vibe. The clientele was of all ages, shapes and sizes, dressed in styles ranging from jeans to party dresses and tuxedos. Exposed brickwork, rustic wooden tables scattered over the floor and a terracotta theme complemented by checked red and white tablecloths gave the interior the appearance of a typical trattoria. But there was a sense of anticipation, a buzz created by the posters and photographs that covered the walls, depicting the club's past and present. Pictures of locals and celebrities mingling illustrating the club's success in bringing people together.

Marco guided her to a seat and, a few minutes later, handed her a glass of champagne.

'To you,' he said.

She shook her head. 'To today,' she said softly. 'It has been a perfect day. So to today and…' She paused and as the singers started to tune up on the stage she felt a sudden, heady sense of exhilaration. What had she said earlier? That she wanted to enjoy this time as a non-princess. With Marco. 'To the night to come,' she said, told herself that she simply meant the time they would spend in the nightclub, knew deep down that maybe she meant something more.

His grey eyes sparked, turned darker with a latent desire and she allowed her lips to curve upwards in a smile she *wanted* to hold allure. And as he clinked his glass against hers, he smiled back, a smile that held a promise, a depth, that made her shiver. 'To the night to come, may it be whatever you want it to be.'

Whatever she wanted it to be. The idea sent a thrill through her; she knew what she wanted it to be, she just didn't know if what she wanted was a good idea. Didn't know if it was brave or foolhardy to say what she wanted, do what she wanted. Because right now all she wanted to do was kiss him, to kiss him and be kissed back, to press her body against his and...

She blinked, forced herself to turn to the stage where the singers were warming up, hoped that music might somehow mitigate, push away, the feelings, the sensations, the yearning in her body.

'The main singer is the owner of the place,' he said and she could hear a hint of strain in his voice, see a tautness in his body as if he too was holding back with an effort. 'And the other members of the band are all family members. They play both traditional Neapolitan ballads and contemporary-style pop and everyone can sing along.'

To her own surprise Sofia found herself doing exactly that along with so many other people at neighbouring tables. All from the singer's ability to somehow draw them in, until everyone was clapping, laughing together with a palpable feeling of fellowship. The next song started and Marco rose to his feet, and she instinctively followed suit. Soon she was lost in the music, the rhythm and the beat of the tambourines, all the feelings and emotions of the day finding expression in the movement of her body.

Eventually she ceased, breathless and laughing, found herself leaning back against the warm, muscular strength of Marco's body as the singers sang a slower ballad that had everyone swaying. Now she closed her eyes, every sense heightened, every millimetre of her, oh, so aware of Marco and the press of their bodies together.

Until she knew that these feelings, this need, this yearning had to be assuaged. Whatever the cost, whatever the obstacles, she could not let this moment pass. And as the last lingering notes trembled through the air she turned, touched his cheek in a fleeting gesture. 'Is it okay if we leave now?' she asked, knowing they had to go before the last vestiges of common sense left her and she kissed him right here.

'Yes.' The one syllable echoed her urgency.

As they exited into the cool breeze of the still starlit sky, she realised it was the early hours of the morning. They walked in perfect synchronicity, propelled by the same sense of urgency until they reached a secluded spot, and she laid a hand on his arm. When he turned to face her, before she could change her mind, she stood on tip-toe and brushed her lips against his.

Heard his exhalation of relief as he pulled her closer into his embrace, his lips demanding more now and she felt a soaring sense of heady exhilaration, a knowledge that there was nothing more important than this, the shocking glorious pleasure his lips evoked. As if everything from the minute she'd set eyes on him in Naples had been leading to this crescendo of desire, this swirl-ing, whirling, dizzying pleasure.

And she knew it couldn't be left at this, because this taste wasn't enough; her whole body was crying out for more.

She pulled back from the kiss, swayed and he reached out to steady her, both their breathing ragged in the balmy air.

'We need to go back to the villa,' she said, didn't even recognise the voice as her own, and he nodded. Turn-ing, they started the walk back, stopping occasionally to briefly brush lips until finally the villa came into sight. Then a few more steps and with a fumble of the keys they were inside and he was kissing her again with an added burning, mutual need. Until he pulled away, despite her small bereft gasp of protest.

'Sofia. I…you…'

She reached out, placed a finger on his lips, her whole being consumed. She heard the break in his voice, knew his need matched hers, understood what he was asking. Knew he needed to be sure this was what she wanted.

'I want this, Marco. I want you. If…if we don't do this, I know I will regret it for the rest of my life.'

It was all she needed to say. He stepped forward and in one fluid movement scooped her up into his arms, and she wrapped her arms round his neck as he carried her upstairs, pushed the bedroom door open with his foot and made his way over to the bed. Laid her down gently and she smiled up at him, her whole body trembling, aching with desire, filled with a need that only he could assuage.

Marco opened his eyes, aware of a deep languorous sense of contentment, shifted slightly to see Sofia, still asleep, her cheek pillowed on one hand, her other hand resting lightly on his chest. The sensation, both sweet and sensual, sent a warmth through his body, triggered memories of the previous hours. Hours filled with a bliss that transcended anything he had experienced before. The passion, the wonder, the intensity, laughter and joy as they had explored each other's bodies and ascended heights of fulfillment.

Yet through the contentment now stirred a sudden anxiety; Sofia had said she would regret not doing this for the rest of her life but suddenly Marco wondered if the opposite could be true. What if she regretted what she had done? After all, she was a Palosian princess, a woman who wasn't even supposed to spend time alone with a man.

The anxiety intensified. Seven years before he'd kissed her and whilst he knew now that hadn't driven her away, maybe it would have. If the guards hadn't found her, would she have left anyway? At some point or another, of course she would. The next day, week, month or year, the conclusion would be the same. Just as it would be now. But now he had done something he had vowed not to do. And he didn't know what the ramifications of that would be. If she regretted it maybe this time she would leave, and he would have driven her away.

As if she sensed his sudden unease, she opened her eyes, blinked and then smiled at him, a smile so sweet something tugged in his chest.

'Good morning,' she said. Then glanced at her watch. 'Or rather good afternoon.' She stretched languorously. 'That is the best night's sleep I've had...ever.' Now her smile widened impishly. 'It must have been all the activity.' The smile retreated slightly as she took in his expression.

'Marco? Is something wrong?' She moved her hand from his chest and shifted away, anxiety clouding the sparkle in her blue eyes. 'Did I do something wrong?'

'No.' Remorse shook him that she should even consider that, even as he understood why she asked. Her whole life she'd been told she was wrong, tainted, not good enough. 'No. Absolutely not. I was worried that *I* did something wrong.'

'You?' For an instant she looked puzzled and then she shook her head.

'You mean you think you shouldn't have, that we shouldn't have...that last night shouldn't have happened.'

'Something like that. You told me yourself that your culture, your traditions, mean you shouldn't even date a man, let alone…'

Sofia gave a sudden chuckle as he broke off. 'Let alone do any of the things we did.' She shifted back close to him again, leant up on one elbow. 'I promise you I do not regret last night at all. I do not believe in or agree with the rules and restrictions my father imposes on Rosa and myself. And if you're worried about the prospects of any arranged marriage, don't be. Most Palosians do not enforce rules as draconian as my father's are. Plus, any prospective husband will be more interested in my title, not any past relationships.' She raised a quick hand. 'Not that this is a relationship.'

Marco pushed away the idea of Sofia getting married. The idea of her being with anyone else sent denial, discomfort and irrational jealousy rushing through him. Which made no sense and he would not spoil 'this' with a dog-in-the-manger attitude. He reached up, twirled a strand of her glossy dark hair. 'So, what is this?' he asked.

'It's an…interlude,' she responded. 'I don't know how long I have here, with you, but I know and you know that it is time limited and I want to make the most of it. I want to enjoy it and look back with no regrets. Neither of us want or believe in love so this is perfect, an opportunity to create something precious, a brief moment in time, that has no impact on our futures.'

Her words made sense. They could enjoy something that could never get spoilt or sullied by the passage of time, or reality. There would be no time for attraction to fade, or incompatibilities to occur. There could be no betrayal of trust. They could simply enjoy their time together without worry or anxiety. And he vowed that he would do everything he could to make sure this interlude was everything Sofia wanted it to be.

'An interlude it is,' he said. 'What would you like to do first? We can go wherever you like.'

'Actually...' Sofia smiled at him '...how would you feel about remaining right here?' She shifted closer to him, her hand still on his chest.

'Hm, I think I could be persuaded. Especially if we...' He tugged her closer and whispered some particularly innovative ideas. 'I believe I know someone who once said attraction is overrated. Well, I'd like to challenge that assumption.'

She chuckled and said, 'Feel free to rise to the challenge.'

And then the chuckle developed into a sudden giggle at the infantility of the innuendo and he laughed too before tugging her into his arms.

CHAPTER TWELVE

AND THAT SET the scene for the next two days; they had picnic meals in bed, spent time sunbathing in the garden, where Sofia sat at the table, sketchbook in front of her, or borrowed his laptop to work. They discussed anything and everything under the sun, from films and books to the pros and cons of velvet cushions, from solar panels to wind energy, politics, and their favourite foods.

They took turns cooking for each other, fed each other olives, compared varieties of lemons and as each hour passed neither of them referred to anything in the real world and Sofia refused to acknowledge the ticking of the clock.

She opened her eyes one morning to find Marco standing by the bed holding a tray. 'Breakfast in bed,' he announced. 'I have warm fresh bread and cheese and strawberries and a chocolate sauce made with a few extra ingredients. A hint of chilli and a touch of vanilla. And I have some very good ideas involving the strawberries and chocolate.'

His words and the suggestive wiggle of his eyebrows made her laugh. But the laughter was accompanied by a shiver of anticipation that clenched her body with desire and she wondered anew how it was possible to feel like this. 'Perhaps we should start with the strawberries,' she suggested.

'Your wish is my command,' he said with a slow smile.

'Even better.' She reached for the jug of chocolate sauce. 'Let's get started.'

An hour later when they were finally eating the bread and cheese, sitting up in the bed, Sofia gave a contented sigh.

'I could get used to this,' she said. As soon as the words fell from her mouth, she regretted them, each word like a douse of cold water, and she struggled to retrieve them. 'You'll have to give me the recipe,' she added lightly, even as she tried to ignore the warning bell clanging in her head, wondered if this was how Pandora had felt when she opened the box. Because until now she would never have believed, never have dreamed, that attraction could lead to such soaring, glorious pleasure. Wouldn't have believed that a physical act could bring such gratification, in both the giving and receiving of joy. The sensations evoked by Marco's touch were beyond description, could reduce her to a trembling, shivering need and yearning. But what was even more heady, more dizzying, was the fact that it was reciprocal, that he felt a desire that matched her own. It seemed impossible that she, a princess of Palosia, could act with such utter shameless, greedy abandon.

But what was most alarming was the persistent feeling that this was about more than attraction. There were times when she would half wake in the night, aware of a sense of safety and security in his arms, her head on his chest, her arm wrapped over his chest, or her body spooned or cocooned against his.

She shook her head, told herself it was the novelty factor, combined with the forbidden-fruit aspect. In the end, this would wear off and leave nothing behind. The life she was destined for might not include this type of attraction but it would include things that were of way more importance. Somehow right now, though, that was hard to believe. The thought of leaving Marco for marriage to some other yet to be identified man made anxiety unfurl in her tummy. Made her want to turn and wrap her arms around Marco, cling to him and never let go. *Never?* What was the matter with her? Now panic added to the anxiety, galvanised her to speak.

'I think we should leave the house, go and see something on Capri.' Perhaps the fresh air would clear her head, shift her priorities back into place. Perhaps seeing Capri, mingling with the crowds, would remind her this was and could only be an interlude.

'Good idea.' She heard the hint of constraint in his voice, wondered if her earlier words had made him think she'd been angling for more of a commitment. Another unwelcome thought and a stark reminder that Marco did not want a relationship. Full stop.

'Great. There are things I want to see before we have to get back to our normal lives,' she said with determined cheerfulness that rang false in her ears. Because right now she couldn't think of a single one, wanted to remain in the villa in a cocooned bubble where she could stop time, let the interlude play on some sort of time loop.

'Sure.'

Now she thought she detected a soupçon of relief and a pang of hurt prodded her. One she recognised as irrational; this was *her* idea. But what if Marco had been feeling claustrophobic? What if he had been humouring her the past days—trying to give the poor princess a good time before she returned home? *Enough*. That wasn't fair because that was the whole point. To have a good time before she went home. 'I'll be ready in half an hour.'

Once ready, Sofia glanced at her reflection, saw how different she looked, suspected it was more than the hairstyle change. There was something in her expression, her eyes, the way she stood; she *felt* different. Presumably it was a temporary thing. Down to some sort of hormonal reaction that would fade in the same way the hair dye would.

Turning from the mirror, she headed to the front door, where Marco stood. His blond hair was shower damp, and he looked so damn gorgeous her heart did a hop, skip and a jump and she had a sudden urge to run to him, wrap her arms around him, pull him straight back to bed. Forcing her steps to slow down, she exhorted herself to calm down. But for the first time in days, she felt a tug of fear that a palace guard would be waiting outside, that this interlude would be ended before she was ready. She would be ready, just not yet.

She told herself not to be foolish, there was no reason to believe a guard could have tracked her down. Even if one had and she had to return today, her sister, her true life, would be waiting. There was no future with Marco; she didn't *want* a future with Marco.

'You okay?'

His voice was deep, reassuring and caring and despite herself, despite everything she knew, she pictured a future with Marco. Waking up with him every day…an image of Marco holding a baby, their baby, a little girl with Marco's blond hair and her blue eyes. *Enough*. She was being ridiculous.

'I'm fine,' she said. 'Just thinking about where to go.'

Before he could respond his phone buzzed, he listened for a few minutes and after a short conversation he hung up, turned to her and she could see the excitement in his face. 'That was my solicitor. They have found your mother.'

Sofia froze, stared at him wide-eyed.

'She has agreed to meet you. *If* that's still what you want.'

'I... I don't know...what I want.' She felt shaky, the emotions of the past few minutes converging.

He put a steadying hand on her arm, and his touch felt so reassuring, so right. 'Then take your time to decide,' he said.

But there was no time. To have got this far and then be thwarted would be unbearable. 'I need to see her,' she said. 'Otherwise, I will always wonder.'

'Understood.' He took his phone out of his pocket and as he started the call, further ramifications loomed. Once she'd seen her mother she'd achieved her goal here. It would be time to go home. Leave here, leave Capri, leave Marco. She pushed the panic down; there was still the villa, still time whilst she figured out the situation on Palosia. Right now, she needed to think about the fact that she was going to see her mother. For real.

'Early evening,' he said after a five-minute conversation. 'We can meet at a solicitor's office in Capri.'

Sofia nodded. 'Thank you,' she said. 'For making this possible.' She glanced outside at the bright early morning sun; already she felt restless, a nervous energy pulsing inside her as she calculated the hours left until the meeting.

Marco studied her face. 'Let's go out. It'll make the time go quicker.'

'I'm not sure I want to risk it.' But then again what if the guards did track her to the villa? 'Plus I don't think I can focus on anything touristy. Or eating anything.'

'I get that. I thought we could find a secluded stretch of beach. We can walk and talk or just sit and look at the sea. Whatever works for you.'

'That sounds perfect.' And once again, it warmed her that he understood her without a need for explanation.

Half an hour later, having stocked up with drinks and snacks, they were back on a boat, a smaller one this time, gliding over the sparkling turquoise waters. And as she listened to the squall of the gulls, she tried to imagine seeing, actually *seeing*, her mother. Speaking to her. The woman she'd pictured so many times, had tried so desperately to remember, never sure if the images she had were real or a figment of her imagination. A slight woman with long dark hair, holding her, stroking her head and singing a lullaby to put her to sleep. Fact or wishful thinking? Perhaps now she'd find out.

She came out of her reverie as the boat bumped to shore.

'We're here,' Marco said and she scanned the un-populated cove, saw that Marco had located one of the very few coves in Capri that boasted sand at all, saw the sun glint off the golden grains and the rockier inland, looked at the loom of the rugged precipitous cliffs per-fectly suited to her restless mood.

Once they disembarked and started to walk, he took her hand in his. 'How are you feeling?'

'Edgy, terrified. Wondering if I've done the right thing,

whether I should have let it lie. Do I really need any answers? She left me. What else do I need to know?'

A shadow crossed his face and she thought she felt him flinch but when he spoke his voice was even. 'I think knowing the answers may help give insight into why she did what she did. But there is a possibility you may not like the answers you get. So, you need to remember something.'

She looked at him, a question in her eyes, and he came to a halt, turned her so she faced him and took both her hands in his.

'That whatever or whoever she is doesn't impact on you. It doesn't add or take away from who you are. You are *not* tainted by her blood. Or your father's. They may have brought about your existence but you have made your character and you have done a wonderful job. You're strong, courageous; you've shown incredible resilience and initiative. You chose to love and protect your sister and your stepmother instead of resenting them. You care about your country and its people. Whatever you find out, whatever the answers are, cannot take away from the wonderful person you are.'

Tears moistened her eyes as she met his gaze, saw, *felt* his sincerity, and warmth blossomed inside her.

'And if you change your mind, decide not to see her, that is okay too. It won't change the person you are.'

'Yes, it will. It will mean I'm too much of a coward to face the truth. Whatever I find out, at least it will be my mother's version, not my father's. Otherwise, I will never know why she left me. How she could have left me to live my life with a man like my father.'

Now she was sure he flinched, but his voice was gentle, as by tacit consent they sat down on the sun-warmed beach. 'I don't know what your mother was thinking but perhaps she thought it was unfair to take you from a life of wealth, take you from your birthright, your country. Especially if she was going to resume a normal life, a life without wealth, without royal trappings. Or perhaps she had no idea what she was running to, her family may not have been supportive of her leaving your father. Maybe she thought that leaving you behind was the best thing she could do for you.'

'Do you think that's possible?'

'Yes. I believe when it is your child's happiness at stake you sometimes have to make incredibly difficult decisions that it is hard for others to understand.'

'Even leaving a child.'

'Even that,' he said quietly. 'I know that's true. Because in a sense it's a decision I made myself.'

She stilled now, studied his face, saw his eyes cloud with a sadness that twisted her heart. But he met her gaze steadily. 'A few years ago, I thought I had a son.'

'I don't understand.' But she sensed he was telling her because he thought it would help her, instinctively knew that what he was about to share was deeply significant. She moved closer to him, hoped her warmth, her proximity, would help him as his had helped her.

'I met Leila when I was twenty-two, at a friend's house. She told me that she'd had an acrimonious split with her partner, that he'd been unfaithful, and then he'd thrown her out of the house they shared. I felt sorry for her and when she asked if I had a spare room she could rent I agreed.

'She moved in and very soon after that she offered to cook me a meal, to say thank you. The wine flowed and we ended up sleeping together; the next morning we both agreed it was nothing more than a mutually enjoyable one-night stand and we could easily continue to be flat-mates. A few weeks later she told me she was pregnant.'

Sofia narrowed her eyes; she could see where this was going, but she couldn't believe anyone could be so du-plicitous.

'At first, I was horrified. I wasn't planning on having children, and certainly not in these circumstances, but then…then I realised that how *I* felt wasn't relevant, it was the baby that mattered. Once I understood that, it felt miraculous that I was going to be a father. It was in-toxicating, exhilarating and I vowed I would be the best father I could be. Leila and I decided to focus on being parents, to stay living together so I could help, could be part of the whole journey. I went to all the antenatal classes, supported Leila as much as I could through the pregnancy. I can still remember the first time I felt the baby kick. Then Leo was born and it was the most in-credible moment of my life, the idea that this precious tiny newborn was my child, my son.

'The next six months were a time of wonder and awe and I felt so grateful to Leila for agreeing to us joint par-enting that I didn't see what was happening. I did notice she seemed different, that she actively discouraged my parents from visiting or being involved with Leo. But I put it down to tiredness, tried to help more. Then one day when Leo was six months old, she told me the truth. Leo wasn't mine. She'd already been pregnant when we met, the whole thing was a set-up. She'd fed me a sob story, orchestrated the one-night stand and then told me I was the father.' He kept his voice even but Sofia wasn't fooled, couldn't even begin to imagine the extent of the shock and devastation Leila's news must have caused.

'Oh, Marco. That's… I'm so, so very sorry. I don't know how she could have done that.'

'She wanted Leo to have a father. A good father. She did it for him because she truly believed the real father, the birth father, would never come good. She wanted what was best for her baby.'

'But that isn't right.'

'No,' he agreed. 'But to Leila it was justifiable. But then the real father contacted her, said he had changed, and to cut a long story short he had.' Sofia knew that there was no way Marco would have let Leo go to a man who didn't check out. 'In the end they got back together and they moved with Leo to Australia. Leila told me I was "off the hook".'

'But I didn't want to be off the hook. It didn't matter to me whose blood was in Leo's veins, what his DNA was made of. To me he was mine. I'd bonded with him, loved him, changed his nappies, watched his first smile, sat up with him at night. He *was* part of me. I wanted to stay in his life, wanted him to stay in mine.'

'But you didn't stay,' she said, her heart wrenching at the enormity of the decision he must have made.

'I didn't. Because in the end I had to try to make the best decision for Leo. If his real father had been a bad person, I would have fought tooth and nail. But he wasn't. Leila admitted she'd made up a lot, exaggerated his faults. I met him, I saw him with Leo. He loved him. So how could I fight for Leo, put him in the middle of me and his real dad? He was only six months old, I knew he would forget me soon enough.'

'But *you* haven't forgotten him,' she said.

'No. And I am sure your mother hasn't forgotten you. She may well spend every day wondering if she did the right thing, just like I do. There are still days when all I want to do is get on a plane and go and see him. Even though I probably wouldn't even recognise him now and he wouldn't recognise me. Leila wanted a completely clean break; said it would be creepy if she kept me posted or updated. That she doesn't want to confuse Leo. That we all had to get on with our lives. Move on. But it's not that easy and every day I question whether I made the right decision.'

Sofia could hear the agony in his voice. So much felt clear now—how could he trust anyone when he had been so fundamentally played and betrayed? And it made it all the warmer, sweeter that he had opted to trust her. 'For what it's worth I think you did, but it must have been heartbreaking for you to do so.' And she couldn't help but wonder if it had broken her mother's heart to leave her. 'And whilst Leo may not remember who you are, what you did for him would have made a monumental difference to his life. You gave him love and security in the first months of his life, and I know you can't regret that. But I am so sorry for what happened.'

'Thank you. I know I need to move on, let it go.'

'I'm not sure that's possible. Leo will always be part of you and maybe it's okay to hold onto that little baby and carry him as a precious memory. But it must be so hard to accept what happened, come to terms with the loss.' She hesitated as an idea came to her and she looked round, saw that there was a stretch of sand near them. 'I know you said your creativity is gone and I understand that. But might it help to make a sand sculpture? Here and now. Try to put all your emotions into the sand and then the tide will take it away.'

There was a silence and she wondered if she'd over-stepped. 'Only if you want to,' she said.

Did he want to? To his own surprise Marco realised he did. He'd only shared his story because he'd wanted to help Sofia, hoped it would make the next hours easier, hoped it would make the meeting with her mother a better one. But talking about Leo, seeing the way she'd listened, had seemed to ease a weight inside him. By allowing some of the buried emotions up, by reliving the past, he had seen the precious parts as well. The love he'd had for Leo, a vision of Leo's nursery with the baby mobiles hanging over the cot. How much Leo had loved them, the way he'd kicked his legs and waved his hands as they'd spun round. The first time Leo had smiled at him. The way he'd splashed in the bath. They were precious mem-ories and maybe he should hold them close to his heart.

And as he looked at the stretch of sand, the waves lap-ping the shoreline, he realised that he did want to make something. Nothing permanent, but something, something that would remind him of the joy Leo had brought him.

Rising to his feet, he held out a hand, she placed hers in his and he felt a fizz, a connection, a bond as he pulled her to her feet. 'We're going to make a butterfly,' he said, hoping that her nervous energy could be allayed by the activity, that it would serve as a distraction from her up-coming meeting with her mother. That this could help both of them. 'It was Leo's favourite baby mobile. Four butterflies that went round and round in the breeze.'

'Tell me what to do and I'll help.'

Marco examined the contents of the rucksack and nodded. 'Right, we have cups, a bottle, and even a straw. Cutlery and a bowl-shaped container. They will all be useful and then the key is having wet sand. We'll make a foundation. Then we build up layers and work from the top down.'

'That sounds like a plan. I'm happy to dig and carry and try to keep the sand wet. Other than that I think my talent lies in sketching.'

'That works,' he said, his mind suddenly busy with the idea of how to use the materials at hand with the vision he had. A way to make clumps of wet sand look like something light and fragile, something that could take flight.

After that time seemed to blur; through it all he was aware of Sofia, of her grace, her ability to do exactly what she had said she would do. Her sheer presence offered a comfort, alongside her instinctive ability not to intrude. She rarely spoke, apart from the occasional question, and after a while they worked in tandem until she unobtrusively slipped away, took her sketchbook out and left him to it.

He had no idea how long he took but finally he was satisfied, stepped back and looked at what he had created.

Sofia came and stood next to him and caught her breath. 'It's…it's beautiful,' she said softly. 'How have you made it look so delicate? And its wings, the patterns, they're so simple and yet so intricate. Somehow, I can see the mobile fluttering in the breeze.' She moved closer to him. 'I can see how much you loved him.'

'I did,' he said softly. 'And you're right. I can't regret that. However much Leila's betrayal hurt me it wasn't

Leo who was to blame and he gave me so much joy.' A joy that outweighed the misery. Maybe that was how his parents had felt about him. 'Thank you,' he said softly and as they stood in the late afternoon sunshine, he felt a warmth tug at his heart.

A warmth that perhaps he should step away from but right now he didn't want to. Right now, he wanted to let himself believe in an impossible dream, that somehow this was sustainable, that this moment, all the moments of the last few days, could be prolonged.

And now as he thought of baby Leo, he hoped with all his heart that Leo was thriving and happy and loved and suddenly, off the back of that, another thought slipped in. Caused him to freeze as the image seemed to go from fuzzy to clear. Sofia and himself, standing together and in Sofia's arms was a baby, a small dark-haired scrap, with clear blue eyes. Their baby. Both of them gazing down at the infant with love.

He allowed himself to linger on the image until reality pervaded and, with a sense of sadness, a regret that pierced, he let it go, dissolve into the shimmering haze of sea and sunshine.

Sofia's position, her identity, her destiny were in her own country, in Palosia. And fundamentally he knew love was not for him, knew he'd never risk watching something beautiful wither and rot, would never put himself in the position his parents had put themselves into. Could never risk the emotional fallout that parenthood could bring.

But what he could do was be here for Sofia today, through the next hours and beyond, for the aftermath from meeting her mother. Admiration surged through him at her courage in facing this and he hoped she would get the answers she wanted.

'We should get going,' he said and she nodded, gripped his hand tighter.

'It's going to be okay,' he said softly.

'Thank you for finding her, for making this happen and for being there.'

'I'm not going anywhere.' The words seemed to reverberate around them, an echo of her words earlier that morning, an intimation of commitment and, just as Sofia had earlier, he hurried to reverse them. 'I'll be waiting right outside the room, and if you need me, just call.'

CHAPTER THIRTEEN

AS THEY APPROACHED the solicitor's offices Sofia could feel her heart hammer her chest, looked up at Marco and he smiled. A smile that exuded such reassurance she felt a semblance of confidence build inside her.

He squeezed her hand. 'It *will* be okay,' he said. 'No matter what.'

They entered the building and were greeted by a receptionist. 'Your appointment is through here.'

'I'll be in the next room,' Marco said and she nodded, and as he walked away she kept her eyes on the breadth of his back. Reminded herself of all the words he had said on the beach, assembled them almost like armour before turning to follow the receptionist.

Heart in her mouth, she entered the meeting room, and came to a halt as the woman sitting at the rectangular mahogany table rose to her feet.

A woman a little bit smaller than Sofia herself, with a cascade of dark hair sprinkled with a few strands of grey. Dark blue eyes, oh, so similar to her own met hers and Sofia stood, stock-still, as the mother of her memories and dreams merged into the woman standing in front of her.

'Sofia?' The words were a whisper and her mother stepped towards her, then stopped, reached a hand out and dropped it, her eyes not wavering from her daughter's face. 'I can't believe it's really you. I have thought about this, dreamt about this.' Her voice cracked and she broke off. 'I'm sorry. I know how inadequate that sounds, that a word does not make up for anything, but I *am* sorry.'

Sofia saw the tears in her mother's eyes, saw Flavia blink them back as she went to sit down. 'I owe you an explanation,' her mother said and finally Sofia found her voice.

'I'd like that.'

The older woman sat down and Sofia followed suit, waited as Flavia visibly gathered herself together, tucked a tendril of hair behind her ear.

'I want you to know that I did love you, so very much, but I struggled. Not with you, never with you, but after the birth I felt so much weaker, so much more vulnerable because now your father had more leverage against me. He used my love for you, would taunt me with the power he had over both of us. That he could divorce me, cast me off, keep you from me and it wore me down.'

Sofia heard the weariness in her mother's tone and, knowing King Fiero as she did, she could picture the scenes, oh, so clearly, see the vindictive triumph on her father's face, and impulsively she reached out and touched her mother's arms. 'It's okay. I understand.'

'In the end… I knew I had to leave. I couldn't think straight; all I could see was a life ahead of me where he would use my love for you and yours for me as a weapon, a tool to grind us both down.' Her mother gave a smile. 'And already even when you were so little you had so much spirit, you were already trying to protect me, and the idea of watching that spirit being broken was too much. Everything became too much; life almost didn't seem worth living, but I knew I could never leave you.'

'Yet you did.' Sofia regretted the words even as she said them, saw her mother flinch. 'I'm sorry. I…'

'No. You are right. And I am not trying to make excuses. I did leave, but you have to believe me when I say I never thought I would never see you again. My plan was to leave, make sure I had somewhere for you and me to live and then I would fight for you, for custody. But I couldn't take you with me, not away from wealth and position and security. From your birthright. Not when I didn't know if my family would take me in, or where I would end up. But your father banished me. He made a case that I was an unfit mother—I was told the best I would get was occasional visitation rights. Your father told me that if I backed off, agreed not to see you again, he would not take out his anger with me on you. He would make sure you were looked after. I agreed. I know how weak that sounds, but I was weak. And every day since then, Sofia, I have wished I could turn the clock back, wished I'd made different decisions, that I'd taken you with me.'

'No.' Sofia shook her head, could see the anguish on her mother's face, knew it was genuine. She remembered Marco's anguished expression when he'd spoken of letting Leo go. 'You were in an impossible position. And you made the decisions that felt like the best thing at the time. You don't know what would have happened if you had taken me. You may have been caught and then I am sure my father would have separated us, would have kept you in Palosia and that wouldn't have benefited either of us.' She reached out again and this time she kept her hand on her mother's arm. 'I understand why you did what you did and I truly hope that the years have been good for you, that you have found happiness.'

'I have.' Her mother gave a small smile. 'Perhaps more than I deserved. I married the man I left for your father. His name is Pietro and he is…kind and gentle, yet he has an inner strength and character that make him a true prince.' Sofia could see her mother's face light up and suddenly an image of Marco filled her mind, his chivalry and strength, and she blinked it away.

'My prince. I love him…and he loves me. I should never have left Pietro; marrying your father was wrong. I did not lie to Fiero but still, what I did was wrong. I didn't understand what it would mean to marry one man whilst loving another, didn't understand the grief, the regrets. Didn't understand how difficult it would be to be touched by someone else when you knew what the act of true love felt like. But no matter what, I cannot regret you, Sofia. I have always cherished the memories I have of my time with you.'

Her mother's heartfelt words warmed her even as she imagined the true horror her marriage must have been. 'Can you tell me about those memories?' she asked, wanting to take away a true picture of her early years, wanting to be able to carry the knowledge of the time she had had with the woman who had given birth to her.

'Of course. I would love to.' Now Flavia smiled, a small sweet smile. 'Now and, I hope, in the future.'

The words were a reminder of reality. 'I hope so too but I cannot guarantee that.'

Flavia nodded, resignation writ large on her face, a face so uncannily like Sofia's own. 'I understand. Then let us make the most of the time we have now.'

* * *

Marco looked around the walls of the small waiting room for the umpteenth time and then resumed pacing, his mind concentrated on Sofia and what was happening next door, half of him wanting to simply go in and see she was all right, the other half knowing he had no right to do anything of the sort. Knowing too that Sofia had the inner strength to deal with this, that this was precious time for mother and daughter to spend together.

The thought was a reminder that after this Sofia would be free to return to Palosia. But that was not a thought for now. It was not a time to worry about the bleakness that it brought. For now, Marco simply wanted to be there for Sofia when she came out, to hold her, give comfort if needed or celebrate or listen.

It was two more hours before there was a gentle knock on the door and then Sofia came in; he could see traces of tears on her cheeks and he moved over and took her in his arms, held her close as he rubbed her back until, finally, she half pulled away, though her hands remained on his forearms.

'I'm all right,' she said. 'It was… I… I want to tell you about it, but…'

'First let's go back home. Back to the villa,' he amended quickly. 'I'll call a taxi. Then when we're back, I'll run you a bath, give you a glass of wine and then I am going to cook you the best pasta you have ever tasted. Then, if you want, you can tell me what happened.'

'That sounds perfect.'

They sat close together in the taxi, hands interlinked, the silence natural and every so often she would lightly increase the pressure of her grasp. Once back he carried out his promise, ran a bath, poured in essential oils, brought her a glass of chilled white wine and headed to the kitchen.

Forty-five minutes later the kitchen door opened and Sofia walked in. Dressed in leggings and one of his T shirts, her hair damp, her face flushed from the heat of the bath, she looked so beautiful his heart twisted.

'Perfect timing,' he said. 'I'll put the pasta in.'

'It smells incredible.'

'I thought I'd keep it simple. I made *lo spaghetto al pomodoro.* Just tomatoes, salt, fresh basil and really good olive oil. Some people say put garlic in, but I think that overpowers the overall taste, so providing I've got really good fresh tomatoes I make it without.' He was talking to distract her, could see the still shell-shocked look in her eyes.

'Thank you.' She looked a little surprised. 'Actually, I am ravenous. I guess emotion makes you hungry.'

Minutes later he placed the steaming bowls on the table along with some freshly grated *Parmigiano Reggiano,* watched with satisfaction as she started to eat, saw a bit of colour return to her cheeks.

'This really is the best pasta I've ever eaten,' she said.

'I'm glad.'

After a few moments she glanced across at him, sipped her wine. 'I'm ready to tell you now. If that's okay?'

'Of course it is. But only if you want to.' He didn't want to force her to talk when he knew her emotions must be in overload.

'I do. It will make it feel real, rather than a dream.'

'Then I'd like to know what happened.'

She looked down at her bowl and then back up at him.

'It was almost surreal. I could see myself in her. In ways that shouldn't be possible. The way she tucks her hair behind her ear, the way she creases her forehead in thought.' She sipped her wine. 'She told me she was sorry, and she explained why she left, why she didn't fight for me. My parents' marriage was one of inequality, a marriage where my father's "love" turned to vindictive hate.'

She reached out and touched his hand. 'I know your parents' love died but at least they were united in their love for you. My father used my mother's love for me as a weapon to threaten her with. In the end she had no real choice but to leave and once she was gone, he made sure that she never saw me again. She did try but, in the end, she gave up the fight because she believed it was the best thing for me. But she has never really forgiven herself. All I could do was tell her that I forgave her. That I understood.'

His heart twisted at her understanding, her compassion, her sheer generosity of spirit.

'Do you understand?' he asked gently. 'I know how very much it has hurt all these years.'

'I think perhaps I still can't fully comprehend that it wasn't possible to fight more, fight harder, or to try to take me with her. But I do understand that she was scared and alone. My father took advantage of that vulnerability. Bullied her, broke her spirit.'

In a way he had never managed to break Sofia's and again admiration swelled in Marco.

'I can see why it was easier to start a new life here and she has. And I am truly happy for her. She married her old love, Pietro, and I could see how much she loves him. She glows when she mentions him and from what she said it is a reciprocal love. They have a son and a daughter. So, I have two more half-siblings.' Her voice held shock and question and perhaps a touch of sadness that he understood. These were siblings who had grown up with their mother. 'They live a simple life and they are happy. But there has never been a day where she hasn't thought of me.'

Her eyes welled up with tears and he moved round the table, put his arm around her. 'That is a lot to take on board. You must be feeling overwhelmed.'

'I am. Overwhelmed and dazed. I've dreamt about meeting her for so long. Now I have and I know that she isn't a bad person. I know her reasons for leaving. But there is so much to process, to think about and I'm...'

'Exhausted,' he said, seeing the tiredness in her eyes, hearing it in her voice. 'Come on. We're going to bed.'

And that night, once they climbed into bed, he pulled her into his arms, her head on his chest, and he held her until she fell asleep, entwined in his arms, close to his heart. Until finally he fell into a deep dreamless sleep.

Sofia opened her eyes, aware that something must have awoken her but unsure of what. Remained completely still, revelled in the sense of cocooned warmth, the safety of Marco's arms around her. Then she heard it again: the buzz of her phone, notification of a message.

She glanced at Marco, saw him stir slightly and gently she eased out of his clasp, breath held, not wanting to awaken him. The only person who could be messaging her, who had this number, was Rosa. Moving as quietly as possible, she sat up, picked her phone up and tiptoed from the room, headed to the kitchen and made her way to the window enclosure.

She glanced out at the pink-tinged sky that heralded the dawn and the coming of another day. Then, taking a deep breath, she looked down, started to read.

Dearest Sofia
Father has found you and he is so very furious. He had a guard following your mother, and that led him to you. I am not sure what he will do next.
Belle

Sofia felt the hammer of her heart against her ribs, her ears already alert for the knock at the door, the inevitable tread of the guards' footsteps. She forced her brain to think. The phone was a new number but both the signature and the code words indicated the messages were genuinely from her sister. In which case her father could have sent the guards the night before. Presumably he was holding fire, wouldn't want to create a scandal. Marco's wealth and position might also play a part in causing King Fiero to at least pause for thought. She returned her attention to her phone, the next instalment.

Eduardo has now stated that he no longer wishes to marry you. He is going to marry Luciana. Father has a plan. You are to return home and continue the pretence of illness. Then in two months you will release Eduardo from his engagement. A few months later you will get engaged to Count Arturion. Father has arranged the marriage.
    Sending you so very much love
Belle

Panic cascaded over her, and she half rose from the chair. All of her wanting, needing, to go to Marco, to wrap herself around him and beg him to never let her go. She forced herself to remain still, told herself not to be foolish.

She had known, they had both known, this would happen. That she would have to return. That her destiny, her duty, lay in an arranged marriage. This interlude had always had an end date baked in.

But all those words, all the logic in the world did nothing to stem the sheer force of the denial rising in her, the soaring sense of despair evoked at the idea of being wrenched away from the man she loved.

Whoa. Stop the press.

The man she what?

Now images of Marco streamed through her mind, his touch, his smile, his scent, his warmth, his chivalry. The way her heart hopped, skipped and jumped at the sight of him, the sense of safety and security he engendered. How he made her laugh, the way his smile caused her heart to leap. She blinked the images away, but however hard she tried to block the knowledge, to dodge the bullet, she couldn't. The truth was blinding in its horrible crystal clarity. She loved him, heart, body and soul.

What was she going to do?

Her phone beeped again and she looked down at the next message.

Saw that it was from her father, or at least issued by the authority of King Fiero.

Sofia, I have discovered your whereabouts. I will give you two choices. To present yourself at the ferry port before eleven a.m. today. Or I will take matters in my own hands.

Sofia glanced at her watch. There was time. But time for what? She had no doubt there was a guard posted within sight of the villa. There could be no escape. Plus, where would she be escaping to? What would she be escaping from now? The only option was to return to Palosia.

She couldn't stay here, could never tell Marco of her love. They had undertaken this interlude on the basis of a mutual rejection of love. The terms absolute. She wouldn't, couldn't admit to Marco that she loved him, wouldn't do that to him. It would feel as if she had somehow betrayed his trust; he'd believed her to be immune to love, believed this interlude was safe.

Marco did not want her love. And he would hate the idea of hurting her, of inflicting pain.

There was no more time. Their time was up. Duty in the shape of Count Arturion summoned her. The thought shattered her; her heart was slowly breaking into pieces. The idea of leaving Marco caused a sear of pain nigh on impossible to bear. But somehow, she had to, because anything else was truly impossible.

How would she say goodbye? How would she hide her feelings from Marco? For a craven moment Sofia looked at the door. Perhaps the best thing for them both would be if she simply left. But could she leave without seeing him one last time?

CHAPTER FOURTEEN

MARCO OPENED HIS EYES, intensely aware that something was missing, that the bed next to him was empty, and when he stretched a hand out the sheets were cool to the touch.

His heart seemed to skip a beat as a sudden sense of panic, of history repeating, assailed him. No, Sofia wouldn't, couldn't, have gone. Couldn't have been spirited away by palace guards whilst he slept through. But the foreboding, dread, sheer panic, wouldn't abate, scrambled all his senses. The idea that she could be gone from his life caused a wrenching sense of loss, made his feelings of seven years before pale in comparison.

As he tugged a pair of jeans on, stumbling in his haste, all he could envisage was the sight of an empty house, and the desolation that would come with it. His brain tried to figure out a plan, work out timings, when it could have happened, what he was going to do. He wasn't ready for her to go. Not yet. There must be a way to circumvent the guards, keep her in his life for longer, to stay in hers. But what if Sofia didn't want that? The question was like an icy deluge of doubt. What if this time she'd chosen to go completely voluntarily?

A few strides later and he registered the smell of coffee. Hope surged as he shoved the kitchen door open with precipitate haste, and relief washed over him as he saw her.

'I… I'm glad you're here. I thought maybe…you'd gone.'

Wariness touched her expression. 'I'm here. I haven't disappeared without leaving a note. Not this time.'

He studied her face, saw its pallor in the early morning sunshine, her eyes smudged with sadness. 'But something has happened,' he said as foreboding unfurled anew in his gut.

She took a deep breath. 'Yes.'

'Are you leaving?' The question jerked out of him, in the desperate hope of reassurance, but somehow the hope already felt doomed. Her expression held the answer. He could see it in her eyes even before she inclined her head.

'Yes. This past week has been…incredible, magical; the type of week I never thought was possible for me,' she said. 'But it can't go on for ever. For either of us.'

Why not? He bit the words back, knew she was right. There could be no for ever for them.

'But why go now?' Why would she want to leave when she had just found her mother, when she was still in the midst of working on the villa, when they were happy together, dammit?

Now her composure seemed rattled and she cupped her hands round her cup of coffee as if for comfort. 'I got a message. Early this morning. From Rosa.'

The foreboding deepened. 'What did it say?'

'My father has found me. He set a guard on my mother. He is furious and I suppose I can see why. If you and I become public my reputation will be ruined. He has demanded my immediate return.'

'What about Eduardo?'

'That is over; Eduardo is going to marry the woman he loves.' Her face lightened slightly. 'I am glad for him. But my father has another plan.'

He waited, saw her hands clench into fists, and he reached out and covered her hand in his. She looked down, briefly covered his hand with her own and then gently pulled back.

'In about six months' time I will marry someone else.'

Now his own fists clenched and he had to force himself to remain still. 'Who?'

'A Palosian aristocrat. He is a massive landowner, owns a huge number of olive groves and he will agree to enter into business with the Crown. In return for my hand in marriage. I know him. He is a good man; he will understand that I have had a previous relationship. But he will not want it to be made public. So it is imperative that no one finds out about us, that we are not seen together. I have to go back. There is no other choice.'

Marco stared at her, his whole mind, his whole body rejecting this idea. Rejecting everything. 'There is always another choice,' he said flatly.

'Not in this case.' Her gaze met his. 'I've already taken too many risks. Realistically at some point someone will recognise either you or me. Then what? Then my marriage prospects are in tatters. I truly don't regret any decision I have made so far; I don't regret my time with you. How could I?' Her voice caught. 'This interlude has been magical. But it has to end here. Before there are any regrets. Before I bring disgrace to my name, prove my father right, demonstrate that I am truly no princess. I don't want misery to outweigh the joy you have brought me. Do you see that?'

'Yes.' That was the worst of it. He did. Understood the importance of her royal duties and obligations, her loyalty to her country and her sister. What could he offer against that?

But there had to be another choice. There had to be. Now he started to pace, desperation triggering ideas, assessing and discarding, until... 'There is another choice, another option,' he said, coming to a halt in front of her. 'Marry me,' he said.

Sofia stared at him as the silence stretched.

'Excuse me?' she said, deciding that her tired, distraught brain must have misheard him. Ever since she'd received Rosa's messages, her mind had been in turmoil. But now, now Marco had thrown a bombshell into her thought process. Her heart leapt, tumbled, flipped as she looked at him.

'Marry me,' he repeated and now his voice was firmer, filled with confidence. 'An arranged marriage with me instead of with a Palosian aristocrat or a prince. I know that I don't have blue blood in my veins, but I do have a lot of money. I am sure I can come to some sort of deal with your father. I could invest in Palosia. In olive oil. In perfumes. You mentioned that Chiara has set up a successful hat business. I could help expand that further, increase exports. Use my platform to help market Palosian goods. We could live on Palosia some of the year and abroad the rest. You'd have your freedom. We wouldn't have to live in each other's pockets. You could go where you wanted whenever you wanted. You could train as an interior designer, still see Rosa.'

His words painted such a beautiful picture, one so

full of allure, that she could almost taste the happiness it would bring. A place on Palosia, walking the oak-lined avenue in the palace gardens with Rosa, hand in hand with Marco leading him through, or better yet getting lost in, the twist and turns of the verdant green walls of the palace maze. A house in Italy, an office in an interior-design firm and, in every scene, Marco was by her side. She blinked, tried to think, really think. Marco was offering an arranged marriage, in which case—

'But what do *you* get from this?'

'Any deal I negotiate with your father will benefit Krafty. On a personal note, I'd gain a relationship I can navigate. Because otherwise what are my alternatives? A series of potential short-term affairs, always seeking a woman who truly doesn't believe in love? Always feeling uncomfortable. Always worried I'll hurt someone. Or you and I can get married. An extension of our interlude, a relationship that can't turn bitter or sour because neither side wants or believes in love.

'You told me all the benefits of an arranged marriage, security, liking, respect. We have all that and we also have trust and attraction thrown in. I know you want a family and I believe we could make that work as well. We would both be truly committed to parenthood and we would also be a unit, offering our children security and stability. And if for some reason our marriage doesn't work then at least we would be able to work out an amicable agreement where we put our children first. We wouldn't be locked into a destructive cycle like my parents. I think this could work for both of us.'

And for one glorious moment Sofia believed it could. Imagined being with Marco all the time, having a baby, *their* baby… Marco cradling the tiny infant, looking down with love in his eyes and herself looking on at the man she loved.

The thought pulled her up short. And the full irony, the horror of the situation burst upon her as she stared at Marco, took in the, oh, so familiar features, the face that she'd seen smile, laugh and frown. The face that had looked on her with compassion, caring, desire… But never love. Because he didn't believe in love. Because he didn't love her. However much she loved him. And in falling in love with him, she'd wrecked everything.

Because she couldn't marry him. Couldn't enter a marriage that was one-sided, though for a deluded moment she'd told herself that she could. That she could hide her love.

Such futile reasoning, which she knew to be wrong. Knew she had to find the resolution to do the right thing. He'd made it plain that the basis of the arrangement, the only reason he was contemplating it, was that he believed she didn't love him. Trusted her to be entering the deal on that basis. She couldn't betray that trust, knew it would make for a marriage of misery, with her hoping every day, every night, that she might make him love her. And you couldn't. You couldn't make people love you. A one-sided marriage couldn't work.

It was only now that the penny dropped and the full ramifications of her foolishness dawned on her. She wouldn't be able to marry Count Arturian whilst knowing she loved Marco. Because a marriage couldn't work if one person loved someone else. That was why she hadn't married Eduardo. Her mother's words echoed in her head. *I didn't understand what it would mean to marry one man whilst loving another, didn't understand the grief, the regrets. Didn't understand how difficult it would be to be touched by someone else when you knew what the act of true love felt like...*

How had she let this happen? So blithely believed she could embark on this interlude and move on? How ridiculous her reasoning felt now. And now...now Marco was waiting for an answer. And even as she heard the crack of her heart, knew she might well spend the rest of her life ruing and regretting this decision, still she knew it was the only thing to do.

'I can't marry you,' she said, keeping her voice even.

'Why not?' His lips set in a grim line.

'Because it wouldn't work,' she said, realising as she said the words that they were the truth. This wasn't only about her; it was also about him. 'You deserve more than to get embroiled in my family's political and emotional messes. All you wanted was an interlude, you don't really want marriage. Or a family.'

Now she could see why he'd made the offer. 'You are trying to do what you have always done. Protect me. But providing me with sanctuary for a week is one thing, committing yourself to a marriage you don't truly want is another. So, thank you from the bottom of my heart, but I can't marry you. So, the sooner I leave, the better.' She knew she couldn't hold it together for much longer. Knew every second she remained with him it would become harder and harder to stick to her resolve. To do what she knew to be right. 'My father has told me I can meet a Palosian escort at the ferry. They will have organised a discreet return to Palosia.' She rose to her feet.

'Sofia, wait. I… I didn't make the offer lightly. Please believe that.'

'I do. But I can't bear the thought of you regretting it. You said to me that you didn't believe that any long-term relationship, arranged or not, can work, because there are no guarantees. That you don't want commitment and you don't think it's fair to risk bringing a child into that or even fair to enter any relationship. I can't and won't have children with someone who is only having a family for me. You can't extend an interlude into a marriage—there are different rules and expectations.' She stepped towards him. 'I truly wish you nothing but happiness and I will never forget our interlude. Not ever. I'll call a taxi.' She pulled out her phone and quickly did that.

'But before I go, I need to give you this.' She placed the sketchbook on the table. 'This has proposed sketches for all the rooms and there are more detailed plans on your laptop, along with suggested outlets and sources.'

'Thank you.' She saw the sadness on his face, and it wrung her heart.

'I'll wait outside.'

'I'll come out.'

She shook her head. 'No. It will be easier if you don't. No one will think twice about your interior decorator getting in a taxi to leave. Job done.'

And indeed, it was. Sofia willed herself not to cry, allowed herself one last touch, one hand placed on his forearm, on the lithe swell of muscles, one hand to cup his jaw with its morning shadow. A light brush of her lips on his cheek—she didn't dare do more. Already his proximity threatened to shatter her fragile resolution.

'Goodbye, Marco. Thank you for all you have done

for me and I will follow your next steps. It's better if we don't stay in touch.'

He inclined his head and she saw his hands clench by his sides as if he was preventing himself from even lifting a hand, and she was grateful for that restraint.

'Goodbye, Sofia. I hope, I wish, that all your dreams come true. I know you will be a wonderful parent and I hope your father appreciates what you are doing, sees your true worth and beauty. You are a true princess. Not because of who you marry but because of who you are.'

She knew she had to go now, that instant, before it was no longer possible for her to do so. And as she closed the door behind her, she thought her heart might crack in two; the pain a burning sear of grief.

Three days later

Marco looked round the villa; he should have left by now but, somehow, he hadn't been able to. Staying here made him feel closer to Sofia. He'd checked the Internet constantly for Palosian news, rewarded with a single photo of a 'convalescing princess', Sofia's hair no longer highlighted brown, but dyed back to its natural colour, her face pale, but at least he knew she was safe.

He sat at the kitchen table, opened the sketchbook yet again, turned to the last page and his heart turned over as he looked at the sketch, saw the words she had written.

Dear Marco
I have drawn this idea without consulting you; I hope
you don't mind. However hard I try I cannot believe
all your passion for your art, all your creativity, is

truly gone. Please know I am not trying to take away
from what you have achieved, your success and your
hard work are phenomenal. But I think there is still
some of the idealistic dreamer inside you, and I hope
one day you let yourself dream again of your art.
     With all my best wishes
Sofia

He looked at the accompanying pictures, the sketch of a
workshop, her handwritten notes—the detail of the picture
showed how much thought she had put into it. The research
into potters' wheels and forges, the maximisation of natural light, the thought for storage and space. The idea that
Sofia had done this for him, that she still believed in the
young man he'd once been, in a talent he had long since
given up on, brought a slew of emotion. Warmth and also a
frustration that all her talent displayed in this sketchbook—
the combination of vision and detail—would be wasted on
some landowning count. The thought twisted his gut with
anger and a bleak, searing desolation. He rose to his feet,
aware of an urge to smash something, punch a wall, do
something, anything, to disperse these unwanted feelings.

The ring of the doorbell was a welcome distraction;
it would be his mother and Lorenzo. He'd asked them to
come and see the villa and he needed to at least show a
good face on it. After all, this was a gift for her, a place for
her and her family to come and relax, enjoy themselves.

Sofia's voice echoed in his head. 'You are her family.
And this is a chance to embrace that.'

He pulled the front door open, saw his mum on the
doorstep and conjured up a smile, tried to keep his voice
normal. 'Just you? I thought Lorenzo was coming too.'

'He's gone for a walk round Capri. I wanted to see you on your own,' Giulia said, her gaze intent as he led the way into the kitchen. She glanced round and headed straight for the coffee machine. 'I didn't want to give you the chance to deflect questions with social inanities. Plus, I thought you may feel more comfortable speaking with just me. I know you and Lorenzo haven't really become close.'

'I…'

'But that's for another day. When I spoke to you, you sounded sad.' She handed him a cup of coffee. 'You look tired and…you look more than sad, you look desolate. Like you did after Leo.' She hesitated. 'After that happened you said you wanted to be left alone and I listened to you. I'm sorry. I was caught up with Lorenzo and, looking back now, I shouldn't have left you alone. I should have been there for you.'

'It wasn't your fault.' He meant every word. 'You did try. Both you and Dad tried. But I wanted to deal with it myself. Anyway,' he added brightly, 'a lot has happened since then. You and Lorenzo have got married, you have a lovely family and…'

His mother shook her head. 'Uh-uh. *I* am not going to be deflected. Yes, I am lucky to have Lorenzo and, yes, I get on incredibly well with his children. *His* children,' she repeated. '*You* are *my* child, *my* family. I know something is wrong and I want to help.' She reached out, touched his arm. 'I am not moving until you tell me what's happened.'

Looking at his mother's determined face, Marco could see she meant it. In truth he wanted to talk about Sofia, needed to work out how to snap out of this. Perhaps his mother could help him find perspective. 'I met someone,' he said. 'And now she's gone and I miss her. But I know I'll get over it and I know it's all for the best.'

His mother frowned slightly. 'Why? Why is it all for the best?'

'Because she didn't want to marry me. I offered her a deal but she—' He broke off at his mother's expression, her mouth agape.

'I'm a bit lost. If you proposed and she refused—that's not a deal.'

'It's complicated.'

'I'll concentrate hard.' Giulia sat at the table and he followed suit, started to explain.

Five minutes later she put her cup down. 'So let me get this straight. You met a princess who was running away from one arranged marriage, but accepted that a different arranged marriage was her destiny. She wanted a week of freedom. You helped her and in that time you and she became involved on the premise it was a temporary fling. Yet when she had to leave you offered to marry her. Why?'

'Because it made sense. I could offer her a better deal. A marriage where she would have real freedom to pursue her dreams, have a family and a career, make decisions for herself.'

His mother looked at him. 'And what was in it for you?' she asked. The same question that Sofia had asked. And suddenly Marco wasn't sure of the answer. What had he wanted, really wanted? The answer hit him. He'd wanted Sofia to stay in his life. But that wasn't the point. This was—

'It made sense. I could have a relationship without the complications of love with a woman I trusted. A relationship where, if anything went wrong, we would be able to split amicably without bitterness. Move on.'

'A marriage completely unlike mine with your father's,' she said softly. 'A marriage with safety nets and rules.'

'Yes.'

'Why did she refuse?'

'She said it wasn't fair to me. That I didn't really want marriage or children. And she couldn't have children with someone who was doing it for her.'

'Was she right?'

'No.' The answer instinctive and instant. Because there was no relief that Sofia had refused. There was only burning regret for what could now never be. Each morning of waking up brought a bleakness and a sense of emptiness at the knowledge he would never hear her voice, never hold her, or see her face light up in a smile. All he wanted to do was fly to Palosia and storm the palace to get to her.

'No,' he repeated. 'She wasn't right. I do want to marry her; I do want a family with her.' The words were so natural and brought up such vivid pictures. Sofia holding a baby, *their* baby, a little girl with a smattering of dark hair and wide blue eyes. The idea brought an upswell of feeling and he stared at his mum in a moment of breathtaking realisation. He loved Sofia.

'Because that makes sense?' his mum asked softly. 'Or for another reason?'

'I…'

'Marco, if you love her, then please, please don't walk away from that love, please don't give her up without a fight, without at least telling her the truth.'

'But… I… I don't want love. And neither does Sofia. She refused my proposal.'

'She refused your proposal of a deal, an arranged marriage. I don't know how Sofia feels about you, maybe she doesn't either. But if you love her, perhaps she deserves to know.'

Marco tried to think. Could Sofia love him? Was it possible? Looking back over the past days, he thought about the connection between them, all the confidences they had shared, how easy and relaxed and happy they had both been. Remembered holding her, remembered the passion they had shared.

'Even if we do love each other, how do I know it is sustainable, that this isn't a mirage, a temporary phase that won't survive reality? How do I know that I won't end up hurting her, or impacting our family?' The thought of bringing pain to Sofia, of seeing her beautiful face look at him with disdain or contempt, was unbearable.

'You don't know. I can't give you a cast-iron guarantee,' Giulia said. 'But I can tell you all marriages aren't like mine and your father's. I am sorry, truly sorry, for what we put you through. With hindsight it was selfish of both of us. And I don't know what happened. Once I did love your father and he loved me. Maybe we didn't work hard enough at it. Love isn't always easy, it has downs as well as ups and your dad and I weren't prepared for that. We never really talked; we never really shared our feelings.

'But just because we got it wrong doesn't mean love can't work. There are no guarantees but that doesn't mean you shouldn't try. I love Lorenzo and I truly believe we will make it. I never take our love for granted and I will work at it, tend it, nurture it and, if need be, I will fight for it. I was scared to risk loving him but in the end the thought of losing him, losing the chance of love, gave me the courage to risk it.'

Marco listened and as he did, he thought of Sofia. They had trusted each other with their very souls, had taken such joy in each other, and he had tried to control that joy, put in rules and regulations and safety nets. Had offered her a deal. He gave a small groan.

'I've messed up,' he said.

'Then go and fix it.' The words were so simple but she was right. Blindingly right. He had to fix this. He loved Sofia and he had to let her know. Before it was too late and he regretted it for the rest of his life. If she didn't love him, so be it. He wanted her to know of his love for her. Wanted to give his love a chance, hoped with all his heart that she would too.

'I will. Thank you. And soon, I want to get to know Lorenzo better and his family. I am so glad you have found love and happiness.' He went and hugged her. 'Thank you again. Here are the keys. You and Lorenzo look round. I have to go.'

Palosian Palace

Sofia sat at the table in the royal bedroom, glanced out of the window, tried to find some solace or tranquillity from the palace gardens, but the bloom and beauty of the terraced flower beds couldn't permeate her fogged senses. The whole world seemed tinged in ash grey, the colour of her crumbled dreams and hopes.

She looked back down at her open sketchbook; drawing had been the only thing to offer peace in the past bleak days. Sketches of Marco. Pictures of Capri, images so indelibly etched on her mind, her heart, her very soul. Memories she knew she would treasure for ever even as she somehow worked out how to rebuild her life. Once the pain, the grief, the desolation of missing Marco eased, each night an escape into dreams of a different life, dreams where he was lying next to her. Only to awake in the morning to the flower-scented breeze from the palace gardens and the dreary, inescapable knowledge that Marco was not there.

A knock on the door heralded the arrival of Rosa and Sofia gently closed the sketchbook, not ready to share the images even with Rosa.

'I came to see how you are feeling,' Rosa said, entering the room with her soft tread, her face full of compassion and love. 'I can sense your sadness.'

How to answer that question? How was she feeling? Heartbroken. Devastated. Furious with herself for the folly of falling in love. Full of the ache of missing Marco.

'Or perhaps it would be better for me to ask what happened. Something happened to you in Naples. You look different. You are different.'

Sofia looked at her sister, tried to decide what she should do. Could she confide in Rosa? Rosa who had her own arranged marriage to deal with at some point in time. With all the added pressure of producing an heir to contend with.

As if sensing her thoughts, Rosa stepped forward, sat opposite her. 'You can talk to me, Sofia. I want to help.'

Sofia looked at Rosa's beautiful face, her eyes wide and sympathetic, and she realised Rosa was right. 'I am different,' she said softly. 'I fell in love, and it has changed everything. How I look at the world. It was one of the most foolish things I could have done, but I did it anyway.'

'And you regret it?' Rosa asked, wonder and genuine

curiosity in her words. 'I know we princesses are not supposed to look for love, whatever the fairy tales say, but do you truly regret it?'

Sofia opened her mouth and closed it again, considered the question. If she could turn time back, would she change anything, forgo the pleasure, the joy, the laughter, the companionship? To never experience any of that would make her world a darker place. Yes, now all she felt was the pain, loss and grief of love unrequited. But being with Marco, experiencing love, had changed her, changed her whole life and given it a new perspective.

'I don't know,' she admitted. 'Perhaps it would feel different if he loved me back. But he doesn't.'

'How do you know? Did he say that?'

'Not explicitly, but I know. He doesn't want love, believes it isn't made to last, that when it goes wrong it causes bitterness, so you are better off without it.'

'All the things you thought until you fell in love with him,' Rosa pointed out, the gentleness of her tone underpinned with an unfamiliar edge. 'Perhaps Marco has changed his mind too.'

The thought poleaxed her.

'Are you willing to gamble your life away on the assumption that he hasn't? Plus, surely Marco deserves the truth. Surely it is good for people to know they are loved?'

'But even if he did love me, there is no future for us. Our father would never permit the marriage. He would banish me and then...'

'Then what?' Rosa said, taking a deep breath as she saw Sofia's eyes widen in surprise. 'Then you would have to leave me? All your life you have protected me. I know you have stayed here in part for me and I love you for it.

But I don't want you to give up your chance of love and happiness for me. In fact, I won't have it. As for your duty to Palosia, our father took away your succession rights. You don't owe him anything.'

Sofia looked at her sister, her beautiful, kind, insightful, selfless sister who she loved so much. A love that would never wither or die. Just as her love for Marco wouldn't. Rosa was right. Marco did deserve to know he was loved and valued. And he deserved the truth from her. Withholding that truth was in itself a betrayal of trust.

As they spoke there was a ping from Rosa's phone.

Her sister's eyes widened. 'I can't quite believe this, but I think it's Marco.'

'How do you know?'

'I'm assuming you told him about our code.' Sofia nodded. 'He's signed it Mark.'

Sofia nodded, remembered she'd written Rosa's mobile number in the sketchbook she'd left with Marco. 'What does it say?'

'He wants to see you, to meet you. He says it's urgent. He will come to wherever you say.'

It could be to discuss the villa ideas, Sofia told herself. Or to discuss the arranged marriage again. Or most likely he wanted to make sure she was all right.

But whatever it was she knew what she needed to do next. She rose to her feet, leant down and gave Rosa a hug.

'Thank you. Please message him back. Tell him I will come to Naples. But now I am going to see Father.'

Rosa's eyes widened in concern. 'But wouldn't it be better to talk to Marco first? Or...'

Sofia shook her head. 'No. It is time I stood on my own two feet.'

Two days later

Marco had never felt this wracked with nerves in all his twenty-eight years, but neither had he felt such heady anticipation. Anticipation laced with dread, a fear that this really would be the last time he saw Sofia. He wasn't even sure how she had managed to leave Palosia, but she had asked him to choose a place to meet in Naples. So here he was, at the place where they had shared their very first kiss seven years ago. Yet as he looked down over the panoramic sprawl of Naples, all he could think of was Sofia.

Anxiety strummed again. Perhaps she would tell him of the impending announcement of her engagement. Worse, perhaps his nightmare of the previous night would come true: Sofia would arrive with the count in tow.

Marco forced his body to relax, scanned the people headed in his direction and his heart skipped a beat. There was Sofia. Simply dressed in one of the dresses she'd bought on Capri, a pattern of purple and blue, her dark hair now a little bit longer. Then she was next to him, slightly breathless from the steep climb, and he couldn't help the smile that tipped his lips. It was a smile that encompassed relief and happiness and she smiled back, a smile that lit her face, and they stood in a timeless moment where anything was possible, an instant of hope, a chance and infinite potential.

But then the nerves returned and he reminded himself that he had no idea of her agenda, of her reasons for agreeing to this meeting. As if mirroring his thoughts, she took a step back and her face became serious, her dark blue eyes full of both wariness and determination.

'So, who goes first?' she asked.

Perhaps he should be polite and let her, but he couldn't. He was here to fight for Sofia, to tell her how he truly felt, and he wouldn't bottle it. Not now. Not when she was standing here and his whole being was filled with his love for her, a burning desire to pull her into his arms.

'If it's all right with you, I'll go first.'

She hesitated and then nodded. 'Go ahead.'

'First I want to apologise.'

'For what?' There was genuine surprise in her voice.

'For offering you a mealy-mouthed proposal for an arranged marriage.'

Was that disappointment that crossed her blue eyes, before she blinked it away?

'You were offering me way more than that,' she said softly. 'You were offering me freedom, an alternative to another marriage. But I completely understand that you are withdrawing that offer. I didn't come here to tell you I'd changed my mind.'

Now it was his turn to blink as he realised she'd got the wrong end of the stick, thought he'd asked to see her to rescind the proposal completely.

'I *am* withdrawing that offer. Because I want to replace it with another.' And now the nerves, the fear of rejection no longer mattered. All that mattered was telling Sofia the truth. 'Will you marry me? Not as part of a deal or an arrangement. Not out of convenience. This time I am offering you my heart, my love, my commitment for the rest of my life.'

Her eyes widened and he saw the disbelief.

'Whatever your answer is, I want you to know that I love you, Sofia. With all my heart. You've changed me, you've made me see everything differently. I've seen how you have navigated life with such strength and kindness and through it all your inner beauty shines. You shone a light in *my* life in Capri, just as you did seven years ago. You light up my world and these past days without you have been bleak. I want to wake up with you by my side for the rest of my life. If you'll have me. You don't need to answer now, please take some time, think about what I have said. I know you don't believe in love, but I promise you my love for you will not change, that it is true and real. But if you don't love me, I still won't regret loving you, because it has brought me joy.'

She stepped forward, reached up to cup his face, her blue eyes holding his gaze unwaveringly and what he saw there made his heart beat faster.

'I don't need any time to think, because the answer is simple. Of course I will marry you. I am offering you my heart, my love, my commitment for the rest of my life. I came here today to tell you that I loved you. To tell you how you have changed my life and my beliefs. You have shown me so much, how to believe in myself and my talent. To see that I can stand up to my father and stand on my own two feet and that does not make me any less of a princess. That my blood is not tainted. I have seen your strength, your resilience and your generosity. In choosing to trust me when there were so many reasons for you to have walked away. You truly are a knight in shining armour, not for protecting me, but for showing me how to protect myself. Showing me the joy of love. So yes, yes, yes! I will marry you. With all my heart.'

In that moment he felt a joy so great he didn't know how to harness it as he reached into his pocket and then went down on one knee in front of her, uncaring of the crowd they were gathering. He opened the box and, taking her left hand in his, he slipped the ring onto her finger, stood up as she held it up, over the city of Naples, so that the sun glinted off the jewels.

'It's beautiful.' She studied the ring and then looked up at him. 'Did you…?'

'Make it? Yes, I did.' To his elation the skills he'd learnt years before had still been there and in the past days he'd thrown himself into creating something he'd hoped Sofia would love. A ring with crossing bands studded with carefully selected colourful jewels interspersed with diamonds that somehow represented to him the idea of her freedom, her beauty and the way she lit up the world.

Now her smile grew even wider and she threw herself into his arms and hugged him. 'That makes it infinitely more precious. I will love looking at it every day for the rest of my life.'

The words brought another smile to his face as he contemplated the sheer happiness of spending the rest of his life with this woman, this wonderful, strong, beautiful woman. 'My creativity is back.' Triggered by her belief in him.

'I am so pleased for you,' she said. 'I know what an important part of you that is.'

'And I know the same for you. And I know how important your country and your sister are to you. We will go to your father and I will do everything in my power to make sure you are not separated from Rosa or Palosia.'

'It's okay,' she said. 'I spoke to my father before I left. I told him I would not enter an arranged marriage. I explained that my time away had changed me. That I was no longer willing to obey his every decree without question and I no longer believed that was where my duty lay. I told him I wanted to show my people that a princess can rule, can be independent and earn her own money. I told him I wanted to work for Palosia and for myself.'

Admiration filled him for the courage it must have taken. 'I wish I could have been with you.'

'In some ways it felt as though you were. Because it was the time I spent with you that showed me it was possible to stand up to him. That and the wisdom of my sister.'

'Did your father see your point of view?'

'No.' Sofia shook her head. 'If this were a film, I suppose he would have. But he didn't. He lost the plot. He forbad me to leave, threatened to make sure I never saw Rosa again.'

'I'm sorry.'

'Don't be.' Now she smiled, a sudden impish smile. 'I said that was his prerogative. But I didn't think the people would stand for that. That I would put my case to them. That for now I was leaving Palosia to visit Naples, that I would do it honestly and openly.

'He blustered, he shouted, and he called security, but I told him that if he secured me in my room word would get out and I would go public with the truth. In the end he let me go. I don't know if he will let me back. But I hope that he will. And Rosa has given me her blessing.

'But whatever happens I needed to tell you that you are loved. And now today you have told me that you love me. From this day forward we will go forward together, and I know there may be downs as well as ups but I know we will navigate every bump in the road. Together.'

He nodded. 'And we will make sure our children have

security and love and that they are brought up by two parents who love each other and them.'

She looked up at him. 'Do you mean that? I know after Leo, after your own upbringing, you may not want children. And if you don't that is truly okay. I love you. I am marrying you because I love you, not for a family, or wealth or security.'

'I know that. And I feel exactly the same. But I *want* to have children with you. I loved Leo so very much and I loved being a father and now, now I can see how wonderful it will be to bring a family up with you. You will be an amazing mother.'

'And you will be an amazing father, just like you were with Leo.'

'Maybe we will have a little girl with your dark hair.'

'And a boy with your grey eyes.'

'Or any combination, any gender, but I want to see you hold our baby. I want to go on family outings to the park. I want the chance to watch our children grow. But most of all, whatever life brings us, I want that life to be with you.'

And now seven years after their first kiss, standing above the glorious vista of Naples, the stretch of history from the ancient fourteenth-century bell tower to the towering recent skyscrapers, he took her into his arms. And as his lips touched hers and they were bathed in the orange glow of a glorious sunset, Marco knew he was the happiest man in the universe.

EPILOGUE

Seven months later,
wedding day on Palosia

SOFIA LOOKED AT her reflection in the mirror, and both awe and wonder flooded her at the thought of the hours ahead. She was going to marry Marco. Here on Palosia. Today she would make vows committing herself to the man who she had grown to love even more over the past months. In those months Eduardo had married his Luciana, despite opposition from his family, and both he and Sofia had insisted on telling the truth. They had announced they had ended their engagement because they both loved other people. But that they would remain friends and they hoped the people would understand and forgive the scandal.

They had all agreed to interviews and between them all they had won the people over. Sofia suspected the majority had been pleased that their royal families were moving with the times.

Marco had handled meetings with the king and courtiers with aplomb, civility and a steely strength that she knew had inspired a grudging respect from all. Even perhaps her father. And with Marco by her side, together they had negotiated a wedding on Palosia, and an agreement that, although she would have to request permission to visit, her father would consider those requests.

She turned as Rosa entered the room. 'You look stunning.'

They both said the words at the same time and exchanged a smile. One of the best parts of the wedding preparations had been choosing the bridesmaid dress with Rosa, and Sofia loved the look her sister had opted for. It was so very quintessentially Rosa. The simple high-waisted floral dress with its floaty style somehow epitomising the sheer happiness Sofia herself felt. The whole perfectly complemented by the circlet of fresh flowers woven into Rosa's silken fair hair that flowed loose around her shoulders.

'I've come to help with any last-minute preparations. And you do look stunning. Beautiful. Radiant, in fact.'

'I feel radiant,' Sofia said. And she knew it was nothing to do with her dress, though she absolutely adored it. This time the choice was truly hers, not motivated by the need to impress. Chosen simply with her love, because she wanted Marco to look at her and see her happiness, and she also wanted to knock his socks off. And she hoped the classic elegance of the dress would do exactly that. It was long-sleeved with a boat neck and made in Chantilly lace, its skirt flaring in graceful folds.

'No doubts?'

'Not a single one. I am truly floating on air. The love I feel for Marco has lit up my life. And I am so happy you are going to be my only bridesmaid.' Rosa would carry the much lighter, less ostentatious train of this gown.

'Are you all right with Father giving you away?'

'Yes. It...felt right.' Sofia didn't believe she and her father could ever be truly close, but she did feel she owed him something. He was Palosia's king and he did have the country's best interests at heart. She wouldn't invoke gossip or scandal by refusing to let him play his traditional role. On some level she appreciated King Fiero's pragmatic acceptance of the marriage even if it was motivated by Marco's wealth and position. Deep down she even still hoped that somehow, some day they could have some sort of relationship.

But regardless of that she now did have new family. In deference to Palosia's traditions she had not moved in with Marco prior to marriage, had mainly lived on Palosia for the time of their engagement. But he had spent time on Palosia and she had made trips to Italy, had met Giulia and Lorenzo and his children. Had stayed for a family holiday at the villa and it had been fun, the type of fun she and Rosa had never experienced. Family meals, board games played amid laughter and banter. Shopping trips with Marco's mother, honest, open conversations.

And Marco's dad had come to stay in Palosia, had reduced her to helpless laughter with his jokes. He had also divulged that he was pursuing a career as an artist, showed them his work, landscapes of the Scottish Highlands, and told them with pride that his work was garnering some recognition. That he had also met a fellow artist, a woman for whom he was beginning to develop feelings.

As for Flavia and her family, Sofia was in touch and after the marriage she hoped to see more of them, hoped that they too would become part of her life.

But nothing could replace Rosa and she looked at her

sister now with a twinge of anxiety at the thought of leaving her, knew how much she would miss her.

Reading her expression, Rosa gave her a gentle smile. 'I'll miss you, but maybe one day Father *will* let me visit you and Marco.'

Sofia frowned. That had been one point King Fiero had been immovable on.

'Your sister is free to call you but she will not be visiting. Rosa's position is now of even more importance and I will not allow her to leave Palosia at this time.'

Somehow the words had sounded ominous, made her wonder what her father had planned for her sister. A marriage, of course, but a marriage to whom?

On impulse, she reached out and took Rosa's hand in hers. 'Rosa. I won't presume to tell you what to do. But I wish, I hope, that you find the same happiness I have.'

Her sister vouchsafed no answer, her brown eyes unreadable. Then she smiled, a smile so sweet it twisted Sofia's heart.

'Right now, it is your happiness I am thinking about; this is your day, Sofia, and all I want today is to see my sister marry the man she loves and start her happy ever after. So, let's go, before Marco starts to worry. And here is your bouquet.'

Sofia took the flowers her sister had chosen and arranged, a glorious concoction made up of the pink and creamy roses that her sister grew and cultivated with such care, daisies and gypsophila, interspersed with sweet peas, lavender and jasmine, the resultant scent somehow redolent of sunshine and happiness. Sofia gave her sister a massive hug.

'Thank you. They are beautiful. Truly perfect.' She

stood still as Rosa made a few last-minute adjustments and then they left, exited the palace into the horse-drawn carriage that took them to the palace chapel. Happiness suffused Sofia as she arrived at the entrance to the ancient stone church, waited for her father to step out of his own carriage to join her.

And as the music started all other thoughts and considerations were gone. She walked forward, her eyes firmly fixed on Marco, and when she saw his arresting look, saw his grey eyes light up as she took each step closer, her heart skipped exultantly, filled with happiness and joy and love as she reached the man she loved so very, very much. Her prince, her happy ever after.

* * * * *

*Look out for the next story in the
Princesses of Palosia duet*

Conveniently Engaged to a Princess
by Suzanne Merchant

*And if you enjoyed this story, check out
these other great reads from Nina Milne*

Their Mauritius Wedding Ruse
Cinderella's Moroccan Midnight Kiss
Bound by Their Royal Baby

All available now!

CONVENIENTLY ENGAGED TO A PRINCESS

SUZANNE MERCHANT

MILLS & BOON

For Jacqui

'For there is no friend like a sister
In calm or stormy weather...'
—Christina Rossetti

PROLOGUE

LUCA MONTENALE STOOD still and forced down a rising tide of panic. He swiped a hand across his forehead, wiping away the sweat which stung his eyes, and turned in a slow circle. Should he go back, or should he go on? Had he last turned left, or was it right? The ancient hedges of the maze towered above him on either side, only a strip of cobalt sky visible between them. And the sun…

He squinted up at it. Heat beat down from directly overhead and that could only mean one thing: it was almost midday, the time he was supposed to present himself at his father's suite of rooms in the palace—shoes polished, hair brushed, face clean. Then they'd go to an important meeting. He hadn't been told why it was important, which was annoying, because he was thirteen and old enough to know. It was safer not to ask questions because his father was permanently in a bad mood. In fact, these days he tried not to talk to him at all.

They were going to meet the King, and he supposed that was important enough. He'd been lectured about 'best behaviour'. As if that was necessary. He knew about good manners and holding polite conversation with adults, who were usually boring and not interested in him, even if he *was* the only son of a count whose family tree was one of the oldest, and richest, in Italy.

Not that his father had had a hand in teaching him his manners, or how to converse with kings. It was his grand-parents who'd done that. But three years ago, his father had taken him away from them to live in his gloomy castle. Although he knew he was old enough not to miss them, he still did, with an ache which never went away.

He was going to be in so much trouble. If he'd been allowed to wear his jeans, instead of stupid shorts like a kid, he wouldn't have hurt his knee when he'd tripped and fallen—and that was before he'd even realised he was lost. He wished he'd never set foot in the maze, but its cool, dark shade had looked mysterious and a bit dangerous, and he'd remembered all the twists and turns he'd taken...until he hadn't.

He pulled his eyes away from the dazzling sun and raked his fingers through his hair. His father's butler, Nico—who had travelled with them from Tuscany and who had told him what clothes he had to wear—had plastered his hair to his scalp with something that smelled disgustingly of damp moss. But it had reverted to its usual thick, unruly waves, one lock flopping over his forehead. He pushed it away.

Standing in the absolute silence of a Mediterranean summer's day, he kicked at a tuft of grass and admitted to himself that he had no idea what to do.

Except the silence was not absolute. He turned his head, listening, and heard it again. Relief, quickly followed by apprehension, flooded through him. What if this was someone who'd been sent to find him? Whoever it was, they'd be angry, because he was keeping his father and, even worse, the King waiting; and angry because he was now unfit to be presented to the monarch in this dishevelled state. He pushed his hands into his pockets and told himself he didn't care.

Luca peered around the sharply trimmed edge of the hedge and huffed out a breath. This must be the middle of the maze, where water from a stone fountain trickled into a circular pond. The sound of the water had been mixed with a soft voice and now he saw to whom it belonged.

If she hadn't been the size of a four-or five-year-old girl, he'd have believed she was a fairy child—if he believed in fairies, which he didn't. She knelt on the stone bench surrounding the basin, her back to him, the grubby soles of her feet showing from beneath the skirt of the lacy white dress she wore. Her hair cascaded down her back in shimmering, fair waves and, as she leaned forward to trail her fingers across the surface of the water, she laughed.

Forgetting that he thought girls were boring, and that he was lost, Luca stepped out of the shadows into the centre of the maze.

'Who are you?' he asked.

Rosabella lifted her hand from the water and shook her fingers. Drops flew off them like a shower of sparkling diamonds and splashed into the pond. Then she turned slowly, sitting on the stone bench so that her feet dangled down but didn't reach the grass beneath them. She wriggled her toes and looked towards the voice that had asked the question.

A strange boy stood there: strange because she'd never seen him before, she thought, not strange, *peculiar*—although his clothes looked funny, and much too smart for being in the garden or playing. His white shirt had long sleeves, buttoned cuffs and a stiff collar. It looked as if it should have been tucked into his grey shorts, but one side of it hung out untidily. His socks were pulled up to his knees, one of which was grazed.

'Who are *you*? And how did you hurt your knee?'

'I asked first. And I tripped and fell.'

'Oh.'

Rosabella studied him. His hair was dark and messy, his eyes even darker, and he was tall. And he *had* asked first. She always tried to follow the rules, because that way her father wouldn't be even more angry with her than he normally was, and she also tried to be kind, because that was what her mother had taught her.

Was this boy like the one her father wished she'd been? Would she have grown tall, had hair like a raven's wing and eyes that seemed to see more than what he was looking at? Instead, she had hair which shimmered with light, like her mother's, and which seemed to annoy her father and her nurse. Everyone, really, except her half-sister, Sofia—and her eyes were plain brown.

'I'm Rosabella,' she said finally. She slipped to the ground and looked up at the boy expectantly. He looked even taller now.

'That's a pretty name. I'm Luca.'

'It means "beautiful rose", because roses are my mother's favourite flowers. Even though they have prickly stems.'

Luca took a step towards her. 'Are you prickly too?'

Rosabella giggled and shook her head. 'You're funny. People can't be prickly.'

She watched Luca glance around the space. The high hedges of the maze enclosed it, and the only way out was the way he'd come in.

'Was it your mother you were talking to? Is she one of the gardeners?'

Rosabella shook her head again. 'She does gardening, but not today. And I wasn't talking. I was singing. To the fish.' She turned her head to look at the pond.

'The *fish*? Now *you're* funny. You can't sing to *fish*.'

Rosabella tipped up her chin. 'I can.' She turned and climbed up onto the stone bench, leaning over the water. 'I'll show you.'

Luca knelt beside her, his fingers curving around the lip of the pool, listening as Rosabella's lilting voice began to sing a song about pretty horses. Bubbles popped, and three golden fish appeared, their mouths forming round shapes on the surface of the water, almost as if they were joining in the song.

'Do they always do that, when you sing?'

He sounded astonished, and Rosa felt pleased. She nodded. 'Mmm. Sometimes the frogs sing too. But it's too hot for them now. It's midday. They're resting.'

Something she'd said made Luca jump off the bench.

'Midday! I'm going to be in such trouble.'

'Why will you be in trouble?' Anxiety clutched at Rosabella's tummy. Trouble was something she'd been told to stay out of, and she tried her best, but sometimes it was difficult to know the difference between it and having fun.

'I'm supposed to go to a meeting, with my father, and I can't find my way out of this maze.'

The tension in Rosabella's tummy relaxed. She couldn't do anything about the time, but she could help him.

'My father also gets cross when people are late. But you aren't lost because I can show you the way.'

She reached out and took Luca's hand. 'It's easy. Come.'

CHAPTER ONE

'WHAT THE...*HELL*?'

Luca Montenale surged to his feet, sending the ornate chair crashing backwards onto the marble floor. His hands shook, making the thick, cream pages of the document he clutched between his fingers rattle.

A movement in the shadowy corridor beyond the door made him shut his mouth on a more expressive expletive. The castle staff, traumatised by the events of the past few days, had hovered around him, offering versions of what had happened and seeking reassurance, from the minute he'd stepped from the chauffeur-driven car yesterday afternoon before the ancient and massive, iron-studded front door.

He wished they'd leave him alone.

He was shocked, jet-lagged and exhausted. The trial in New York had lasted for weeks and, although he'd been sure he would win his client's case, nothing could ever be taken for granted. The verdict in their favour had been a relief, and he'd been looking forward to a quiet weekend, catching up on sleep and the newspapers, before returning to his head office in Rome.

Instead, a white-faced employee had met him at the entrance to his offices. His father, with whom he'd hardly exchanged a handful of words for over a year—and those had been angry ones—was dead. He'd taken his habitual post-lunch nap in his armchair in the drawing room and simply not woken up.

Way to go, had been Luca's first thought, hotly followed by a spike of annoyance bordering on anger. His father, the Count, the latest in a long line of custodians of this castle in Tuscany, had made his and others' lives hell for so many years, he'd hardly deserved a peaceful death.

'Sir?' The shadowy presence in the passage materialised into his father's—his *late* father's—elderly butler. He gestured towards the toppled chair. 'Is there anything…?'

Luca shook his head, as much to try to order his thoughts as to dismiss the man. 'No, thank you, Nico.' He dropped the sheaf of papers onto the desktop and waved him away.

'Very well.' Nico backed out of the door, his eyes sliding back to the chair. 'If you're sure, Count Montenale…'

Count. Luca pinched the bridge of his nose between his thumb and index finger, closing his eyes. Would he ever get used to the title? It made him feel like a different version of himself, and not one he wanted to know.

For as long as he could remember, there had been no love lost between his father and him. He might even have said for ever. His mother had died in a fall from a horse when he was two and he had no memory of her at all. It was said that his father had been furious, rather than grief-stricken. He'd forbidden her to ride the horse, but she was wilful, headstrong, and had refused to be told what she could and could not do.

'She defied me, and she paid the price,' his father had frequently said. 'I will *not* be defied.'

The iron will he'd imposed on his son when he'd summoned him back from the care of his grandparents on his tenth birthday seemed designed to crush any defiance before it started—to bend him to his will and force him into a shape closely resembling his own. Luca had fought against it with unwavering determination. He did not want to be like his father, and he had not intended to allow him to dictate how he lived his life. It seemed unjust that a man could determine how his son lived just because generations of sons before him had followed the same path.

His grandparents had been kind, fair and loving, always trying to help others. He wanted to be like *them*.

As soon as he'd been old enough, he'd broken away. Able to use the fortune his mother had bequeathed him, which his father could not touch, he'd gained the qualifications he wanted and climbed to the top of the legal profession with astonishing speed. He defended the defenceless when he could, and stood up for the rights of men and women whose voices would not otherwise be heard.

His father had never forgiven him for leaving the family estate. He'd accused him of abandoning his family, bringing shame on the ancient name of Montenale, and had hinted at retribution.

Luca rubbed his eyes and looked up at the massive portrait that dominated the room. His father returned his stare. The artist had captured his likeness admirably: the silver mane of hair swept back from the broad forehead; the frown between the heavy brows; the imperious nose and the mouth set in a straight, fierce line. But the eyes were the most compelling element of the picture. Deep and dark, they glared at Luca, and the expression they held seemed to be one of thinly-veiled triumph.

It took an effort of will, but he dragged his gaze away from those eyes and back to the document he'd dropped. He might have broken free of his father's control in life, but there on the burgundy leather top, signed and stamped with the thick, wax seal of the Montenale dynasty, lay the evidence that his control reached to trap him from beyond the grave.

Luca heaved the chair from the floor and sat down at the desk again. He gathered up the pages, which he'd found filed away with his father's papers, and ran his practised eye over them, even though he'd known what he'd find from the instant he'd read the first paragraph.

Twenty years ago, when Luca had been thirteen, his father had signed a contract promising him in marriage to Princess Rosabella of Palosia on the occasion of her twenty-fifth birthday. Scanning the print, which wavered and swam in his shocked vision, he calculated that date to be in three months' time.

He shoved the papers away and flung himself back in the chair, massaging the back of his neck where the rigid muscles felt as hard as iron. The whole idea was so preposterous as to be laughable, except that he knew it was deadly serious. This was a legal document, and it would take delicate negotiations to extricate himself from its grip.

He would never agree to a marriage of convenience. Such a thing went against the moral convictions on which he'd founded his career: freedom of choice, the importance of being heard and the defence of the persecuted. Neither he nor his proposed bride had been given a choice in this matter, or the opportunity to voice their opinions on it. To agree to it would undermine him professionally. He'd be regarded as a hypocrite and his career would be compromised.

Was this the threat his father had hinted at during their furious arguments? At least, Luca thought grimly, his sudden death had robbed him of the opportunity to gloat at his son.

The clearest memory Luca had of his visit to the kingdom of Palosia was of meeting the little daughter of one of the gardeners. She'd led him, unerringly, out of the maze when he was lost. He'd been reprimanded by Nico for being late, had his shoes cleaned, his painful knee scrubbed and been told to brush his hair, before being handed over to his angry father and ushered into the austere presence of King Fiero.

Later that day they'd returned to Tuscany. His father had seemed to be in a rare good mood on the flight and had ordered champagne. Now Luca knew why.

He flipped open his laptop and emailed his PA in Rome, asking her to investigate flights to Palosia, before composing a letter to King Fiero, requesting a meeting. He could have undertaken this awkward task by email, but good manners dictated that he should do the King the courtesy of meeting him face to face. The visit shouldn't take more than a few hours and he would only need to meet the King. It was simply a matter of unravelling a business deal, and there was no reason at all why he should meet the princess.

CHAPTER TWO

PRINCESS ROSABELLA CHECKED her watch. There was enough time to plant out the three remaining lavender plants into the herb garden. She firmed the rich, dark earth around them and then rose to her feet, bending to brush dust from her skirt. She stretched, easing muscles which were stiff after spending the morning bent over the flowerbeds.

The gardens surrounding the gleaming white palace on the hill fell away in ordered terraces. Flowers bloomed in a riot of colour, roses scrambling over pergolas and archways. The hedges of the maze—one of the original features of the gardens which had survived centuries of neglect—formed a dark-green block of linear orderliness amongst the vibrant exuberance of summer.

Lifting her eyes, Rosa could see the jumble of pastel-coloured houses of the nearest village clustered in the valley, while above them rose forest-clad mountains, their peaks shimmering in the heat. A sliver of sparkling sea glinted in the distance.

The sultry stillness was broken only by the sound of trickling water from one of the many fountains and rills that dotted the gardens, and the harsh call of a bird of prey, just visible, riding the thermals high above her.

Later, when the afternoon had cooled, she'd return to water the plants. She'd need the solace of the garden then.

Before that could happen, she'd have to endure what was sure to be a massively awkward lunch meeting with her parents and the man they thought was going to take her off their hands, be her husband and provide a male heir to the kingdom.

She'd dreaded this day ever since her father, the King, had told her that her husband-to-be was coming to meet her and, subject to the paperwork being put in order, there was no reason why their wedding shouldn't take place as soon as she turned twenty-five in September.

'But we've only just had Sofia's wedding,' she'd argued, and then wished she'd said nothing. The subject of her half-sister's marriage was guaranteed to anger her father. She'd shunned the men he'd chosen for her and instead had married for love. The King had grudgingly agreed to allow the wedding to take place on Palosia; and, even though it was not a Palosian tradition, Sofia had insisted on having Rosabella by her side as her bridesmaid.

Rosabella knew that the brave face the King had put on events had been a perilously fragile mask. He regarded Sofia's defiance of his wishes as a loss of face on his part, but she was loved by the people, and he'd feared a backlash of negative public opinion if he denied her the wedding on Palosia she so badly wanted.

Rosabella had hoped to gain more time, because the longer her marriage was delayed, the greater the chance that something might happen to prevent it. And then she wouldn't have to tell her father that like Sofia, she refused to enter into a marriage of convenience. The idea of confronting him with this bombshell terrified her. She needed more time to gather her courage to do it.

'You, Rosabella,' he'd replied, disdain colouring every syllable, 'Are my *second* daughter, of my *second* wife. It's not as though you can expect this marriage to be a celebration. It's a legal contract between two people.' His hand had swept downwards in a dismissive gesture. 'Nothing more.'

Rosabella understood only too well what this marriage would be. And, if she hadn't, his use of the word *second* would have told her all she needed to know. Second-best was all she'd ever amount to. Her father had made sure she'd always known that she held no power and could not expect any man to want her for herself. Born a girl, she was of no use to him whatsoever until she produced a son. By ancient law, women could not rule the country, but they could produce a male heir.

She should consider herself fortunate that he'd been able to broker any marriage for her at all. A rich Italian count, the inhabitant of one of the most beautiful castles in Tuscany surrounded by ancient and productive vineyards, had wanted more than he already had. The allure of connecting his family to the royal line of Palosia had been too much for him to resist, and he'd promised his son as her husband long before her father had ingrained in her the knowledge that she completely lacked beauty or grace.

It would be an important alliance, her father had said. Rosabella knew that what he hadn't said was much more pertinent. Once married to the so-far nameless and faceless son of the Count, she would be taken away from the only life she'd ever known. Her mother, despised by the King for not producing a son, would be left without the protection which until now Rosabella had provided.

Rosabella flicked her long braid over her shoulder and tugged her straw hat low over her eyes. While her mother had always encouraged her to spend time in the garden, learning about the wonders of the natural world and benefitting from the effects of fresh air and sunshine, she'd been a stickler for making sure her fair skin was protected.

She glanced down at her hands and frowned at her nails, which were ringed with dried earth. Sighing, she dropped her garden trowel and fork into her basket and turned towards the Queen's private quarters. She could already imagine the exclamation of horror that she knew her mother's lady in waiting, Luisa, would utter when she saw her. It was going to take every minute of the hour she had left to make herself look presentable for her future husband. Except, he wasn't her future husband, because she was going to refuse to marry him, or anyone else of her father's choosing.

From the age of four, Rosabella had been told by her father that she would marry the man he'd chosen for her and be grateful for it. She was too chubby, he'd said, when anyone praised her round, rosy cheeks. Too tall, he'd spat, when she'd reached a height from which she could look him straight in the eye. Too thin, he'd sneered, when the hand-me-down dresses from her half-sister had had to be adjusted to fit her. And she was too fair—just like her mother, he'd added.

What red-blooded man would want a fair, slip of a girl who looked as if she might break if touched? No-one, that was certain. He knew, because he'd learned that lesson from marrying her mother.

All these faults would have been regarded as assets if she'd been the boy her father had so badly needed. As a child, she'd tried her best to please him, desperate to make up for not being what he'd wanted her to be. If she rode her pony fearlessly, dived from a high rock into the sea or hit a tennis ball with all her might, surely he'd notice, pay her attention or perhaps even praise her?

But he'd simply snapped at her to try to be ladylike, because he didn't know what he'd do with her if the marriage he'd arranged fell through. There was no chance at all of finding anyone else who would be willing to take her for his wife.

She'd understood from an early age that she had to do as he wished even though her parents' marriage was a disastrous example. Her father lived in a perpetual state of simmering anger, and her mother had retreated to her quarters years ago and took hardly any part in the life of the palace. Her failure to produce a son and heir had come to define her, and her relationship with the King, and she'd poured her energies into restoring the neglected palace gardens and setting up charities to promote education for women and children.

Rosa accepted that her marriage of convenience could only ever be loveless. After all, if her own father could not bring himself to love her, what hope was there that a perfect stranger might feel differently? Absolutely none. Although her mother cared for her, and told her she was beautiful, it was her father's admiration, attention and *love* which she'd craved so fiercely. When she married the son of the Italian count, would her father finally be pleased with her? *Only if you produce a son,* a voice whispered in her head. And, even then, it would not be his daughter he'd be pleased with, but his grandson.

Everything had changed for Rosabella when her beloved half-sister had rebelled. She'd refused to marry the man of their father's choice and had run away, to find her mother who'd abandoned her as a baby and been banished by the King. And then she'd married the man she loved. *Truly loved.*

Rosabella shivered, despite the heat that bounced off the cobblestones between the beds of herbs. The joy and emotion that radiated from her sister and her new husband seemed magical. This was how two people marrying each other should look, she realised. They had eyes only for each other. The glances they shared, the gentle touch of his hand on her arm and the sense that they might set each other alight with the warmth of their feelings had showed Rosa a whole world which she hadn't dreamed existed. In the depths of her soul she knew that no man would ever—*could* ever—love her like that and she'd made up her mind, then and there, that she would never marry.

The reality of a loveless, convenient match suddenly felt abhorrent. She'd glimpsed the love between Sofia and Marco and she would never settle for anything less. She'd rather continue to work in the garden and protect her mother from her father's wrath than do a strange man's bidding in a foreign castle, away from everything she knew and loved.

How she would ever find the courage to tell her father of her decision was something she hadn't been able to think about, but now, with her potential husband here, the problem had become urgent.

The King had ruled her life, and that of her half-sister, with an iron rod. Never once had she defied his will. The idea made her stomach churn with anxiety. She was terrified of his anger, which she knew would be incandescent. What if he banished her, as he'd done to Sofia and her mother? What if he prevented her from ever seeing her own mother again? Apprehension crawled over her skin. Somewhere she was going to have to find the strength to face up to him and tell him she was ruining his plans.

Sofia had found that courage, strengthened by love. Unlovable as Rosa was, would she be able to emulate her?

Precious minutes slipped away while she stood, staring at the view, lost in fearful thought. Being late for an appointment with King Fiero was unthinkable. Rosabella picked up her basket of tools and broke into an unladylike run, plunging through the arch into the dim shadow of the courtyard.

Luca did not see what hit him. The bright sunlight striking the white marble paving was dazzling, even though he wore sunglasses. He'd decided to take a stroll through the palace gardens before lunch. He remembered the maze and smiled to himself, deciding to avoid it. The little girl who'd helped him escape all those years ago would be grown up now, as he was, and no longer singing to the fish.

The impact almost knocked the breath from his lungs. There was a crash that sounded like metal objects hitting the marble slabs, and a cry. Acting purely on impulse, Luca's hands clamped around a pair of slender arms. The owner of them swayed and he tightened his hold.

'Hey,' he said, 'Are you alright?' He risked releasing one of the arms then raised a hand to remove his shades and slip them into a trouser pocket. Hands pushed firmly against his chest, and he looked down.

'Yes, thank you, I'm alright.' The voice was breathy and definitely feminine and he could feel the rapid rise and fall of her chest against his shirt. 'I'm late. If you'll excuse me…'

'Of course.' Luca dropped his hands and stepped back, putting a little distance between them, but registering how pleasant her nearness had felt for those few seconds and how delicious she smelled—of lavender and warm sunshine.

The woman swiped a forearm across her forehead, leaving a streak of dirt. She glanced around, then crouched, gathering up her trowel and fork and reaching for the straw hat that had bounced off her head.

'Allow me.' Luca quickly bent to help her. Her fair hair fell in a thick braid over her shoulder, and in the vee at the neck of her linen smock he caught a glimpse of smooth skin. As they stood, she raised her eyes to meet his.

He felt as if he'd been hit again, in the stomach this time. He narrowed his gaze and studied her face. What were the chances? He did a quick mental calculation. She looked about the right age. Her long fair hair was tamed in a braid, but her eyes… He was sure they were the same wide-spaced, soft brown eyes he remembered.

So she'd grown up to be a gardener. He supposed her mother had retired by now and she'd taken over her duties. He shook his head slightly, not quite believing the coincidence of meeting her again so many years later.

'Thank you.' She was turning away but something made him want to keep her there for another minute.

'You're…you're still here.'

She turned back and a puzzled expression clouded her eyes—those brown eyes.

'What do you mean? Do I know you?'

'Yes. That is, I *think* we met a long time ago.'

A frown creased the skin between her brows. 'I… I'm sorry. I don't remember you.'

Luca pulled a hand across the back of his neck and shook his head. 'No, you probably don't. You were just a little girl, but you led me out of the maze when I was lost.'

She nibbled her bottom lip, her eyes on his face. 'Oh. Perhaps I do remember something about that. It *was* a long time ago. You said you were…*in trouble*?'

'Twenty years,' he said decisively. 'It was twenty years ago. You're…your name is…' He searched his memory. 'Something to do with roses?'

Her face cleared and she smiled slightly, the faint indentation of a dimple showing in her left cheek.

'Yes, it is. But, if you'll excuse me, I'm already late.' She held her basket in one hand and the brim of her battered straw hat in the other. 'I'm sorry I crashed into you.' She stepped backwards, away from him. 'Thank you for helping me.'

'You sang to the fish,' he said. 'It was a song about pretty horses.' The memory surprised him, surfacing from nowhere.

A smile lit her face, the dimple deepening. 'Yes,' she said. 'It probably was.'

With that, she walked quickly away. She placed the basket on a stone bench, tugged open a pair of French windows and disappeared.

Luca watched until she'd vanished into the dark interior of the palace, the door clicking shut behind her. After a moment he pulled out his sunglasses again and walked through the archway into the garden.

The hazy memories of his previous visit to Palosia suddenly shifted into sharper focus.

Rosabella turned and backed away from the French windows until she was sure she couldn't be seen from the courtyard—or, to be specific, seen by the tall, dark-haired stranger who stood there and appeared to be watching her.

She wondered who he could be, and she puzzled over the fact that he'd remembered her after their chance meeting… had he said *twenty* years ago? Perhaps being lost in the maze had frightened him as a boy and the incident was burned into his memory. Maybe he'd been visiting the King with his father and had now become an envoy in his own right, here to discuss some political matter.

She had no idea about affairs of state. Whenever she'd showed an interest in anything to do with the governing of Palosia, the opinions of the people or the preservation of the precious, unique natural habitats of the island, she'd been slapped down and reminded to confine herself to matters befitting a girl.

If her father needed proof that she was unladylike and lacking even the smallest amount of decorum, she'd just provided it. Not to run, when she should walk, was one of the first points of etiquette she'd ever been taught. Crashing into a visitor with enough force to almost knock him off his feet and the air from her own lungs must rank amongst the most cardinal of sins. Luckily, he'd kept her upright. Falling in a heap at his feet would have been even more undignified and embarrassing. She rubbed at her upper arms where the warmth of his hands lingered and wondered why, in the moments when she'd been pressed against him, she'd felt somehow protected and safe. It wasn't a familiar feeling.

As she watched, he pulled his shades from a pocket and put them on, then disappeared through the archway.

Rosabella heel-toed her dusty rope-soled espadrilles from her feet and wriggled her toes. The quick tap of footsteps approached along the passage.

'Princess Rosabella? I've been searching for you. Wherever have you been? The time…'

Rosabella turned, ready to face the worst. 'I was in the garden, Luisa. I needed to…'

'Oh!' Luisa stopped, dismay spreading across her habitually impassive, unshockable features. 'Well, I shouldn't have expected anything different, I suppose, but just this once I thought…' Her tone was resigned. 'Never mind now; come along, we don't have much time.'

She glanced at the tall grandfather clock that ticked steadily in an alcove, eating up the seconds. 'We'll just have to make the best of it.' She shook her head, and Rosabella felt a needling of guilt. Her dirty fingernails and messy hair that resisted being tamed wouldn't make things easy for Luisa.

'You mean the best of *me*. I'm sorry, Luisa. I thought I had enough time, but…'

Luisa pursed her lips. 'I've known you all your life, Rosabella. When have you ever had enough time to do everything you wanted to do in the garden, especially when there was something else waiting which you *didn't* want to do?'

Rosabella pushed her hands into the pockets of her skirt, hoping Luisa hadn't seen her nails, and studied her grimy bare feet. 'What do you mean?' Was she *that* transparent? She'd tried hard to hide her feelings about the impending ordeal.

'I mean this meeting with your parents. I know you've been dreading it.'

Rosabella nodded. 'Yes, you're right, I *have* been dreading it. But, now that it's here, or rather *he* is here, I *do* want to do this. I want to get it out of the way as quickly as possible.'

CHAPTER THREE

LUCA FOLLOWED THE stiff-backed courtier from the magnificent suite of rooms he'd been given in what he presumed to be the guest wing of the palace. Deep carpets muffled their footsteps until they emerged into a soaring atrium with marble-clad walls and tiled floors decorated with jewel-coloured mosaics. They crossed the space beneath a crystal chandelier and entered an antechamber of even greater opulence. Rich rugs cushioned the floor and light reflected from a dozen gilded surfaces.

The man ahead of him bowed. 'His Majesty, King Fiero of Palosia,' he announced. 'Sir, I present the Conte Luca Montenale.' He stepped back smartly.

The King, who stood beside a wide, ornately carved desk, extended his right hand.

'Welcome.' He inclined his head and it seemed to be with an afterthought that he turned slightly and indicated the presence of a pale, anxious-looking woman who hovered near the windows, as if uncertain of her place. 'Her Majesty, Queen Chiara,' he said.

Luca bowed over the King's hand, and then towards the Queen. 'An honour,' he murmured, hiding his surprise at her presence at this meeting. Perhaps she would withdraw after this initial introduction. Moreover, the King seemed far from pleased to see him. Deep lines furrowed his forehead, and his lips were pressed together in an angry, straight line.

Had he somehow discovered that Luca was here to cancel the marriage of convenience, rather than to act on it? That was impossible. Luca had told nobody the reason for his visit to this island state, or even of the existence of the marriage contract. Had he displeased him in some other way? Perhaps his late father...

Suddenly, Luca wished he'd taken a little time to consider his actions rather than rushing in uncharacteristic haste to a meeting with this formidable man. But he'd been so shocked to discover what his father had done, and so keen to disentangle himself from its implications, that he'd wanted to resolve the issue and free himself without delay.

But King Fiero's daughter would soon be twenty-five and he would be ready to put plans in place for their marriage. He would have been anticipating this moment for the past twenty years. He was going to be furious, disappointed and, quite possibly, feel humiliated. And his daughter, the princess, would have been anticipating this day almost all her life.

Zipped into a compartment of his luggage was the original contract, and now he wished he'd studied it in greater detail, as he realised he didn't even know her name. For a man like him, reading and understanding the detail of every case or transaction was of paramount importance. This was an embarrassing omission, and he felt ashamed. He'd never believed in making excuses for sloppy behaviour. He could only think that the shock of his father's death, coupled with the discovery that he was promised in marriage to an unknown foreign princess, had affected his usually razor-sharp and incisive mind and prompted him to act in such an out-of-character, impulsive fashion.

King Fiero's eyes remained fixed on his face. 'My condolences on the death of your father.'

'Thank you.' Luca nodded.

'My daughter is late,' the King rasped. 'I apologise. I'll...'

'Your *daughter*?' Luca sucked in a breath. He hadn't expected the King's daughter—Luca's supposed future *wife*—or the Queen to be present at this meeting. Once again, he berated himself for not having been more measured in his approach; for not having made clear that he'd only expected to meet the King on this brief visit, to pave the way towards cancelling the agreement his father had made on his behalf.

Presenting facts had never been a problem for him, but this was different. His decision would impact on the lives of the King, Queen and their daughter in a negative way. It was never going to be easy, but conducting the discussion in the presence of the Queen and the princess would make it much more difficult.

'Yes, my daughter, whom you are going to marry.'

Luca imagined that the girl's options were limited, if her father had been determined to settle her future from such an early age. He felt a twinge of guilt at what he was about to do. The princess's dreams of marriage would lie in ruins when he walked away from this meeting. His guilt was followed by a surge of anger towards his father, who had brought about this whole, disastrous situation. Nevertheless, he would not allow sentiment to cloud his judgement or alter his decision.

Luca heard the click and swish of a door opening. The King turned and the Queen's gaze, which had been fixed on a spot on the floor, moved towards the sound.

He turned his head.

A young woman sank into a low curtsey before the King, her head bowed.

'You're late,' snapped the monarch.

'Your Majesty, I apologise...'

'Get up.'

There was a soft whisper of silk as the fine, pale green fabric of her dress settled about her hips. It fell from a fitted bodice into gentle folds, to just above her ankles. A conservative, high neckline, and sleeves that reached her wrists, only served to direct his attention to the soft curves that were tantalisingly visible beneath the fabric—curves which he could, all too easily, imagine pressed against his own hard, honed body.

Your Majesty? Was this woman seriously expected to address her father with such stiff formality? And the King's tone had been harsh to the point of displaying blatant dislike.

Another wave of guilt assailed him. Perhaps he, as her promised husband, was her only hope of escaping what appeared to be a tyrannical father.

Her slender neck was bent, her eyes downcast. Thick, fair hair formed a glossy, complicated knot dotted with seed-pearl clips in the nape of her neck. Larger pearls gleamed in her earlobes. She appeared to be composed, but the way her long fingers plucked at her skirt hinted at anxiety.

'Up,' repeated the King.

The movement as she stood was smooth and practised. She clasped her hands together in front of her and raised her head.

For the second time in two hours, Luca felt as if the air had been punched from his lungs. He tried to breathe in, but his shirt and suit jacket suddenly felt tight and restrictive. He wished he could loosen his tie. What had happened to the oxygen in the vast room? Could he request that a window be opened? His head spun, his brain trying to find a logical explanation for this feeling of confusion but coming up with nothing.

Because the brown eyes fringed with long lashes that had lifted to his face and then dropped again were unmistakeably those of the little girl who'd sung a song to the fish about pretty horses... and of the grown-up gardener who had crashed into him earlier in the day, sending her tools and hat flying.

No wonder he could imagine the soft contours of her body pressed against his own. Less than two hours ago, that was exactly where they'd been. Their body-to-body contact might only have lasted a few seconds, but the pleasure of it had been imprinted firmly on his memory.

The King's voice sounded distant, and Luca fought to engage his brain to make sense of his words.

'My daughter, Princess Rosabella...'

Rosabella. He remembered her name now. *It's because they're my mother's favourite flowers.*

Finally, he found his voice, but the only words his brain could come up with were far from the courteous, formal ones that would have been expected.

'It's you,' he said.

If her father expected her to curtsey to this man, he was going to be disappointed in her yet again. Rosabella engaged all the strength of her core muscles to stop herself from swaying on her feet. Silently, she gave thanks for the fact that she'd won the argument over her shoes. Luisa had favoured cream courts with a heel—high enough to lend some sophistication to her outfit—but Rosabella had insisted on wearing the pale-gold ballet flats. They were comfortable and safe, and today she needed comfort and safety as she never had before.

She'd had many years to imagine what her intended husband might be like. When she'd asked her father if she might see a photograph of him, he'd brushed her request aside with an irritated flick of his hand.

At first, when she'd been much younger, she'd thought he might be a dashing prince, or a knight, who would ride a white horse, sweep her off her feet and carry her away on his galloping steed, like in one of the stories she'd loved to read.

But as she'd grown up and reality had taken hold, she'd imagined he must be small and weak—a man who bent to his father's will, as she did, never permitted to express an opinion or follow his own path. Surely only such a man would have agreed to marry her when she had nothing to offer beyond her royal lineage?

Never had her imagination been so far off the mark. She kept her eyes downcast and gripped a fistful of the silk of her dress in each hand.

How could this man be her intended husband? There must be some mistake. This was the man she'd collided with not two hours ago, who'd held her arms and stopped her from falling, and against whose hard, broad body she'd been pinned for a few brief, confusing seconds.

She wanted to release her grip on her dress and feel the place on her upper arms where his strong hands had supported her, but she was frozen with shock.

Could it be true that they had met twenty years ago when he'd been lost in the maze? It must be, or how else would he know that she'd sung her favourite lullaby to the fish?

The silence in the room seemed to stretch and shrink around her, becoming more brittle by the second, and she knew her father would expect her to do something to break it…but what?

She'd wanted to get this meeting over with. She'd made her decision to refuse to go ahead with the marriage, and she'd needed to tell her father while she was being propelled forwards on a wave of resolve. But in that brief instant, when her eyes had met the dark ones of the man in front of her, her determination had shaken and shattered around her.

This was not a man marrying her because his father had decided on it, or because he had no other choice. His broad-shouldered stance, confident demeanour and direct, take-no-prisoners stare would have given him the pick of hundreds of eligible, beautiful women, and the choice would be his alone. Neither his father, nor anyone else, would influence him. If he chose her, it would be a true marriage of convenience, solely on his terms. She had nothing to give him but her name. If he married her, it would be because it suited him. There could be no other explanation.

These thoughts tumbled through Rosabella's head as she stared at the floor, her heart thundering in her chest and her blood pounding in her ears.

It's you, he'd said. Had that been disappointment? Surprise? *Disbelief?* Or all three?

'*Rosabella!*' The King's voice cracked across the silence, harsh with displeasure. 'Where are your manners?'

Her head snapped up. 'I… I'm…'

'This is Count Luca Montenale. Please greet him appropriately.' She saw her father turn towards the Count, his slight shrug seeming to say, *I've done my best. It's over to you.*

Rosabella forced herself to take a deep, necessary breath. Consciously she relaxed her tense fingers and smoothed the crumpled fabric of her dress. She straightened her spine, raised her chin and dared to seek out those dark eyes again.

There was no disappointment in their depths. There was surprise, certainly, and a trace of disbelief. But what else she found—which astonished her—was his look of interest, as if he wanted to know how the little, bare-footed girl in the maze and the grown-up woman who looked like a gardener could possibly be the princess, his future wife.

'What do you mean, "it's you"?' barked the King. 'Have you met before? How? When…?'

One corner of the Count's mouth kicked up; had she imagined it or had that slight movement of his head been a deliberate shake of denial?

We'll keep it between ourselves.

She understood his meaning as clearly as if he'd spoken the words out loud. As if he knew exactly how her father would react to being told he'd found her, bare-footed, singing to the fish; and that she'd cannoned into him while running in an unladylike manner, late for this meeting.

He reached out and lifted her hand, bowing low over it so that his dark head hid from the King's view the fact that he brushed the pad of his thumb in a feather-light touch across her knuckles.

She might have found the gesture forward or presumptuous, but instead his touch filled her with reassurance, as if to say she could feel safe with him and he understood some of the turmoil of her thoughts.

He held her hand for mere seconds, then straightened up and let it go. Glancing towards the King, he moved to her side and offered her his arm, instead.

'Forgive me, Your majesty,' he said, his voice smooth. 'I simply meant I've waited a long time to meet your daughter. Come, Your Highness.' He inclined his head towards the doors that stood open at the far end of the room, beyond which lay the terrace and the view down the tree-lined walk towards the fountains. 'Perhaps you and I need to take time to get to know each other a little.'

Rosabella looked at her father to see how he had reacted to the Count's suggestion. Would he feel sidelined and therefore furious? He probably wanted this marriage to go ahead badly enough not to display any anger towards her future husband.

He'd reserve that for later, when she'd disappoint him yet again by failing to produce a son, just as her mother had.

A movement made her look towards the windows, and for the first time she became aware of her mother's presence. She'd taken a step forward and raised a hand, as if about to say something. But her hand fluttered down to her side again and she dipped her head, avoiding Rosabella's eyes.

For as long as she could remember, Rosabella's mother had warned her against believing any man who made promises of everlasting love and happiness. She'd said she knew, from her own bitter experience, that such promises would always either be conditional or simply untrue. If Rosabella doubted her advice, all she needed to do was reflect on how her father, the King, treated her. Her earliest memories were coloured by his words of disdain and disapproval. In withholding the fatherly love she'd craved, he'd convinced her that she was unworthy of any love at all.

The Queen's ancient, noble family had fallen on hard times when she'd been a girl and her father had seen a way back to fortune through marrying his daughter into the royal family of Palosia. The King, furious at the betrayal of his first wife, had divorced her and married Chiara with almost unseemly haste. He'd promised to adore her for ever and had showered her with luxurious gifts. Chiara's upbringing had been sheltered and she had been raised to be a dutiful daughter and wife. She'd had no reason to doubt the promises made to her.

But the King's adoration had been conditional on Chiara producing a son to inherit the throne. The birth of Rosabella had been traumatic, almost costing the Queen her life and robbing her of the ability to have more children.

Thwarted again in his plan to produce an heir, the King had quickly turned away from his wife and disappointing baby daughter, moving them to an isolated wing of the palace and made sure their paths crossed as infrequently as possible.

The Queen had raised Rosabella to be meek and obedient, but she had not tried to shield her from her own disillusionment with the idea of love and the institution of marriage. She'd explained that the King regarded Rosabella as nothing more than a useful commodity, a bargaining tool that he had used in arranging a marriage of convenience for her. She would have to go through with the marriage, but she must enter into it with no expectation of love.

This tall man who now stood beside her, with the broad shoulders, solid, sheltering chest, the deep, dark eyes which seemed to look into her soul and read her emotions and the firm yet sensuous mouth which had hinted at a smile, was the last person on earth whom she could, or should, trust. He might try to convince her that she was safe with him but believing him would lead her straight into a position of weakness and disappointment.

His agenda was obvious: he wanted to separate her from the presence of her parents so that he could ply her with empty promises of devotion and duty. She sent a swift glance of gratitude towards her mother, even though her eyes remained downcast. The Count's gallantry had made her drop her guard for a few dangerous moments, but the memories of her mother's warnings had brought her to her senses.

He didn't want to get to know her at all. Why would he? Legally, she was his already. There was just the wedding itself which had to happen before he could take her away to his castle in Tuscany. Once there, he would hope she would quickly produce a son, which would mean he'd be free to carry on with the life of his choice, leaving her isolated, just as her mother had been.

If she refused to marry the Count, what could her father

do? He would be furious, but she was prepared for that. He could send her away. That idea made her tummy drop and her heart race with fear, especially if it meant she could no longer see her mother, but she would have to find the courage to face it.

He could make her life hard and unhappy, but entering into a loveless marriage, far from everything she held dear, would be worse. Her parents' own marriage was the perfect example.

The one thing he could not do was force her to say, 'I do'. That knowledge was the most powerful weapon she possessed.

So instead of taking the Count's proffered arm, Rosabella folded her hands together in front of her. She lifted her chin a fraction and took a step away from him.

'No,' she said, audibly this time. 'I don't think we do.'

CHAPTER FOUR

LUCA KEPT HIS expression impassive. He inclined his head.
'As you wish.'

When their eyes had met, he'd seen her surprise and confusion, but he thought he'd also seen something like...*hope*?
Was that because she believed he would rescue her from
what seemed to be a toxic atmosphere in this palace? It might
be sumptuous and beautiful, set like a glittering jewel in the
lush landscape of Palosia, but the reality of it was cold and
forbidding, lacking in any feeling of welcoming warmth or
friendliness. Life within its boundaries, in spite of all the
comforts and the vibrant gardens, might feel like a prison.

Whatever he'd seen was quickly obscured, like a camera
shutter dropping down over her eyes or an inner light being
extinguished. She'd stiffened as he'd moved beside her, as
if she found the idea of his touch frightening or distasteful.

He remembered how she'd crashed into him earlier, and
the firm, almost desperate way she'd thrust herself away
from him. As he'd walked along the garden paths afterwards,
between the flowerbeds alive with the sound of bees, beneath
the trees where birds sang, his thoughts had been on her,
rather than on his surroundings. He'd puzzled over her reaction. Had she been embarrassed that she, a palace gardener,
had collided with a stranger and possible guest of the King?

Now that he knew who she was, he was more intrigued

than ever. What had happened to the beguiling and enchanting girl who'd taken his hand so readily in the maze, to make her shrink from the touch of a man—even just a touch that had been accidental and stopped her from falling onto the paved courtyard?

Luca had never been short of female attention, or lacked the company of a beautiful woman when he'd needed one on his arm. But his career had taken precedence over any desire for a lasting commitment. Having broken the ties with his father, he'd had to prove that he'd done the right thing. He'd been disillusioned by many of the women he'd met. Their interest in him seemed driven by what he was worth and what he would one day inherit, rather than in what drove him to do what he did, and his commitment to defending the disenfranchised.

Bitterly, he reflected on the fact that the only interest his father had shown in him over the past ten years had been to enquire occasionally whether or not he was in any sort of relationship. What would have happened if the answer had been yes? How would his father have informed him that he was not free to marry a woman of his choice because he'd been unknowingly engaged to a princess since the age of thirteen?

He should be glad that the Princess Rosabella had given him the cold shoulder, he thought wryly. If she was indifferent to his attentions, it would make the task of telling the King he could never marry her that much easier.

But something didn't feel right. He watched her as she exchanged a murmured word with her mother. Her spine was ramrod-straight, her head held high. The hem of her silk dress swung, brushing against her legs—legs that looked as stiff as poles.

Her body language spoke of conflict and anxiety rather

than of any pleasure or excitement. He thought of the wide smile she'd given him when he'd reminded her about singing to the fish, and how she'd swung away, carrying her basket and hat.

If he hadn't seen that version of her, he wouldn't have believed it existed. It was as if, in scrubbing away the dirt of the garden, putting on her silk dress and taming her hair into a regal style scattered with pearls she'd dressed herself in a layer of protective armour which held her in its stiff, formal shape.

And protected her from her father. Or from her prospective husband. An irrational desire to discover the secrets behind the impassive mask of her face took him by surprise.

He'd planned to spend no more than one night on the island, extricating himself from the net in which his father had seen fit to entangle him. But the flash of unguarded emotion in Rosabella's eyes when she'd recognised him told him that something much more complex and intriguing lay beneath the face she was willing to show him, now that she knew who he was.

She'd shut it down quickly, but not quickly enough. He'd built his professional reputation on his ability to read people. The merest flicker of an expression glimpsed across a crowded court room could give him the lead he needed to probe a defendant's story, getting them to unwittingly reveal something vital in a case.

He pushed his hands into his pockets and lifted a shoulder, casting a deliberately rueful glance towards the King. *Just give her time*, his look implied. His fingers flexed. The sudden image he had of removing those pearls and feeling her silky hair between his fingers surprised and irritated him. This was no time for the inconvenient, unexpected desire that tightened his muscles and pushed up his heart rate. He was here to escape from the deal in which his father had tied him up—*damn him and his obsessive need for control*—not to entertain thoughts of seduction.

If Rosabella didn't want his attention, he would never force it on her—or any woman, for that matter. But he felt a connection to her which he could not explain and he wanted to explore it.

The King frowned and shot an angry glance at his daughter's back. A flick of his hand acknowledged the uniformed man who stood at the door.

'Your Majesties, Your Highness, my Lord—lunch is served.'

For Rosabella, the formal lunch couldn't end quickly enough.

She'd expected to be seated next to the Count. Instead, they were placed opposite one another, meaning there was no escaping the gaze of those dark eyes, which she suspected saw far too much.

She pushed food around her plate, every mouthful she attempted tasting like sawdust, needing a gulp of wine to wash it down.

'What's the matter with you?' hissed the King, while Luca's attention was taken up with trying to engage the Queen in conversation. 'Eat.'

Rosabella turned sharply towards him, angry at his words and tone, but knowing she could never let it show. 'I'm not a child, sir. And I'm not hungry.'

'You're behaving like a spoilt teenager. I don't care if you're hungry or not.'

'Your Highness.' The deep, authoritative voice made Rosabella turn her attention back to the Count. 'Allow me to speak for the Princess Rosabella. This occasion is an unusual one, for both of us. It's not surprising if she's lost her appetite.'

Secretly grateful for his intervention, Rosabella watched as his strong fingers closed around the delicate stem of his wine glass. He raised it and took a mouthful. Why did she find it impossible to drag her eyes away from the smooth skin of his throat as he swallowed? How could such a simple, ordinary action feel…sensuous?

He replaced the glass on the table, and she realised he'd been watching her from beneath his lowered lids. Now he raised them and she felt the full force of his gaze. She tried to pull her eyes away, but he'd captured them in his, trapping her. Her cheeks heated and she knew her discomfort would be clearly displayed in the flush she could feel seeping across her pale skin.

The impossible idea that she should drop a bombshell into the middle of this excruciating meal came to her, but she dismissed it. If she announced now to her father that she had no intention of ever agreeing to marry the Count, or anyone else of his choosing, the thing which she dreaded and feared would happen: the King would be furious and humiliated; he'd possibly banish her from Palosia or make sure she stayed here, a virtual prisoner, for ever.

The Count would be free to leave and stop wasting his time on pointless conversation. He might be angry too, she thought, to have his plans to marry her thwarted, whatever his reasons might be for wanting the union to go ahead.

The one thing she was sure of was that he only wanted to marry her for some self-serving reason of his own. She'd been told often enough that nobody else would ever want her. What nobleman or billionaire would be interested in tying himself to a plain girl who wore flat shoes and preferred digging in the garden to shopping or jet-setting?

But, even as she entertained the tempting idea of deliberately sabotaging her own future right here in the elaborate dining room, watched from their portraits on the walls by imperious ancestors, her resolve drained away.

While she felt afraid of her father's rage, it was the idea of how such a scene would upset her mother that caused her to bite her lip and swallow the words that she longed to say. Her gentle mother, who avoided confrontation at all costs and who devoted her life to making a difference to impoverished women and children, would hate to witness such an argument. It would be far better to wait until she could talk to her father in private, when she'd worked out exactly what to say and didn't feel forced into it by the awkwardness of the situation in which she now found herself.

A taut silence settled around the table. Rosabella wondered if her father would break it with a crushing comment, but a glance at him showed his mouth clamped shut and his eyes on the Count. Her coffee cup rattled in the saucer as she picked it up.

'Perhaps Princess Rosabella could show me something of the gardens after lunch?' That voice sent another ripple of… what?…through her and, despite wanting to avoid his eyes, she looked at him again. 'Their reputation is widespread, and I'd be most interested to see them.'

'Very well.' In her peripheral vision Rosabella saw the King nod.

She felt a conflicted gratitude to the Count. He'd smoothly broken the tense silence and turned the attention of the King away from her. But she'd have much preferred it if he'd suggested walking with her father alone. Right now, she longed to escape to her rooms, shed her formal clothes for her comfortable gardening ones and lose herself in a distant corner of the rambling estate where no-one would find her—and especially not the Count, with his missing-nothing eyes.

She'd thought his eyes were dark-grey, almost black. But

now she thought they might be the colour of the midnight sky, or that shade of obsidian which was almost blue in its blackness.

Get a grip. The colour of his eyes was of absolutely no interest to her, because after today she'd never have to look into them again or have them study her with that expression of compassionate interest that threatened to make her reconsider all the resolutions she'd made.

CHAPTER FIVE

ROSABELLA FOLLOWED HER father and the Count down the curved steps that swept from the terrace to the gardens.

As they'd risen from the table, her mother had pleaded a headache and retreated to her quarters. Rosabella wished she could have followed her.

The two men reached the foot of the steps and turned onto the path between the avenue of ancient oaks. In the distance, the marble fountains gleamed. The Count appeared to be deep in conversation with the King and she wondered how he managed to talk with what appeared to be such ease with her father, who was known for his abrupt aloofness, not his conversational skills.

If she turned in the opposite direction and melted away into the terraces of flower beds on the other side of the palace, how long would it be before she was missed? There were numerous arbours covered in roses and jasmine where she could hide.

But, while part of her longed to escape, another part of her felt pulled towards the Count. He was so completely different from the man she'd expected him to be that she still felt confused. It was as if she'd received a package but, when she opened the box, found it contained something intriguing and exciting instead of the rather dull object she'd anticipated.

The Count's calm confidence unsettled her. It spoke of

a man who almost always got what he wanted and would fight for it if challenged. He was here to claim her, and he didn't doubt at all his right to do so. As far as he was concerned, the deed was done. Only the formalities remained to be concluded.

Yet she'd had no say in this marriage. This felt like a story from the past, and not a good one. Hadn't her parents' marriage been brokered in this precise way? She shuddered to think of how her mother had been treated when the possibility of her producing a son had been wiped out by Rosabella's own birth.

When she'd first become aware as a young girl of the turmoil her arrival had caused, she'd been overwhelmed with guilt. How she'd wished things had been different. How much better all their lives would have been if she'd been a boy! When she'd understood that she was the cause of the Queen's inability to have more children, the guilt had intensified. Irrational as it was, that guilt had never left her, and she'd tried to assuage it by being everything her parents could ever have wanted.

It had been a waste of emotion and energy, because the one thing they wanted was the one thing she could never be.

As she watched the interaction between her father and the Count, anger at her situation mounted. Her father appeared to be listening to him intently, and she remembered the futility of the years she'd spent trying to be interesting enough, clever enough or beautiful enough to warrant a glance or a word of praise or encouragement from him.

She was determined that the Count would never see the emotions that seethed beneath her meek exterior. She would be cool towards him. Her composure would not slip again, as it had in those few seconds when she'd realised who he was and she knew he'd read the confusion and longing in her eyes.

The two men paused while her father explained the perspective of the tree-lined walk leading to the focal point of the fountains, and Luca half-turned to look back over his shoulder. He smiled, and it took all her determination to crush her natural instinct to smile back. He moved to one side, creating a gap between himself and her father, and gestured to her to walk between them, but she gave a slight shake of her head.

Rosabella welcomed the shade cast by the trees. When she'd dressed for lunch, hurried and fussed over by Luisa, she hadn't expected to walk in the gardens afterwards and she hadn't brought a hat. The briefest exposure to the August sun could turn her fair skin pink and make the faint sprinkling of tiny freckles across her cheekbones and nose stand out.

The gardens were quiet beneath the blanket of the afternoon heat, as if all living creatures had retreated to the deep shelter of the trees and shady arbours. Normally her father would shut himself in his study with his books at this time of day. Evidently, he was anxious to please or impress his visitor.

The demure high neck and long sleeves of her silk dress felt restrictive, and she longed to be able to feel the air against her skin, even if the breeze was a warm one. Up-to-date, fashionable clothes were readily available in the shops of Palosia, these days, as tourism had increased, but her father insisted that Rosabella dressed conservatively in long sleeves and skirts. Nothing even faintly revealing was permitted.

As they neared the fountains, the cool sound of water splashing from marble conch shells into the surrounding pool made her feel even warmer.

King Fiero slowed his pace. 'I'll rest here.' He indicated

a bench beneath the trees. 'Show his Lordship the fountains, Rosabella.'

Rosabella wanted to say that the Count could see the fountains very well without help from her, but she pressed her lips together and nodded. Luca kept a respectful distance from her. He would know that her father had positioned himself where he could keep an eye on them, and he would be sure to observe decorum.

The view was spectacular. Beyond the fountains, the gardens fell away towards the valley, the terraces becoming increasingly wild until they merged with the woodland below. Further away, the mountains thrust jagged peaks of rock into the bleached sky. Luca imagined that in winter, snow would soften their outlines and lend a bite to the wind that whistled across the island.

From what he'd seen, Palosia was a perfect universe all of its own. There were towering mountains, verdant valleys, clear rivers and streams and beaches of fine, white sand. The azure Mediterranean encircled it all, isolating it, yet also linking it with other nearby islands, and the mainland of Europe was not too great a distance away to the north. Luca didn't think he'd ever been anywhere which more closely resembled his idea of paradise.

He turned towards Rosabella and swept an arm in an arc, encompassing the vista.

'I've always thought Tuscany beautiful, but this...' He shook his head. 'This is more dramatic, more varied, more... unique.'

Was this the reason why she was cold towards him? Did she dread being taken from her home and forced to live somewhere new and alien? Perhaps she'd be relieved when he announced he was cancelling their engagement.

If that was so, then he should feel pleased about what he planned to do. Why, then, did something make him feel the tiniest bit of regret that he would not be marrying her and making her his?

He dismissed the thought. He'd been seduced by the sumptuous palace, the glorious gardens and the attention that King Fiero had paid him, nothing more. The castle in Tuscany, which was now his, was known as one of the grandest in Italy, with its Renaissance frescoes, marble statuary and flourishing vineyards that produced some of the most famous Italian wines.

He wanted for nothing and yet here, on Palosia, he felt that something in his life was lacking. It was because he'd just wrapped up that difficult case in New York and had not yet had the opportunity to start on the next one, he told himself. His life consisted of moving from one challenging brief to another. That was how he liked it.

The sudden death of his father had been shocking, but he would have dealt with it with swift efficiency if the startling matter of his engagement to a princess had not come to light. Knowing that his father had kept this secret from him, waiting to spring it on him when he saw fit, infuriated him. All the measures he'd taken over the years to escape and build his own successful life, had been futile. His father had held the trump card all along.

Well, it was a pity the old man hadn't stayed alive long enough to see that he would never agree to this archaic and ridiculous arrangement. Just as his father had failed to control his wife, he'd fail to control his son. If he hadn't forbidden his mother to ride that untamed horse, she wouldn't have felt the need to defy him. Luca imagined how his mother must have chafed against the constant restrictions her husband had imposed on her, and how her frustration had finally made her do something so wild and dangerous that she'd paid for it with her life.

People said Luca had inherited his free spirit and determination to be independent from her. Looking back, he supposed he'd been a constant reminder to his father of how he'd failed to mould his young wife to the shape he wanted. Agreeing to marry Luca to a woman of his choosing must have felt like a way of keeping him in line.

He'd be kind and considerate to Princess Rosabella, but agree to *marry* her? Never. It was his father's attempt to force him into obedience and that made it the last thing in the world he would do.

Luca dragged his eyes from the stunning view in time to see Princess Rosabella quickly avert her gaze from him. His expression was probably grim, reflecting his thoughts, and he dipped his head, trying to find a smile to give her to defuse the tension that crackled between them in the warm air.

The heat felt suffocating. He slid his jacket off his shoulders and spread it on the marble seat that encircled the fountain.

'Shall we rest here for a few minutes? The outlook is magnificent.'

He watched as her conflicted expression gave way to one of acceptance, and she nodded and sat down carefully on his jacket after a quick glance in the direction of her father. The marble figures of the fountain blocked the King's view of them. Was that why she'd agreed to sit with him?

Her spine was straight and stiff. As he sat down near her, she kept her eyes fixed on the distant mountains rather than turning her head to meet his. Her flushed cheeks made him think her silk dress was much too warm. The slight tilt of her nose, her fine jawline and her luminous dark-chocolate eyes stirred something in him. Then his memory landed on an angel on one of the frescoes in the castle in Tuscany. If her hair could be freed from its restraining pearls and pins and allowed to float down her back in its natural waves... Luca was surprised to find that he wanted to liberate it himself.

'How long will you be staying?'

The question surprised him. Was this her attempt at polite conversation, or was she genuinely interested? If so, he wondered what she hoped to hear.

'I'll return to Italy tomorrow morning.' Although, after his meeting with King Fiero later this afternoon, he might have to leave tonight.

'Oh! So soon? I thought...'

Her stiff formality slipped for an instant, but only an instant, and it was impossible to tell whether that was relief in her voice or disappointment. What could he say that might make her relax enough to deliver another one of the smiles she'd given him when she'd walked away from him earlier?

'If there were fish in this fountain, would you sing to them?'

There was a flash of surprise in her eyes as she turned her head towards him.

'There are no fish in this fountain, so...' She lifted her shoulders and dropped them again, then glanced up at the cupids and their conch shells endlessly splashing water into the marble basin. Whatever she'd expected him to say, it hadn't been that.

'I said "if". Would you?'

'I've grown out of that. It was a long time ago.'

'Even if I asked you to sing?'

'Especially if you asked me to sing.'

He watched her dark lashes sweep to her cheeks. The bones of her knuckles gleamed white as she gripped the edge of the seat, supporting her rigid, upright posture.

'Why is that? It was so joyful and carefree.'

Finally, she lifted her gaze to his face. 'Perhaps at the age of four I was joyful and carefree, Count Montenale. But, as I said, I've grown up.'

'And grown out of joyfulness? Yet when I saw you earlier you seemed closer to that child than you do now.'

'That was before I... Before we...'

The sideways glance she sent him from under her lashes was quick, and she shook her head.

'That was when I still thought you were a gardener and you thought I was...who?'

She released her grip on the edge of the bench and twisted her fingers together in her lap.

'I don't know. Perhaps just another envoy come to petition the King for something. I never thought that...'

'That the person you crashed into might be your future husband?'

He heard her sharp intake of breath. 'No, I never thought that. You were...you are...'

He waited but she was silent, staring down at her interlaced fingers.

'I'm what?' he prompted.

'You're just not what I expected.' When she eventually spoke, her words came in a rush.

Luca leaned forward, resting his folded arms on his knees. He kept his eyes on the distant mountains, feeling she was more likely to engage with him if they didn't make eye contact.

'Then what...or *who*...were you expecting?' He felt intrigued and a little mystified. 'You did know I was coming?'

Her teeth worried her bottom lip and a faint frown creased the space between her brows.

'Yes. And I...don't know. I just wasn't expecting someone like you.'

'What am I like?'

'Do you always ask so many questions?'

He turned his head to look at her then. 'I'm a lawyer, Princess Rosabella. Asking questions is what I do most of the time.'

Her startled eyes flew to his.

'A *lawyer*? But… I thought you were an Italian count.'

'The two are not mutually exclusive.' He smiled. 'I know because I'm both. Except I'm still testing out the "count" bit.' He saw the question in her eyes. 'My father passed away recently. I've inherited his title, so I am the *new* count. It still feels strange.'

'I'm sorry. When…?' There was compassion in her voice.

Luca shook his head. 'Perhaps that's a story for another time. But how come you don't know more about me? After all, we've been engaged for twenty years. Have you looked me up on the Internet?'

It occurred to him, for the first time, that she might not have access to the Internet, unbelievable as that seemed. There was Internet on Palosia, but she appeared to be so protected, so unworldly…so controlled by her father.

Unease stirred in his gut. He'd had to fight that particular kind of control. It had been a lifelong struggle to hold onto his determination and self-belief. For a young woman isolated in this palace, it would have been very difficult.

He saw her emotions shut down again. The hint of compassion that had sparked in the dark depths of her eyes was wiped out and her expression reverted to one of cool indifference. She turned away from him, her chin lifted.

'Until my father introduced us, I didn't even know your name.'

Shock took him by surprise, momentarily shredding his careful composure.

'What?'

She rose quickly. 'I need to go. The sun is too hot, and I don't have a hat.'

'Of course.' Luca was on his feet in an instant, his good manners restored, but his thoughts were in turmoil, trying to play catch-up, although nothing made proper sense. He didn't like that. His lawyer's brain needed facts to be clear and logical. Mysteries needed to be explained as quickly and efficiently as possible. Surprises were unwelcome because they meant he'd failed to anticipate something important. 'Surely your father…?'

He knew she was telling the truth. There was something in her gaze and her manner that spoke of simple honesty. He was good at recognising that when he saw it.

Why had her father hidden the identity of her proposed husband from her? Having briefly observed King Fiero's dismissive behaviour towards his wife and daughter, he thought he knew the answer. Queen Chiara and Princess Rosabella were unimportant women who didn't need to be kept informed about what he had planned for them, and he obviously had no expectation that they wouldn't always obey him.

Now he heard King Fiero's authoritarian voice summoning them. Uncertainty flickered across the princess's face and then anxiety quickly replaced her look of cold distance.

Without thinking, needing to reassure her, he put a hand on her arm. Her attention, twisted towards her father, slowly turned back and she appeared to freeze as her eyes fixed on his fingers where they lay across her forearm. Then her shocked gaze lifted to lock with his.

'It's okay.' He kept his voice even and soft, but the sound of it seemed to jolt her into action.

She snatched her arm from under his hand, folding her

arms tightly across her body and shaking her head. 'No! It's… not. At least, it won't be okay if I don't answer him at once.'

'I apologise. I'm truly sorry. I only meant to reassure you, not to offend you.'

Colour that he was sure had nothing to do with exposure to the sun stained her pale cheeks and she dropped her gaze, shaking her head again.

'I'm…not offended. But…'

The King's voice came again, calling her name. Luca watched her inhale a deep, shaky breath, and then she walked away from him, out of the bright sunlight and into the shade. He had the strangest feeling that somewhere in the vicinity a light had been extinguished.

He picked up his jacket and shrugged it on, straightening his shirt cuffs and doing up one button, keeping his eyes on Princess Rosabella. He watched as she stopped in front of her father and heard him bark a question at her. He could see her shake her head from where he stood. King Fiero's eyes sought him out, boring into him as he walked towards him.

Luca refused to quicken his pace, or apologise to this man for keeping him waiting. Mostly what he wanted to do was to tell him, right here and now, that he could shred the document that he'd drawn up twenty years ago with his own treacherous father because he would never, ever consent to a marriage of convenience, and that he'd be leaving Palosia as soon as possible.

But long experience made him breathe in and pause. Acting on impulse was never advisable. While he wanted to bring this unfortunate episode in his life to a quick conclusion, as he watched the princess walk away from him he felt an unwelcome need to find out more about her. If he left now, in anger, what repercussions would that have for her and her future?

And did it really concern him? The aim of this visit to Palosia was to extricate himself from the agreement their two fathers had drawn up, not to involve himself in the life of the princess he had no intention of marrying.

But before he could leave he would have to make sure that no harm would come to her because of his actions. In his profession, he gave a voice to those who had none; should he be willing to speak for Princess Rosabella, who no longer had a voice to sing to the fish about pretty horses?

He needed to take a step back and focus on what he'd come here to do. Morally, he felt bound to tell King Fiero immediately that he was not going to marry Princess Rosabella, but as soon as he'd done that he'd no longer be welcome on Palosia. He'd have to leave immediately. Anything other than his swift extrication from the agreement could lead to him becoming entangled in the affairs of this family and giving his father a voice in the way he lived his life.

So why did he feel a burden of responsibility for the princess's welfare? As he watched her walk away, the thought hit him that he might never see her again. A shaft of regret stabbed him somewhere in the region of his heart, but he made up his mind to ignore it.

CHAPTER SIX

WHEN THE FIRST pale fingers of light crept around the edges of the heavy curtains at the windows, Rosabella gave up all hope of sleep.

She kicked off the bed covers, slid to the floor and padded across the thick carpet to the window, pulling back the drapes. The valley below the palace was shrouded in mist but the sky above the mountains was streaked with gold and pink, promising another warm day, just like yesterday.

Only no other day would ever be like yesterday. Reliving it in every detail had kept her fitfully awake through the dark hours of the night. That, and the knowledge that *he* was sleeping somewhere in the palace.

Colliding headlong with the stranger, and that fleeting sense of being *protected* as his hands had stopped her from falling, then the shock that had threatened to immobilise her when she'd discovered his identity, had played in her mind on repeat. She'd thought over and over again of the moment when their eyes had met as he'd bowed over her hand, and all her convictions about the evils of a marriage of convenience had seemed to tremble, on the brink of collapse.

With no facts to go on before now, it had been left to her imagination to conjure up an image of the man who was willing to marry the graceless, plain, frankly unladylike person she was. He'd be older, austere and dismissive of her, interested only in the prestige that marrying into an ancient royal family could bring him. And he'd expect her to produce an heir, and spare, in rapid succession.

Then he'd leave her in some remote wing of his castle, thinking she should be grateful to him for rescuing her from a lonely, single life. That was how her parents' marriage had played out, and she had no other example with which to compare it.

If the Count had been anything like the man she'd imagined, it would have been easier to remain steadfast in the face of her father's anticipated anger.

But he wasn't. Not at all. His manner had been warm, his actions considerate and he seemed to have a genuine interest in her. If his presence on Palosia was merely to finalise the details of their marriage, he'd hidden the business side of his visit well.

His calm gaze seemed to see into her soul and understand her thoughts. She could get terrifyingly lost in those dark eyes, but losing herself with him wouldn't be frightening because he made her feel...*safe*. The way a corner of his mouth tipped up a fraction when he was amused did something unfamiliar and strange to her insides. With her eyes caught in his, she'd had the unsettling thought that she could give up all her idealism about marrying for everlasting love in a heartbeat if she could marry this man.

If being his wife would mean feeling the warmth of that searching gaze resting on her face, and the reassuring touch of his hands on her arms again, she wouldn't care if it was merely a marriage of convenience. Perhaps, sometime in the future, she'd be able to persuade him to change his attitude to her; to see her in a different light...

The insanity of her thoughts had lasted seconds. She'd pulled herself back to the reality of meeting the man who wanted to marry her for his own materialistic reasons. His sincerity had to be a mask, his warmth and interest fake. How could it be anything else, when he'd only just met her?

Besides, she knew very well that no man would ever want to be with her for *herself.* She'd been taught that from an early age.

She thought of her sister and the joy she'd found in marrying the man she loved, and who loved her back without reservation or condition. She remembered the humiliation and misery her mother continued to endure for failing to match up to her father's demands. If she couldn't marry for love like Sofia had done, she'd never marry at all. And since even her own father could not love or even tolerate her, no other man ever would, obviously.

Until the Count had laid his hand on her arm, it had been fine, she told herself. Her determination to maintain an icy demeanour had held firm after that first meeting, and following the few minutes they'd spent together at the fountain she'd been within seconds of excusing herself from his presence. The touch of his fingers on her forearm, even through the barrier of her silk sleeve, had changed that.

Rosabella turned her back on the glory of the early morning revealing itself beneath her window and paced across her bedroom floor. She stopped in front of the full-length mirror, in its elaborate gold frame that hung on the wall.

It would be perfectly obvious to anyone who chose to study her closely this morning that she'd had a restless, largely sleepless night. Her fair hair, which had been pulled into a sleek knot yesterday, flowed over her shoulders and down her back in a tangle of curls. Rubbing her eyes had made them red and there were dark smudges beneath them.

Growing stronger by the minute, light gleamed through the windows behind her, illuminating her body through her translucent cotton nightgown. She studied her curves and planes, trying and failing to imagine how anyone could ever find her attractive. Her legs were too long and her breasts too small. While there was an acceptable curve at her waist, her hips could never be described as 'childbearing', and surely that was what any husband would require?

The convenience part of a brokered marriage would mean the swift arrival of children, preferably at least one boy. And if she failed to provide those essential commodities…well, she'd have failed as a wife and a woman. She only had to look to her mother to see what would happen next.

Then her fingers strayed to the place on her arm where Luca's hand had rested until she'd recoiled in shock. The cause of the shock was the fact that he'd touched her. The way it had affected her had made her freeze, her eyes scanning his face to see if he was experiencing something similar.

When she'd reached the sanctuary of her room yesterday afternoon, she'd tugged the silk dress over her head, sending hairpins and pearl clips flying in all directions, and studied her arm. She'd felt almost disappointed not to see the marks of his fingers branded on her skin. Her heartbeat and ragged breathing had taken long minutes to return to something like normal, although she'd told herself that her breathless, flustered state was the result of walking too quickly in the heat.

His touch had only lasted seconds, but a pulse of energy had travelled up her arm and down into the pit of her stomach, triggering an intense tightening, hollowing sensation that had alarmed her. Yet she longed to feel it again.

He'd be leaving this morning. Rosabella ran her fingers over the skin of her forearm and then pressed her palms flat against her abdomen. Once she'd confronted her father, would she be ready to accept that she'd never see the Count again? Would he be angry? Or would he shrug her off as forgettable, and find some other royal bride who would willingly marry him and do his bidding?

The thought caused a strange tightness around her heart. If she could have just one more chance to experience those strange, electrifying sensations he'd stirred in her, she knew she'd seize it.

Even though she'd longed to be able to change back into her gardening clothes yesterday afternoon and lose herself in the terraces, when she'd reached her room she'd felt too wrung out and confused to want to leave it again.

She'd tried to read but the words on the page kept blurring as her mind returned to Luca. She'd made a huge effort to be rational. He'd only touched her to reassure her, and he could have no idea of how that had made her feel. If he had, he'd have found her reaction amusing. A corner of his mouth would have quirked in the way that sent a tingle up her spine…

There seemed to be no escape from her thoughts. She'd asked Luisa to bring some soup to her room but she hadn't even been able to eat that.

Now, frustrated, she pushed her hands into her hair and pressed her palms against her temples. Enough! Much more of this and all her resolutions would crumble to dust. The Count had not asked to see her again after she'd walked away from him, and for all she knew he was already back in Tuscany. She'd put him out of her mind before these endless thoughts drove her to distraction.

Today she'd request a meeting with her father and tell him she wouldn't be marrying anyone. In the meantime, she'd take herself to one of the furthest corners of the garden so that she wouldn't have to see or speak to another soul for hours. Gardening would calm her mind and allow her time to think and plan. Although she'd already decided what she would say to her father, she could spend the morning perfecting her speech and preparing answers to the questions he was bound to fling at her.

Luisa had stuffed her dusty linen skirt and smock into the laundry basket but Rosabella pulled them out and put them on again, relishing the comfort of the worn fabric compared with the expensive silk she'd had to wear yesterday.

Opening the tall windows that led onto a narrow balcony, she took her hairbrush and a ribbon out into the early-morning sunshine and sat down at the little table from where the view stretched all the way to a glimpse of the distant sea.

She pulled up her feet, sat cross-legged on the chair and began the slow task of teasing the knots out of her hair. When it was finally tangle-free, she brushed it, finding the long, slow strokes soothing.

As her nimble fingers wove the final strands of her braid and tied the ribbon around the end, there was a knock on her bedroom door. Luisa swept in with a swish of her skirts and the crackle of her starched apron and Rosabella could tell at once that she was bringing more than just the coffee and fruit she had for breakfast every morning. She deposited the tray on the table in front of Rosabella and planted her fists on her hips, shaking her head.

'Thank you, Luisa, but I can see you want to tell me something. What's wrong?'

'It's your clothes, Princess Rosabella.' The disparaging look she cast over her matched the tone of her voice. 'They will not do.'

Rosabella conjured up a smile, surprised that she was able to, considering the way she'd been tormented in the night by thoughts of the Count, and was now mentally trembling at the prospect of the meeting she anticipated having with her father.

'They're perfectly fine for what I'm planning to do in the garden this morning.'

'But I put them in the laundry basket. They need washing.'

'And I took them out. There's no point in washing clothes which I'll only get dirty again.'

Luisa sighed. 'After you marry the Count, you'll have no use for them.' She waved a hand dismissively. 'You'll have gardeners to do all that work. You'll wear beautiful dresses and polish on your nails and…behave like a princess.'

Rosabella drew in a breath to tell Luisa that her fantasy was doomed but remembered in time that she had to keep her decision a secret until she'd revealed her intentions to her father.

Instead, she shook her head. 'Well, there're gardeners here to do the work, yet I enjoy doing it myself. And since my marriage to the Count has not happened yet, I can spend today in the garden.'

She poured coffee into the delicate cup, inhaling its rich aroma. She studied Luisa over the porcelain rim. 'But commenting on my clothes was not what you were going to do when you came in.' She swallowed a mouthful of the dark, hot liquid and sighed. 'Perfect coffee, thank you. Now, what was it you were going to say?'

Luisa folded her arms. 'I wish I had come in a little earlier. I could have saved you the trouble.' She indicated the smooth braid that lay over Rosabella's shoulder. 'I will have to undo that braid and put your hair up again.'

Rosabella laughed. 'Since when did a gardener need a fancy hairstyle?'

'Ah, this morning you may admire the gardens, but you will not be doing any digging or getting your hands dirty. You will be going for a walk with the Count.'

Shock made Rosabella gasp. She choked on a mouthful

of coffee, spilling some of it over her linen smock. The hot liquid trickled down her front, soaking through the fabric.

'The *Count*?' The cup rattled against the saucer as she replaced it. 'But…he's gone. Or, he's going this morning.'

Luisa unfolded the damask napkin from the tray and used it to mop at Rosabella's top. 'This is hot, Princess Rosabella. I hope it didn't burn you.'

Rosabella plucked at the soaked fabric, pulling it away from her skin. It was hot, but she hadn't noticed. She pulled up her knees and wrapped her arms around them, gripping her fingers together to hide their shaking.

'No, you must be mistaken, Luisa. Yesterday we walked in the garden, through the oak avenue to the marble fountain, where we sat for a while. The Count…well, he said clearly that he would be leaving this morning.'

She swallowed, aware that she was talking too much, but wanting to relive the moments at the fountain. She bit her bottom lip.

'Leaving? Today?' Luisa shook her head and waved a hand in a dismissive gesture. 'Of course not. He will want to get to know you a little, so we must go and choose a dress for you to wear, and do your hair again, so that he will see you at your best.'

'But he *said*…'

'Perhaps you misheard or misunderstood. It was very hot yesterday and you were upset and flustered when you returned to your room—a touch of the sun, perhaps.' She leaned forward and looked closely at Rosabella's face. 'Mmm, those freckles…'

Rosabella unlinked her hands and wiped her palms over her face, as if she might be able to rub out the offending freckles. Then she stopped and turned her face towards the morning sun.

'What if I happen to like my freckles? I won't try to hide them.'

'Very well, but eat some fruit. You will need energy for your walk. The grapes are delicious.'

Rosabella eyed the bowl of fruit but did not feel tempted.

'Who,' she asked, suddenly suspicious, 'Told you that the Count was staying longer than he'd planned and would like to walk with me? Because, if it was my father, it might simply be what he *expects*.'

'It was Paulo. When he served the Count his breakfast, he was specifically requested to send a message to you. He told Paulo he would be staying for perhaps a week.'

'A *week*?'

CHAPTER SEVEN

Luca stood on the gravel path, just beyond the archway, a few steps from where Princess Rosabella had crashed into him the previous day.

A breeze ruffled his hair, but the sun was already warm on his back and he knew the temperature would climb quickly towards noon. But for now the day was perfect, with crystalline air and a matchless blue sky. The distant sound of voices floated up to him from the village far below, and somewhere he heard a church clock begin to strike. He counted the chimes to ten.

Ten o'clock was the agreed time for his meeting with Princess Rosabella. He had been here for five minutes already and, although he told himself that to be late would have been impolite, he knew the truth was that he was impatient to see her again. He pushed his hands into the pockets of his jeans, determined not to check his watch. To be seen doing that would also be considered impolite.

But as the minutes ticked by doubt began to niggle at him. What if she didn't show up? She'd been shocked when he'd touched her arm yesterday and, although he'd apologised at once, she'd walked away without looking back. Perhaps what he'd taken for shock had been annoyance or dislike. There'd seemed to be some confusion when he'd enquired about her later, but eventually the Queen's lady-in-waiting had sent a message to say Princess Rosabella was indisposed. The warm day had been too much for her delicate constitution.

Luca had frowned at that information. What did 'indisposed' actually mean? Was she ill? Or did she simply not wish to see him? Also, Princess Rosabella did not seem delicate to him. He'd felt the wiry strength in her upper arms when he'd steadied her and had secretly admired her upright posture and firm step as they'd walked through the avenue of oaks.

It had been the sight of her straight and determined back that had made him change his mind about leaving Palosia so abruptly. Although she seemed determined to project an image of strength, he suspected there was something much more complex going on beneath the surface.

She'd been shocked by his touch, yes, but after her initial confusion she'd tried to cover it up. That she'd had to try meant she was determined not to let him know he'd stirred any feelings in her, but he strongly suspected that he had. She'd frozen, and he'd seen the confusion in her eyes when she'd dragged them away from his hand to meet his gaze, and, if he was not mistaken, he'd also seen a want or need for something that went deep. He wondered if she had any understanding of her reaction and what it had communicated to him.

When had the simple touch of his fingers ever elicited such a marked response from a woman? Stupid question, he told himself, because the answer was 'never'. He thought about the last woman he'd dated. She'd been a finance executive, with a head for numbers and a body honed and toned to perfection by hours with a personal trainer and a dedication to avoiding carbs. Her response to him had been cool over dinner, and then clinically controlled later in his bed.

The episode had left him feeling dissatisfied on every level, but he'd realised that, in the life he lived, he'd come to expect nothing more. The memory of the sudden bright flash of sensation he'd felt when he'd held the princess upright was more vibrant than any other encounter he could remember. The recognition seemed to link them when their eyes had locked over their hands in the King's antechamber had made him feel curiously charged.

There was nothing to compare between those brief moments and his most recent cold and mechanical date in New York. Was it simply because Princess Rosabella was inexperienced with men? Or was it her natural spontaneity that came across to him as fresh and unspoilt? Whatever it was, her response intrigued him.

The King had been surprised when he'd said he'd like to stay for a few days so that he and the princess could become better acquainted. Without saying as much, he'd given Luca the impression that he felt it an unnecessary waste of time—as if to say, what difference would it make, once they were married, whether they knew each other or not? But he'd shrugged his shoulders and agreed, and also stipulated that Luca and Rosabella could spend time together on condition that they were supervised by a chaperone.

Luca mused that he could have taken offence at the inference that he was not to be trusted alone with the princess but had decided it was not worth the trouble it might cause. His intention was not to seduce her but to make sure that when he announced he was not marrying her she would not be blamed. He would use their time together to explain gently the reasons why he could not stand by the marriage agreement. She would be perfectly safe with him.

Impatience got the better of him and he pulled a hand from his pocket and glanced at his watch. Ten minutes had passed since he'd heard the church clock in the valley, and…

There was the sound of a light step on the gravel behind him and he turned.

* * *

She trod carefully across the courtyard, hearing only the faintest click of the French windows as her chaperone closed the door—grimly resentful at being made to trail around after the count and the princess for the morning, if her frown was anything to go by.

She stepped around the corner into the archway, still hidden by deep shade, and stopped in her tracks. All the imaginings that had plagued her during the night immediately faded into insignificance. He was *more*…so much *more*…than the image her mind had preserved, even though all she could see of him was his back.

Slim black jeans, slung low on his hips, accentuated the length of his legs and the power of his thighs. When had anyone ever worn *jeans* in the palace of Palosia? A narrow tan leather belt was threaded through the loops. A pale-grey cotton shirt with a fine white stripe did nothing to disguise the width of his shoulders and she could see that he'd rolled the sleeves up to the elbows. Thick, dark hair curled slightly at his nape, and the sight of it did odd things to her fingers, making them want to feel if it was as thick and soft as it looked. His hands were pushed into his pockets and she quickly buried her own in the deep pockets of her dress in case they ignored her silent pleas to behave.

What was happening to her? When had she ever had this powerful urge to touch someone who was virtually a stranger, and definitely a man from whom she must keep a cool distance?

If she could make him not want to marry her, the future would be so much easier. It would mean she could avoid the confrontation with her father which she knew was going to rip a hole in the fabric of her life. So, formal and polite, but cold, was how she should be. Wasn't it?

But how could she be unmoved and cool when her heart had leapt into overdrive, hammering against her ribs, and a warm tide of something she did not recognise flooded her whole being, making her knees feel stupidly weak?

As she watched, he pulled his left hand from his pocket and she caught a glimpse of a strong forearm and the flash of a gold watch as he bent his head to check the time. She knew she was late, but she'd have been later still if she'd given in and allowed Luisa to undo her braid and perform a gravity-defying miracle with her hair.

Sharp fingers belonging to the chaperone nudged her in the small of her back and gave her a little push towards the sunlight. 'Go on. Greet him,' her voice hissed in Rosabella's ear.

Her sandals crunched on the gravel as she stepped forward, and he turned. The view of his broad back and long, powerful legs had not prepared her at all. The top two buttons of the grey shirt were undone and Rosabella's eyes fixed, mesmerised, on the smooth tanned skin of his throat, neck and the hint of dark hair that showed below it. Somehow remembering it was rude to stare, she dragged her gaze upward and felt the warmth of those calm, all-seeing dark eyes land on her face. His hair had a mussed look, as if he'd raked his fingers through it, and some of it flopped forward over his forehead.

Quite simply, she stole his breath away.

She wore a wide-brimmed straw hat that cast her face in shadow, but her luminous brown eyes, fringed with long lashes, shone from beneath the brim. They rose from where she appeared to be staring at his chest and met his own.

Her sunshine-yellow linen dress with heart-shaped neckline hugged the slight curves of her body but fell in soft pleats from her slim hips to her calves. Three-quarter length sleeves ended in buttoned cuffs. She stood a little way from him and it looked as if her feet, in bronze leather sandals, were ready to turn and run at a second's notice; she was as unsure and jumpy as a startled fawn.

His first instinct was to put out a hand to stop her from fleeing, but that hadn't gone well yesterday. Calling on a store of control he normally reserved for difficult moments in the courtroom, he kept his arms at his sides. The last thing he wanted was to scare her off before they'd exchanged a single word.

'Good morning, Princess Rosabella. What a beautiful day for a walk in these glorious gardens.'

A faint flush stained her cheeks. Her mouth opened, feather-soft beneath a slick of balm, and the tip of her tongue touched her bottom lip. Luca felt a punch of reaction so strong that he feared he had visibly flinched.

Small earrings in the shape of daisies fashioned from crystal shone at her earlobes. He was irrationally pleased to see that she wore her hair in the long braid he'd first seen the previous day. A pale-gold silk ribbon secured the end of it. Her hands were buried in the deep pockets of the pleats of her dress.

She nodded and he found himself entranced by how her earrings sparkled. 'The gardens are beautiful in all weathers and seasons.' She drew a hand from a pocket and touched the bow that tied her plait, drawing his eyes to her slender fingers. An image of them entwined with his own danced in his imagination.

'Your hair...' Luca bit his lip. He'd only have himself to blame if she was offended or frightened away by this personal comment, but the words had escaped in response to the fascination her hair held for him. At lunch yesterday he'd spent some time wondering how that amount of lustrous hair had been tamed and confined into the pleat resting at the nape of her neck. The thoughts had distracted him from his conversation with the King and then he had castigated himself for allowing them at all. He was here to extract himself from a frankly mediaeval agreement which sought to bind him to this girl for ever, not to fantasize about her hair.

That little frown he'd seen yesterday creased her forehead and she looked stricken. 'Oh!' She flicked the thick rope of the braid over her shoulder. 'Luisa wanted to put it up but there wasn't time...'

'No,' he said quickly. 'I mean, I like it like that. It's beautiful. It's a pity to hide it in a formal style.'

Her lips curved in a slight smile, and he remembered the promise of a dimple in her left cheek.

'Thank you. But I don't believe this can be an informal walk, in spite of my hair style.'

'Oh, I think it can. Although...' He glanced behind her to the figure of a woman in the shadow of the arch.

She dipped her head. 'My chaperone will make sure it's kept formal enough. Did you request her, or was she my father's idea?'

'It wasn't mine, but your father expressed surprise that I might want to get to know you, even though he intends for you to marry me.'

'No, he wouldn't see the point. After all, surely there'd be enough time afterwards to make my acquaintance? Perhaps he thinks if you find out too much about me beforehand you might change your mind.'

He looked for a sign that she was teasing him but found none. Her gaze was steady and serious.

'Surely he would want you, his daughter, to get to know her proposed husband a little too?'

She dropped her eyes and shook her head. 'No. In his opinion, that would be an even greater waste of time.'

Regret stabbed at him as he thought about what he intended to do. Would he shatter all this girl's precious dreams of marriage and freedom from the seeming tyranny of her uncaring parent when he abandoned the agreement their fathers had struck? What kind of future would he condemn her to?

But then he remembered why he had to do it. The shock of discovering what his father had done, plotting and dictating how he should lead his life, would burn for ever. Had he honestly believed that he could force his son to go through with it?

Anger strengthened his resolve. His mother had fought against the iron bonds her husband had forced on her, and her rebellious reaction had killed her. As an adult, he'd wondered if she'd been given the choice between living the rest of her life under the relentless and stultifying control of her husband, or dying on a wild, exhilarating last gallop, which she would have chosen.

After his mother's death he'd been sent to live with her elderly parents. They had raised him in a home filled with love and gentle kindness, teaching him to care for those less fortunate than himself and always to consider the feelings of others. But on his tenth birthday his father had demanded his return. He'd stood in his father's study, confused and afraid before this man who was virtually a stranger, to be told that his real education was about to begin and from then on he would do his bidding and no-one else's.

But the principles his grandparents had instilled in him had prevailed and his own fight for independence had begun that day, alongside the education his father had deemed fit for his heir. It had been a long and bitter battle, culminating in the estrangement of father and son.

There was no way, ever, that he'd give up what he'd fought so hard for and go ahead with the marriage his father had tried to bind him to. To do that would feel like surrendering his soul.

Mentally, he shrugged off her words with a smile. He pushed a hand through his hair and shook his head. The question he'd seen in her eyes when she'd raised them again had died, and he thought she had possibly hoped he would vehemently deny what she'd suggested.

The code of scrupulous honesty by which he lived bound him to speak the truth, so he said nothing. Better to remain silent than to voice his growing dislike of her father. He glanced over at the woman who had been instructed to protect the princess's honour. She had most likely been told to report back any conversation they had to the King.

So he half-turned away from Rosabella, his eyes sweeping over the distant view and the nearer terraces of the gardens.

'I suggested ten o'clock as I thought we could explore the gardens before it grows too warm. I hope this isn't too early for you. I understand you suffered from the effects of the heat yesterday.'

'Oh! Yes, I… It was very warm.' She dropped her gaze. 'Thank you for your consideration.'

'And you had neglected to bring a hat for protection.' He glanced at the intricately woven straw hat she wore. 'I'll ask you to lead the way, princess, since you have a lifelong knowledge of the gardens.'

'If we're to stop walking before it becomes uncomfortably warm, we'll only see a small part of them.'

'I believe the weather on Palosia is reliably settled at this time of year, so perhaps tomorrow we can explore further? That is, if I'll not be taking you away from any official duties.'

'It could always be arranged for the head gardener to show you around, if necessary.'

'Surely that would defeat my purpose?' He kept his voice gentle. 'After all, it is you I wish to know, not the head gardener, even though I'm sure his knowledge is faultless.'

Without replying, Rosabella turned on her heel. 'If we take this path, we can follow a circuit around the flower garden and through the orchard terraces.'

Luca fell in beside her, leaving enough space between them to placate their chaperone. Her delicate floral scent was unlike any of the perfumes with which he was famili-ar. It had a lightness and freshness which its elusiveness somehow made alluring. He wanted to ask her about it but decided to steer clear of a question that she might find too personal. He didn't want to jeopardise any chance he had of getting her to relax a little in his company.

He realised that what he desired most from the morning was to spend the next two hours with her, and he was de-termined not to do or say anything at all that might frighten her away or upset her. He wanted to know more about her, listen to her soft voice telling him about the plants and flow-ers and ask her what had led her to sing to the fish—and what had made her stop.

If he was still here in a few days, perhaps they'd have reached a level of familiarity with each other that would allow him to comment on her perfume.

He put a brake on his thoughts. They could never be-come familiar with one another. He needed to banish from his mind that image of their intertwined fingers. It was un-likely he'd still need to be here in a few days. With his honed skills of communication and negotiation, he'd tell her why he couldn't marry her, and then tell King Fiero too.

He'd accomplish what he needed to do in less than a few days and be gone.

Walking with the Count at her side made Rosabella self-con-scious. The distance between them felt charged with some-thing like magnetism, and she held herself stiffly to resist the invisible force that tugged her closer to him.

What reason could he have for wanting to get to know her better? It was absolutely unnecessary, although it demonstrated a concern for her feelings which she thought was kind.

The repellent image of the man she'd expected to meet was fading rapidly from her memory in the presence of Count Luca. His consideration confused her, and she thought again of how her determination had wavered in the aftermath of the tangle of emotions that had assaulted her when he'd touched her, and how she'd longed to feel that jolt of electricity and that curious warm, melting sensation in her stomach again.

But that had been during the long night when her thoughts had become a jumble of wants and forbidden desires which she didn't understand or recognise. It was much easier to be rational and reasonable in the bright morning sunlight.

She could be herself in the gardens, without reservation or pretence. She knew every inch of the land, including the secluded places cooled by trickling rills of clear water and shaded by giant tree ferns, where she could escape from the heat of the sun and the eyes of the palace staff. She had no intention of showing any of those places to the Count.

But, instead of feeling the sense of calm and peace which she always found among the flowers and trees, she felt like an exhibit, or a tour guide—as if he would use this time to judge her and, naturally, find her wanting in all the areas which he'd think were important.

She lacked the skill in making polite small-talk and wouldn't know how to begin to attract the interest of a man. Those were social skills that she'd never been taught. Since her future had been determined from the age of four, it had been deemed unnecessary for her to learn them. And now she had no interest in acquiring them. After all, what use would they be to someone who intended to spend the rest of her life tending these beautiful acres?

Besides, she knew she was plain. She had freckles that came out with the sun, and wild hair which had to be tamed in a braid or a complicated knot, held in place with sharp hair pins.

When Count Luca discovered her lack of grace, coupled with the lack of beauty which he would already have noticed, perhaps he'd stop trying to get to know her and go home to his castle in Tuscany. He'd been kind to say he liked her hair, but for all she knew that was a standard compliment that men paid to women. To everyone else, her hair had only ever been a source of irritation.

If he really did intend to remain for several days, she would have to delay telling her father that she would not marry him. While he was here, staying in the palace, her father would never take any notice of what she said. In fact, if her father thought she was going to embarrass him and cause an unpleasant scene, he might insist that the marriage take place immediately. A prickle of apprehension ran down her spine at the thought.

Within a few days she could be tied to this man for life—taken away from everything she knew and treasured—and her mother would be left alone and defenceless. She couldn't afford to take that risk. She squashed the traitorous thought which had briefly sparked in her brain the previous day, that she would submit to a marriage of convenience if it could be to this man.

That, she told herself, had only happened because of the shock she'd felt when she'd found he was so…different from what she'd expected.

Why, then, had her response to seeing him this morning been even more intense and visceral than yesterday? She was over the shock of seeing him, she told herself. What shocked her now was the behaviour of her own body.

His voice was as reliably deep and measured as she'd remembered it, and the tiny lift at the side of his mouth when she'd referred to their chaperone had sent a dart of forbidden pleasure plunging through her, exactly as she'd known it would.

Now they were walking side-by-side along the gravel path, and she was in charge of showing him some of the garden. Her heart returned to a rhythm more in keeping with someone taking a quick walk, rather than an athlete in the final stages of a marathon, and she returned both her hands to her pockets in case he noticed that they shook a little.

The path curved to the left as it began to slope downward, and Rosabella trod carefully. A slight unevenness in the gravel and the stiff way she held herself threw her a little off-balance and her arm brushed against the Count's. She pulled away sharply, putting more distance between them, but the memory of how it had felt when his hand had rested on her forearm ambushed her again. That delicious rush of shivery sensation must be addictive, she thought and, though she'd spent much of the night dwelling on how his touch had felt and affected her, she knew that the only cure for addiction was total abstinence.

That was all very well in theory. Putting it into practice felt impossible.

CHAPTER EIGHT

THE SUN WAS at its highest, the shadows at their shortest, and Luca and Rosabella were the furthest they'd been from the palace all morning.

Sometime during their walk, the determined pace which the princess had set had slowed to a stroll. Their initial occasional stops to admire the fragrant, waxy blossoms of a frangipani tree, or the red velvet flower of a hibiscus, became increasingly frequent.

Again and again, Luca found himself astonished by Rosabella's detailed knowledge of the flora of Palosia, and her enviable ability to describe it to him with an uncomplicated fluency. He watched her stiff demeanour soften as she lost herself in the place where she obviously felt at ease and in control. As they walked along grassy paths between the borders filled with flowers, she'd reach out to remove a drooping daisy or snap off the pepper-pot seed pod of a poppy, shaking it to sprinkle its seeds onto the earth.

She glanced at him over her shoulder. 'Many of these plants seed themselves. We have to be vigilant, or the beds become too crowded, but a poppy seed pod is so perfectly designed for its purpose, I can't resist shaking them out.' She'd straightened up, dusting the palms of her hands against the fabric of her dress.

Sometimes she almost seemed to be talking to herself

about what they were seeing, but if he asked a question her reply was informed and immediate.

Watching her was almost bewitching. They reached the upper slopes of the citrus orchard, where glossy-leaved orange trees grew in rows, their branches covered in developing fruit.

A few minutes later Luca pointed to a beehive beside the purple haze of a lavender hedge. 'Do you make your own honey?'

'Naturally, we do. The hives are moved according to where the blossom is at its best. Then, when the honey-comb is harvested, we know that it's orange-blossom honey if it's from the orchard, or lavender honey if the hives were near the lavender walk.'

She reached down to pick a flower spike, crushing it be-tween her fingers, and then holding it out to him on the palm of her hand. He inhaled the floral, faintly herbal scent, tak-ing care not to lean too close to her. He wanted to close his hand around hers as she held the crushed bloom, but he kept his hands in his pockets.

'Mmm. It's exquisite. The honey must be exceptionally good.'

'Honey from Palosia is rare and prized.' She dropped the petals to the ground. 'If you like, I'll ask the head gardener to give you some to take back to Tuscany.'

'I'd like that very much. Thank you.'

The moment felt intimate and precious, as if she'd finally accepted that he was a real person who might like a simple thing like honey, not a stranger who'd come to finalise the business of marrying her. It seemed as if they'd moved beyond formality, and the unspoken thing that hung between them.

Their eyes met and for the first time she didn't look away. The air was warm, and thick with the sound of assiduous bees and the call of birds, but Luca felt that the beat of his heart and the rush of his blood must be loud enough for her to hear. He had the strangest feeling that if he reached out and cupped her cheek in his palm she might not recoil.

Fascinated, he watched her guarded expression change to one of confusion and then, he was sure, to one of curiosity. He hardly dared breathe.

A loud cough broke the spell. Luca almost heard the snap as the tension in the air broke, and with a jolt he remembered the presence of the chaperone. He exhaled a long breath. For a moment in which time had appeared to stretch, the world had shrunk to just the two of them and the emotion that hummed between them. He'd completely forgotten that their every move was being observed.

He'd allowed the intoxicating scents and sounds of the garden to overwhelm his senses and cloud his famously sharp mind. The fact that he was the focus of attention of this beautiful princess had not helped him to maintain his equilibrium. He was a world away from his usual comfort zone, he rationalised; immersed in an exotic environment, in the unlikely position of getting to know the woman who was meant to become his wife.

It felt crazy. He had to get his thoughts and feelings back into some sort of balance before he did something he'd regret that would make the task at hand much, much more difficult. Apart from the practicalities of having to extract himself from the absurd marriage deal, he wanted with all his heart not to do anything that would allow Rosabella to believe he might have feelings for her.

Naturally, he did not. He'd met her barely twenty-four hours ago, unless he counted their brief encounter twenty *years* ago, and that would be ridiculous. This impulse to touch her, to feel the softness of her skin under his hands, to *kiss* her even, was all the result of the romantic location, the heady scent of the blossom and the presence of a beautiful princess. What man would *not* want to kiss her?

He clenched his fists in his pockets. Frustration tugged at him, but he knew he could do nothing to release it here. Later, when it was cooler, he'd go for a run in the hills, or swim fifty laps of the pool he'd glimpsed from his windows. Better still, he'd arrange a meeting with King Fiero and get this over with before it became more complicated than it already was.

The chaperone coughed again, and Luca looked over at her. She tapped the watch on her wrist.

He returned his full attention to the princess. Her bottom lip was caught between her teeth. She looked cool and calm, but he could see the rapid beat of the little pulse at her throat.

'I think,' he said quietly, 'We're being given our instructions. It must be midday.' He glanced up at the sun, almost directly overhead. 'And we still have to walk back up to the palace. I'm afraid I've kept you out in the heat for too long.'

Rosabella shook her head. 'No, I'm perfectly used to it, although it's our custom to stay out of the sun during the hottest part of the day. Yesterday, I…'

'Yesterday you didn't have your hat.'

'Luckily, I remembered it today.'

She turned towards him, and at last he was rewarded with the wide smile she'd handed him the previous morning. He thought it hinted that they were complicit in something.

The walk back up to the palace was steep, and once they'd left the citrus orchard behind there was little shade. Their chaperone puffed up the slopes ahead of them, obviously satisfied that her duties were complete. Only once did she look back to check on them.

Despite the heat, Rosabella felt filled with a strange exhilaration. The morning had flown by, and she found herself wishing that it wasn't over yet. Count Luca had expressed interest in every aspect of the things she'd shown him and had asked searching, intelligent questions.

It was enjoyable to hold a conversation with an adult who was not one of her parents or a member of the court. The ever-present dull ache of missing her sister flared. This man who walked beside her, attentive to her words as well as her physical comfort, sharpened her awareness of everything. He seemed to enjoy her company and to find the things she said interesting. How he made her feel was new and exciting. She must make the most of his company, while she could.

Once he'd gone, and she'd told her father she would never marry for convenience, to cement an alliance or to satisfy the ego or ambition of a man, she could expect a life of doing... probably very little. She had not been allowed to pursue her dream of becoming a garden designer, or anything else. Further education, her father had thundered, was wasted on women. All they needed to do was be wives and mothers, preferably to sons, but some of them couldn't even get that right.

How thrilling it must be for her sister finally to be able to fulfil her ambition to forge a career in interior design. Rosabella had become more and more responsible for her fragile mother's care. Her role in the charities her mother had founded, to help women and children access education and develop skills that would allow them to support themselves, would steadily increase.

Not that she minded. She loved her twice-weekly visits to the workshop they had established, where they'd revived the centuries-old craft of making hats from the left-over straw from the wheat harvest. The women wove intricate hats that they were beginning export to far corners of the world. A small school had been set up as part of the enterprise where the workers' children were taught by volunteer retired teachers.

What had begun as an experiment was now a thriving business, and Rosa found the days she spent there deeply fulfilling. Working with the women, taking orders from foreign buyers and sourcing materials and new designs made her feel alive and useful—as if she was doing something useful, rather than just marking time until her twenty-fifth birthday, when her life was due to change dramatically.

Would her father allow her to expand her role at the workshop when she refused to marry a man who would never love her back? Given his views on education and employment for women, it was unlikely, but it was something for which she was prepared to fight. She'd been denied the opportunity to follow the career of her choice, in garden design, but she could help other women realise their potential and achieve their ambitions.

Perhaps the rewards she'd reap from helping others would, over time, help her to accept a life without love.

She'd be at the hat workshop in two days' time, and the thought brought a little warmth to the coldness which had settled around her heart as they reached the top of the steps, near the archway. Was this the moment when she really would bid farewell to Count Luca for the last time? Although Luisa had said he planned to stay, there was nothing to stop him from changing his plans. He might have found the morning…okay, her company…boring. His interest in the gardens had most likely been fabricated, just to give him something to talk about with a freckle-faced, unsophisticated woman.

The confidence she'd felt walking and talking with him began to crumble and she stood, tongue-tied and awkward, waiting for him to make an excuse to leave.

The chaperone disappeared through a side door to the

palace. Did her father honestly believe that she had been necessary? After all, he'd spent enough time telling her that no man would ever fall in love with her, and demonstrating, by his habit of ignoring her at all other times, that she was unlovable. Why did he think that the Count might be the exception to prove that rule?

Then she remembered how her half-sister's disappearance had unfolded. King Fiero had been left humiliated and furious by Sofia's defiant desertion. He was not going to let that happen again.

Rosabella tried not to think too often about her beloved half-sister because the ache of loss was almost too much to bear. Sofia had been her friend, companion and protector, often standing between Rosabella and their father when he'd raged that she was a useless girl who should have been a boy. She'd been afraid that Rosa's mother would abandon her, as her own had done.

The times they had been apart had been hard, but she'd always come back. Not this time, though. She had married the love of her life and gone from Palosia for good. Rosa was happy for her—she truly was—but that didn't stop her from missing her, every day.

Sofia had deserted Prince Eduardo, the man the King had chosen for her, at the altar. Marriage to him would have cemented an important alliance between Palosia and the prince's own ancient dynasty of Sarcos, on a neighbouring island. Then she had found Marco again. Her sister's bravery had given Rosa the courage to make her own decision. She wasn't yet sure from where she'd find the great courage she'd need to carry it out. She would not marry the man her father had chosen for her either, but sadly, in her case, she had no-one like Marco to find.

With anyone else the silence which stretched between

her and the Count would have felt awkward, but it seemed he was comfortable enough not to feel he had to fill it. She looked across the valley, where heat shimmered on the clay-tiled rooftops of the village below. The mist had cleared from the mountain tops, leaving their rocky peaks etched against the clear blue sky. The distant sea shimmered, the sunlight dancing off the glittering waves.

A prickle of awareness brought her attention back to the Count, and she knew he was looking at her. Feeling his eyes on her made her chest feel unnaturally tight and she took a big breath, trying to ease it. She swallowed hard, as if she might be able to stop the sensations that rose through her, threatening to morph into words which she'd be embarrassed by and regret later.

'Thank you for this morning, Princess Rosabella. I've enjoyed it much more than… I can express. May I ask you something?'

She went still, dreading what might be coming. Was he about to ruin the hours they'd spent together by mentioning the marriage? It felt to her as if they'd both avoided the subject by silent mutual agreement, but perhaps she'd completely mis-read the situation. She had no experience of how these matters worked. How could she respond to him with honesty when she had no intention of going through with their wedding?

But he surprised her.

'Where did you learn about horticulture? Your knowledge seems extensive, at least to a layman like me. Have you been to university? Studied botany?'

Relief washed over her and she smiled, even though her lack of formal education was something she regretted and resented. This question was an easy one to answer.

'From my mother. She rescued these gardens from years of neglect and she has passed on her knowledge to me.'

'Ah.' He nodded. 'I remember you telling me, all those years ago, that your mother was a gardener. What you did not tell me was that she was also the Queen.' A half-smile teased his mouth. 'I simply assumed that she was one of the team of gardeners which must be needed to keep this estate in order.'

'Twenty years ago, if that was when we met as children, she would only have wrestled a small part of them back from nature. The maze had been here for centuries, and she restored that first.'

'Does she still manage the gardens? Yesterday, she seemed...frail.'

Rosabella looked down at her feet. Her sandals were dusty and a stalk of grass was lodged under one of the straps. They weren't suitable for the sort of walk they'd done, but Luisa had prevailed in the shoe battle that morning and insisted she wear them, rather than her canvas plimsols.

'No.' She bent to tug the stalk free and rolled it between her fingers. 'She walks on the level paths sometimes, and she sits in the shade of the old linden tree.'

He followed her gaze and saw the tree she indicated. Its twisted trunk was gnarled with age and there was a wooden bench beneath it in the deep shade cast by its canopy.

'She no longer plays an active part but her knowledge is boundless.'

'Did she study the subject? I'm afraid I'm rather ignorant of the achievements of your family.'

Rosabella laughed. 'She's entirely self-taught. I think my grandfather's attitude towards education for women was even more antiquated than my own father's. Her life was completely sheltered until she married him, and not a lot changed.' She shrugged. 'I think she found solace...'

She stopped, wishing she could take the words back. She'd said too much. The way her father treated her mother was shameful and private, not something to be discussed with a stranger. If it wasn't for the fact that the citizens of Palosia sympathised with her and loved her for the charitable work she did among them, King Fiero might well have divorced her and taken another wife in his bid to have a son.

'Solace?'

Any hope she'd had that he might have missed what she'd said evaporated on the warm air. She took a quick step back, putting what she hoped was a safer distance between them. She'd allowed him to get too close, not just in body but in mind. He'd made her feel too comfortable, and she'd dropped her guard. If the chaperone hadn't reminded them of her presence in the orchard...

She didn't know what might have happened, because she had nothing on which to base her imagination, but she'd *wanted* something to happen.

Was it wrong of her to long to discover how it felt to be wanted, or cherished, even if it was only once in her life?

She felt a shiver of apprehension. He'd have soon discovered that she had no experience or expertise in the art of flirting. That, she thought bitterly, would have been a quick route to persuading him that he really did not want to marry her.

A breeze had picked up and it lifted the brim of her hat. She put a hand on the crown to keep it in place.

'I need to go. Thank you for your company this morning...' She found she didn't know how to finish. Should she say goodbye, as if she did not expect to see him again? Flustered, she spun round and walked away.

He didn't call after her, yet he'd mentioned tomorrow...

Luca watched her retreating. Her steps were hurried, her back stiff and straight. So much effort seemed to be expended in keeping up the appearance of strength and determination, that it had the effect of making her look achingly vulnerable.

On their tour of the garden, he'd been fascinated to see how she'd unwound, bit by bit, until he'd found it easy to converse with her and ask questions about the plants, trees and flowers. The garden was obviously her happy place. Her mother had found *solace* in her restoration project. Had she passed on that solace to her daughter? And why did either of them need it?

Palosia should have felt like an island paradise, yet the King was bad-tempered, the Queen frail and anxious and Rosabella did her best to hide her vulnerability behind a shield of stiff control. What he'd believed would be a quick, if rather brutal, transaction between himself and the King could turn into something much more complicated if he allowed his concern for the princess to get in the way.

He did not owe them anything, he told himself, although he admitted that money might have to change hands if he was to extricate himself from the proposed marriage. He was okay with that, and the quicker he put his plans in motion the better.

But a weight of responsibility pressed down on him in the form of the future welfare of Princess Rosabella. If he'd chosen a different path in life, it might not have affected him in this way, but he was a lawyer who defended members of society who were defenceless against the lot life had dealt them. For him, it was an impossibility to stand by and watch another human being suffer if he could do something to alleviate that suffering.

While this family of ancient noble lineage appeared to have it all—wealth, a home of such opulence that most people could never dream of, security and an island kingdom of stunning beauty and abundance—unhappiness pervaded the very atmosphere of the place. It had been obvious how Rosabella's spirits had lifted, her whole demeanour changed, when she'd talked to him about the garden. Amongst the flowers and trees, she was in her true element, filled with enthusiasm for and a love of nature.

Standing in the citrus orchard, he'd felt a surge of feeling for her, and the urge to cup her cheek in his palm, to feel the petal-softness of her skin, had been almost overwhelming. The look in her eyes had told him she had wanted something too. But as they'd climbed back towards the palace, and a parting of their ways, he'd watched her revert to her cool, guarded self.

It was a cardinal rule never, ever to become personally involved with a client. Crossing that line clouded judgement, destroyed impartiality and closed the gap that was essential to maintain clear-sightedness. It was something of which he had never been guilty. He ran a tight ship, and it ensured his continued reputation as one of the best.

He watched Princess Rosabella vanish through the French windows across the courtyard and huffed out a sigh of frustration. What was going on with him? Why was he finding this difficult? Everything should have been done and dusted by now and he should have been back in his castle—which he would hardly call home—at his penthouse in Rome, or even on his way back to New York.

Why was it that not one of those prospects filled him with even a hint of pleasure? Could he make allowances for this feeling of wanting to tear up the rule book because the princess was not a client, and therefore the rules did not apply to her? She was meant to become his *wife*, damn it.

His brain stalled at that thought. The idea that he'd even permitted it to form felt dangerous, putting all he held true and certain in jeopardy. She could never be his wife. Never. His father had duped him for twenty years and had gone to his grave believing he'd defeated him. Luca would go to his own knowing he'd triumphed over the control and bullying that had robbed him of his mother. The rage he harboured for his father was corrosive, but he welcomed the bitter taste it brought to his mouth. It served to focus his mind.

He couldn't—*wouldn't*—allow concern for this enigmatic princess to undermine his stated purpose.

Later, Luca asked the valet who'd been assigned to see to his needs to have his hire car brought to him. He urgently needed to put some distance between Rosabella and himself, and strenuous physical activity was the quickest way he knew to suppress inconvenient desire.

Since he'd originally planned to stay on Palosia for less than twenty-four hours, he hadn't packed for a holiday. He decided to drive down to the village, buy swimming things and find a beach where he could swim until he'd worn himself out. That way he just might be able to clear his mind of the image of deep-brown eyes, faint freckles on a straight nose and hair he longed to loosen from its restraining braid and run his fingers through before cupping her face in his hands…

He slammed the car door and pressed the ignition button, then he lowered the soft top. Getting the wind in his face might help. The solid roar of the engine was satisfying as he released the brake and pressed the accelerator. This car was something solid and predictable which behaved as he expected it to. He could control its power and speed and the direction it would take.

The realisation that his own mind and body were not so reliably biddable shocked him.

CHAPTER NINE

WHEN LUISA CARRIED Rosabella's breakfast tray onto the balcony the following morning, she brought no message from Luca.

From behind the dark protection of her sunglasses, Rosabella studied her face, searching for clues but coming up with nothing. Luisa's face was impassive, and Rosabella refused to bow to her own need and ask for news of him.

Luisa ran her eye over Rosabella's clothes and clicked her tongue in what could have been frustration.

Rosabella rose to the bait. 'What is it, Luisa? If I've offended you, I apologise, but please tell me what I've done so that I can make sure I don't do it again.'

Luisa smiled. 'No, of course you haven't offended me, and if you had I'd certainly explain how. It's just…' She sighed. 'You have so many pretty clothes.'

'Since I'm planning another day in the garden, I don't need anything pretty.'

'You were in the garden yesterday, and you wore that lovely dress.'

'That was because I had to play hostess to my father's guest.' She bent a leg up and hugged her knee. 'Today, I'll be working.'

'But the Count…'

'Since he has not asked to see me today, I presume he's left. And without saying goodbye.'

She wished she hadn't said that. It might sound as if she cared, and she didn't.

On her way back through the doorway, Luisa turned. 'I don't know what he plans to do today, but he hasn't left—not yet. There might still be time.'

Rosabella snapped her head round to look at her, all kinds of scenarios rushing through her head. 'Time for what, exactly?'

'Oh, time for him to say goodbye. After all, his manners are beyond reproach.'

The work of tying in the thorny stems of a climbing rose that scrambled over a wrought-iron frame was hot, hard and scratchy, but the scent of the pale-pink blooms intensified as the day grew warmer and more than compensated for her aching shoulders.

Rosabella ducked under the dense growth into welcome shade, where water trickled into a stone basin. She dropped her hat onto the paving stones, pulled off her gardening gloves and wiped the beads of perspiration from her forehead. Then she scooped up water in her cupped hands and splashed it over her face. She sighed as the cool drops trickled down her neck. She tucked a strand of hair behind her ear, then she sat down to rest on the cushioned swing seat to admire the view over the flower garden.

'Is this a good time? It looks as if you're taking a break.'

Every muscle in Rosabella's body stilled, apart from her irritating heart, which began to hammer against her ribs. It felt as if her chest might not have enough space for it. Her lungs squeezed and her breathing quickened. The fingers that she'd pushed into her hair at her temples were stiff. His voice took her thoughts to the dark, amber honey that they harvested from the hives near the meadow, where the buck-wheat grew wild.

She was dirty and sweaty, and a scratch on her arm was caked with dried blood. Luisa's words beat in her brain: *You have so many pretty clothes.* She was most comfortable in what she wore now, but her skirt and top showed her exactly as she was. They didn't provide a disguise, like a pretty dress did. She lowered her hands and slid her fingers into her pockets before turning.

Luca stood at the entrance to the arbour. She blinked, because the light beyond him was dazzling and all she could see was his silhouette against the summer sky. But the shape of those wide shoulders was already imprinted on her mind.

'I… Yes.' She tried to swallow the constriction in her throat, to find a voice that sounded more like hers. 'That is, yes, I'm taking a break.' She lifted her shoulders. 'But a good time for what?'

Her mind, which had frozen along with most of the rest of her, leapt back into action. What did he want? Did he want to talk about the marriage? Or had he come to tell her he was leaving, as good manners dictated that he should?

He stepped out of the light into the shade and Rosabella remembered that this was one of the places she was not going to show him. She'd decided to tidy up this arbour today because it was in a remote corner of the garden where she'd felt sure she'd be undisturbed. After the stress of the last two days, she craved time to herself to reset and put her thoughts and feelings back where they belonged, under control.

He looked a lot more relaxed than she felt. The black jeans he wore were comfortably worn-in; his grey tee-shirt clung to his shoulders and the flat planes of his stomach and abdomen, not hiding anything of his physique.

'Oh,' he said, his tone light. 'Just to continue our conversation from yesterday, but without…' He glanced over his shoulder towards the entrance.

Rosabella's eyes followed his. 'You mean…there's no-one *else* here?'

'Uh-huh.' He shrugged. 'No chaperone.' His lips lifted at the corners and her stomach dropped, doing a curious loop-the-loop on the way. It settled low down, leaving a hollow where she felt it should have been. She was convinced the beat of her heart could be heard. It could definitely be seen, if he looked.

'How did you find me?' Did he suspect she'd been hiding from him? The physical exertions of the morning had given her mind time and space to consider, and she'd convinced herself that she really didn't care if the Count had left. It would mean she could now tell her father her decision. She was tired of putting off the confrontation and afraid that, with each day which passed, a little of her determination would ebb away.

He made her feel things she'd never felt before, but then she'd never had the opportunity. Perhaps that sense of the world receding and her focus narrowing to one specific point, or feeling she'd willingly do anything he asked of her when he looked into her eyes was perfectly normal when a man touched her arm. To *want* to do anything for him.

The often-present longing for her sister squeezed her heart a little more tightly. They'd always talked to each other, and she wished she could talk to her about this. Sofia knew about love, courage and following one's own path. She'd be able to reassure her and tell her that these feelings meant nothing at all.

'I asked one of the gardeners. He said he'd seen you heading this way.' His eyes dropped and she knew he'd seen her chest rise and heard her sigh of annoyance. 'Did you not want to be found? I can leave.'

'No, please don't.' She shook her head and a lock of her hair fell across her forehead. 'It's just that I feel as if someone is always tracking my movements. I'm probably over-sensitive.'

Her cheeks were flushed and there was a damp patch on the front of her shirt, making it stick to her skin. He sat down on the stone wall at the front of the arbor to distract himself. She seemed oblivious to the effect she was having on him. He felt as warm as she looked, only it wasn't from the sun or hard work. He stretched out his legs and crossed them at the ankles, resting his hands behind him on the stone parapet in a show of seeming relaxation.

'I wanted to ask you,' he said, raising his eyes to her face, 'About your hat.'

Rosabella glanced down at her straw hat. It was the battered one she only wore for gardening, unlike the elegant, broad-brimmed and intricately woven one she'd worn the previous day.

'Which hat?' Her brows drew together. 'That one, or the one I wore yesterday?'

'Both.' He leaned forward and propped his folded arms on his thighs. 'Yesterday afternoon I decided to explore a little. I drove down to the village in the valley. I went swimming in the sea, I…'

'Swimming?'

'Do you like swimming?'

She nodded. A spark, possibly of longing, lit her eyes. 'I love swimming. But I haven't swum in the sea for a long time. When I was a child, I used to challenge myself to dive off the rocks into the sea. I thought that if I climbed higher and dived deeper, my father…' She stopped and gave a quick shake of her head.

'You thought what—that he'd be afraid for you?'

She laughed, and there was bitterness in the sound. 'That he might *notice* me.'

He nodded, understanding far more from her few words than she probably realised. The anger that had gripped him last night—so fiercely that he'd had difficulty stopping himself from barging into the King's study and tearing up the despicable marriage agreement under his nose—roared back.

Last night, he'd returned to the palace, tired from a strenuous swim in the surf and a couple of miles of running on the beach, followed by a meal at a beachside café. He'd put his thoughts in order and settled his mind. He'd decided he would talk to King Fiero in the morning. Having made his case clear to the monarch, he would ask permission to dine with Princess Rosabella and explain to her, in as gentle a way as possible, why they could never be married. And then he would leave.

He'd showered and then done what he should have done as soon as this situation had come to light. He'd settled down to read the marriage document from beginning to end with as much detachment as he could muster. It was imperative that he had all the facts at his fingertips when he approached King Fiero.

At first it appeared to be a straightforward document, if a contract for a marriage of convenience could ever be called that. He and the princess were to be married when she turned twenty-five. He frowned at the nearness of the date. Just how much notice of the event had his father been planning to give him? And what would have happened if he hadn't returned to Tuscany and found the document when his father had died? The fact that they were estranged was an open secret and nobody would have been surprised if he hadn't attended the funeral. Would King Fiero have sent a couple of his acolytes to New York or Rome to find him and bring him to Palosia to fulfil his, or rather his *father's*, side of the bargain? He'd smiled grimly at the idea.

But then he'd got onto the small print, and he'd stopped smiling.

It seemed Rosabella would leave Palosia as soon as they were married, to live with him in Tuscany. The expectation of a male heir was clear. When the anticipated boy was two, he'd be taken from her, along with any rights his parents had, and returned to the island to be raised by the King as his heir.

The prince, if one was born, would have no memory of his mother. Luca knew that with the authority of one who'd lost his own mother at that same age. The difference was that he'd been cared for by his kind and thoughtful grandparents, in a home filled with love and mutual respect. In his mind, their marriage and relationship was a shining example to him of what love and commitment looked like.

If he ever married, it would be for love and for ever, not to appease a king who clearly saw his daughter simply as a nuisance to be removed from his life. But also someone to provide an heir, or to fulfil the egotistical longing of his father to ally his name with that of an ancient kingdom.

What sort of lonely, frightening life would a little boy taken over by King Fiero have? He had only to look at the frail, shadow of a woman that was the Queen to understand the effects of the man's unreasonable expectations and bullying tactics.

Even if he *wanted* to marry Princess Rosabella, the terms of this agreement would make that impossible. He could never agree to it. He did not want to marry her, but he was beginning to realise that he cared about her.

Now he stood up abruptly, trying to keep his fury at bay. If he gave vent to it and said what was on his mind, he would frighten her. He dragged a hand over his face and felt the scrape of stubble on his jaw. He'd slept badly, with this appalling information churning in his mind, and then had fallen into a fitful sleep as dawn had begun to lighten the sky. He hadn't bothered to shave when he'd finally risen, and had drunk two cups of strong black coffee.

It was late morning when he'd stepped out into the sun to find Princess Rosabella. He'd felt an irrational need to reassure himself that she was alright—though what harm could possibly have come to her in less than twenty-four hours? And yet, what if her father had been dissatisfied with the report back from their disgruntled chaperone? What if Rosabella had been deemed to have been too forward with him, or perhaps not forward enough? Not all damage had to have a physical face, he thought grimly.

If the princess would agree, he needed to get her away from the claustrophobic and watchful atmosphere of the palace. He'd only be able to talk freely to her where she could forget about the possibilities of staff eavesdropping on their conversation.

He spent too long wrapped in his thoughts and now she was watching him, two faint lines between her eyebrows, as if she was trying to predict what he might do or say next.

'You mentioned my hat?' Her voice was soft, as though she felt she had to tread gently or risk him cracking in some way.

He nodded, dragging himself back to the present, and the realisation that whatever he did, he'd be destroying her happiness. The weight of that knowledge would be impossible to carry and ever feel free again.

'I went into a boutique to buy a towel and swimming trunks. They had straw hats like yours on sale, and I noticed that they were made on Palosia. They're very beautiful. Can you tell me about them?'

Rosabella bent, retrieved her gardening hat from the stone paving and handed it to him. It was woven from coarse straw, with a rounded crown and up-turned brim. An iridescent blue feather was stuck under the green ribbon that was tied around it.

'Hats have been woven on Palosia for hundreds of years, but the art had been all but lost by the turn of the century. It's thanks to my mother that it's been revived.'

'Your *mother*?'

Her expression had become guarded. 'Why would you want to know about hats?'

He conceded to himself that her question was a fair one. Why would he want to know? But it wasn't really the hats; it was Rosabella he wanted to know about.

'Because you wear them, and I'm interested in you.'

Her watchful expression vanished but the incredulity which replaced it tugged at his heart.

'I thought you were here to finalise things…with my father. Not to be interested in me.'

He nodded and tried to keep his tone neutral. 'I accept that my intention was to discuss matters with your father. But now I want to discuss things with you. Only, not here.' He looked around, spreading his hands. 'I'd like to take you out—have a proper conversation. Obviously, I'd have to ask permission from your father, but I can't see that he'd refuse.'

'No, he wouldn't refuse. But he might make sure he had eyes and ears at the next table.' She reached out and took her hat back from him, turning it in her hands. 'But,' she said, 'If you really want to know about the hats…'

Her voice wavered, and he wanted to remove the hat, take her hands in his and make her lift her gaze from where it was fixed on a spot on the stone slabs beneath their feet, and meet his. 'I have another idea.'

CHAPTER TEN

ROSABELLA BUSIED HERSELF with the display of hats in the reception area of the Palosia hat workshop. A volunteer receptionist manned the desk, next to the double doors which led to the small manufacturing unit. She'd positioned herself between the desk and the entrance so that she could greet Luca when he arrived.

If he arrived.

She glanced at her watch for the tenth time. It was five minutes past the time they'd arranged and she decided to give him another five before concluding that he definitely wasn't coming.

Today was one of the two she spent at the charity each week, and it was her favourite time. One of the palace drivers had dropped her off at eight o'clock that morning and, as usual, the time had flown.

Until now.

She'd done her usual round of the busy factory floor, where some women were weaving straw into braids and others were turning those braids into rudimentary hat shapes, using wooden blocks of varying sizes. In a separate room, the final designs were being created. Some were bespoke orders, while others were destined for boutiques, such as the one the Count had visited, or to fulfil orders from abroad.

Finally, she put her head round the door of the crèche and

then the school room, where the children of employees were cared for and taught.

The glass entrance door swung open again but she did not look up. She was bound to be disappointed.

Luca saw her immediately. She stood before a display of elegant hats woven of fine straw in different colours. They were the sort of hats which could have been seen at any famous race meeting or royal garden party, and a far cry from the battered model which Rosabella had worn in the garden.

She was dressed in a soft linen skirt and a cream blouse with a rounded collar. Her hair was pulled into a messy bun, secured with clips that sported tiny butterflies. His eyes followed the movements of her elegant hands as she adjusted the position of a particularly spectacular, bright-red hat.

'Good morning.'

She looked up and their eyes clashed, and he was rewarded with another of those wide, dimpled smiles he craved.

'You came.' She stood up, straightening her skirt and putting a hand to her hair.

'Did you doubt it?'

'No…yes. To be honest, I did think you might change your mind.'

'Why would I do that? I wanted to see you. And to learn about the hats.'

She took him on a tour of the premises, answering his questions. The industrious atmosphere impressed him, and the childcare facilities impressed him more, but what intrigued him the most was the difference in Rosabella. Rather like the changed person she became in the garden, she was engaged in what she was doing, ready to talk to him with passion and without reserve about what she showed him. She knew all the workers and their children by name and demonstrated care and respect for them. Her interest in them was obviously reciprocated. Many of the women asked after the Queen with concern.

When they'd concluded the tour, he bought them coffee from the work canteen and carried the tray out into a small garden. Tables and chairs were grouped under shady trees and tubs of crimson geraniums marked the edges of the paths.

'My mother established this outdoor space.' Rosabella led the way to a table, stopping to pick a yellowing leaf from a plant. 'There's a children's play area too.' She nodded towards a climbing frame and swings. 'For Palosia, at the time it was innovative, but many other businesses have followed her lead.'

They sat opposite each other and Luca placed a mug of coffee in front of her. 'Thank you. My mother is much loved and respected.'

'Yes, I can see that. Do you know what motivated her?'

Rosabella's face clouded and she dropped her gaze, tucking a strand of hair behind an ear.

'I suppose she…needed a distraction. She started by beginning to restore the palace gardens, and then she had this idea.'

'A distraction from what?' He tried to hold her gaze, but she looked away. He watched her chest rise on a deep breath and he thought she was going to shake her head and rebuff his question. She wrapped both her hands round the coffee mug, her knuckles whitening, raised it and took a sip before replacing it carefully on the table.

'From the fact that my birth had robbed her of the chance to have any more children. And I wasn't a boy.' When she looked up at him again, her expression was stricken. She shook her head. 'I'm sorry. I shouldn't have said that. It's not something you need to know.'

There was a deep sadness in her that he wanted to understand, and perhaps alleviate. Understanding people who had been traumatised by events over which they'd had no control was something he did very well. He should be able to do it for Rosabella. The connection he was beginning to feel to her should make it easier, but instead he found himself hesitating, searching for the right words, aware that getting this right was terribly important—although the reason he felt that way hovered at the edge of his mind, just out of reach.

'Rosabella… May I call you that?'

She nodded, the line of her jaw tense, her hands still gripping the mug. 'Most people call me Rosa.'

'Rosa, then. And you must call me Luca.'

She darted a look at him. 'I…don't know if I can.'

'Try. You'll see it isn't so difficult.' Very gently, he lifted her fingers away from the mug. 'I'm afraid you're going to crush that mug.' He placed her hands on the table. 'Say it, just once. Nobody else is listening.'

She took a couple of breaths. 'Luca?' she whispered, and then half-smiled. 'Luca.'

'See?' He lifted his own mug and swallowed a mouthful of coffee. 'Not so difficult. Now, tell me why you've taken your mother's guilt and regret onto your own shoulders. Because I think that is what you've done.'

Luca thought he knew the answer, but he knew that persuading victims to articulate their feelings themselves could help to rationalise their thoughts.

Rosabella's eyes were fixed on her hands, and he had the strong feeling that she wished he'd kept holding them. He'd wanted to. He'd wanted to turn her hands over in his and stroke his thumbs across her palms and the pale insides of her wrists, but he knew how alien a man's touch was to her. Most of all, he wanted her to feel in control.

'Because it was my fault.'

He had to lean in to hear her.

'Why else?'

'How we're born and whether we're girls or boys are two things over which we have zero control. Someone has imposed that guilt on you all your life.' He leaned back in his chair, mentally reaching for the self-control that would enable him to keep anger from his voice. 'I'm guessing it was your father,' he ground out, his jaw rigid.

What looked like a self-deprecating smile curved her lips and she nodded. 'Of course, logically I know I wasn't to blame, but emotionally… Until quite recently 'what if' was something I asked myself frequently.'

'What did you wish could be different?'

'I wished—still wish—that my father did not resent us… my sister and me, or our mothers.'

Surprise made Luca's eyes snap back to hers. 'You have a *sister*?'

'A half-sister—Sofia. Her mother was our father's first wife. She was very beautiful, but not of royal blood, and she ran away after Sofia was born, back to her true love.' She nipped at her bottom lip. 'My father divorced and banished her and married my mother very quickly afterwards, needing a son to secure the succession, since the law of Palosia states that only a male can rule. But he got me, and after that my mother couldn't have any more children. So, you see… well, you see how it could be blamed on me.'

Luca did see, very clearly, and he wanted to punch something, or someone. His hands curled, his fingernails biting into his palms. The reason for Rosabella being offered in a marriage of convenience from an early age suddenly made sense, given the restricted and old-fashioned world of Palosia. And the draconian clause enabling her father to take away a baby son from her, to be raised by him, was the brutal attempt of a man who needed to keep control at all costs trying to order things to enable him to exercise it.

'Where is your sister now?' He hardly dared ask the question.

'She refused to marry the prince our father had chosen for her when she discovered he loved someone else. The union would have cemented an important alliance, but she left her fiancé at the altar, fled to Naples and found the man she'd loved since she was twenty—when she ran away to search for her mother. In the end, she married…for love.'

Her voice cracked and Luca wanted to put his arms around her, stroke her hair and hold her hands—anything to sooth that ragged break in her voice that said almost more than her words could.

After that disaster, the King would have felt humiliated and out of control of his own family and his kingdom. No wonder, then, that Rosa was subjected to such close scrutiny and her movements so restricted. The King was doing everything humanly possible to prevent a repeat performance and to ensure that, if Rosa gave birth to a son, he would have control over him.

'Are you in touch with Sofia? Where is she?'

'Yes, but she and Marco, her husband, are both involved in their businesses. Sofia is an interior designer now, and he's the CEO of Krafty. He set it up as an online marketplace for small businesses and entrepreneurs, but it grew very quickly. Marco is hugely successful.'

'Sofia is married to Marco Stewart?' Luca blew out a breath. 'That's amazing. In my legal work I frequently cite Krafty as a model for relationships between management and employees. They have an excellent record in that regard, and for their equal opportunities ethos. It's massively successful on a global scale. Marco Stewart is a very wealthy man.'

'When Sofia first met him, he was a poor artist training to be a sculptor. The thing is, Sofia didn't believe in love. Her mother abandoned her when she was one, so she always felt unloved and unlovable. Our father didn't help, banishing her mother and wiping Sofia from the line of succession, even if she had a son. But she had the courage to stand up to him and for her rights. Love found her and she embraced it, in spite of everything.'

Luca felt an unfamiliar sensation in his chest, as if his heart were being squeezed tight and his lungs crushed. He sucked in a deep, deliberate breath, trying to ease the feeling. Was this what Rosa hoped for? That love would find her, even though she was being forced into a marriage of convenience designed to ensure the succession and bolster the ego of his now dead father? He remembered the flash of what he'd interpreted as hope in her eyes, and he needed to take another breath.

She had all the qualities anyone could wish for: beauty, kindness, generosity and thoughtfulness. And, from his tour of the factory, he'd learned that she cared very much for the people of Palosia. He did not doubt that she had a deep capacity for love. Not only would she make a wonderful partner, but she'd also be a great ruler, if her narrow-minded and autocratic father could only see beyond the boundaries of the antiquated and self-centred conventions that bound him.

Rosa deserved all the love in the world, but he could not give it to her. By binding Luca to her in a betrothal of convenience to boost his own ego and wealth, his father had made sure of that. Anger churned in his stomach. Rosa needed someone to love her unconditionally, not a husband who had been forced on her for the sake of convenience. The battle he'd fought against his father's control had been hard won, and he wasn't about to concede defeat by consenting to the marriage agreement.

* * *

Luca's lips were pressed together in a straight line, his jaw taut, and anger seemed to fight a battle with compassion in his dark eyes. But Rosa's attention was dragged away from his face to the drumming of his fingers on the table. His breathing was steady but deep, as if by concentrating on every breath he was controlling whatever it was that had angered him.

She wished he'd continued to hold her hands. Luca's hands on hers had been gentle yet sure. The touch of his fingers had sent *that* sensation buzzing up her arms and down into the pit of her stomach, where it had settled into a feeling of yearning and anticipation of what might have come next, if circumstances had been different.

Above all, his light caress had rekindled that sensation of being safe. Perhaps that was why she longed for it to continue. The urge to lace her fingers through his, to anchor herself to him, to prolong that sense of security, was powerful.

The coffee was cold but she lifted the mug and took another sip, just to give her hands something to do in case they reached over to cover his drumming fingers. She glanced across at him and he closed his eyes for a second, then leaned back in his chair and raked his fingers through his hair, before folding his arms across his chest.

His fingers tapped against his biceps. He'd rolled up his shirtsleeves to the elbows, revealing tanned, muscled forearms and a slim watch on his wrist. Dazedly, Rosabella wondered about the time and, as if reading her mind, Luca glanced at his watch.

'It's just after midday. How soon can you get away?'

'Get away?' She wasn't sure she'd heard him correctly. 'I don't "get away". The palace driver will collect me. If there's any shopping I need to do, he'll take me to the appropriate stores and wait for me, then he'll take me back to the palace.'

'Seriously?'

She nodded. 'When Sofia ran away the first time, I was sixteen and still very much restricted to the palace and the gardens. But when she fled from her wedding my father became even more paranoid. He's convinced I'll try to run away too, to join Sofia. It's a little better since Sofia married, but he keeps track of what I'm doing. That's why the garden, and the two days a week I spend here, are so precious to me.'

She looked at him, hoping he might understand. 'He knows where I am, so I'm left alone and I can feel a little…free.'

Luca leaned forward and rested his forearms on the table, holding her gaze with his.

'With your permission, I'll cancel the driver and take you back to the palace when you're ready. When *we're* ready.'

'But my father…'

'I'll send a message to your father with the driver. He may not like it, but he'll accept it. He agreed we should take time to get to know each other. Besides, he won't do anything to jeopardise his relationship with me. He wants this too much.'

He gestured between them, and Rosa liked the way it made her feel, as if she had an equal say in what they were doing. 'And, if he is angry with you, I'll deal with it.'

The initial tide of anxiety that had washed over Rosa ebbed a little, to be replaced by a stirring of excitement which she hardly dared to acknowledge. Could she do this—go off with Luca while nobody else would know where they were, or what they were doing? It felt frightening. She remembered how she used to push herself to do scary things when she still thought she could earn her father's admiration, or simply his attention. Could she push herself to do this, when she knew it might anger him, even though Luca would let him know?

'Well?' Luca raised an eyebrow at her. 'Was it presumptuous of me to book a restaurant for lunch?'

The idea of being seen in a restaurant with a stranger was
alarming but was also exciting. Besides, Luca no longer felt
like a stranger to her. She'd spent longer with him and talked
to him more than almost anyone else she could think of, outside her family and the staff at the palace. When he reached
across the table and took her hand, she knew she'd throw
caution to the winds of Palosia—because with her hand in
his she could face her fears and she'd be safe.

CHAPTER ELEVEN

THE DOOR OF the low-slung car closed with a soft thud, and Luca strode around the front of it and slid in behind the wheel. He turned to look at Rosa, who was fumbling with the seatbelt.

'Allow me.' He took the buckle from her and clicked it into place. Then he reached into the door pocket and pulled out a leather case containing a pair of over-sized sunglasses.

'Yesterday afternoon, when I had the idea of taking you out, I bought these for you.'

'I already have sunglasses. They're in my bag.' She reached into her tote.

'Yes, I know you do, but these are about twice the size of yours, and one of the latest designer models.' He removed the glasses from their case, unfolded them and handed them to her.

'Oh…thank you. That was very kind, but why do I need extra-large sunglasses?'

'You'll see. Now, is your hat secure?'

'It will be, when I've undone my hair. Why?'

Rosabella pushed the sunglasses onto her face and began to pull the butterfly pins from the loose bun at the back of her head. Luca turned away and busied himself with his own seatbelt as her fair hair began to fall over her shoulders like spun silk. He gripped the steering wheel in both hands and pushed himself back into his seat. At the touch of a button the engine came to life with a throbbing roar, then he reached for another button and the soft top of the car began to retract.

'This is why.'

He heard her soft gasp. 'Luca, no!' Rosabella's fingers curled around his forearm, gripping tightly.

'What is it?' He turned to look at her but her eyes were hidden behind the enormous dark lenses of the sunglasses. Was he taking this too fast? It was a lot to expect of her, but he was afraid she might lose her nerve and ask to go home if he gave her too much time to think about where she was and what they were doing.

He halted the retraction mechanism of the roof. 'It'll be okay, Rosa. I'll look after you.'

Her grip on his arm eased a little.

'Yes, I know you will,' she said, softly. 'But with the roof down I'd feel so…exposed.'

'Mmm. I understand why you feel that way but look at it like this…' He lifted her hand away from his arm but continued to hold it lightly. 'With the roof and the tinted windows closed, everyone is going to want to peer in to see who is hiding inside. If we let it down, very few people will give a second thought to the couple in it, sensibly protected from the sun by sunglasses and a hat. A few might look at the car, because it's unusual and powerful, but nobody will expect to see Rosabella, the sheltered princess of Palosia, in plain sight, and so they're unlikely to recognise you.'

He placed her hand in her lap and picked up her hat from the footwell, fitting it carefully onto her head. Her smooth forehead creased as she considered his words, and he could see indecision at war with determination in her expression.

Then she nodded. 'Okay. I suppose that could be true.' The tremor in her voice made his chest ache. He didn't want her to feel anxious or stressed. What should be an easy, fun excursion might be a massive ordeal for her. 'But…'

'But I promise that, if you aren't comfortable, we'll put the roof up again. You just have to say the word.'

He watched her face as he pressed the button again, seeing her jaw clench and her shoulders stiffen, but this time she didn't try to stop him. He eased the car into the stream of traffic as the roof folded itself away.

At the first set of red traffic lights, his theory was proved correct. A few passers-by glanced at the driver and his passenger before sliding covetous eyes over the sleek black body and silver trim of the car. When the lights changed to green, he pressed the accelerator and relished the deep roar of the engine and thrust of power as they pulled away from the surrounding traffic.

Soon they'd left the town behind them and were climbing up a switch-back road that swooped higher and higher up the mountainside, revealing spectacular views of valleys and the coastline with every turn. A warm breeze blew into their faces laden with the perfume of summer flowers. Sliding a sideways look at Rosa, he could see that she was smiling. He hoped that meant she was beginning to relax.

The restaurant he'd chosen was at the top of the mountain pass, with sweeping views down to where the sea churned against the rocks. Luca hit the button to kill the engine and at first silence descended on them, until the song of birds and the chirp of insects intruded on it. He unclipped his seatbelt and turned to face Rosa.

'Did you enjoy the ride?'

Her answer came in the form of the wide, spontaneous smile she gave so rarely. She nodded. 'Oh yes, I did. Thank you. It was unlike anything I've ever done before. I'm already looking forward to the drive down again.'

He laughed, tipping his head back against the head rest. 'We'll go down a different way and then follow the coast road until we can cut back across the island to the royal estate.'

A smart *maître d'* welcomed them, and if he recognised Rosa he was too discreet to show it. He led them across the restaurant, weaving through tables of diners, out onto a stone terrace to a table in the corner. There were views up and down the coast, but their position was shaded and given privacy by a climbing rose that rambled over a wooden trellis above them. He handed them leather-bound menus and a wine list and rattled off a list of special dishes of the day.

Rosabella opened her menu but quickly snapped it closed again.

'Isn't there anything you'd like?' Luca berated himself silently. He should have tried to discover what she liked before presenting her with a complicated menu like this. He recalled how she'd pushed the food around her plate and hardly eaten anything at all at the palace lunch on the day they'd officially met. Perhaps she had very specific tastes, or even food intolerances.

'No, it's not that.' She shook her head. 'This may sound ridiculous to you, but I've never had to choose from a menu before. I have no idea where to begin. I'm sorry.'

Luca took the menu from her hands and placed it on the table. 'It's I who should apologise. It was clumsy of me not to have realised that.'

Rosa removed her hat and shook out her hair. He reached out and took the hat from her and hung it on the back of a vacant chair.

'Thank you. Please don't apologise. You probably can't even begin to imagine how exciting and strange this is for me.' She glanced over her shoulder, along the terrace, as if to check that they hadn't been spotted or followed. 'It's strange, in a wonderful way, just to be here alone. It's liberating.'

Her voice dropped and she frowned. 'Having lunch at a restaurant may be an everyday thing for you, but it's the sort of normal thing which my father's rules have prevented me from doing. It's what he is so afraid of.'

The anger Luca felt every time he thought about how her life had been restricted, her experiences curtailed, coiled in his stomach again. His eyes fell on the collection of bright butterfly clips she'd pulled out of her hair and put in the pocket of her blouse. Rosa herself was like a beautiful, delicate butterfly trapped in a net, longing to find freedom in the sunshine and fresh air.

As they'd driven up the mountain the breeze had whipped warm colour into her cheeks, and her eyes shone, despite her frown. Suddenly Luca wished, very much, that he could set her free.

Their eyes met. 'You're not alone, Rosa. You're with me.'

Her lashes fluttered down to her cheeks. 'Alone with you, is what I meant,' she murmured the heat in her cheeks deepening.

'I want you to enjoy your day out, without thinking about your father. He's very afraid of losing control of you, just as you say he lost control of Sofia. He's made sure you're never exposed to temptation in case you give into it. He fears that a taste of freedom will become an appetite you can't suppress. And, talking of appetites, shall I order for both of us? You don't have to eat anything you don't like.'

Rosa loved it all, from the artisan bread dipped in superb local olive oil, to the delicate home-made pasta in a spicy sauce and the fresh strawberries served with bowls of thick cream and sugar to dip them in.

She ate with relish, having an appetite which felt sharpened by the fresh air and the sense of indulging in something slightly illicit. Was this how Sofia had felt when she'd abandoned Palosia and found Marco again? As if she'd cast off shackles and seized control of her own destiny?

Just for this one day, she wanted to enjoy how it felt to be free. She had no doubt that, when her father heard Luca had taken her to a restaurant unchaperoned, he might forbid her from returning to the workshop for her scheduled day later in the week. Whatever Luca thought, King Fiero would not be willing to allow her to test the limits of her freedom without payback. Her days at the hat workshop were the highlight of the long weeks, especially during the winter when there was less to do in the garden.

Out here, at the top of the mountain, eating delicious food with Luca, she felt brave and invincible. She'd tried to obey the rules all her life, but the emotion swelling in her heart right now did not feel good or obedient. It felt like rebellion, and it felt empowering and glorious.

Except, confronting her father wouldn't be like this. Her stomach dropped at the idea of the interview she would have to have with him: the rage he'd fly into, the threats he'd issue. It would be frightening, and her father would use his skill with words to shred her determination, to cut her down to something small, worthless and as useless to him as she'd ever been. When she told him she refused to enter into a loveless marriage, he'd pour scorn on her romantic notions of love and demand to know where she thought she was going to find a man who might love her.

She had no illusions about that, and she'd tell him so. She knew she would never find anyone to love her, but she'd rather live out her life on her own than be contracted to a man who married her for the wrong reasons—to satisfy greed or ambition, or to provide the heir her father needed.

But nothing he said, or did, could make her marry anyone. She had to find a way to sustain the bravery she felt now, until all this was over.

The thought that the day would soon end and she'd have to say goodbye to Luca tore at her heart. This day of freedom with Luca would be the day she looked back on all her life. His deep eyes seemed to see into her soul and his gentle touch set her nerve endings alight with a fire which burned to her core, melting any resistance she might have. These vivid memories would keep her going through darkness and despair, if necessary. She'd cherish them so that she could always remind herself of the joy to be found in the world in simple, every-day things.

She could not marry Luca, because he would never love her, but she'd never forget how he made her feel and would forever be grateful for the memories they were making on this day.

'Hey.'

Rosabella's attention snapped back to the present, where the warm breeze lifted the ends of her hair and the sun scattered diamonds on the sea below. The concern she saw in Luca's eyes made her heart squeeze. She smiled at him, grateful for it.

'Hey to you too.'

'Are you okay? This has been quite a day for you. Please tell me if you feel you've had enough of adventure, or when you'd like to go home.'

'Go home?' Surely he didn't believe she wasn't enjoying herself? 'No, not yet… I was just thinking.'

'I could see that.' His mouth did that little lift at one corner that she loved. 'Good thoughts?'

'Mostly. I'm trying to make sure I remember everything, so…'

Luca leaned back in his chair and his gaze on her face felt warm. 'Do you remember our meeting in the maze, twenty years ago?'

She smiled, surprised. 'A little, yes.' She traced a pattern with a fingertip in the condensation on her glass of iced water. 'I remember a boy—a boy who seemed very tall to me—being in trouble and lost and I showed him the way out.'

He leaned forward, resting his folded arms on the table. 'That was me.' His eyes held a deep intensity which she couldn't quite understand. 'I was in trouble because I was being taken to meet your father and I was going to be late.'

'You were being taken to meet your future father-in-law, you mean.'

He nodded. 'I was, but I didn't know that. Not then.'

'When did your father choose to tell you?'

Luca's mouth compressed and he turned his face away from her. She saw the grip of his hands tighten on his forearms before he dipped his head.

'He never did. I found out after he died—two weeks ago.'

Rosa felt her eyes fly wide. She'd assumed he would have known for as long as she had that their futures had been decided for them.

'But how is that possible? Why didn't he tell you? I've known for almost as long as I can remember, although I didn't know it was you.'

He was quiet for so long that she thought he wasn't going to answer at all. Perhaps this signalled the end of her glorious day out. He'd drive her home in silence with no explanation forthcoming. What had she said to annoy him so much? She shifted uncomfortably on her chair, wanting to leave, but then he took a long breath and looked up at her.

'My relationship with my father was not happy. He obsessively controlled every aspect of my life, and I rebelled against him. I thought I'd broken the hold he tried to have over me...'

'Luca, I'm sorry. You don't need to tell me this.'

'Yes, I do. You need to know about me. What I'm like. It'll make things easier for you.'

An urgency in his tone made her swallow her protest. She gripped her hands together in her lap.

'My father and I had barely spoken for a year, and before that all our exchanges had been angry. I'd left the family estate and carved out a career for myself, independent of him or my ancestry, and that infuriated him. I felt he was withholding something from me, which he planned to use against me at some time in the future. I assumed it was something to do with my inheritance.'

His smile was grim. 'When he died, I discovered how wrong I'd been. I found out I was engaged to a foreign princess from a country I barely remembered.'

Rosa needed to breathe but her lungs refused to expand beneath the weight she felt pressing on her chest. There was a buzzing in her ears, and she wondered, in an oddly detached way, if there was a swarm of bees passing by. When she heard Luca's voice again, it seemed to come from a distance.

'Rosa, are you alright?' She felt the touch of his hand on her arm, and thought fuzzily how good it felt, and then that she shouldn't get to like it too much because it couldn't last long. 'Rosa...?'

Finally, just as a shadow encroached at the edge of her vision, she gasped, and much-needed oxygen reached her brain. She blinked. 'I'm sorry. I was shocked by what you said. I...'

Luca lifted her water glass and held it to her lips. 'Have some water. Just a sip. You're very pale.'

She shook her head. 'I'm usually pale. It's my complexion. It makes my freckles stand out.' Her words felt muddled. She inhaled another deep breath. Why had she mentioned her freckles?

'I've never noticed them until now, and I think they're beautiful. I'm sorry I had to shock you in order to see them.'

The tenderness in his voice was more than she'd ever heard, from anyone, before. Rosa took the glass from his fingers and swallowed a mouthful of water. 'I just assumed you'd always known. And to find out like that…it must have been shocking.'

'Did you ever wonder why I hadn't tried to communicate with you?'

'No. I was never given the chance to communicate with *you*. I thought you were…'

He arched an eyebrow, his gaze narrowing. 'What?'

'Mmm… I thought you must be like me. Bound to do your duty by your family.'

'I understand why you'd have been forced to accept your duty, especially after your sister defied your father's wishes. All his hopes for an heir now rest with you.'

She massaged her temples with the tips of her fingers. 'To escape my duty to my family and Palosia would be impossible. My life is here and the path I must take has never been in doubt. But…'

She was suddenly dangerously close to telling him that she would never marry him, but she pulled back. What if her admission angered him? He might insist on bringing the day of their marriage forward, to the earliest possible date, on her birthday. If he told her father, she'd be watched every moment of the day and night, in case she tried to run away, as Sofia had.

And yet she was sure Luca cared about her. She saw compassion and comprehension in his dark eyes, but she was not equipped to know if he was sincere. Her mother's warnings echoed in her head. He said he'd look after her, but how could she trust him? Her mother had believed her father's promises and declarations of love, but they'd all been conditional on her producing an heir.

For the first time ever, she questioned her mother's words. Her opinion of marriage had been formed by the way her husband had treated her and, like Rosa, she had no other experience with which to draw a comparison. But not all men were like her father. Sofia had found love with Marco and was ecstatically happy. Perhaps Luca was genuinely kind and considerate.

It felt as if a cloud had passed in front of the sun, dimming the brightness of this precious day, but when she turned her head she could see that the sea still sparkled and the waves still gleamed, foamy and white. She felt utterly confused, but amidst her confusion one thing stood out: more than anything, even if she never saw Luca again after today, she wanted to believe that he was trustworthy and honourable.

'I'm sorry I shocked you.' His voice was gentle. 'Can we not let it spoil the day?'

Luca felt her withdraw from him and it twisted his heart. Once again, he hadn't made allowances for the unnaturally sheltered upbringing she'd had. He should have anticipated how much his revelation would shock her, and he should have considered his words much more carefully.

He needed her to know what he was like. How he'd been taken from the loving home of his grandparents and returned to the castle in Tuscany without warning. How his stubborn determination not to be controlled had infuriated his father, led to bitter arguments and, eventually, estrangement from him. How he'd never known his mother and had always blamed his father for her death. If his mother had lived, perhaps his father would not have been able to arrange this marriage of convenience, or hide it for so long.

Watching Rosa across the table, and seeing the emotions shadowing her face, he wondered if his mother had fought an inner battle with herself, before deciding to defy her husband and ride that dangerous horse. And why, when she'd had a two-year-old son, had her duty to him not been stronger than her need to exert her own will? His grandparents had always insisted that she'd loved him dearly—but, if she'd loved him enough, surely she wouldn't have put herself in danger?

His father had got the heir he wanted, but had she been happy to accept her role of wife and new mother, her independence curtailed, her horizons narrowed? Perhaps she'd been unbearably frustrated and had rebelled against that as much as against the strict controls her husband had imposed on her.

Luca had always felt proud that he'd inherited his rebellious, independent spirit from his mother. King Fiero had gravely restricted Rosa's life, just as his father had tried to curtail his. Both had lost a young, beautiful wife for different reasons, and fear of losing more might have driven their subsequent behaviour.

Perhaps his father had imagined that, by binding his son to the marriage, he'd be securing himself against what the future might hold. He'd never know what had motivated the actions of either of his parents, but considering them from a different point of view made him feel uncertain, and his convictions not as unshakeable as they'd been until now.

He couldn't allow anything at all to interfere with his rock-solid opinion that the idea of this proposed marriage was the result of the greed and ambition of the two men who had brokered it. If Rosa understood how the events of his life had shaped him, perhaps she might understand the reasons why he could never marry her, and be less hurt by his abandonment.

Somehow, it had become important to him that he hurt her as little as possible. He'd watched her bloom over the past few hours like a beautiful, delicate flower unfurling its petals in the sun, and it had warmed his heart and touched him in a way he was reluctant to explore. What if he began to have feelings for her that went beyond not wanting to hurt her when he refused to marry her? What would he do about that?

The anxiety which had gripped her at the prospect of spending the afternoon with him, and possibly being recognised, had melted away and been replaced with openness and enjoyment. It was deeply rewarding to think he could make her happy and he wanted to keep her this way. He'd already been planning how to spend more time with her, but now he wondered if she'd agree to it. Her expression had become distant, and the smile to which he might just be becoming addicted had vanished.

A few petals drifted down to the table on the refreshing afternoon breeze from the rose-covered pergola above them. Luca picked one up and studied it. It was pale pink, darker at the edges, and smooth as satin. He rubbed it between his fingers, picking up its delicate, sweet perfume.

If he brushed his fingers across Rosabella's cheek, would her skin feel equally soft? He wanted to find out and his heart flipped as he imagined reaching across the table to touch her. The thought that she might recoil was what stopped him. He'd already demonstrated impaired judgement more than once today.

'When we met in the maze,' he said, finally catching her gaze again, 'You said you'd been named Rosabella because roses were your mother's favourite flower.'

In the silence that followed he felt as if she was weighing something up, and that her decision would be very important to him. He waited, giving her time, hoping to see the faint lines between her brows smooth away and a trace of her smile return. Her fingers which had been busy pleating the linen napkin stilled, and her face cleared. He released the breath he hadn't realised he was holding.

'Yes.' She nodded. 'I'm surprised you remember that.'

'Do you have a favourite flower?'

He thought she'd have a quick answer, but she glanced at him from beneath her lashes and shook her head. 'I think I do, but then I change my mind. There're so many to choose between, I never have a favourite for very long.'

'Well, then, what would your favourite be today?'

'Maybe roses? Because now they'll always remind me of…this. And you.'

'Even though I almost spoiled the day?'

She smiled, and his heart soared. 'I won't let anything, or anyone, spoil this day.'

CHAPTER TWELVE

MORE THAN ONCE on the drive back, Rosa slid a sideways look at Luca. His eyes were hidden behind dark shades, his mouth serious, with no hint of a lift at the corners. Since their conversation at lunch, he'd been quiet.

The road rose steadily through a series of twists and turns towards the hill on which the palace stood. Luca's hands on the wheel fascinated her. His strong fingers seemed to hold it lightly, but his touch was sure and decisive. The muscles of his thighs flexed beneath the denim of his jeans as he pressed the accelerator, releasing a burst of power and speed from the car.

Rosabella swallowed, her mouth dry, and shifted her gaze away from him to watch the countryside speed by the window. Why did watching his hands on the steering wheel make her remember their touch on her upper arms and wish she could feel it again? Or make her remember the feel of his rock-hard chest beneath her palms? If she put a hand on his thigh, how would it feel?

The gleaming palace came into view above them. Isolated from the outside world in the warm car, close to Luca, she wished the journey could continue for ever, but she knew she had to end it now.

'Luca?'

'Mmm?' He glanced across at her. 'Are you okay?'

'I'd like you to stop, please. There's a place just up ahead, next to a gate.'

'Sure.' He braked, slowing the car steadily, and pulled off the road, where a wooden gate was fitted into a gap in the wall.

As the throb of the engine died away on the still air, he unclipped his seatbelt and half-turned towards her, raising his eyebrows in a question.

'Care to tell me why? We'll be there in a few minutes.'

All at once his presence felt overwhelming. His shoulders blocked out the light. He shifted, flexing one knee and stretching an arm across the back of her seat.

'I…don't want to be seen arriving back with you.' She released the buckle of her own seatbelt and put a hand on the door, fighting the feeling that she wanted to stay here with him, cocooned in a world of their own. She needed to put more space between them before this pull that urged her to close the gap became too strong.

The way these unfamiliar feelings seemed to take control of her, threatening to allow her body to act against her better judgment, was frightening and confusing. Her mind knew exactly how she should behave but her body had developed a will of its own.

Luca regarded her in silence for a moment, before nodding. 'Okay, if that's what you'd like. I did send a message to your father, so he'll be expecting me to bring you back.'

She shook her head. 'It would still raise eyebrows and the staff would speculate. I'd rather avoid that.'

These memories needed to be kept safe, to belong to her alone. The idea of the gossip that would begin to circulate if it became known they'd spent hours together, unchaperoned, and how the facts would be picked over and discussed, made her angry.

Luca removed his sunglasses and dropped them into his shirt pocket, resting a forearm across the top of the steering wheel. His eyes were soft. 'Don't look so fierce.' He smiled. 'Where would you like me to drop you off? You shouldn't walk on the road. It wouldn't be safe, or seemly.'

Rosa tipped her head, indicating the gate. 'That gate leads into the orchards. I can make my way from here up through the garden.'

He leaned forward. 'It looks as if it's locked.'

'Oh, it is, of course. But I know the combination.'

'Do you often let yourself in or out of it if you want to keep your movements secret?'

'No, of course not. I'd never…' She stopped, seeing the quirk of his mouth and the gleam in his eyes. 'Are you teasing me?'

'I am.' His smile sent heat barrelling through her, melting the barrier she'd been about to put up. Teasing was something new to her, and it felt fun and intimate. 'Except for today, when we definitely want to stay under the radar. And, just to keep things above board, I'm going to deliver you safely back into the garden. Nobody can object to that.'

Rosabella wished she could think of a light-hearted response, but her mind had stalled. 'Thank you,' she said. 'Nobody will see me…or us.'

'You're sure you'll be alright?'

'Yes.' Something inside her warmed at his concern. She turned her face towards him. 'Thank you, for the most wonderful day.'

He smiled, again, his eyes crinkling at the corners. 'When will you next be going to the factory?'

She ducked her head and pulled her tote and hat onto her knees.

'On Thursday—the day after tomorrow.'

'I've had a look at a map of Palosia and there's a beach I'd like to explore. It's remote but I think it's accessible. Will you come with me—on Thursday?'

'To the beach?' Rosa pressed a hand against the place in her abdomen where she felt the stirrings of panic.

'You said you like swimming.'

'I… I do. But I haven't swum in the sea for so long. I don't think…'

'You don't have to swim,' he murmured. 'Just be with me.'

'Won't you have gone by Thursday?'

He frowned, running a thumb along his jaw. 'I'll have to leave on Saturday. I'm booked on a flight from Rome to New York on Sunday.'

Something caught in her throat and she swallowed. The reality of the situation felt hard and unforgiving. He would leave on Saturday, and she would never see him again. He'd be furious to be rejected by a shy princess with no other prospects, but he'd soon find someone else, someone worldly and experienced, who could be the wife he needed.

'Well? What do you think, about the beach?'

The beach… She imagined the fine, white sand tickling the soles of her feet and the azure of the water deepening to inky blue where it lay in the shadows of overhanging rocks. She could almost feel the push and pull of the waves, with their foamy crests.

Soon, her life would become…what? She'd had a taste of freedom and normality with Luca, but she knew it would never be repeated. She doubted she'd ever be allowed to leave Palosia, even to visit Sofia and Marco. She'd have to return to marking out the weeks with charity work, caring for her mother and helping to maintain the gardens.

It was difficult to remember that she'd been resigned to

her future until she'd crashed into the hard wall of Luca's chest and he'd stopped her from falling.

She was falling, anyway—falling for him.

But she couldn't give those feelings the oxygen they needed to breathe or grow. She had to stifle them now. Even if she fell in love with Luca, she would not agree to the marriage because he would never be able to love her back. He would find being shackled to a woman to whom he was indifferent frustrating, and he'd want his freedom.

She accepted that she was unlovable. Just because a handsome, charming man had paid her attention for a few hours shouldn't make her doubt it. A loveless marriage was unthinkable. But a marriage in which she loved Luca and he didn't love her back would be much, much worse.

'What do you think?' His voice sounded rough, edgy.

Rosabella dragged her thoughts back to the man who sat so near to her and yet was so utterly out of her reach.

'What do I think?'

What would he say if she told him where her thoughts had been? There was no room for love in a marriage of convenience, and it wasn't necessary for him to spend time with her, even if he had asked for the opportunity for them to get to know each other. All he needed to do was agree on the formalities with her father, so was he simply being polite? She couldn't believe that he really *wanted* her company, but perhaps being with her was a convenient way to fill the time until he returned to New York.

'Yes. About the beach?'

Was it so wrong to want to feel that all-consuming security that his body provided again? Could anyone blame her for snatching a few hours of excitement? She thought of Sofia, and she knew exactly what she'd say if Rosa asked for her advice: *Yes! Go for it!*

'The beach sounds like a wonderful idea.'

'Good. I'm glad you think so. I'll inform your father that I'd like to take you out, again.'

Was he glad, or simply being kind? She wished she had some way of knowing.

'I must go.'

'Yes.'

But she didn't move. She could feel the warmth of his body so close to hers, and hear his steady breathing, a reassuring counterpoint to the way her own was becoming uneven and quick.

'Rosa, I...'

There was a new intensity in his voice and suddenly she was afraid of what he might say. If he'd changed his mind about the trip to the beach... She leaned forward to open the door but her shaking fingers slipped on the smooth metal of the handle.

Luca stretched across her. His forearm pressed against hers as he released the door easily. All her attention focussed on the place where their arms touched. His skin was tanned and smooth, against the fairness of hers, his arm corded with muscle. His hands and fingers looked strong and capable.

Capable of what? How would they feel, stroking over her face or body? The need to discover whether reality matched up to her imagination swelled inside her. She wanted to prolong the contact but that thought frightened her. If she turned, she could press her cheek against the crisp cotton of his shirt and inhale his scent of pine forests and citrus groves, which she could never quite get enough of when he was near.

Most of all, she could press her hands against him and feel that...*safety*. As if he'd always catch her when she fell, or that he'd never let her fall at all. His fingers lingered on the door handle and then brushed across her hand and arm with a feather-light touch as he moved away.

Her chest felt tight, and her heart thrummed against her ribs. She'd been thinking about his touch, longing for it, but afraid of the idea of it. Yet somehow, in the confined space of the car after the day they'd shared, the intimacy of the gesture didn't shock her. It felt normal and right.

If only the fear of rejection didn't stop her from acting on what her body wanted her to do.

Luca pushed the driver's door open and walked round to the passenger side.

The few seconds it took him were not nearly long enough. He needed minutes—scrub that, he needed days—to nail this down. He was practised at ordering his mind. It was an essential skill in his profession. And it was how he'd had the gritty determination to lead the life he wanted, not the one his father had decreed.

His body had always been biddable, so what the hell was going on with it now? And what was it about Rosa that sent it into overdrive, out of control and rushing headlong towards disaster?

Was this going to prove to be his father's ultimate victory over him? The grim irony that he could end up wanting the one woman in the world he would never allow himself to have, because his father had chosen her, was not lost on him.

He pulled open the door. Rosabella swung her long legs out of the low car, clutching her tote and hat. Luca extended his hand and she took it. His fingers closed around hers as he helped her from the car, and he felt as if he could finally breathe out with relief because, at last, he was holding her hand. Then it seemed the most natural thing in the world for him to draw her close, brush his mouth against her temple in the lightest of kisses and hold her, briefly, against his side.

He wanted to pull her into his arms and feel her soft body relax and melt against the hot, hard planes of his. And then he wanted to wrap her hair around his hand, tip her head back and kiss her until neither of them could remember what day it was.

But he released her. He sucked in a long, steadying breath. These thoughts and feelings were inconvenient and impossible. And disrespectful. In a few days he'd be gone, having severed all ties with Palosia and its antiquated customs and restrictions—the ones in which his father had so deviously entangled him. There was no place for him in this world, or for Rosa and him in any world at all. He needed to get back to his own life, and quickly, hopefully without leaving too much damage in his wake.

What, in the name of all things sensible, had made him suggest taking Rosa to the beach? She was vulnerable and innocent, and the quicker he got out of her life, the better it would be for both of them. She needed care and gentleness—*commitment*—not the bitterness his upbringing had left in him, or his soul-deep distrust of the idea of love.

If his father had loved him, surely he would never have entangled him in this impossible web of obligation? If his mother had loved him, would she have gambled with her life when she must have known she might lose it? His grandparents: they hadn't had a choice. They'd had a bereft two-year-old thrust upon them with orders from his father to care for him, until he'd decided he wanted him back.

If he married Rosa, and they had a son, they'd be under pressure for the boy to be taken from them to be raised by King Fiero as his heir. Even if he wanted to marry her, he could never enter into an agreement which would put pressure on them to remove a child from its mother. He'd had the benefit of the love of his grandparents, but the wound left by the death of the mother he didn't remember remained raw.

Just as well, then, that the chances of him marrying her were significantly worse than a snowball's in hell. He should stop this—now.

But his eyes caught Rosa's and held, and he knew he wouldn't do that. Why deny her a little more pleasure? And why deny that he wanted to spend time with her? She was utterly different from any woman he'd ever met, and he found her beguiling and intriguing. When she was relaxed, she was delightful company—fresh and spontaneous—and he loved that he was able to give her that. And, when she looked stressed, he wanted to hold her and erase the worry from her beautiful face. Why was that wrong?

Because it was dangerous, his inner voice told him.

Her eyes were bright, her lips parted in surprise, and he wanted more than anything to cover them with his own and find out how sweet and warm she would taste. He took her hand again. 'I enjoyed the day too. Thank you.' He bent his head and kissed her fingers which were interlaced with his.

'Until Thursday.'

She turned abruptly, the late-afternoon sun sparking golden highlights in her hair. He kept a hand hovering at the small of her back, his fingertips just brushing the waistband of her skirt as she punched numbers into a keypad on the gate post and disappeared through the gate. It slammed shut behind her.

For minutes he watched the place where she'd gone. Frustration at his inability to resist seeing her again made him thrust his fingers through his hair. He swore softly. He didn't understand this. He lived his life within certain rules and he was busy breaking them. When last had he ever not listened to the voice that told him to back off; that he was getting in too deep; that he might lose control of a situation?

His sense for detecting trouble was impeccable, but Rosa had scrambled it. He might have inherited his need for independence from his mother, but the iron grip he had on his emotions stemmed from the cold and unsympathetic upbringing of his father. The idea that he might not win this internal battle was unthinkable.

He slid back into the car and gunned the engine, revving it and pulling onto the road in a shower of gravel then turning downhill, away from the palace. The island roads, with their steep inclines and sudden bends, were perfect for indulging his love of speed and pushing his driving skills to the limit. He needed to focus on something immediate and taxing, away from the girl he'd come here to jilt.

He'd left Tuscany with the intention of dealing with this situation in a few hours. The only person he'd needed to meet with was King Fiero, but that plan had gone to hell from the moment he'd connected, literally, with Rosa. This should have been handled purely as a business transaction. He'd never made the basic error of allowing emotion to interfere with business.

Until now. A situation that should have been quick to resolve had turned into something much more complicated, in which desire was intent on sending the wrong messages to all the wrong parts of his body. He was playing with fire, but the pull of the heat was irresistible, and that was dangerous.

Danger could be addictive.

CHAPTER THIRTEEN

ROSA SHADED HER eyes and studied the beach. In the years before Sofia had first run away to try to find her mother, when the two of them had had freedom to explore their island home—although always accompanied by a member of the palace security detail—this beach had been a no-go area.

From above, it looked like a tiny piece of paradise. Gentle waves lapped at a perfect crescent of white sand and two rocky promontories curved out on either side, protecting the bay and keeping the water calm in most weathers. But the only way to reach it was to scramble down a steep slope, covered with boulders, thorny scrub and tall pine trees. The island abounded in beautiful, safe beaches and to risk breaking bones, trying to reach this one, was unnecessary.

But today they didn't need to scramble down to it because, when he'd collected Rosa from the factory, Luca drove to the tourist marina and hired a motorboat. They strolled along the jetty, Rosa cautiously confident, after their previous outing, that her disguise of a floppy straw hat and big sunglasses would be effective.

The boat was sleek and powerful, with a canopy providing shade. Once they left the protection of the marina, Luca opened up the throttle and they bounced over the ruffled sea, with spray flying over the bows. Rosa laughed; she loved it. Luca seemed to be as skilled behind the wheel of a speedboat as he was behind the wheel of a car. After skimming over the sea for ten minutes, he cut back the speed and turned towards the coast.

Now she watched from the boulder he'd helped her climb onto while he made the boat secure. He'd pulled off his grey T-shirt, and his swimming shorts were slung low on his hips. His broad chest looked as solid as it had felt under her hands, and the way the defined muscles of his arms and shoulders flexed and stretched as he tied a mooring rope firmly around a rock made her clench her fingers and think about running her palms over them, exploring their shape and feel and adding them to her growing store of memories.

She'd never been even remotely close to this amount of beautiful, male skin and muscle. She envied the relaxed way in which he carried himself and how he seemed to be totally at ease and unselfconscious.

Rosa had changed into her modest one-piece swimsuit in the factory bathroom, then had pulled her linen dress back on and tucked her underwear into her bag.

Not that she planned to get wet. The thought of stripping off her dress in front of Luca, even though her black one-piece was not at all revealing, made her cheeks flush hot and her heart lurch.

Luca jumped onto the rocks. 'Are you okay? Not seasick?'

She laughed, tipping her chin up to look at him. 'Not at all. That was so much fun.'

She followed him carefully until he jumped down onto the sand and held out a hand to her. Then somehow he continued to keep his fingers loosely linked with hers as they walked along the edge of the water, their shoulders bumping.

A thrill ran up her arm and down into her middle, making something in her stomach tighten and warm. Should she untangle her fingers from his and put more space between them, or should she leave them there, where she wanted them to be? What would he expect? She wished she knew how she should behave. She longed to appear carefree and relaxed but every cell in her body seemed to be on high alert and aware of the man next to her who swung her hand in his. Perhaps he'd simply forgotten to let go her fingers.

Luca stopped and crouched to smooth out a patch of sand and then pulled her down to sit beside him, releasing her hand. Even though his shoulder continued to brush hers, she felt bereft at the loss of the contact of his fingers as they sat, their feet in reach of the ripples that washed onto the beach, in an almost hypnotic rhythm.

She leaned back on her hands and buried her toes in the damp sand.

'Do you know this beach?' He bent up his legs and propped his elbows on his knees.

'I knew it was here, but it was dangerous to access it from the land, and I've never been on a boat.'

He turned to look at her, his dark brows drawn together. 'You've lived all your life on an island and you've never been on a boat?' He shook his head. 'If I'd known, I would have hired a bigger one. We could have gone further—taken a picnic.'

She pushed herself upright, dusting the sand from her hands and smiling. 'No. This is perfect. If we went further and returned too late, there'd be a search party out looking for me and I'd be in all sorts of trouble. And so would you.'

He shook his head, a dark lock of hair landing on his forehead. 'Not me. Surely it's acceptable to take the woman I'm—?'

'Luca.' She knew her voice sounded impeded and that he'd pick up on it. He seemed to be acutely attuned to her anxieties and insecurities.

'What is it?' He turned towards her, his eyes full of concern.

'Can we please not talk about that? This is such a beautiful place—so unspoilt.'

He raked his fingers through his hair, mussing it more than the wind on the boat had already done. 'And talking about the fact that we're supposed to marry each other will spoil it?'

Rosa pulled her bottom lip between her teeth, frowning, wishing she could be honest with him. But telling him now that she could never marry him would fracture this beautiful day into a million tiny pieces, and she wanted to keep it whole and perfect, to look back on in the future.

'Maybe.'

His narrow gaze was intense, locked onto hers. She tried to pull her gaze away and stare out to sea but the connection between them was too powerful. Her attention was dragged back to his, as if connected by an invisible thread which wouldn't allow her to look anywhere else.

He scooped up a handful of sand, fine as powder, and let it trickle through his fingers. 'If that's what you want, Rosie.' The gentleness in his voice reassured her. He wasn't going to insist on a discussion she didn't want to have. 'May I call you Rosie?'

The lump which formed in her throat stopped her from speaking, so she pressed a hand to her chest and nodded, despite thinking this was no time to start calling each other by familiar names. As soon as he discovered that she'd refuse to marry him, he need never think about her again. Her name would be scrubbed from his mind. From his *life*.

'Would you like to go in for a swim to cool off?' He stood up. 'Either that, or you need to find some shade. You must take care not to get sunburned.'

Rosa nodded, torn between wanting to be honest with him and not wanting to spoil the day with a confrontation. Already the easy atmosphere between them had become charged, and the sight of his tanned, sculpted chest and taut abdomen made her stomach clench and awareness prickle along her nerve-endings.

She dropped her gaze and began to walk along the edge of the water, treading carefully in the soft, wet sand, to where overhanging rocks cast some shade. It was very warm. Sweat trickled between her shoulder blades and pricked her scalp. She lifted her heavy hair off her neck and puffed out a breath, wishing she could be like Luca, unconcerned about baring her body, and could pull off her dress and plunge into the water. She watched as he waded in and then dived beneath the surface, shaking his head as he came up again, flicking his hair back so that a shower of drops arced through the air.

With a body like that, of course he wouldn't mind others looking at it. He flashed a smile at her and raised a hand, and then he struck out, swimming across the bay with long, easy strokes, his powerful arms cutting cleanly through the water. It was years since she'd swum in the sea and the lure of it was strong. She could smell the saltiness of the water and almost taste it on her tongue.

Luca kept swimming until he reached the end of the headland. She watched him pull himself onto the rocks, shake water from his hair and stretch out on his back, his arms folded behind his head.

Perhaps he was far enough away for her to be safe for a few minutes. She'd watch carefully and leave the water as soon as he dived back in. She dropped her hat and sunglasses, grabbed the hem of her dress and tugged it over her head. Before she could over-think it, she ran into the water, letting the shallow waves swirl around her ankles, delighting in the refreshing coldness.

She waded in further until a larger swell brought the water over her knees, around her thighs. It was cold enough on her heated skin to make her gasp, despite the warm sun on her back. She dipped her hands into the sea and let the water run through her fingers, then she took a deep breath and dived in, twisting as she surfaced to float on her back. The sun was dazzling so she closed her eyes. It was sheer bliss, rocking in the gentle swell, supported by the water. She forgot about protecting her face from the sun, forgot about…

Abruptly, she pulled herself upright, planting her feet on the sand beneath her and looked up to check on Luca. He'd vanished. She scanned the rocks for a sign of him, and then the water, but found none.

Then with a splash, he emerged beside her. Rosabella stifled a scream of shock and wrapped her arms around her body. A swell caught her off-balance and she staggered backwards.

Luca's hands caught her shoulders. His grip was just as gentle and firm as she remembered. Her palms splayed out across his chest and, in some detached part of her brain, she thought how much better it was, being able to feel his naked skin beneath her fingers rather than through the fabric of his shirt.

She was close enough to see drops of water clinging to the fine, dark hair that roughened his chest, and an insane urge to drop her head and press her mouth to his skin ambushed her.

He held her steady, but then, instead of releasing her, he eased her towards him until his firm stomach and the long, hard muscles of his thighs pressed along the length of her body as he continued to hold her.

The sun sparkled on the surface of the water and she blinked up at him, dazed. His head dipped and her gaze slammed into his. If he let her go now, she'd slip beneath the surface, her limbs reduced to a shaking mass, but, if she stayed where she was, she would drown in the dark depths of his eyes that seemed to see what she wanted before she knew it herself.

Either way, she was doomed.

'Luca.' Was that *her* voice? It was husky with a need she didn't understand and wouldn't have been able to articulate.

'Mmm?'

She heard the rumble in his chest through her palms, because her ears were filled with the sound of his deep, steady breathing, the beat of her own heart and the rush of blood through her veins.

Dreamily, she moved her hands, searching for his heartbeat, curious to know if it was as wild as her own, and her palm brushed across the hard bead of a nipple.

His sudden, harsh intake of breath shocked her, and her head jerked back.

'I… I'm sorry. I didn't mean to hurt…'

One of his hands released her shoulder and slid to cover hers where it lay on his chest, pressing down. The other slipped across her shoulder blades and down to the small of her back, exerting a gentle pressure that eliminated any space left between them. She circled her free arm around his waist, astonished at how easy it was to make the movement.

'Don't be sorry, Rosie.' His voice had a ragged edge. 'You didn't hurt me. It's just…' His attention dropped to her mouth as he sucked in another sharp breath. 'It's just that I want… I *need*…to kiss you. But I'm so afraid of hurting you.'

'You won't hurt me, Luca.' She lifted her face towards him and saw a mix of confusion and conflict in his eyes. She wanted to resolve whatever internal battle he was engaged in, but mostly she wanted this to last for ever.

His glance moved up and fixed on hers. He lifted his hand and traced his index finger across her bottom lip and then shuddered as she opened her mouth and sucked on his fingertip.

'Dear God, Rosie,' he breathed, tipping her chin up with

his finger, and she could feel the moistness from her mouth on its tip. 'I shouldn't do this. It's not…'

'Luca, please. I want you… I *need* you…to kiss me.' She rose onto her toes, dragging her body against his, feeling every muscle in him tense beneath her touch. He coiled her braided hair around his hand and gently eased her head back, his gaze fused with hers.

'Rosie, are you sure?' His voice was a whisper against her lips.

'Yes. Oh, yes.'

As his mouth finally found hers, sensation swamped everything else. His kiss was tentative, then firm but gentle. He eased away from her for a moment, pressing his lips to her forehead, but she reached up and buried her fingers in his hair, pulling him down again. He breathed in, his chest expanding against hers and then he claimed her again, his mouth moving restlessly, easing her lips apart to allow his tongue to stroke against hers.

Rosa felt as if she'd finally found something she'd been searching for all her life. As if everything she'd ever done, every thought she'd ever had, had been leading up to this moment. As if she'd found home and never wanted to leave its safety again.

And yet it also felt shockingly new, unbearably exciting and erotic, and her body screamed for more, although more of what she didn't know. She just wanted this not to stop; to see where it would take them both.

How was it possible, she wondered in the last lucid moment before a surge of need and white-hot physical desire swept her away, to feel so completely safe in the arms of this rock of a man, yet at the same time teeter on the edge of something terrifying and dangerous?

CHAPTER FOURTEEN

HE HADN'T MEANT to kiss her. It was wrong and he needed to stop. Perhaps he could have, if the communication between his brain and his body hadn't malfunctioned. But who was he kidding? Somone had pressed 'override' and that some-one was him.

Rosa tasted just as sweet and warm as he'd imagined she would, since that moment when their bodies had collided and he'd held her briefly against him. Because it was no use pretending he hadn't thought about it every time he'd seen her and most of the time when he hadn't.

He'd persuaded himself that he wanted to get to know her better so that he could explain to her, in as reasonable and gentle a way as possible, that he could never marry her. And he did want that. She deserved to be treated with care and respect. Her father had agreed with his suggestion with scepticism, no doubt thinking that it was easier to humour him than to object. Luckily her father couldn't see him now.

He wanted to make sure she'd be alright when he left her. But he wanted this so much more. The hot sun, the dazzling light on the sea and the cold water seemed to have induced a kind of madness in him. He felt driven by a need simply to be here with her, in this moment.

He felt as if he'd known her all his life. He smiled against her mouth at that thought. Technically, he'd known her since he'd been thirteen years old. Imagining her in his arms, her mouth beneath his and more, had been the subject of his waking and sleeping dreams for days.

She should have *stayed* in his imagination, but even as he acknowledged the folly of what he was doing he knew that, whatever happened in the next few minutes, days, or the rest of his life, he would never regret this.

She was warm and soft, her arms around him taut, her legs against his thighs long and lean. Her fingertips trailed over his back, straying innocently into the zone at the base of his spine, which sent a charge of electricity to his groin.

He tried to suppress a groan, but knew he'd failed when her whole body tensed against his, her hands came up to bury themselves in his hair and she began to kiss him back with an unpractised, wild fervour that threatened to part him from every last vestige of his shredded self-control. She swayed against him as the sea swirled around them and on the next swell he slid his hands behind her thighs and lifted her, so that her chest was pressed against his and her legs wrapped around his waist.

The contact, the friction, between them was building to beyond bearable and he sank to his knees. She gasped against his mouth as the cold water lapped at their shoulders.

With a monumental effort, Luca pulled his mouth from hers and cupped her face in his hands. 'You're cold. I'm sorry...'

She shook her head. 'No. I'm so warm, against you.' She pressed closer to him and then lightly licked along his jaw, making him clamp it beneath her tongue. 'And you taste so good.'

He tightened his arms around her. 'Try to be still, Rosa.' His voice hissed through his clenched teeth. He rested his forehead against hers, his chest heaving as he fought for control.

She pulled back her head and he saw the focus returning to her wild eyes. Her arms slid from around his neck and her hands came to rest on his chest. Her gaze dropped.

'Luca, I'm sorry. I'm doing this all wrong. But I…'

His heart squeezed as she shook her head, avoiding his eyes. 'No, no, you're not. Rosa, look at me. *Look at me.*'

But she shook her head again. He slipped his hands into her hair and drew her towards him, cradling her head in the place where his neck met his shoulder. She began to shiver. Holding her tightly against him, Luca stood and carried her out of the sea. He gently allowed her body to slide down his until her feet touched the sand.

'I'm sorry,' she said again. 'I should never have…'

He kept holding her against his chest and circled his other arm around her waist, holding her firmly. He dropped his cheek to rest on the top of her head.

'You should never have…what?' He turned his head and kissed her hair. 'Come to the beach with me? Gone swimming?' He took her hands, drawing them up to his chest.

'All of those things. But mostly I shouldn't have kissed you.'

'I was under the impression that I kissed you first.'

'But I kissed you back.'

'Mmm. You did.'

'And I did it all wrong, so you wanted to stop.'

'It was I who was in the wrong. I shouldn't have kissed you. I wasn't going to but—'

'But I threw myself at you.'

She looked stung, hurt and crushed, and she turned away from him, brushing her fingers across her eyes.

'Rosie, it's not like that. Listen to me.' He reached out and circled his fingers around her wrist. 'Please.'

She pulled away from him, but she stopped walking away,

digging her feet into the sand and wrapping her arms around her body. Her body, which had fitted so perfectly against his own that it felt as if they'd been cast in moulds to match each other. He'd felt the hard peaks of her breasts through the fabric of her swimsuit, and the restless shift of her thighs around his waist had almost driven him over the brink.

This was wrong, and torturous. He'd tantalised her, while fighting his body to prevent them from going any further. He'd always considered himself a match for temptation; he'd always been able to walk away from it. He still could, he told himself, but this was way more difficult than anything he'd ever had to do before. This would mean hurting someone. And hurting someone whom he realised he cared about more deeply than was safe or sane.

'What?' Her voice trembled. 'What more is there to say?' She scrubbed at her face with the heels of her hands. 'I just feel so…*ashamed.*'

From the way she'd responded to him, Luca had no doubt that she'd never been kissed before, and now he needed to make sure that she didn't look back on it as something shameful or secretive. He inhaled deeply, steadying himself, because he needed to hold her and reassure her, but his body wouldn't want to stop at that.

Stepping behind her, he put his arms around her waist. The top of her head fitted perfectly beneath his chin.

'Wanting to kiss someone is nothing to be ashamed of, Rosie. It's a way of expressing your feelings when you can't find the words. It's a way of communicating with actions.'

She turned her head and pressed her cheek to his chest. 'I wanted to kiss you. But you wanted to stop. And I feel ashamed, because I wanted more and you didn't.'

'I wanted to kiss you, too. And I didn't want to stop, Rosie.'

She twisted in his arms, backing away, pressing her hands against his chest. Her eyes were shiny.

'Please, Luca, don't lie to me. I can bear most things, but I don't want to have to bear that. Be honest with me, even if the truth hurts.'

He reached out and brushed away a tear that had escaped with the pad of his thumb, afraid that his touch might send her running from him. She flinched but she didn't pull away.

'Why,' he asked, cupping her cheek in his palm, 'Would you think I'm lying? I didn't want to stop, but if we hadn't stopped then I wouldn't have been able to.'

He waited, watching her eyes dip and rise to his face again, her teeth catching her lip and releasing it, her chest lifting in a shaky breath.

'I don't believe you,' she eventually said, her voice barely above a whisper. 'Because nobody will ever want to kiss me, so why should you?'

If this was how a mix of fury and compassion felt, he didn't like it. It was confusing as hell. He wanted to punch something, or preferably someone, but at the same time he wanted to focus all his energy on making her feel safe and desirable. *Lovable.*

'Who,' he asked, fighting to keep his voice level, 'Has made you believe that about yourself? Because it's so far from the truth, it'd be laughable if it wasn't so cruel.'

Knowing that pulling her close would catapult him straight back into the danger zone, but not caring, he slid his hands down her sides, feeling her shiver as his fingers traced over her rib cage, then wrapped her in a tight embrace.

'I've always known I'm not lovable, Luca,' she said into his chest. 'My father has always made that clear. That's why he arranged for me to marry you. He said I should be grateful he'd found a husband for me.'

'Believe me, Rosa, that is criminally untrue. You're beautiful, kind, gentle and generous. Men would be lining up to marry you in their dozens, if your father hadn't kept you under such insane control. My own father was a greedy, ambitious man who saw our marriage as a way to advance his status as a member of a royal family.'

He adjusted his arms around her, settling her closer. 'Along with you, your father gave him several vineyards which adjoin what is now my estate in Tuscany, increasing its value enormously—and to seal the deal an emerald mine in Brazil, on the birth of a son.' He tried to keep distaste out of his tone.

Rosa tipped up her head, squinting into the sun. He lifted a hand and shielded her eyes from the glare.

'He's giving so much away. What's he getting in return for me?'

Luca smoothed a hand over her hair, tucking a stray curl behind her ear. He took his time, choosing his words carefully.

'There've only been boys born in my family for generations. It's no accident that King Fiero sought out the Montenale name when he decided to secure his lineage. The promise of a son is all he wants—our son.'

CHAPTER FIFTEEN

LUCA RETRIEVED HER things from the shade and Rosa put on her hat and sunglasses. She pulled the silk ribbon, crusty with dried salt, from the end of her braid and Luca helped her to unravel her damp hair. He brushed his fingers through it, spreading it over her shoulders and down her back.

She knew it would dry in unruly curls and waves, guaranteed to give Luisa a headache if she saw it, but that felt trivial. They sat on the sand until her swimsuit was dry enough for her to pull on her dress again, and then they walked along the beach to the boat.

The return journey held none of the fun Rosa had felt earlier. The breeze had freshened, whipping up waves that lifted the boat then dropped it with a thud into troughs. Rosa clung to her seat, feeling cold and slightly ill. She shivered.

Luca lifted a hand from the wheel and reached for the towel he'd used earlier to brush sand from his body. He dropped it over her shoulders, then quickly took control of the boat again as it lurched over another wave. She gripped the towel in her fists under her chin, grateful for the protection it gave from the sharp wind.

Luca, she thought, had to be one of the most thoughtful and kind people she'd ever met. It was difficult to remember that he was also the tough, ruthless lawyer who fought tirelessly for the rights of his clients. And that he'd come to Palosia to discuss the business details of their marriage deal.

Had her father ever treated either of his wives with this sort of care and attention? She supposed he must have, in the early days of courtship and marriage. She knew her mother had been overwhelmed by his extravagant gifts and promises.

Promises and gifts were easy to give. But the way Luca paid quiet attention to her, and took notice of her needs almost before she was aware of them herself, was a much rarer and more precious thing.

If she ever fell in love, it would be with someone who had similar qualities of gentleness, kindness and quiet strength. Someone who made her feel safe and protected enough to allow her to explore her own strengths and desires, knowing he'd always be ready to catch her if she fell. Nothing could be further from the cold, businesslike arrangement her father had committed her to.

In her heart she wanted to believe Luca's kind, sweet words, because she desperately wanted him to be an honourable and honest man. But, even on a sun-kissed day at the beach, his words couldn't wipe away the years of her father's negative opinions, and her mother's insistence that she should never, ever trust a man.

Were his words simply an example of what her mother meant? He'd gain wealth and prestige by marrying her. If she'd listened to her head, she would have maintained the aloof attitude she'd adopted when they'd met in her father's antechamber. She'd have refused to walk with him in the garden or show him around the hat factory. Most of all, she would have turned down this trip to the beach, which had led her to behave in such a shameful way.

But if she hadn't agreed to spend time with him… Her heart squeezed at the thought. If she'd stayed in her rooms, refused to meet him… No, she didn't want to begin to imagine that scenario. Because if she'd hidden herself away, refused to get to know him even a little, she'd have been denied the memories of these precious and incandescent hours together.

Her freedom could be limited, her life made lonely and bleak, but no-one could steal her memories. Even though her heart felt in danger, she was glad she'd listened to it. That knowledge gave her a feeling of quiet strength.

Rosa was glad to reach the privacy of Luca's car. They'd returned the boat to the marina and walked back along the jetty, but she felt stressed. It was probably just her over-active imagination that made her think heads turned in their direction, eyes speculative as comments were made behind hands. It was because she felt embarrassed and ashamed, despite Luca's attempts to reassure her. She convinced herself of that.

She climbed into the car and sank into the comfort of the leather seat. Luca stared straight ahead as he started the engine and she tried to look anywhere but at his lovely, strong hands gripping the wheel or releasing the handbrake, so close to her thigh. Watching his hands would only make her remember how they'd felt on her body, or cupping her face, and make her wonder how she was ever going to get used to having to live without those sweet sensations.

Without him.

To her relief, he did not suggest lowering the roof. She wanted to hide behind the tinted windows. And she wanted to hide from him.

What must he think of her? She cringed. She wanted the journey to be over. She wanted this pain to end. Because she knew when she exited the car she'd be saying goodbye to him. It was no use to think otherwise. Tomorrow she'd request a meeting with her father and change the course of her life, for ever. Every moment she spent with Luca now simply prolonged the agony of knowing that she wanted to be with him but could never agree to marry him.

She was lost in her thoughts when he braked and pulled the car off the road.

'I thought you'd probably want to go back through the gate again.' He nodded towards the locked gate in the stone wall.

'Oh. I…yes, I suppose so.' She reached for the door handle, but he put out a hand and took her fingers in his.

'Rosie.'

She didn't want to look at him but found she couldn't look anywhere else. His eyes, dark with some emotion she wasn't equipped to understand, caught hers and held them.

'I should go.'

He nodded. 'Do you have a phone?'

Surprised by his question, she stumbled over her words. 'Yes, but it's not much use. Anyway, why do you want to know?'

He shook his head. 'I suppose I just want to know that I can contact you.' He ran the pad of his thumb across her knuckles. 'Do you mind if I look at it?'

Rosa dug in her tote, under her underwear, to find her phone. It felt as though changing into her swimsuit at the factory had happened in another life. She held out the phone to Luca.

His brows drew together. 'That is your phone?' He didn't take it from her. 'If you'd rather not…'

'I don't mind.' She shrugged. 'It's very basic, I know. It can only make and receive calls and texts. It's not "smart".'

He took the phone from her and turned it over in his hands. 'Do you have any access to the Internet?'

'No, although it's been available on Palosia for years. And I know that this phone is not secure. After my sister ran away, my father made sure of that. I didn't have a phone at all for a while. Then I was given this one. I don't use it much. I'm sure all my calls and messages are monitored. My sister phones me on it sometimes. That's the best thing about it.'

'Right.' He nodded. 'Do you mind if I take your number?'

'Why do you want it?'

'Because I'd feel better if I know I can contact you, even if everyone else knows about it before you do.'

'Okay. I don't really like to use it, apart from the calls from Sofia. It's just a reminder that very little about my life is my own.'

Luca was silent, but he pulled out his own phone and entered her details into it.

'Thank you.'

She shoved the phone back into her bag. 'Now...'

'Just in case you're thinking otherwise, Rosie, I've loved being with you. I want you to know that. I don't want you to feel embarrassed, or ashamed or any of those negative things. You're beautiful, and *today* was your own.'

Hearing him say those words did something to her, as if he'd read her mind and understood about the memories. Suddenly, she wanted to show him that she'd do her best to banish the negative thoughts and beliefs that had been ingrained in her for so long. She felt a surge of that inner strength she'd unearthed.

'Then will you do something for me?'

'Anything in my power, yes.'

'Will you drive me back to the palace, to the main, big entrance door? I'm tired of being the obedient princess who always follows the rules and does as she's told. I don't care who sees us, or what they think.'

The words sounded braver than she felt, but it was too late to rethink them or take them back. Luca stared at her for a moment, then one corner of his mouth tugged upwards, and it was all she could do not to put out her hand, cup his jaw and touch her thumb to his quirked lip.

'Absolutely, Rosie. And I will handle any fallout we receive when we turn up unexpectedly together.'

She shook her head. 'No. *I* will.'

The tug at his mouth turned into his devastating, full-blown smile. He pressed the ignition button and eased the car onto the twisty road, heading up the hill towards the palace.

They stopped in a shower of gravel under the palace portico. The huge oak door, studded with metal, was closed and the forecourt was deserted. Luca strolled round the bonnet of the car and pulled open her door, taking her hand to help her out.

She swung her bag over her shoulder. 'Thank you.' She felt the tremor in her voice but hoped he couldn't hear it. She would walk away as if she expected to see him again, even though it felt as if something was tearing her heart apart.

He leaned forward to kiss her cheek. 'Thank...'

Behind them the door crashed open. Her father stood framed in it for a long few seconds, and then strode towards them, one of his secretaries hurrying in his wake.

'I don't need to ask where you've been,' he thundered, thrusting a mobile phone in front of Rosa's face. 'Because I can see for myself, along with the rest of the world.'

All the moisture left Rosa's mouth and her twisted heart suddenly beat painfully in her throat. She removed her sunglasses and looked at the phone. On the screen was a photo of Luca and her, walking along the jetty at the marina. Her bag swung from her shoulder, her hat shaded her face and her sunglasses hid her eyes. Luca was beside her, carrying a small backpack, his shorts and grey tee-shirt not hiding any details of his built physique. His head was bent towards her. There was no mistaking their identities.

Is this the man the King is forcing our Princess to marry? Shouldn't she have a say in the matter? the caption screamed.

There were already hundreds of likes and comments.

She tried to swallow past the dryness, trying to find her breath. She felt exposed, stripped of the unique feeling of safety being with Luca gave her. An echo of the words he'd spoken, in his deep, reassuring voice, hammered in her head: *today was your own.*

Today was suddenly tarnished. Luca's reassurance had strengthened her fragile self-belief. His words had given her the courage to return to the palace openly with him, ready to face her father and tell him of her decision.

The day which had been her own—*their own*—was no longer something she'd be able to revisit in her memory, delighting in the wonderment of being in Luca's arms, tasting the salt on his skin, feeling his lips on hers and his strong, insistent heartbeat under her palm.

Someone had recognised her and snapped her picture then shared it with hundreds, possibly thousands, of others who would now be picking over every detail and expressing their opinions on it. Moreover, the caption would add fuel to the embers of the fire of the succession debate, which only needed something like this to fan it into a little flame that might then flare up into a bigger, much more dangerous blaze.

The people of Palosia loved Queen Chiara and disagreed with the way the King treated her. She'd worked tirelessly for the poor of the island, setting up charities for women's education and employment. The hat business was one of her great achievements, but there were others. She'd established beautiful, open spaces where everyday citizens could relax in safety, and a botanical garden that was fast becoming internationally renowned for its collection of the flora that it protected, unique to the island.

The fact that she was unable to have more children was widely known, and sympathy for her ran deep. It was said that, if the King divorced her and married again in his quest for an heir, there would be a groundswell of outrage that might result in his removal from the throne.

He'd moved Queen Chiara and Rosa to a remote part of the palace and had never denied the rumour that he might end his marriage. That threat, unspoken though it was, had kept Rosa in line, obeying her father to protect her mother.

All these thoughts flashed through Rosa's mind as she stood, frozen, staring at the picture on her father's phone. What if this was the spark that would reignite the debate about the succession only going through the male line? What if the rumble of dissatisfaction with the King's rule and his autocratic treatment of his family became a roar? Would it all be her fault?

'Rosie.' Luca's voice in her ear was low and steady and his use of the name that only he had ever used melted a little of the iciness inside her. The warmth of his hand on her arm sent a current of energy through her. 'It'll be okay. You're strong enough,' he murmured.

Luca was right, she thought, but he'd *made* her strong enough, with his kind words and encouragement. She could choose to believe her heart, that he was honourable and truthful. He made her feel worthwhile, as if she counted for something more than she'd always believed—and surely only the truth could make her feel the surge of strength and power she felt flowing through her now? Her fearful heart regained something closer to its normal rhythm and swelled with gratitude and another deep, unfathomable emotion. She raised her chin and met her father's furious gaze.

'What have you got to say about this?' The King's voice was lower, but no less angry. His eyes bored into hers and he swiped at the phone screen. Rosa saw there were other pictures, of the two of them boarding the boat and heading out of the marina, and then of their return, windswept and damp, with her hair a tangled mass.

Rosa returned his stare with an unwavering one of her own. If she saw a flicker of uncertainty cross his face, it was gone in an instant. 'I will not speak to you while you're so angry. Let me know when your temper has cooled. I will have something to say then.'

'How dare you defy me?' His voice rose again. 'What made you think you could disappear for hours on a boat, with a man you scarcely know? Answer me now.'

'Possibly the very same sentiment which made you think you could make me marry him. The boat trip lasted a few hours. Marrying him would be for life.'

Summoning all her strength and courage, Rosa walked past her father and away from Luca. The brush of his hand on the small of her back gave her the impetus she needed to keep going, through the door and into the hushed, cool palace.

Luca turned to face the King. He folded his arms across his chest and regarded the other man steadily from his superior height, waiting for him to speak.

The King's breathing was laboured in the silence, and he seemed to fight to control it.

'You, Montenale,' he rasped, 'Have treated me and my family with disrespect. I expected better of my future son-in-law.'

Luca raised a brow. 'In what way have I disrespected you, Your Majesty?'

The King huffed. As Luca had thought, he was not accustomed to having to explain himself. In a court of law, he'd have been able to pulverise the man's arguments in a few sentences.

'You said you wanted to take her out for lunch, but instead you disappeared with her in a boat.'

'That is correct, but I consulted with the princess beforehand, and it was done with her permission.'

'*Her* permission? She doesn't get to make decisions about what she can and cannot do. *I* make them. *Always.*'

Luca shook his head. 'Apparently not. She is perfectly able to make her own decisions.'

'This is the result of your influence.' King Fiero tapped the phone. 'Behaving like a woman with no morals, putting ideas into her head about independence.'

'I can assure you that Princess Rosabella does not need me to put ideas into her head. She has a plentiful supply of her own.'

The King's eyes bulged with anger. 'When she's your wife and she tries to assert her will, you'll think differently.'

Luca raked his fingers through his hair, rocking back on his heels. 'Contrary to what you believe, I didn't come to Palosia to claim the princess to whom I've been in an engagement of convenience for the past twenty years. When I discovered the existence of the agreement my father made with you, I was astounded that such a thing could be thought fit in the twenty-first century. On consideration, I recalled my father's antiquated and intransigent opinions regarding the liberation of women, and on meeting you I quickly realised he'd found someone who shared his views. Or, rather, I think you found him. The propensity of the Montenale line to produce male children is well known.'

King Fiero opened his mouth to interrupt but Luca held up a hand. 'We have a meeting scheduled for tomorrow morning. I'll be leaving Palosia on Saturday.' He bowed his head. 'Thank you.'

Luca got into his car and took his leave. When he glanced in the rearview mirror as he took the first bend in the driveway, a little too quickly, the King still stood where he'd left him, staring after the car. The temptation to fling in the man's face the fact that he could tear up the marriage agreement had almost shredded his control but, faced with his rage, he'd known that Rosa must hear his reasoning from him, not some twisted version the King might invent. He had to tell her first.

He exhaled heavily. He would head up into the mountains on the far side of the valley to find one of the hiking trails marked on his map. Then he'd go for a punishing run. The reserves of self-control he'd been forced to tap into to resist Rosie had proved to be only just deep enough, and his body still ached with frustration. The longing, the nameless *need*, to make them part of each other was all-consuming. If she hadn't stopped kissing him, thinking it wasn't what he wanted, he believed the thread of control that had been stretched tight would have snapped.

He had to pound all those thoughts and needs out of his mind and body so that he could meet King Fiero tomorrow with all his attention focussed where it needed to be. It was not going to be an easy or pleasant discussion. He would have to have all his wits about him, and have his negotiating skills at their sharpest, without his thoughts wandering to places to where he needed to forbid them from going.

But first, this evening, he had to see Rosie again one last time.

CHAPTER SIXTEEN

THE WALK THROUGH the palace to her rooms was a familiar route along marbled passages and colonnades, past court-yards where fountains played and ferns grew in cool, green shade.

Rosa frowned, bewildered. How could everything be so unchanged? All the familiar rugs, pictures and ornaments looked just as they had all her life—and yet she felt they should have taken on new shapes and colours, and the distances should have grown or shrunk, because she saw them through new eyes, experiencing them from a changed per-spective.

The feeling that she hadn't been able to identify, but which filled her up so completely it had left no space for fear of her father or trepidation about the confrontation she needed to have with him, suddenly revealed its nature to her. The touch of Luca's hand, his words of encouragement and belief in her ear, had opened her eyes on a new world.

She loved him. She loved him, but she could never marry him, because he didn't love her. Uniting their two families would grant him lands, riches and a royal wife, and all he would have to do was make sure he gave her a son.

What a sweet deal it was for the Count Luca Montenale. Why would he think he had to do anything more? Bring-ing love into the equation wouldn't enter his head. He was wealthy, successful, revered in his profession and stupidly handsome. Love was just a word to be bandied about, just a feeling that could not be described or pinned down. He'd have no use for that.

And yet she loved him for the way he'd made her feel: safe, interesting and cherished. And for the way he'd given her the strength and courage she needed to confront her father—to tell him that she refused to marry the man she loved.

How could she bear to do that now? She knew he was the only man she would ever love, and yet tomorrow she would deny herself the chance of being with him. She'd need all her courage. The thought that she might give in to her feelings and agree to her father's demands and Luca's expectations scared her. What irony that she must now use the courage he'd given her to tear herself from him for ever.

The passion and longing their kiss had unleashed in her felt unfathomable. The way Luca had held her, caressed her and claimed her mouth with a fervour that had felt almost desperate, made her want to believe he had found it as earth-shattering as she had. Yet that could not be true because she knew in her heart he could never love her.

How could he, when she was unlovable? What if trusting her heart had been the wrong choice to make? What if she gave in to these feelings, agreed to the marriage, to be with him, and then found her head had been right all along and he was only in it for what he'd get out of it? To love him and not receive his love in return would destroy her.

By the time she reached her quarters she thought she might be sick from the pounding in her head and the flood of emotions that confused and frightened her. Guilt at how she'd behaved with him in the sea, a longing to feel safe in his arms, grief that she never would again and anger towards her father for his egotistical belief that he could manipulate her life in this way all fought for her attention and threatened to drown her.

She paced the floor, then stopped at the window. It was early evening, and the heat faded as the light drained from the sky. The distant mountain peaks glowed pink in the setting sun. She turned away, unwilling to witness the beauty of nature when she felt as if part of her was dying. She buried her face in her hands.

Then she raised her head, straightened her spine and took a deep breath. She was not dying. This would not defeat her. She couldn't let it. There was work to do with her mother's charities and in the garden, and nobody would ever know that her heart had been broken. She wouldn't allow anyone to have that satisfaction.

There was only one person in the world she wished she could talk to, and that was Sofia, but she strongly suspected that her conversations and messages were intercepted. She wasn't going to open her heart to Sofia, only to have others listening in and reporting back to her father. Anyway, Sofia and Marco would have seen the picture on the Internet by now, just as her father and thousands of other people had.

She copied Sophia's number into her address book, then switched the phone off and put it in a drawer in her bureau, deciding to let it run out of battery and never use it again. It would be better to have no phone than to worry about it being hacked if she used it.

She took a hot shower, sluicing away the sand and salt that still lingered on her skin and washing it out of her hair. Then she sat on her balcony and ate some of the supper Luisa had brought her, thankfully without asking any questions. There was no doubt that news of the confrontation she'd had with the King would have reached every last person in the palace by now. Speculation on it, and the social media debacle, would be rife.

Pink, violet and indigo infused the sky and the pale slice of a crescent moon rose over the mountains. Scents of lavender and roses wafted up on the warm evening air and Rosa knew that the one place she would find solace was in the garden. Pulling a cashmere pashmina around her shoulders for when the temperature cooled, she made her way quietly to the French windows and let herself out into the courtyard.

As she slipped under the archway she paused and glanced back at the palace. A handful of windows glowed with light but the only sounds came from the garden: the soft hoot of an owl, a mouse rustling in the border and the distant trickle of water.

Luca had returned hot and tired from his run but not feeling better in any way. The prospect of escaping from Palosia and returning to his normal life should have lifted his spirits, but instead it filled him with an unfamiliar kind of sadness.

He had to speak to Rosie. Before he saw her father, he wanted to tell her the truth. He owed her that. A rush of emotion had almost floored him when he'd listened to the firm, calm way she'd addressed the King. Her response had taken courage and determination. He knew she had both, and now he also knew she was not afraid to use them. At what had been a moment of extreme vulnerability, she'd dug deep and not capitulated to her father's anger and attempted bullying.

He felt proud of her and humbled by her bravery. It was more than pride, but he couldn't allow himself to admit to what he truly felt. It was safer to keep it hidden, even from himself.

Now he stood at his window and wondered how he could find her. He'd wanted her phone number because the idea of not being able to contact her had triggered a feeling of panic in his chest. She'd warned him that her phone was insecure, and he wasn't about to advertise to whoever it was on the King's staff who listened in to private conversations that he wanted to see her.

He could ring for the man who'd been assigned as his valet and ask him how to find her, but that would probably be a quicker way of advertising his intent than using the phone. He could prowl the passages of the silent palace, hoping for a miracle...

But then he saw that he wouldn't need to. Rosie appeared at the French windows through which she had disappeared on that first day and walked quickly across the cobbles on the far side of the courtyard.

His heart bumped in his chest. Even in the dim evening light her beauty shone. Her hair flowed down her back in waves, briefly gleaming in a shaft of light shed by a lantern on the wall. Her slim form, swathed in a shawl, moved with easy grace as she approached the archway, and then she paused and looked back over her shoulder.

Luca stood stock-still, holding his breath, wondering if she would see him. But she slipped into the darkness of the archway and disappeared.

Without making a conscious decision, Rosa's feet took her towards the rose-covered arbour in the far corner of the garden where she'd tried, unsuccessfully, to avoid Luca earlier in the week. It felt like a lifetime ago.

From the arbour she could look out over the flower garden, bordered with shrub roses, where she'd picked the flowers for her sister's wedding bouquet. If she couldn't talk to Sofia, this was the next best thing. She could remember every bloom she'd chosen, from the pink and creamy roses with their satiny petals and light, fresh scent, to the sweet jasmine and clean, woody lavender. There'd been daisies for simplicity and gypsophilia for delicacy, while the perfume of sweet peas had been strong and heady.

In the evening light she could barely see the terraces of flowers, but the mingled scents that wafted up to her on the warm air made her feel closer to Sofia. She settled herself on the cushions of the swing seat, pulled off her plimsols and wrapped the soft shawl around her shoulders. The rhythmic swaying of the seat was soothing. She let her eyes close while she breathed in the perfumed air and felt the peace of the garden surround her.

'Rosie?'

She jerked upright, her brief moment of tranquillity shattered, and her fists closed on the edges of her shawl, pulling it tightly around her. But then her muscles relaxed and her shock drained away. This wasn't her father, or one of his emissaries come to find her.

Only one person called her by that name. It felt right, and not at all surprising, that it was Luca, even though when she'd walked away from him earlier she'd believed she would never see him again.

She turned her head against the cushions. 'How did you know where to find me?'

He moved closer, a defined shadow in the twilight. 'I saw you crossing the courtyard from my window. Finding you here was a lucky first guess.'

'You didn't think of trying the maze?'

'Luckily not. I'd be wandering its paths until morning. May I sit next to you?'

'Of course. Why…?'

'I had to see you, Rosie. There's something I need to explain.'

He sat, leaving space between them. She tucked her feet up under the skirt of her dress and turned a little. His sharp jaw looked cleanly shaven, and his dark eyes gleamed in what little light there was. Her heart did the little leap and then beat painfully against her ribs, just as it always did when he was near.

'Have you spoken to your father?' He sought out one of her hands and folded it in his.

'No. I'll have to talk to him tomorrow. Why?'

'I rather lost it with him, after you left earlier. I felt so impressed with how you managed the situation. You were right to walk away. I was also angry with him, and I should have let myself calm down, but I didn't.'

'What happened?' Her voice was a whisper. He wished he could freeze time and remain here with her like this for ever. But he had to tell her.

'I walked away before it became too heated. But I'll meet with him in the morning.' He pressed his mouth to her palm. 'I want to tell you before I see him…'

'What?'

'That I cannot marry you.'

He heard the hitch in her breathing. The silence around them seemed to gather and thicken. Then her breath stuttered. 'Why?'

He hated that he was going to hurt her.

'This proposed marriage feels like a trap my father set for me and, although he didn't know he was going to die, it's as if he's trying to control me from beyond the grave. As if he's scored a final victory over me, after all the times I defied him.'

He could feel useless anger towards his father building in his chest. 'I can never comply with it. I came here intending to tell your father to go to hell, and then—'

'Why didn't you?' Her voice rose. 'Why didn't you tell him as soon as you arrived?' She twisted towards him. 'Then none of this…'

'Believe me, that was my intention. I could have done it by email, but I thought I should meet your father. After all, it's something he's been counting on for twenty years. It seemed only good manners to tell him, man-to-man. I thought it would take a couple of hours.' His breath caught. 'But then I met you. I didn't think I would. It didn't seem necessary, but there you were, and I remembered you from twenty years ago…'

'How did *that* change anything? Surely meeting me simply confirmed that you were right to refuse to marry me?'

'Don't, Rosie, please. Don't let what your father has told you all your life become what defines you. You're so much better than that. You're worth so much more.'

'All I've ever been told is that nobody will desire or love me, so how else could I be? I had to wait to be married to someone—*you*—to cement a business transaction between two men who cared nothing for me. That *is* what has defined my life.'

He could hear the tremble in her voice and knew she was fighting to keep tears back.

'All you have to do is make sure I have a son to satisfy my father's obsessive need for an heir.'

'Shh, Rosie, listen to me—how much do you know about the agreement they made?'

Her shoulders jerked on a sob.

'Absolutely nothing. Like I told you, I didn't even know your name until I met you.'

'So you don't know that if we honoured that agreement should you—we—have a son, then when he is two years old we would have to relinquish him to live here, with your father, to be raised as his heir?'

Her head jerked round.

'*What?*'

'I didn't read the full agreement until after I'd arrived here, otherwise I don't think I would have paid your father the courtesy of a visit. Even if I didn't care about my father's actions, I could never go through with it under those terms. My mother died when I was two and I was sent to live with my grandparents. Then on my tenth birthday, with no warning, I was taken back to the estate in Tuscany to be brought up by my father. I will never, ever subject a child of mine to an experience like that.'

'I'm sorry, Luca. I didn't know.' She shivered. 'To lose your mother so young… Of course you'd never agree to give up a child of your own. I…can understand your reasons for refusing to comply with the agreement. But were your grandparents kind?'

'Yes, but they lived in a house belonging to my father and were bound to do what he wanted. I can see how he would have thought a marriage of convenience, which would bring him assets and a link to royalty, would be perfectly acceptable.'

'I still don't understand why you didn't just tell my father immediately.'

'Like I said, I met you.

'And I wasn't prepared to like you.

'I met you, Rosie, and I felt as if I'd found something incredibly rare and precious. I wanted to get to know you. I remembered what a bright, happy little girl you were. I wanted to discover what had changed you so much.'

He reached out to brush the backs of his fingers across her cheek. 'And why you no longer sing to the fish. I thought you'd probably been waiting for most of your life to meet me, be married and have children, and I was going to destroy all those dreams. I've meant every single one of the things I've said to you, but…'

He shook his head. 'I cannot agree to the terms of this deal. I wanted to find a way to tell you gently that I couldn't give you what you want. What you need.' He stroked a hand over her hair. 'But, instead, I've fallen in love with you.'

Rosa's mind threatened to spin out of control, unable to absorb what he was saying. She needed air, space, time, but there wasn't any. Luca had said he loved her, but he couldn't marry her and was leaving tomorrow…and she needed to show him that she loved him too, even though they could never be together.

He twisted to face her as his free hand brushed her hair off her face and cradled her cheek. He rubbed his thumb over her bottom lip. It only took the slightest turn of her head to press her mouth to his palm. His skin tasted clean and smelled of soap. She thought hazily that he must have showered the salt away, as she had done.

She pictured him in the shower, water cascading over those sculpted muscles of his chest and shoulders, running down his washboard stomach, and something clenched and snapped inside her. The longing to feel his skin against hers, with nothing between them, was overwhelmingly powerful. She wanted to make another memory to store away.

After tonight, he'd be gone from her life. Once he'd broken off their engagement, her father would never permit him to return to Palosia, even if he wanted to come back. And, whatever Luca said about her finding someone else, no-one else would ever love her. At this moment, in the sweet-smelling darkness, she wanted to know how it felt to give herself completely to the man she loved.

She felt his fingers slide into her hair, cradling the back of her head as he leaned into her.

'Luca…'

'Mmm?' His forehead rested against hers, his fingers feathering across her cheeks and down to her collar bones, easing the edges of the pashmina apart and probing the sensitive places of her neck and throat.

'Make love to me. Please.'

Luca stilled, aware that his breathing was growing uneven and aware of the fragility of the grip he had on his control. He needed to stop this, but overriding all his thoughts was the deep, visceral need to make her his. It expanded from somewhere deep in his core and obliterated sense and logic.

His awareness shrank to this place, this moment and the feel of Rosie's soft curves, the scent of her skin and the small sounds of need in her throat. He wanted to kiss her so that, if she ever kissed another man, she would think of *him*. If anyone else ever touched her, it would be the imprint of *his* fingers she remembered and longed for.

Because he loved her. It was the only thing in this tangled web that made any sense.

'Rosie, no…'

'Please, Luca. This is the only chance I'll have…*we'll* have. Please, kiss me.'

He pulled in a shaky breath. 'You're lovely. You're absolutely enchanting and I want you more than anything I've ever longed for or desired.' He brushed his mouth across her lips and drew back again as she arched towards him, her head falling back, the creamy skin of her throat a soft gleam in the half-dark. Her eyelids closed over her shiny eyes.

He cupped her head in his hands, holding her steady while he kissed her again, more firmly, opening the seam of her lips with his and sliding his tongue into the sweet warmth of her mouth. It was heaven. Hell would come later, when he had to leave her.

Her hands were buried in his hair as she kissed him back, and then he broke away from her mouth to drop a line of light kisses across her shoulder and along the neckline of her cotton dress to the shadowy dip between her breasts. He heard her soft gasp and reached up to stroke her cheek.

'We can stop, Rosie. Just tell me…' He wasn't sure how he'd stop, but he'd find a way. He would never do anything she didn't want, or anything to hurt her. She was precious and beautiful, and he wanted with all his heart and soul to protect her, and *love* her, for ever.

'I want this,' she whispered. 'I want you. Now. Because, when you're gone, I'll always have this to remember.'

He raised his head and found her mouth again.

Afterwards, he held her in his arms as their breathing calmed and, after thundering against each other, their hearts quietened.

He'd hesitated, then covered her mouth with his when she'd cried out, hating that he'd hurt her, but she'd pulled him closer again. Then his name had become a mantra that she'd breathed over and over, until finally it had become one sharp cry of pleasure, followed by his own groan of release.

She shivered and he pulled her shawl over them. Later the air chilled with a dewy dampness, and he helped her to dress. Then he eased her onto his lap and held her close again, her head tucked into his shoulder.

'I'm sorry.'

She struggled upright, away from him, pushing her hands against his chest. His fingers looped lightly around her wrists.

'Sorry? How can you be sorry, Luca? I wanted you and I think you wanted me.'

'Rosie, listen to me. Please.'

She wriggled off his lap. Her legs felt weak. Luca stood too, towering over her, holding her hands against his chest. 'Tell me why you're sorry.'

'I'm not sorry that we made love. It was beautiful.' There was a crack in his voice. 'More than beautiful. I love you and I'm sorry that I can't marry you.'

Rosa slid her hands from under his, even though she longed to keep them there.

'I've felt so safe with you, Luca, but suddenly nothing about this feels safe.'

'Rosie.' His voice was quiet, insistent. 'I love you, yet I cannot marry you under the terms of the agreement our fathers made. If I could find a way for us to be together, free from these obligations…'

She shook her head. 'I don't want a marriage that's been pre-arranged for the convenient satisfaction of two massive male egos either, even if one of them is no longer with us. Have you thought about how it looks from my point of view?'

'Yes, of course I have.'

'Then can you tell me how a marriage of convenience could ever become a love match?'

She'd seen both her father's marriages fail when no heir had been born, her parents becoming lonely and embittered. Sofia's mother had loved her, but she'd left her as a baby to return to her first love. For much of her life, Rosa had feared that her own mother would leave and return to her family. She didn't know if Chiara loved her enough to stay, because she knew she was unlovable. How could she bear it if her childhood fears came true, and someone who professed to love her abandoned her?

'Because if we were free to choose each other it wouldn't be a marriage of convenience, Rosie. It'd be a marriage filled with love.'

Doubt and fear crowded in on her. It could never be the sort of union she dreamed about, like the one between Sofia and Marco. The past would always cast a shadow over them. It was much safer to be on her own. On her own, she'd have control of her life, even if it was narrow. She wouldn't have to fear not having a son, or being left for someone else, or leaving her mother unprotected.

Yet would it be worth it, if a way could be found? Did she dare to believe that might be possible? She needed to be on her own, to have space to think. Luca's presence made that impossible. The longer she stood so close to him, his male scent filling her senses, his hard body now promising so much more than security and comfort, the more likely she was to believe in what he said.

'I need to go, Luca.' She finally found the will to drag the words out of herself.

'I'm afraid to let you go, Rosie.' His voice shook.

Hot tears scalded her eyes. Those few words, spoken with such a depth of feeling and emotion, told her more about his love for her than anything else. But she couldn't take the risk. He'd made her feel valued and precious, and had made love to her with such gentleness and passion that she'd treasure the memories for ever. But she had to remember what she would tell her father tomorrow: she would never marry anyone unless they loved each other equally and deeply. And she couldn't allow herself to believe, absolutely, that the love Luca promised would be for ever.

She shook her head. 'And I'm afraid to stay,' she whispered. She took a step backwards. 'It could never work,

Luca. There's too much in our past to allow us to have a future together.'

Then she turned and began to run.

A shadow fell across the earth where Rosa was digging. The flower bed had already been weeded and dug over once, but physically exhausting herself was the only way she could think of to cope with the grief that overwhelmed her every time she stopped to rest. She'd wrestled with it all night, unable to shake the conviction that she'd let something very precious slip away.

She stood up, wiping her hands on her thighs, and faced her father.

'He's gone.' He sounded breathless, seething. 'He's broken the agreement his father made with me.'

Despite the amount of cold water she'd splashed on her face earlier, she knew the signs of sadness and a sleep-deprived night were obvious but, since her father rarely looked at her, properly, it was unlikely he'd notice. For once, she felt grateful for his indifference.

She lifted her shoulders a little. 'Yes.'

Her father's eyes narrowed. 'You knew? Did he speak to you? What did he say?'

He looked curiously diminished, haggard and slightly stooped. This morning, Luisa had hinted at the eruption of uncomplimentary comments about King Fiero on social media. The people were calling for change, she'd muttered, before hurrying away.

This might be her fault, but perhaps in the end it would be for the good of Palosia if it instigated that change. Her father had been impervious to criticism all his life, but perhaps he was feeling the heat at last.

'He said he couldn't marry me, but that shouldn't surprise you.'

'Obviously you didn't please him, for him to give up all that you would have brought him.' He scowled.

'He's a man who is highly successful in his own right. He needs none of the trappings, or the problems, that marrying me would bring. He has everything he wants without that.'

'And it doesn't bother you, that you've squandered the chance to provide Palosia with an heir?'

For the first time in her life, she stared him down. 'No, it doesn't, especially since, if you had your way, that heir would be taken from me at the age of two to be raised by you. Did you believe you would get away with that? A solitary future doesn't scare me at all, but the idea of a loveless marriage of convenience is terrifying. I will *only* marry for love.'

'Love,' he spat. 'What do you know of love? Your half-sister's marriage has filled your head with fantasies.'

'No. It has shown me that a marriage of equal love and respect between two people is possible and, above all, joyful.'

She turned and walked away. She felt no urge to look back. Instead, a sense of liberation filled her, lightening her step and even lifting her heart a little.

CHAPTER SEVENTEEN

LUCA FROWNED AND dropped his phone onto his desk.

He'd known hell would come later, but he hadn't expected the pain to intensify rather than diminish as the days passed. He'd thought getting back into his life in New York would make the memory of events on Palosia fade. Instead, they were sharper than ever.

He'd worked for two weeks solid, and his brain felt fried. The hit he usually got from success in court had failed to deliver and, instead of feeling happy at the latest victory, he was simply exhausted. Add to that the fact that he couldn't get hold of Rosie, and he was setting himself up for a major all-fall-down.

This morning he'd snapped at his PA when she'd brought him coffee, exactly the way he liked it, and suggested he might take a break.

'What would I do with a break? Any useful suggestions?'

Her eyebrows had disappeared beneath her glossy fringe but she hadn't answered.

Later, however, he'd found a brochure for high-end spa breaks in the Caribbean on his desk. He'd dropped it in the bin.

He pushed away from his desk, strode to the expanse of glass that was his office window and looked out at the iconic skyline. The buzz of New York no longer fired him up. Instead of skyscrapers and Central Park, he wanted mountains, beaches and…

He didn't need a spa break. He just needed to speak to Rosie and know that she was okay. Then he could move on.

What if her father had blamed her for the way Luca had cancelled their engagement and was meting out some sort of punishment? Had her phone been confiscated, leaving her with no means of talking to anyone, not even her beloved sister? How would she cope with that? Every time he tried to call her, he was met with silence. He was a breath away from throwing the phone at something—or someone.

It was his job to defend people, stand up for their rights and speak for them, when necessary. He told himself he needed to do that for Rosie, but then, judging by the way he'd seen her face down her father, perhaps she no longer needed his help.

But if he was honest, which he always was, speaking to her would never be enough. The depth of his longing for her touch, her kiss, just *her*, was bottomless and beyond the realm of all his previous experience. As a result, he had no idea how to deal with it, and his frustration was building with every day, every hour, which passed.

For the first time since he'd freed himself from his father's control all those years ago, he felt dissatisfied with his life. He wanted something different. The admission shook him. He'd glimpsed heaven in Rosie's arms on Palosia and he craved more of it.

He was in love, for the first time ever. Love was meant to bring joy, he thought, but it was agony. He thought he'd be able to get back to work and park the tumultuous emotions he was experiencing somewhere safe, to be visited when he felt better equipped to examine them. But that wasn't how it had worked. They ruled his life, waking and sleeping. Everything reminded him of her and he knew, with absolute certainty, that he wanted her in his life full-time.

He'd told Rosie he loved her, but in the next breath told her why he couldn't marry her. His reasons were sound, and he'd never change his mind about them, but how it must have hurt her—made her doubt his sincerity, believe that cruel nonsense that she was unlovable. She'd pushed him away, panicked and fled. That he hadn't gone after her was an error that would haunt him for ever.

He needed to speak to her, desperately. He pressed the heels of his hands into his eyes, but immediately imagined her standing in front of him in her gardening clothes and hat, giving him that rare smile that made him want to kiss her and which he'd pay a king's ransom to see again.

Something connected in his tired brain. If he wanted to see her smile—see *her*, damn it—he had to stop wishing. He retrieved his phone from across the desk and scrolled through his diary and commitments. There was nothing that couldn't be handled by someone else for the coming week, because he only employed the best.

He sent a request to the travel department and buzzed his PA.

She came in, looking mutinous. 'If you're going to…'

He held up a hand. 'I'm really sorry about earlier. I'm not myself.'

'I don't need you to tell me that. You've been like a bear with a sore head ever since you returned from Italy. Your father's death has affected you deeply.'

'Yes, it has.' *If only you knew.* 'And I've decided to take your advice. I'm taking a break. But, before I disappear, please get one of the partners in the Rome office on the line. I have something unusual for them to tackle…'

* * *

Looking back and wishing that things were different was a waste of time and energy. Besides, there were things for which Rosa was grateful. The groundswell of opinion in Palosia towards allowing a female to succeed to the throne was one of them. It seemed her father had finally, and reluctantly, bowed to public pressure and might consider initiating changes in the ancient laws. It wouldn't happen overnight but it had to be a good thing for their small kingdom.

The inner strength that she'd found with Luca had not deserted her. She felt as if it had always been there, waiting for the right moment to show itself, and his kind attention had been the catalyst.

She also felt the beginnings of tolerance for her father. In making her choice, she'd removed any leverage he had over her. She could protect her mother and increase the amount of charity work she undertook. It was fulfilling and rewarding.

But she hadn't yet learned to limit the scope of her imagination or her emotions. The gut-twisting longing persisted. A spotlight seemed to shine on the memories of Luca, illuminating those few days, picking them out in vivid Technicolor. Every word they'd spoken, every touch, every sigh, was imprinted on her memory. The memories showed no sign of fading or losing the ability to wring her heart.

A phrase, a scent, the taste of salt on her tongue… There was no telling when she'd be hit with longing so powerful that she gasped.

Finally, longing for the comfort of her sister's voice, she called her from the hat factory.

'What's happened, Rosa? Why doesn't your phone work? And you sound…different.'

There would be no use denying it, and it was a relief to

be able to talk about Luca. Sofia listened in silence as Rosa told her everything…well, not exactly *everything*.

'And he said he loved you?' Rosa heard the change in Sofia's tone. 'Since you're the most lovable person on the planet, I'm not surprised. Whatever our father says.'

'But I didn't know whether to believe him or not.'

'Why would he say it if it wasn't true?'

'I don't know. I was shocked and confused. He said he couldn't submit to a marriage of convenience, but he wished there was another way.'

'He's right about the agreement, Rosa, and it was honourable of him to be honest with you. So I don't believe he was lying when he said he loved you. What did you say?'

'I said it would never work. I didn't see how it could. The past would always intrude.'

'You could choose to let the past go. If the agreement was cancelled, you could start afresh. Love is one of the most powerful things in the world, and with the love of a good man your life would be transformed. After all, I know. And it sounds to me as if Luca is a good man. He's prepared to stand up for what is right, in his professional and his personal life.'

Rosa gripped the phone more tightly, squeezing her eyes tighter still. 'I should have told him…' Her voice caught.

'What, sweet sister?'

The endearment, always loved, now made her want to cry.

'That I love him too.'

'You *didn't*?'

'No. I tried to…*show* him. But my feelings frightened me. I felt so vulnerable.'

Sofia was silent for a moment. When she spoke again, there was added weight to her voice. 'Rosa, you once told me that it's good for people to know they are loved. Do you remember?'

'Y…yes, I do.'

'And you said Marco deserved the truth. Your wise words that day changed everything for me…for us. They granted me the clarity to see what I needed to do. Marco and I are eternally grateful to you.' Rosa heard the wobble in her sister's voice, but then Sofia continued. 'Now you need to take your own advice. Can you contact Luca?'

'He has my number.' She remembered the phone lying in her bureau drawer, the battery dead. 'But I don't have his. And I turned my phone off after he left and let the battery die.'

'Okay…' There was a grim note in Sofia's voice. 'I lost count of how many times I tried to phone you after those photos appeared on social media. How do you know Luca hasn't been trying to contact you?'

'Why would he?'

'Because he *loves* you,' Sofia said gently. 'Love isn't something you can switch off when it suits you, like your phone. Charge it and switch it on, Rosa.'

That conversation had been two days ago. She'd followed Sofia's advice, but her phone remained silent. Despite her determination to ignore the steady march of time, she knew it had been three weeks and two days since Luca had left.

Impatient with herself, she threw off the bed covers and pulled open the curtains at the window. The sky was a deep, velvet blue quilted with stars, and she knew the air would have the crispness that came with September, heralding the earliest signs of autumn.

She pulled on a dress and then picked up the pashmina she'd left folded on a chair for the past three weeks, allowing herself a moment to bury her face in its soft folds, because in her mind it still held Luca's clean, soapy smell.

Then she let herself out into the garden.

Luca pulled the hire car off the road and into the layby. The rush of silence when he cut the engine seemed almost tangible after the constant, twenty-four-hour cacophony of the city that never slept.

He remembered the code for the locked gate after having watched Rosie punch it in, but he still felt a rush of relief when the gate clicked open. The grass beneath the fruit trees cushioned his footsteps as he climbed steadily up the terraces.

Above him crouched the silhouette of the palace, light illuminating a few windows. He didn't know how he'd find Rosie, but he was determined that he would.

He paused where two paths crossed, debating which one to choose, and then he heard a sound that simultaneously tore at his heart and sent it soaring. The maze was dark on this moonless night. He kept one hand on the spiky hedge to guide him through its twists and turns.

At the centre, he stopped. A clear, sweet voice singing about pretty horses floated on the night air.

'Rosie?'

Her voice wavered and died. Starlight glimmered off the cascade of her hair as she turned.

'Luca?'

He closed the space between them in three strides.

'I came to find you.' He stopped, afraid to touch her in case he frightened her away. 'I had to know that you're alright. I've tried to contact you...'

She put out a hand and touched his chest.

'The phone felt like a trap, and I didn't think you'd want

to contact me after what I said. So I switched it off. But Sofia persuaded me to turn it on again, just two days ago.'

'I gave up trying to call you. I decided to come to Palosia instead. And you were right—there *is* too much in our past, and we can't erase it, but the marriage deal is being dissolved. We'll be free of it, free to do as we choose.'

'Yes, I demanded that my father cancel his side of the agreement and the notion about handing an heir to him. I told him I choose to remain single. I choose to help the people of Palosia through my charity work, and to help protect the unique habitats of our precious island. And I'd never choose to marry for convenience. Only for love.'

The need to touch her after these weeks of missing her became too much and he reached out, taking her hands. 'I choose you.'

She stilled, her dark eyes luminous. 'Luca.' She breathed his name. 'That last night…it's tormented me.'

Fear that she was going to say she regretted their love-making gripped him. 'I'm sorry, Rosie. I should have been restrained. I hurt you.'

'No. I should have told you what I'd been wanting to tell you.'

He searched her face. 'What should you have told me?'

'That I love you. But I couldn't see how we could make something new and beautiful out of our past.'

He pulled her against him, kissing her hair and then resting his forehead against hers. 'I've missed you every minute we've been apart, with every cell of my body, and I've been so afraid for you. I had to come and find you.' He kissed her, slowly and gently.

'How did you know where to find me?' she asked when he lifted his lips from hers.

'I didn't. I heard you singing. You've found your voice.'

'Yes, I have. And I'll never be silenced again.'

He smiled against her mouth. 'The courage you showed, facing your father, was inspiring. It made me realise that I was being a coward.'

'But it was you who gave me the strength to stand up to my father.'

He shook his head. 'I was afraid of love. I feared that my mother hadn't loved me enough, or my father at all, and my grandparents only from a sense of obligation. I refused to acknowledge my true feelings for you and, when I did, I told you that I couldn't marry you. My obsession with refusing to allow my father to control my life clouded the truth. But I realised that, if I denied my love for you, he would have scored the ultimate victory. He'd have stopped me from being with the only woman in the world I want. I'm not letting that happen.'

'Does this mean that our twenty-year engagement is over?'

'Mmm. Do you think we can start again?'

'What do you mean?'

'I've made a career out of trying to improve the lives of others, but I've been afraid to examine my own. Acknowledging that I love you makes me feel vulnerable, but I do—unconditionally and completely. I'd love you just the same if you were the gardener I mistook you for, and not the daughter of a king. I love you for your generosity of spirit and your kindness and care for others. I'll care for you and protect you for ever. There're no certainties in life, and we'll have challenges to face, but I'll be by your side through anything... if you'll marry me.'

'Oh, Luca. Yes.' The raw emotion in her voice made his chest ache. 'I was so afraid of loving you. But your love has given me the courage to love you back without fear. We can love each other freely, on our own terms. You, and your love, are safe with me.'

Their kiss was deep and long. Luca trailed his fingers

over her shoulders to span her narrow waist in his hands, holding her hips against him.

'Do you think your father is still awake?' he whispered when they broke apart. 'Because I think we need to tell him our plans.'

'He may be, but tomorrow will be soon enough to tell him. We can keep tonight for ourselves.'

'In that case, I have to ask something of you.'

'What?'

'To lead me out of the maze—because without you I'll be lost for ever.'

Rosie laughed and took his hand. 'Come; I'll show you how easy it is.'

'And then I'll show you how easy it is to love you. Over and over again—for ever.'

EPILOGUE

ROSA SCANNED THE congregation in the palace chapel. Everyone wore a smile—even her father. Seated beside him, her mother looked happy too.

All of Marco's big family was there, and her heart swelled, knowing that Sofia had been welcomed into their midst with such warm generosity.

They had all gathered for the baptism of one-month-old Angelica Sofia Rosabella, Sofia and Marco's daughter, and the atmosphere in the chapel hummed with joy.

Sofia and Marco wore the happiest smiles of all. They stood at the carved marble font, and Sofia cradled their perfect baby girl in her arms. Downy, dark hair curled at the edges of her lace bonnet, and her grey eyes, just like her father's, gazed up unblinkingly at her parents. Sofia rocked her gently, smoothing the silk christening robe that had been worn by generations of royal babies of Palosia.

Rosa's eyes caught Sofia's, and they exchanged a warm smile.

Sofia had kept her hair short, and Rosa loved the way the glossy bob curved along her jaw as she bent her head over her baby daughter. When Marco had taken Sofia to his villa on Capri to hide from the men King Fiero had sent to find her, he'd cut her long hair into a bob as part of her disguise.

The King had surprised everyone by being besotted with

his baby granddaughter. He insisted that she be christened on Palosia and that, even though they lived in Italy, Sofia and Marco should have a home on the island. It was as if, confronted by the reality of a new generation, he was able to see his own place in the world more clearly, and accept that there were some things he couldn't control.

As for the things he could, he was doing something about them. He was changing the law of succession so that a woman could rule. He had officially recognised the valuable contribution Queen Chiara had made to the lives of the people of Palosia, and agreed to support the movement that advocated tertiary education equally for girls and boys.

Much remained to be done, and for Rosa her relationship with him would always be difficult, but her generous spirit allowed her to regard him with increasing tolerance.

Luca's hand brushed against hers and she entwined her fingers with his, feeling that current of strength, security and love—so much love—that his touch always brought her.

They had been married seven months ago in the private chapel of Luca's castle in Tuscany. They hadn't wanted a grand wedding, happy to make their vows in the company of family and a few trusted friends.

The bodice of Rosa's antique ivory silk wedding dress had hugged her curves then fallen in liquid folds to the floor, sparkling with gems and gleaming seed pearls.

When Luca had lifted her veil, his eyes had shone unnaturally brightly, and a muscle in his jaw had flexed. 'My love,' he'd whispered, taking her hand.

Her engagement ring was tucked safely in a pocket of Luca's suit, ready to return to her as soon as he'd slipped her wedding band onto her finger. She'd missed the weight and sparkle of its rose-pink diamonds.

They'd invited Queen Chiara to move to Tuscany with

them, but she'd refused. Her place was on Palosia, she'd said. With Rosa leaving, she'd have to pay more attention to her charities and gardens. Her selfless demonstration of loyalty and service had helped to motivate King Fiero to initiate change, both in his public and personal life.

Luca bent his head towards Rosa. 'Are you alright? Not feeling tired?'

The wide smile she gave him was the one he always craved. His hand tightened around hers.

'I'm fine. But thank you for your concern.'

He dipped his head further and brushed his lips across her temple. 'Nothing is more precious to me than you. And now…'

She nodded, because the service was about to begin and there was no more time for words. But the understanding between them needed none. They had their own very precious secret that they would keep for a few weeks yet. They didn't know if their baby would be a boy or a girl, but they knew that one day he or she would rule Palosia with the blessing of the people.

Their hearts were full to overflowing with love.

* * * * *

MILLS & BOON®

Coming next month

SECOND CHANCE UNDER THE MISTLETOE
Kandy Shepherd

'It's less than two weeks until Christmas. Can we make the effort to get to know each other in that time? Even acknowledge that we could become friends of a sort? You know, bond over our shared care of Clem and her baby?'

'Friends? Do you think so?'

Jon paused. 'Perhaps not quite friends, although we were friends long ago.'

'We were never just friends,' Natalie said slowly.

An awkward silence fell between them. Was she remembering the fierce passion that had immediately flared between them, the overwhelming obsession they'd had for each other? First-time love. He had never forgotten it. Although he'd had serious relationships since, even been married, nothing had ever come anywhere near the intensity of those youthful feelings. No one else had engaged his emotions so deeply. 'You don't know how to love,' his second ex-wife had accused. But he had loved Natalie, deeply and completely. Perhaps there hadn't been any love left in him for anyone else.

Continue reading

SECOND CHANCE UNDER THE MISTLETOE
Kandy Shepherd

Available next month
millsandboon.co.uk

COMING SOON!

We really hope you enjoyed reading this book.
If you're looking for more romance
be sure to head to the shops when
new books are available on

Thursday 23rd October

To see which titles are coming soon, please visit
millsandboon.co.uk/nextmonth

MILLS & BOON

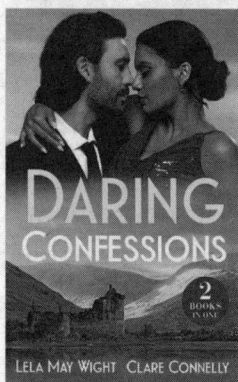

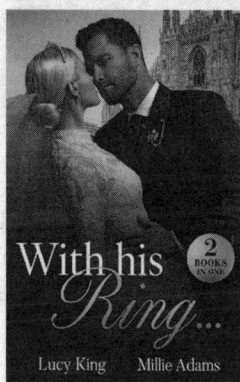

afterglow BOOKS

Afterglow Books is a trend-led, trope-filled list of books with diverse, authentic and relatable characters, a wide array of voices and representations, plus real world trials and tribulations. Featuring all the tropes you could possibly want (think small-town settings, fake relationships, grumpy vs sunshine, enemies to lovers) and all with a generous dose of spice in every story.

♪ @millsandboonuk
⬡ @millsandboonuk
afterglowbooks.co.uk

#AfterglowBooks

For all the latest book news, exclusive content and giveaways scan the QR code below to sign up to the Afterglow newsletter:

SCAN ME

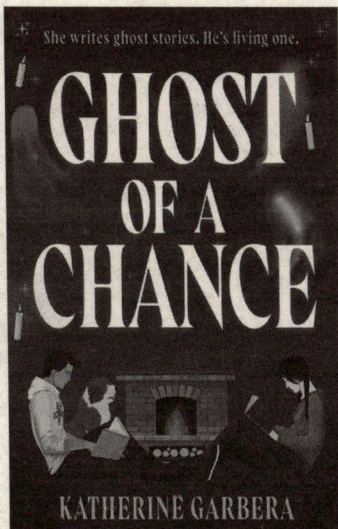

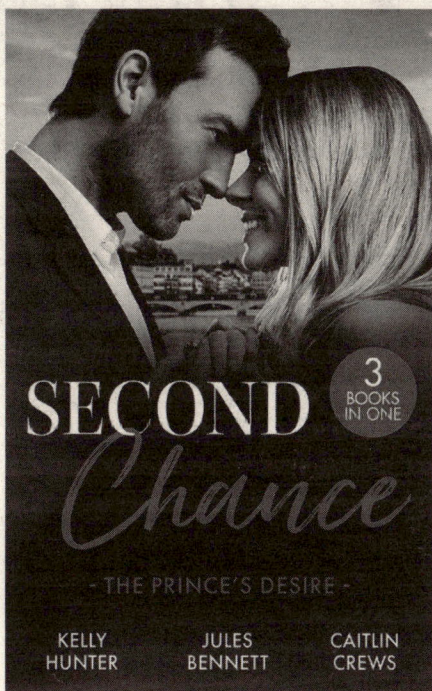

LET'S TALK
Romance

For exclusive extracts, competitions and special offers, find us online:

f MillsandBoon

X @MillsandBoon

⊙ @MillsandBoonUK

♪ @MillsandBoonUK

Get in touch on 01413 063 232